# *Chapter 1: Where now?*

ADVISE JOB MPIKA J/
REPATRIATION SO
IMMEDIATELY STOP MI
STOP

Rick's whoop brightened up the study room.

'Come on then. Tell.'

Twenty young students at Kenyatta Teachers' College took a break from cramming for their finals to listen. Rick, a little older than the others, was the leader of the pack. This was likely to be entertaining.

'You won a Ferrari.'

'You got a date with Miss India.'

'It's that carrot top girl you've been grinding on about, right?'

He kept shaking his head until he finally told them what they didn't want to hear.

'I got a job in Zambia.'

'Why Zambia, man? I thought you said stick with you.'

'Yea, stick with me and you'll go far, you said. Now what?'

It was true. Whenever something needed to be organised for the students' benefit, Rick could turn on the charm. Things happened around him and everyone liked him. Nobody pressed him for an answer. He was one of three Indians in the group of forty Kenyan Africans and one Canadian exchange student. The camaraderie was warm but unrest was seeping across the border from Uganda and emanating over the radio waves of Rick's CIA issue radio, a relic of an abandoned past life.

'We got to grab our chances.' Rick announced, regretting his outburst. 'Come on. Onwards and upwards. Exams to pass and places to go.'

As everyone stuck their noses back into their notes, Rick thought, 'Borders to cross and fair lady to win back.' He would have to contain his excitement until the exams were over. Thank goodness he'd got the teaching job in Zambia but what was he going to do about his passport? He couldn't be repatriated to Kenya. Would Ella think he wanted to marry her for entry into UK? She'd run a mile. What was he thinking of? He hadn't seen her for months and she might have gone off with that dairy farmer.

Ricardo Fonseca, exams over, tucked his pristine white shirt into his smart cream trousers and gave the thick waves of his shiny black hair a last nervous sweep with the comb he always kept in his hip pocket. He fitted his suitcase into the front trunk of his Beetle and piled his hockey stick, tennis and badminton racquets, balls, shuttlecocks and sports bag on to the back seat. There was a slight frown on his handsome face and he sighed as he struggled to fit his tall, athletic frame into the driver's seat. As a Gemini, Rick aka Ricardo aka John Francis enjoyed his aliases. He was Ricardo to his family and on official documents. His student mates called him Rick. He wouldn't admit to the baby-talk Rickoo. Poor Ella had been thoroughly confused. She had been introduced to him and fallen in love with him as John Francis the teacher, discovered he was a spy whose real name was Ricardo and then he asked her to call him

# The Cosmopolites

## – ELIZA JANE GOÉS –

FASTPRINT PUBLISHING
PETERBOROUGH, ENGLAND

www.fast-print.net/store.php

# Cosmopolites
Copyright © Eliza Jane Goés 2010

ISBN 978-184426-843-6

First published 2010 by
FASTPRINT PUBLISHING
Peterborough, England.

An environmentally friendly book printed and bound in England by
www.printondemand-worldwide.com

**Mixed Sources**
Product group from well-managed
forests, and other controlled sources
www.fsc.org  Cert no. TT-COC-002641
© 1996 Forest Stewardship Council
FSC

PEFC Certified

This product is
from sustainably
managed forests
and controlled
sources
PEFC™
www.pefc.org
PEFC/16-33-415

This book is made entirely of chain-of-custody material

*To Gerry – He Knows Why*

# The Cosmopolites: Chapters

Rick. She called him Ricky – mostly – unless she was annoyed.

He'd managed to get through on the phone to Ella at her school three hundred miles away. She'd been dragged out of class, been told off by the young headmistress and had snapped at Rick for not getting in touch for *so* long. The line had gone dead as he yelled that he would pick her up after school that day. He hoped she'd got the message. So he was smartly dressed and combing his hair. He would pop into see her in Kericho on his way home to his family in Kisumu. It was just a social visit for old times' sake. They'd been through so much together, some of it life-threatening. He'd play it cool. Ask about Mike. Wish them well. Oh no. His heart was lurching. Not him. His thoughts tumbled around as he drove round the familiar bends of the spectacular rift valley escarpment, remembering how Ella had been overwhelmed by the beauty of this country he took for granted. He realised he loved the smell of the charcoal burning, the voices of the young goat herds and the colourful traditional dress of the Masai warriors who stubbornly resisted western influence. But it wasn't his country and it wasn't Ella's.

He wouldn't go to smoky, cold and unfriendly Britain and add to the shock to the system that a thousand Asians like himself were inflicting on the place every week. He had too much pride. It was December 1970. His passport had an endorsement which read *Holder is subject to control under the Commonwealth Immigrants Act.* This was not dated. It was also in that purple ink used for those stamps which decided the fate of countless migrants who had found themselves in situations which were not of their own making.

'Who dragged your parents here in the first place?' Ella had asked while in one of her feisty moods.

'So what. It makes no difference now.'

The British had indeed brought the Asians, including his own Goan family, across to East Africa to do the jobs they did not want to do and that the Africans were not yet trusted to do. Ricky knew a smattering of his own Konkani language and very little Portuguese so he did not relish the idea of going back to Goa and probably could not without an Indian passport. His father, Santos, had insisted on the children having British passports. Agnelo, Ricardo's older brother had made up his own mind and plumped for a Kenyan passport, convinced that this would allow him to stay indefinitely in Kenya. Ricardo's British passport meant he might be asked to leave at short notice at any moment.

That was why Ricardo had found himself a job as an education officer, a fancy term for a teacher, with the government of The Republic of Zambia. There was still, however, a problem with his status. Zambia would not allow him to enter their country without a further endorsement which stated that he had a country of residence to return to on completion of his teaching contract. Although his national status was described as *British Subject: Citizen of the United Kingdom and Colonies,*

in that same blurry purple ink, it was obvious from his 'University of the BBC World Service', as he liked to call the endless hours he spent listening to his radio, that he would not exactly find the red carpet if he tried to migrate to England. Enoch Powell with his rivers of blood speeches had put paid to that.

It appeared that the Zambians were well aware of that lack of welcome. Ricardo, therefore, turned to the British High Commission in Nairobi for help; they proved more than happy to stamp his passport with a new endorsement. *This is to certify that the holder of this passport Ricardo John Francis*

*Fonseca is entitled to an entry certificate to travel to the United Kingdom and will be issued with one on application to the nearest British Government representative.* Of course, at the time, they did not expect him to take advantage of that entitlement.

He wanted Ella to know all this so she wouldn't feel he wanted to use her as a UK passport. He could get there under his own steam, he would say, not that he wanted to go there anyway. What was he thinking of? She probably wasn't interested. They hadn't exactly dumped each other but neither had they kept in touch since he'd left the neighbouring school to study in Nairobi. He'd heard her parents had come over from Scotland and visited Mike Kilpatrick's family, on their posh colonial dairy farm, at Christmas time. That wasn't a good sign. But he had to try.

A bunch of waving, cheering schoolgirls, some singing a song he didn't know, escorted Rick and Ella off the school campus.

'I wrote that song,' she said. 'They think it's about you.'

Rick's heart leapt. 'Is it?'

'Pff,' she said. After all he hadn't been in touch for almost a year.

Rick noticed her auburn hair and coppery lipstick were especially shiny. He didn't know she had gone home at lunchtime to shower and get dolled up for his arrival. She *had* got the phone message but pretended she hadn't. She wasn't going to give him an easy time although she couldn't stop fancying the pants off him. What was it about big brown eyes and snowy white linen shirts – and unruly hair that wouldn't obey a comb?

They talked and talked. No, he hadn't got the message to say her parents holiday plans had changed and couldn't meet him. Yes, her parents had spent a day with Mike's family but she hadn't arranged that. Yes her flight home was booked. When had he decided to go to Zambia? Did he want to go? Of course. Did she want to go? Silence. No, she didn't love Mike Kilpatrick.

'And do you love me?' Rick blurted out.

'I don't know. I haven't seen you for ages.'

To cut a long story short, by next morning, the casual 'drop in to see you for old times' sake' had moved along deliciously and the two were cosily breakfasting on slices of pineapple.

'Come and meet my family.'

'Okay but give me a week to wind up here.'

She got her week and made the visit to the family, as one of Rick's many European, or *mzungu*, friends. To Rick's parents there didn't seem to be any threat of romantic complications as, like the others, this girl was on her way home and safely out of reach. Rick had other plans so he popped the question.

'I have to find out if my soul is in the soil of Scotland, the land of my birth,' Ella had said melodramatically. Ricky hadn't worked out if this was tongue in cheek by the time she had gone – possibly forever. There was always something more to discover about that girl.

He had packed her off at Nairobi airport complete with a coppery tan on her pale skin, even more freckles, battered suitcase and that damned guitar which had to go everywhere with her, and set off hurriedly back to Kisumu for Christmas in the bosom of his family – his last Christmas before heading for a new life, five thousand miles away in Zambia,

As his greenish–blue 1967 VW Beetle, as opposed to Ella's blueish–green 1968 VW Beetle, bombed over the top of the potholes along what passed for a road on its way across the savannah, Ricardo put all thoughts of never seeing Ella again to the back of his mind and turned to more practical matters. He wasn't succeeding. Strains of 'Leaving on a Jet Plane' and 'Malaika' were causing him to choke up in a very non macho way that he could never admit to.

There were a few loose ends to tie up in Kericho before he could go on to Kisumu. For example he hadn't been able to pay a rather large grocery bill from the time he had been 'teaching Science with a Political Science degree' at a school near Ella's. In fact, he had been an undercover CIA agent protecting Tom Mboya. Well the protection hadn't worked as the guy had been assassinated so Rick had abandoned all political aspirations and concentrated on positive activities, including becoming a teacher, before he lost all faith in humanity.

Needless to say, despite their friendship with Ricardo, the *dukawallahs* were getting rather impatient - after a year. He decided he'd pop in to the shop en route to Kisumu and explain how he'd been studying in Nairobi and had been forced to sell his beautiful finned1968 Ford Anglia and buy a cheaper 1967 VW in order to finance his course. He couldn't get any financial help for a second qualification, he would explain, and he had never intended not to pay his bill.

Now he could pay his bill if he sold the VW. Ramesh and Mitul, the two brothers whose father owned the shop (and provided them with employment) were looking curiously at the green car,

'Did you buy that off that *lal* haired teacher at the girls' school?' Mitul asked.

'No,' Ricardo replied, 'she sold hers back to Joginder Singh.'

'It looks the same,' Ramesh said.

'Almost but not quite,' Ricardo replied, with a smile, as he remembered the fun he and Ella had had trying to open each other's cars with the wrong keys.

'So you're still chasing her are you?' Ramesh laughed.

The two started teasing their old mate mercilessly until finally Ricardo butted in and said,

'She's gone back to UK so that's probably that. Anyway what about a straight swap - my car for your bill? Hey, I didn't need to stop off here you know. I could've sloped off to Zambia and you'd never have known. See what an honest chap I am. But you'll have to drive me to Kisumu before you can have it.'

By coincidence the local MP, Winston Kipkeino, was in the shop while this discussion was taking place. He said that he just happened to be looking for a car so agreed to pay Ricardo KSh 4000 for his VW which just happened to be what the shopkeepers were owed.

After a bit of haggling over practicalities, everyone shook hands on the 'deal' - but something stopped Ricardo from handing over the car keys. He dangled them between the shopkeeper, Ramesh and the African, ex head teacher, now the Honourable Winston Kipkeino, Member of Parliament for the Kericho District.

'Ramesh, I can give you the keys or give them to Winston. What's it going to be?' Ricardo said willing him to do the right thing – and enjoying a touch of the melodramatic - as usual.

'Oh, let Winston have the keys, I'm sure he'll pay me,' the hapless Ramesh replied, slightly cowed by the arrogance of this proud African in high office, who had just demonstrated his generosity by offering to arrange and pay for a taxi to take Ricardo and his luggage home to Kisumu just in time for Christmas.

Ricardo was vaguely aware that there might be a flaw in the proceedings but he was in a desperate rush to get home and his bank balance couldn't stand a taxi fare so he had been relieved when Winston had solved his problem. Many years later Ricardo was to bump into the family of Ramesh and Mitul in Peterborough, England, and find out what had finally happened.

# Chapter 2: A Reflective Journey

Blissfully unaware of the outcome of the deal just done, Ricardo settled down in the back seat of the RVP (Rift Valley Peugeot) *matatu* (mini bus taxi), which Winston had paid for, and allowed himself the luxury of a bit of inner reflection. He usually hated this, being a man of action, but since getting to know Ella, who called it 'in between' time, he occasionally found himself slipping into it. The other ten African passengers were dozing so it was a perfect opportunity.

He was thinking of his boisterous and flamboyant family, who forgave him all his eccentricities; they lived in his beloved Kisumu on the shores of Lake Victoria where he had grown up. He hadn't seen nearly enough of them over the past few years and now he was heading for Zambia which seemed like the other side of the world. He thought of Ella's words about her soul being in the soil of Scotland. He doubted whether his soul was in any soil anywhere, even Kisumu, though he would probably miss the place.

He thought of his father, Santos Fonseca, who loved to tell his children the story of how, in 1938, he had got a ticket with a recruit number from a British Shipping

Company in Goa which would allow him to join his cousin Basilio in Mombasa. He had joined hundreds of other young men from Goa on the same ship. He told his children that all these young men had shared a dream, which was to make their fortune and go home to Goa to retire. In telling the tale he hoped he was passing on that same dream to his children. However, as children do, Santos's children grew up to have different dreams.

Ricardo thought of how his father had, almost, gone back to his home village Cortalim, in the still Portuguese Goa, to find himself a wife to bring to Kenya so that the food and customs he had grown up with would continue unchanged and uncontaminated by outside influences. As he and his brothers grew up they tended to rebel against this preservation, at any cost, of 'Goanness'. About a year before, after one more confrontation about some petty comment, there had been yet another angry outburst. Ricardo couldn't even remember the issue.

'What utter garbage. Hasn't he read any Goan history?' Agnelo, Ricardo's big brother and the avid reader in the family, had asked. 'Goa has been changed and contaminated by outside influences for thousands of years and it's likely to change again if India has anything to do with it.'

'How come you know so much about it?' Ricardo had asked him. His Political Science degree in Canada had only touched on Goa's past.

'Elementary, my dear Ricardo, elementary. I just read the right History books,' was Agnelo's condescending reply.

'Come on then Sherlock,' goaded nineteen year old Jos who was planning to be on his way to England before they 'shut the doors' as he put it. 'Tell us how it's changed. Not that you'll catch me going back there.'

'Yes, tell us Nelo,' little Rosie said. 'I don't know anything about Goa except people go to Mass every Sunday and eat all the stuff we eat like xacuti and sorpotel, and don't wear saris and stuff – and that's why Mum says *we* have to do that too.'

Agnelo was delighted to have an audience though he would have to make it simple enough for Rosie to understand. Ever since he had agreed, as the eldest son, to leave school and take a job to help out with the family finances, he had been a frustrated student. He had never made Ricardo feel that he resented the fact that his younger brother had won a scholarship to study in Canada – but Ricardo had always felt uncomfortable because his clever big brother had not had the same chance of an education as he had.

'Three thousand years ago – approximately,' Agnelo began as eight year old Rosie plonked herself on his lap to settle in for the long story, 'Goa was known as the land beyond the end of the Earth and the only people were the tribal jungle people who worshipped their ancestors. Some of their descendants still live in what's left of the forests, I've heard. One day I might go there and find out if that's true.'

'Are we descendants of them, Nelo?' Rosie asked earnestly.

'Maybe Rosie,' Agnelo answered gravely, 'but probably not. They were supposed to have been tiny and very black.'

Then, the story goes,' continued Agnelo, ' a man called Parashuram, which means axe man in Sanskrit, shot an arrow into the sea and the Konkan coast rose up to create Goa – a land which could only be approached from the sea. Anyone who wanted to go there from Bombay, South

India, Persia, Arabia, Africa and finally Europe had to get there by boat.'

By this time, fifteen year old Carlos had come to join the other four siblings in the boys' bedroom which was set up with its four single beds for the rare occasions when all four brothers were home at the same time.

'Shh,' said Rosie, 'Nelo's telling us where Goans come from.'

Carlos raised his eyes and chanted in schoolboy fashion, 'Fourteen hundred and ninety eight, Vasco knocked on India's gate.'

'That doesn't happen for ages yet,' Jos added. 'They're still in the trees so far.'

'Who are?' asked Carlos who'd missed the first bit of the tale.

'The Junglies who lived in the forest and spoke to their ancestors,' Rosie said impatiently, getting it not quite right.

'Anyway, to go on,' Agnelo continued, 'the myth tells us that the Konkan coast was formed when it rose out of the sea. I suppose that's where the language Konkani came from – though I'm not sure about that – and soon people from all over the world came to settle on the sandy beaches. They didn't often see the forest aboriginals as most of them just ignored the newcomers and let them get on with things.

The first settlers were Hindus, Brahmins in fact, who farmed the land, and around the same time the Buddhists came and brought literacy. Then the Turks came along and ruled Goa until the Portuguese came.'

'Were they Hindus too?' little Rosie enquired.

'No, they were Moslems – called Moors at that time,' Agnelo the wise one told his little sister. 'They liked to conquer all the lands they visited – unlike the Venetians who only came to trade and then went away again. The Moors once ruled Portugal, you know, which was perhaps why the Portuguese wanted to conquer Goa.' Agnelo was pleased to see that his captive audience were spellbound, which spurred him on. He had done his reading and wanted to share his knowledge.

'I think we'll leave out the Goa Inquisition, shall we Nel,' Ricardo interrupted. He had done some reading too and knew enough about the horrors to know that Rosie would be upset or she might recount the tale and get into trouble with their parents. He'd picked up some knowledge of the Spanish and Portuguese sixteenth century atrocities while he was in Canada and had been astounded to learn that most people in Portugal and Goa knew little about it or denied it had ever happened.

When he first came home from Toronto he had brought up the subject of St Francis Xavier being an evil, racist, Jesuit bully, a fact that he felt had escaped his parents' awareness. His father had lost his temper and accused him of blasphemy and his mother had cried.

'No, Rickoo my son,' Father had said in his halting English which was catching up with his fluent Portuguese and Konkani after all these years in Kenya. 'The man was saint and he made so many miracles. You don't know. He saved lives and when he died his body did not rot. How you can say he evil?'

Ricardo had been horrified by the reaction and wondered how they could have been so brainwashed. He decided that he would never again upset the *susegad* - that wonderful Konkani word for 'cool, calm and collected serenity'. He remembered having the secret thought that *susegad* might have been the final state of calm acceptance after the forced repression of the old religion and acceptance of the new one. This had disturbed him rather a lot so he had kept it to himself.

'Come on, Nelo, tell us who came to Goa next,' Rosie pleaded.

'As I said, there were all kinds of different people living in Goa, 'Junglies', as you say Rosie, Hindus, Buddhists, Moslems, Christians and Jews, but Adil Shah who was the son of the Sultan of Turkey was in charge next. They say he was a good leader who tried to bring everybody together through music, Hindus, Moslems, Christians and Jews – or was that his son? I can't remember.' Agnelo mused, a little unsure of his facts.

'Then Vasco da Gama came and all the Goans became Catholics like we are today,' Rosie added, keen to show that there was something she knew about her Goan heritage.

'Well, it wasn't quite as simple as that. He *did* come to Goa for a short time. The King of Portugal had wanted him to take over the spice trade in the East, but the things he brought to exchange weren't rich enough or beautiful enough for the Indians, so Vasco da Gama went home. He was famous because he was the first European to reach India by sea. It was a man called Alfonso d'Albuquerque who conquered Goa killing Moslems and destroying mosques and Hindu temples so that they could build Christian churches on the same sites. But not everyone was converted to Christianity. Albuquerque left the villages to carry on their Hindu customs except one – which he banned.' Agnelo paused for effect.

'What was that?' was Rosie's predicted response.

'Sati,' her big brother said gravely, 'That's the custom of widows throwing themselves on the funeral pyre of their dead husbands.'

'That's horrible,' Rosie said with a cringe. 'I'd never do that.'

'Some say the wives wanted to go with their husbands because it was worse to stay alive and be a widow and an outcast,' Agnelo went on. 'Anyway it doesn't happen now.'

"I know,' little Rosie continued. 'Siti Patel's granddad died a long time ago and her granny's not outcasted at all. She works at the hospital.' Everyone laughed at their cute little sister who was the adored baby girl who had finally arrived after four boys in the family.

'Anyway,' continued Agnelo, 'there were all these Portuguese sailors who didn't have wives so Albuquerque made them marry the Indian women – some say there were four hundred weddings in the first year. Then all these families were Catholic but it wasn't enough for the King of Portugal. He arranged to send the big guns to convert more people and he wanted it done in a hurry.'

'How did they do that then?' piped up Jos who was pretending not to listen as he lay on his bed with his knees up and crossed and his eyes closed.

'That's too long a story – we'll skip that for now,' Agnelo replied, dodging the issue. 'You've all heard about Saint Francis Xavier, the Patron Saint of Goa, haven't you?'

Of course they all had. Every year on December 3rd all the Goans celebrate the feast of St Francis Xavier, *Goycho Saib* (Lord of Goa) and *Goycho Pia* (Father of Goa) whose partly mummified relics (minus a toe, an arm and some other parts which were sent to Rome or acquired by followers) lie in a glass casket in Bom Jesus Church in Old Goa. Like all good Goan parents Santos and Olga had taught their children how privileged they were to be custodians of the body of such a wonderful saint who would keep all Goans together wherever they were in the world. He would also answer all their prayers whatever these were. He was their inspiration and protector and their faith was unshakeable.

'Right,' Agnelo went on, 'Francis Xavier, who was Spanish and not Portuguese, and another man called Ignatius Loyola founded the Jesuit movement and they were the best people in the world at converting people to Christianity. They converted more people than anyone could have imagined so they were both made saints.'

'Hmmmm,' was Ricardo's response just before he switched off.

'So is everyone in Goa Catholic now?' Rosie asked.

'No,' Agnelo answered. 'More than half are Hindu and since 1961, more and more people are Hindu since India took Goa back from the Portuguese and more and more Goans have scattered all around the world.'

'So if our name is Fonseca, does that mean we've got Portuguese blood?' Carlos asked, waking up to take a bit of interest.

'Not necessarily,' Ricardo contributed. 'The Jesuits made up a lot of rules and one was that nobody was allowed to have a Hindu or a Moslem name if they'd been converted to Christianity.'

'So,' said Carlos thinking hard. 'Our ancestors could have been Hindu, Moslem, Buddhist and only maybe with a bit of Portuguese. We haven't found out much have we?'

'Aww,' little Rosie wailed, jumping off Agnelo's lap and staring at him with steely eyes. 'I *still* don't know where we came from!'

'Never mind Rosieoo, Posieoo,' her big brother Ricardo said giving her a hug. 'You know what? It doesn't matter where you came from. It's where you're going that counts.'

Rosie's reply with a little crumpled face was, 'OK fine –
but I don't know that either.'

And everybody laughed.

Olga, their mother had been eavesdropping from the
adjoining room and was waiting in the wings to make her
contribution. She wanted to have one last word.

'Have you heard of the Beggar's Banquet?' Olga asked.
'It happens before weddings in Goa. Your granny told me
about it, God rest her soul. The Goa people believe if you
don't give food to the poor people, the evil spirits who are
their ancestors will put the evil eye on the new couple and
their babies. So you see, after all these religions and their
temples and mosques and 'Se Cathedral' the biggest
Catholic Church in Asia, the local people go right back to
their roots. They're afraid of the wrath of their ancestors.
Strange isn't it? All I know,' Mother continued, 'is that
there's been peace for a long time and I think it's because
Francis Xavier is looking after us. Never forget that –
wherever you go in the world. He'll look after you because
you are Goan.'

Her brood of five stayed silent, each interpreting that
tale in their own, probably very different, ways.

As Dad had said before, it was very important for these
young men who had come to Africa to return to Goa to
find a wife who could help to preserve the food and
customs. All the other young Goan men he knew had done
this, but Santos Fonseca loved to boast that he was 'the only
one' who hadn't had to go further than Nairobi to find the
beautiful, nineteen year old, Olga Gama Pinto.

Santos had stolen Olga's heart but the sway of the caste
system transferred from Hindu to Goan Catholic culture
had reared its ugly head. Olga's father worked for the
British Colonial Government and had sent his sons,

including the famous martyr Pio, to Goa for a 'proper' education. He was not about to allow his daughter to marry a bank clerk who had just fallen off the boat in Mombasa. Santos had a fight on his hands which he eventually won, but not without using all the panache and charm he could muster and a few 'tales' of eminent relatives in Goa. His success at winning the fair lady was fairly remarkable at the time as there were many similar lost battles since tailors weren't good enough for bakers or railway workers weren't good enough for chefs and so on. Filing clerks were considered superior to teachers Ricardo noted mentally with a rueful smile – because they could be classed as 'business' people and therefore likely to become rich – which of course teachers never could. Outside the academic and professional groups, plutocracy definitely ruled. To be rich was to be respected and if you were not rich enough you had to spend to give the impression that you were rich so in the end, you ended up even poorer. This amused Ricardo on reflection as he was able to detach himself from this mind set.

'I wonder if all this nonsense was the reason why Uncle Pio became such a rebel,' he asked himself and the familiar pain in his soul reminded him of the day, while he was still a young undergraduate, that his Auntie Emma had arrived in Toronto a widow with three children, because greedy people of some complexion did not want to be exposed by yet another activist who was fighting to relieve poverty.

*

As the RVP continued to trundle along, Ricardo, his memory jogged, was making plans to make a very important visit for the last time ever, before he set off for new pastures. He simply had to go to Rusinga Island to visit the grave of a man he had admired and whose life he had wanted to save. Ricardo's association with Tom Mboya had been cloaked in secrecy because of his temporary recruitment as a CIA agent whose job it had been to protect this popular but outspoken politician, known to be a 'man of the people'. He had been unable to join the throngs of mourners who had caused riots in every town along the route between Nairobi and Kisumu near the exquisite little island on Lake Victoria where his body was finally laid to rest on land belonging to his Luo family. Tom had been gunned down outside a Pharmacy around midday on a July Sunday in 1969. Rightly or wrongly the Africans of various tribes believed that the people closest to Jomo Kenyatta their President had been involved in the assassination of the hero they believed would improve the conditions of the poor people across the country.

Ricardo had reason to believe that this was not entirely true and he felt very strongly that he wanted to mourn the loss of this popular and brave man. His only regret was that Ella had gone back to Scotland and could not share these moments at Tom's graveside. She too had become inadvertently involved in thwarting an earlier attempt on Mboya's life and had briefly met him and been inspired by his charisma.

★

The RVP lumbered off the tar road announcing its arrival in Kisumu by hitting the rocky murram streets on the outskirts of the town.

'*Hapa tafadhali,*' shouted Ricardo dragged out of his reverie. 'I want to get off.'

A one hundred and eighty degree spin on the brakes and a cloud of dust later, Ricky and his luggage were deposited outside Kisumu Stores run by V J and K P Shah, neighbours of the Fonseca family in the Indian section on the outskirts of town along the road towards the village of Nyangoma Kogal on the shores of Lake Victoria.

In 1970, seven years after Kenya's independence, there were still very clearly segregated neighbourhoods. People felt comfortable with this or so it seemed. There was the African area, the Indian area and an upmarket area which was racially integrated where the few Mzungus who were left lived alongside Africans and Asians – but they had one thing in common. Regardless of their race they were wealthy.

K P Shah Junior of Kisumu Stores was behind the counter, perched on a high stool, cigarette in hand.

'Hey Rick. How we don't see you so much? Thought you went London. What's with the suitcase? You back for good?'

'Just for Christmas, you know – family and all,' Rick replied in similar lingo. The two had been to Kisumu Boys School together and K P had gone straight into the family business at sixteen.

'We never found another right inner for the Kisumuwallahs, you know,' K P said spotting the hockey stick poking out of the now dusty blue sports bag. He didn't know it was bound for Zambia. 'How about a game on Sunday – two o'clock vee Eldoret?'

Ricardo jumped at the chance. The Kisumuwallahs were the 'All Asian' (meaning Goans and other Indians) hockey team who took on other 'All Asian' teams from other towns in Kenya. Lower down the league were the separate Goan, Sikh, Moslem and Hindu teams who, in Kisumu at least, played match after match and could barely find an outright winner between the Sikhs and the Goans with the other two trailing. The Daal- Bahts (lentil and rice eaters) were usually at the bottom of the league and got teased that rice and daal didn't give them enough strength to whip the meat eaters. The competition was lively but the lads were the best of mates, especially when it came to finding the best joint team to tackle other town teams. They weren't going to let a turban or a gold cross interfere with choosing the best players.

'Sure K P, I've been playing in my Nairobi team lately and I've done a bit of centre forward. I'd love to,' Ricardo said, delighted to find that not much had changed in his home town.

Kisumu in the 1960s was known as the Indian town and in fact there were more Indians than Africans, for a short while, at that time – and a buzzing town it was with a population of almost two and a half million. The busy Lake Victoria port had links with Uganda, Tanzania, Rwanda, Burundi and Zaire with few restrictions for the traveller who had a passport to stamp. Also Kisumu was at the end of the southern branch of the Mombasa to Uganda railway for the building and administration of which so many workers had been brought over from all parts of India.

In one area of town a Sikh Gurudwara and a Hindu Temple had grown up close to each other and in another area an Ismaili Mosque, The Aga Khan hospital and a mosque had grown up near each other. With half a million Catholics and around sixty Catholic priests in Kisumu Diocese, the religious needs of Goan Catholics were also well catered for.

Schools were a problem, however, for those who wanted to educate their youngsters within community traditions. As a result many of the Indians of all faiths went to school together, regardless of creed or caste. A privileged few were able to go to the Dr Ribeiro Goan School in Nairobi or the Aga Khan or Sikh schools in Kisumu. Little

Rosie, however, could go to St Theresa's Secondary for girls which would please her parents. K P, Ricardo and countless other Indians of all backgrounds hadn't been aware that there was any such problem and had grown up happily together forging firm friendships.

'What time do you finish K P?' Ricardo asked fishing for a lift.

'Dad's in the back of the shop – I'll see if he can take over,' K P said disappearing out to the back and coming back with a grinning K P Senior.

'Ricardo. Good to see you. Habari?' he said.

'Mzuri, Mr Shah, Habari iako?' Ricardo replied.

'Mzuri tu, Hakuna matata,' the older man said, 'Ngoja – wait - K P,' he added before going to fetch two boxes from the back. 'These are what your mother wanted K P – and Ricardo, take these to your family. I'm sure we'll be seeing your mother with her tray of sweets soon. Wish them a Happy Christmas.'

Inside the box for Ricardo's family were all kinds of savoury snacks like ganthia, sev and cheura and a selection of sweets like halwa, ladoo and jilebi in a separate box with a lid that Ricardo opened straightaway because he couldn't wait.

'Thank you, Mr Shah; I haven't had these for a long time.'

'No problem, Ricardo, we have so much in stock. But tell them they must eat it fresh, eh.'

'Don't worry, they won't last long,' Ricardo said, stuffing a jilebi in his mouth as K P Junior dragged him out of the shop to drive him home in the shop pick up truck, leaving his father to drive home in the car. Things were profitable for shopkeepers in those days.

# Chapter 3: Kisumu

Night had fallen by the time Ricardo arrived home unannounced but the light on the front verandah was shining expectantly casting shadows through the morning glory (his mother's pride and joy) as it clambered over the trellis. The pungent aroma of sorpotel was wafting through the air making his mouth water as he came through the gate and along the path past the huge avocado tree whose fruits, sadly, were rejected by the Fonseca family. It was good to be home.

Santos Fonseca, now in his sixties, with a proud paunch but still with all his hair, was swinging on a rocking chair enjoying a pre-dinner drink away from the hustle and bustle of the family.

'He's here,' he shouted through the open front door and gave his second son an enormous Goencar bear hug. It was almost a desperate hug. Another son was slipping away – this one to Zambia.

Olga Fonseca, young for her fifty years, jet black hair tied back in a bun at the nape of her neck, Spanish style, pulled off her apron as she ran.

'That crow's never wrong. He came and sat and sat. I knew it was for you,' she said hugging him.

'Is that true?' Ricardo addressed the whole family as they appeared in hierarchical order, as always, for their greeting hug – Agnelo, Jos, Carlos and finally Rosie.

'Absolutely,' Jos laughed. 'She's been talking about it all day. I don't know what kind of state we'd be in if you hadn't arrived.'

Ricardo was going to say it was a pretty sure bet he'd be home for Christmas but instead he humoured his Mum.

'Amazing eh? Who needs telephones?' Unfortunately, he'd touched on a sore point. Olga had been nagging to become one of the few households in the area at the time with a phone. This one had back fired on her. Rosie was leaping up and down with excitement pointing to a pile of big containers.

'Look Rickoo, I helped Mum to make all the Christmas kunswars; neuris, dodol, dos, bolinhas, and… and… your favourite korbolams – and the bibique's been outside on the ngiko for about a day and a half.'

'Brilliant, Rosie,' Ricardo answered. 'Are you going to feed the five thousand with all that?'

'Only the Goaencars,' Mother interrupted, 'and maybe the Shahs next door… oh and the Patels and the Kalasingas.'

'And the whole world,' Dad grumbled. 'I know your mother.'

'Oh, by the way, there's a box of stuff from the Shahs,' Ricardo said remembering he'd left everything out on the verandah.

'Come on Carlos, Rosie, help me get my stuff in,' Ricardo yelled using his big brother's unquestionable right to boss his younger siblings around.

'We'll put the kunswar on the trays in the morning and we can all help to take them round. It'll be so nice for everyone to see that *all* my family are here for Christmas. Then, in the midst of all the excitement, she burst into tears. 'I don't know when I'm going to see all my sons together again if ever,' she sniffled.

Unfortunately there was some truth in what she said so there wasn't much anyone could say.

'My voucher's arrived,' Jos said by way of explanation for Mum's tears, 'and I leave for London Heathrow at the end of January. As some sort of excuse he added, 'I have to go Rick. There aren't any jobs for me here – and if there was a job, I've got the wrong colour and passport. There isn't even a nice available girl with a rich father.'

'When are you off to Zambia then Rick?' Agnelo asked rather too quickly.

'They fly me to Lusaka on the 19th and then on to some place in the north with an airstrip called Kasama,' Ricardo said. 'The school's called Mpika Boys' School; it's a new World Bank School and we're going to be the very first lot of teachers. I'm not sure if they've even finished building it.' He couldn't contain his excitement and for a while it rubbed off. Little Rosie was excited about something too and she couldn't wait to blurt it out.

'Agnelo's getting married,' she called out.

'Fantastic,' Ricardo cried shaking his brother's hand vigorously. 'Who's the lucky girl and how come you kept it so quiet?'

There was a stony silence and Ricardo realised that his father had left the room.

'The wedding's on the 29th at Our Lady and St Joseph but not, I'm afraid, at the G I,' Olga announced much too calmly. Even more calmly she added, 'It will be very small.'

'The 29<sup>th</sup> of what?' Ricardo gasped, thinking he might miss the celebrations.

'December,' Olga hissed. 'That's next week. We didn't want you and Jos to miss it.'

'Shotgun,' sixteen year old Carlos hissed with perhaps a touch of glee – and then wished he hadn't. The looks were killing him.

Agnelo looked crestfallen.

'We'll be all right,' he said after a while. 'I love her. She's a lovely girl.'

'Who is she then?' Rick asked too cheerfully. 'And when am I going to meet her?'

'Do you know the Lobo family? It's Maria.' Agnelo told his brother looking into his eyes searching for approval.

'Ah,' Rick said knowingly. 'Then it's probably a good thing … well … you know… that you have to hurry.'

The problem was clear. The Lobo family were Christian Brahmins and Maria's father was an eminent solicitor. Never in a million years would they have allowed their daughter to marry into the Fonseca family under normal circumstances. Later on, in confidence, Ricardo quizzed his big brother. It turned out the two had been seeing each other for years.

'Did you plan this then?' Ricardo asked his big brother for whom he had a healthy respect.

'No, in all honesty, I didn't want things to happen in this way – but Maria did. She said it was the only way,' Agnelo disclosed looking crushed.

'Come on big brother, you're supposed to be happy. Stuff these petty Goencar attitudes. You wait; when this baby comes along they'll all be goo gooing together.'

'I hope so, little bro,' Agnelo said with a weak grin. 'The trouble is it's affecting everything. The Lobos are saying they're going to emigrate to Canada to avoid the shame. Can you imagine? It isn't the old man so much. It's the mother who's the snob. She'd never have let us get married if we hadn't pushed it.' The two brothers guffawed a bit at the double meaning before Ricardo pointed out, 'It's your life and if Maria's the girl for you, that's fine. You know I wish you every happiness – and I can't wait to meet her. The last time I saw her was in a little white dress with hockey stick legs underneath.'

'You know Jos was seeing Anastasia for a while,' Agnelo started.

'De Souza?' Ricardo interrupted.

'Yep. They put a stop to that.' Agnelo continued

'What for - Oscar's Dad's best mate, for heaven's sake?' Ricardo shouted both in surprise and anger.

'Shh, keep your voice down,' Agnelo whispered. 'It seems that administrators can't marry into tailor's families. For bank clerk, read administrator nowadays.'

'Who decided that one?' Ricardo added.

'Both lots did. They agreed that it would be 'for the best' if Jos and Anastasia didn't see each other again.'

'And they went along with it?' Ricardo said, a bit disappointed that his younger brother hadn't put up a fight.

'I reckon they couldn't put up with the hassle,' declared Agnelo. 'It's what elbowed Jos in the London direction, I think. Dad won't believe that though. Rick, you don't know how lucky you are to get away. You can choose any girl you like.'

'It's not as easy as you think big bro,' Ricardo confided. 'The girl I fancy has gone back to Scotland so I'll probably never see her again.'

'But you never seriously considered you might marry her did you?' the older brother assumed.

'Why not?' Ricardo was feeling even more rebellious. The two young men tried to imagine the old man's reaction and laughed. Then they recounted all the stories of the many unsuitable but lovely girls they had encountered on their way through school and college – and for Ricardo through university in Canada. It took them a long time as any girl would have found it hard to choose between those two attractive and fun-loving brothers. There were the Ismaili girls – absolutely no chance, Moslem girls – ditto, Hindu girls, - even worse, African girls – not for marrying and European girls – only for fun until they went home to their families.

'I only once tried to date a Goan girl,' Ricardo said. 'I was only seventeen and her father pinned me to a chair for an hour's lecture on the birds and the bees and then told me I hadn't a chance anyway because master bakers and bank clerks don't mix. What a farce!' The two brothers had lowered the level of the whisky bottle rather a lot so their laughter woke up their mother who came shuffling through to send her two eldest sons to bed so they could be of some use next day.

'It's Christmas Eve tomorrow, boys. We need to be busy,' she mumbled, half asleep.

'Sorry Mum, we just had a lot to catch up on.'

Agnelo was feeling too emotionally cowed to respond with much more than an irritated, 'Ok then, we're going.' And in Ricardo's direction, 'I suppose you've noticed Dad hasn't talked to me since you arrived. It's been going on for days.'

'I would have thought he would be more understanding about it.'

'I think he likes Maria but he thinks we're bloody fools - or *I* am for getting her pregnant. He reckons it's put the kibosh on Carlos's chances of getting into Doctor Ribeiro to do his A levels.'

'That's rubbish. He wouldn't have got in anyway. We don't class as being the right people,' Ricardo pointed out. 'What I can't understand is why some of those Goencars think they're so much better than Hindus because they wear western clothes and go to Church and don't have a caste system. The Goan caste system seems to be even worse.'

'You know what it might mean, if Carlos doesn't get into Ribeiro?' Agnelo continued. 'He's already talking about going with Jos to do his sixth form in England. He's down for getting straight ones in his Cambridge Lower, you know, the first boy for years, so he shouldn't have a problem.'

'That leaves Rosie on her own with Mum and Dad. No wonder Mum's upset.' Ricardo observed. His own situation was looming into the horizon. They'd probably go mental if they thought there was a possibility of him marrying Ella; they had liked her but only as just another of Ricardo's many Mzungu friends.

Ricardo recalled the fun they'd had when Ella had come to visit for a few days, after they'd become (secret) lovers. As usual, with her easy manner, Ella had got along well with everyone especially Rosie who loved Ella's stories about funny things that had happened at Kipsigis Girls' School. Their main criticism was that she was scruffy and couldn't be presented at church on Sunday in her not very well stitched kitenge dress with its bat sleeves and her leather chapals. Ella considered any footwear other than rubber flip flops 'dressed'. She did have some clean jeans and a T shirt in her bag but these were not suitable for church. The solution was found. Oscar de Souza, Santos's best friend and tennis partner of old, was visiting and, as a master tailor, was carrying a tape measure in his back pocket. Two seconds later, Ella's arms were in the air as she was measured up and asked one question,

'What's your favourite colour?' Oscar had asked.

'Probably green,' Ella had replied rather puzzled. She was the only one that didn't know what was going on.

Rosie, Ricardo and Ella had gone down to the bazaar and found some black shoes with a slight heel and no open toes. Ella hated them and was to remember the blisters they gave her for a long time despite them being half a size too big. Her Scottish feet had never been weathered into wearing shoes without socks or stockings. In Africa it was too hot for those so flip flops or open sandals were her answer.

That evening Oscar had arrived with a little sleeveless tailored dress with darts in all the right places and a hem which was demurely on the knee (unlike her other mini dresses of sixties fashion). It fitted her in all the right places like no other dress she had bought had ever done – and it was in a shiny material with an emerald green pattern on a white background. Everyone else had been delighted with the transformation and even Ella had begun to feel comfortable after a while.

She had wanted to pay for the dress but Oscar had refused to accept any money saying that Ricardo had told them she was a very kind friend and colleague. Instead, she asked if she could order two more dresses which he could charge his going rate for – one long and one short – she'd been shamed into taking more care of her appearance. Next day, Saturday, she had gone to the shop to choose some black and white material for the sophisticated long dress and some green polka dot material for the short dress – and could it please, she had asked, be a couple of inches shorter than the first one. She could pay him in advance and Ricardo could pick the dresses up the next time he came home. Everyone of course had politely invited her to come and fetch them herself. It had been so nice to meet another one of Ricardo's friends.

The most memorable and amusing part of the weekend, however, had been the trip to Our Lady and St Joseph church.

Roads, in Kisumu, were not the best in the world in 1969 and very often there were drainage ditches up to six feet deep or more located quite close to the edge of a road and there was no particular pattern as to where these might be. Parking was equally haphazard. You simply drew up and stopped at a reasonable distance away from where you wanted to walk. You just had to make sure you were well away from the middle of the road.

Ricardo had wanted to take his visitor as close to the Church as possible since she was decked out in her new dress and borrowed white shawl with which she could cover her head and or shoulders as she wished. He had drawn up swiftly and jumped out expecting Ella to do the same thing. She had - except she had opened the front passenger door and stepped confidently into fresh air and landed neatly at the bottom of a six foot culvert. She couldn't move or speak, not because she was hurt but because she was paralysed with laughter.

'Has anyone seen Ella?' Ricardo had asked flummoxed.

'I'm down here,' a slightly winded and giggling Ella finally managed to say. 'I can't get out. You'll have to help me.'

Fortunately the weather was dry so most of the red dust brushed off but it was a rather ruffled Ella, rather than the perfect one that all the effort had gone into, who joined the Fonseca pew at Our Lady and St Joseph Church for all the Kisumu Goaencars to stare at curiously.

The two brothers laughed at that memory before they went off to bed. Later, in the dark, speaking from one single bed to the next, Agnelo whispered, 'Stay happy, Rick. Keep your relationships uncomplicated.'

Ricardo was going to look back and wonder if that was the moment when he had decided never to marry a Goan girl. He had sampled freedom beyond the restrictive customs and traditions that were crippling the older members of the Goan community and especially his parents. He hated to see them suffer but he saw no way forward for himself except escape. He had become a cosmopolite free to adopt any nation who would accept him. After all, there was nothing new about the concept of having one foot in the East and one foot in the West; he was a Goan.

His thoughts drifted towards a red haired girl with green eyes who was examining her own Scottish roots at that very moment.

★

Next morning, on Christmas Eve, the family made themselves so busy with preparations and visiting, that there was conveniently no time to dwell on any tensions. Only Dad was stomping around being not very useful looking as if his world had come to an end.

'I think I'll have a chat with Dad,' Ricardo said. 'I'll see if I can talk some sense into him.

He found his father pacing up and down outside on the verandah like a caged lion.

'It's time to think of going back to Goa, son.' Santos said very seriously. 'There's going to be nothing left for us here soon. Rosie can do her schooling there. What you think?'

'I think,' replied Ricardo, 'that you should wait for a while and see how things work out. And I think you'll love your new grandchild.'

'Herumph,' was all that the stubborn old man could produce. 'And what's going to happen to you, my son? There are no Goans in Zambia that we know. Maybe we find you a good girl in Goa when we go.'

'It's not time to worry about that now, Dad,' the son, feeling more like the father, said. 'For now, just remember that the world is changing and we all have to change with it or nobody's going to be happy.'

'Hmph,' was his Dad's reply.

Midnight Mass, the Christmas tradition that no self-respecting Goan would ever miss, ended with a few surprises for the Lobo and Fonseca families which were to restore their faith in human nature – or at least the Goan community. Amid the usual gregarious hugs, handshakes, kisses on cheeks and cries of, 'Happy Christmas', congratulations for the two families on the wedding of Agnelo and Maria filtered through with offers of help with catering, a cake, venues, photography, flowers, decorations, music – or anything at all. Invitations would not be necessary. It had all happened by word of mouth.

The two sets of parents were astounded. Where they had expected criticism and perhaps ostracism they had instead found friendship and support. The news of the heartbreak that Max and Antoinetta Lobo and Santos and Olga Fonseca had subjected themselves to had spread like wildfire. A meeting had been called and a decision made that nobody was going to allow them to do everyone out of a good wedding. They were to be offered the G I (The Goan Institute) as a venue, complete with the Christmas decorations and any other help they needed to make it an occasion to remember.

The original plan had been to have a small church service with the immediate family, and a meal at the Lobo 'residence' which was in the upmarket former European area of town. This was now taken out of their hands and, before they could protest, there was a guest list of three hundred, including workmates and neighbours from the other Indian communities and a few Europeans and Africans. The only stipulations were that if you could bring a dish or contribute anything towards the day, could you please do so. It was understood that Max and Santos might be getting a few bills – especially Max as he was known to be worth a few shillings.

The only items which had been pre arranged were the priest, the Church, Maria's cream dress and veil with gold trimmings and mantilla and two bridesmaid's dresses in gold satin for Maria's two sisters, Caterina and Alvira. Oscar de Souza had run those up with his usual efficiency. Within the community it had been easy to find a florist, a baker, live musicians, a photographer and a shopkeeper with an off licence so the entire occasion was very well catered for. Hakuna Matata. No problem.

The Fonsecas were to host an evening at their house to take the place of the traditional custom (in Goa) of *Bhikarenchem Jevonn* or the Beggars Banquet as Olga had named it. The houseboys were invited to eat first and then they could take home a can of beer and a *potli* (doggy bag) of food. Olga had insisted on this taking place. She couldn't possibly risk the effect of some *pessao* (evil spirit). Their children, however, wouldn't allow Olga and Santos to tell anyone that this was the reason for their generosity. After the servants had gone, the two families and a few select friends enjoyed a meal and some drinks together. It all went swimmingly well which led to a few differences being sorted out.

Max and Antoinette Lobo had insisted on hosting an open house for snacks and cocktails in the garden of their large house so that Maria could display her trousseau and give anyone who wished to the opportunity to bring a gift for the happy couple. Max's elderly aunt would act as a scribe to record all the details of the presents. (This custom usually improved the quality of the gifts.) This had been a very practical suggestion as the newly weds would be living at the Lobo house until they had sorted out their own accommodation.

By the actual Wedding Day, everyone was exhausted apart from the bride who – because of her condition – had not been allowed to stress herself. She looked lovely in her empire line dress which hid the little story behind the rush.

The church ceremony at Our Lady and St Joseph was short, simple and traditional with a couple of well known hymns, the vows and an address from Father Carey, the Irish priest. The much larger than expected congregation included Indians of all faiths, some Africans and a few Europeans all of whom were connected to the families in at least some small way. Many of them were unexpected guests but Ricardo noticed that his father was smiling (or really smiling) for the first time since he'd got home.

This was followed by photographs outside the church and a quick drive or short walk to the Goan Institute round the corner.

The Christmas decorations were still up in the otherwise bare but large hall and a very long table down one side of the room was groaning with dishes ranging from starters at one end, main dishes in the middle and sweets at the other. One separate area near the sweets was labelled 'Vegetarian'. Some good person had even organised 'table heaters' to keep the curries warm and muslin cloths with beads around the edges to keep the sweets protected from flies.

Antoinetta Lobo and Olga Fonseca couldn't believe their eyes. Olga whispered to her son's new mother-in-law, 'I'm ashamed that I thought these people would turn their backs on us. Look, it's like a 'bring a dish' wedding.'

Antoinetta was a harder nut to crack however. She sniffed loudly and said, 'I'm still not sure Maria had enough time to consider if she was doing the right thing.'

Olga's reply was sharper than her usual, 'Then she'll just have to get on with it won't she,' and she left it at that. She was sure Antoinetta was still smarting from her daughter not netting at least a lawyer if not a doctor. She also thought to herself, 'Just you wait, Antoinetta Lobo, you'll see just how successful my Agnelo's going to be.'

Then there was no time to be petty. The young girls were descending on the guests with little paper plates with a selection of one each of samosas, king rolls, dhanya chutney sandwiches, bhajias, potato vaddas and several other starters from different Indian cuisines – plus a splash of tamarind chutney and a slice of lemon. If you were vegetarian you were handed an empty plate so you could go to the table and fill it yourself.

The live band meantime had struck up – glad of the chance to rehearse for the New Year's Eve Dance which was two days later – and the bride and groom did a little twirl before being joined by a few others.

Drinks were being served in the corner manned by the shopkeeper with the off licence and a willing band of teenage boys eager to sample the goods. Max Lobo had agreed to pick up the tab which in retrospect he realised had been rather a foolish thing to do.

Next an army of ladies armed with ladles and large spoons lined up behind the food table and a long queue formed for food to be served to them. The military operation was perfectly executed and soon the muslin cover over the desserts was removed so that anyone who hadn't stretched their stomach linings to the limit could enjoy some rasmalai, gulab jamons or anything from the mountains of kunswar left over from Christmas.

Half way through the evening the couple began to say their goodbyes so all the guests formed an arch by joining their hands in couples from one end of the room to the other for the two to walk under and say their farewells to each and every guest. This took a very long time - but the band played on.

Mr Will Smith, general manager of Homa Bay Cruises and his wife Emily thought it was the most delightful event they had ever attended though Emily did whisper to her husband, 'I think there's going to be another happy event soon – by Easter I'd say. Ah well.' She had only just noticed.

The rumour was that, for their honeymoon, Maria and Agnelo had booked into Whitesands Hotel in Mombasa.

Ricardo's thoughts turned to Ella. Had he lost her forever?

Later on it transpired that the instigator of the 'bring a dish' community-spirited wedding had been K P Shah Senior of Kisumu Stores. The whole community had to go in there at some time for something or other so he'd had the perfect opportunity to spread the news. Of course his sales had spiralled over the period as had those of his cousin who just happened to be the owner of the off licence.

However nobody was going to let that detract from the fact that it had been a wonderful wedding.

And there was another thing to think of; within the community it was perhaps wise to keep the banker and the solicitor on your side. You never knew when you might need them.

★

Now that the wedding was over and some rather subdued New Year celebrations at the G I, the family seemed happier and Dad had stopped all his pacing up and down and his talk of going to Goa.

Ricardo and Jos were both using Agnelo's vacated bed to pile up the stuff they'd need to take to London and Zambia respectively.

Jos at least knew that his cousin Manuel was going to meet him at the airport and take him to a place called Peterborough where they would be lodging with a Patel family who needed the rent they could afford to pay.

Ricardo didn't know what he was going to find in Zambia or how he was going to travel the last one hundred miles from Kasama to the rural school he had been assigned to. He had no idea who his colleagues might be or if he would be accepted. He suddenly felt very lonely – even within the bosom of his very warm family.

He sat down and wrote a very long letter describing the wedding and all the other recent events and his feelings related to them. He also wrote about his intention of going to Rusinga Island. 'I wish you could be there too,' he wrote. (Ella had met Tom Mboya and had been around and may have saved his life when he had escaped an assassination attempt.) He described his fear of stepping off the plane in the middle of a strange country where he knew not one soul and ended his letter with, 'I hope you are finding out if your soul's in the soil over there – or not. All my love, Ricardo John Francis.' (Ella would understand the significance of the John Francis bit from the exciting clandestine days of undercover work.)

He addressed the blue airmail envelope with its red white and blue striped edging to Miss Ella Mackay, Hillside Farm, Balnahuig, Nr Altnabervie, Caithness, Scotland, U K. That seemed like a very long address especially considering that he only had to write R J F Fonseca, P.O. Box 34, Kisumu, Kenya as the sender's address.

When it was time to leave his family, Ricardo was more than ready to go and feeling excited. The wedding, however, had helped to restore his faith in the various Asian communities in Kisumu and helped him to put back a few roots which gave him a clearer sense of his identity. He found time to indulge his mischievous side, which was never very far from the surface, and had a photograph of himself and Maria, his brother's beautiful bride, framed.

'That'll keep the ladies in Zambia at arm's length. I'll tell them my wife's coming to join me soon,' he announced to Jos, Carlos and Rosie. 'All except one lady maybe,'

'Ha,' pounced Carlos. 'Who's that then?'

Ricardo tapped the side of his nose and replied. 'The right one.'

He could embark on his new life carrying happy memories of his family. Maria's parents and his own had decided to work on their friendship for the sake of Maria and Agnelo. For Olga the thought of a new baby was taking away the pain of the loss of three and perhaps soon four of her sons to the outside world. Young Rosie seemed to be taking everything in her stride as usual and was probably looking forward to the time when she didn't have to be at the beck and call of four big brothers.

Ricardo would always be a Goan and proud of it, but thinking of the wonderful people from other Indian communities, who had helped his family out, he'd always be proud of being an Indian too.

But now Ricardo had to become part of the Goan diaspora, a wanderer in the wider world, a cosmopolite. But he needed a companion to help him along the way.

# Chapter 4: Culture Shock in Reverse

Ella Mackay's departure from Kenya by night flight from Nairobi airport was in stark contrast to her arrival in Africa via dawn over the Nile valley. Instead of the orange blaze of sunrise above the clouds, and the excitement of the pilot bringing the plane down for his passengers to see the familiar bend in the River Nile with its green ribbon edges, the descent through the murky clouds into a damp winter morning at Heathrow was dismal.

She was glad she (or had it been her Mum?) had had the presence of mind to pack her old red duffle coat with its tartan lining and wooden toggles for this moment. It hadn't seen the light of day for two and a half years in the heat of Africa but now she was glad of it as she walked through the wind and sleet into the Airport terminal. She wondered why heads were turning until she caught sight of her reflection in a large window. Her red coat was standing out against the greys, blacks and browns that everyone else seemed to be wearing and her recent tan and shiny hair were glowing – despite the bags under her sleepless eyes.

Ella began to notice the pale, care-worn faces of the Heathrow public. They looked ill compared to the sun drenched Mzungus she had been spending time with in Kenya and there was hardly a black or a brown face to be seen. It felt very strange. Was this culture shock in reverse? She had been warned that this might happen.

She was missing Kenya already – the blue skies, the hot sun, giraffes swaying across the main road, the smell of charcoal fires and exotic spices, pawpaw, mango or pineapple for breakfast, the sound of the waves crashing on the Mombasa beach and the sight of a golden sunrise spreading across the Indian Ocean at dawn. Was it only two days ago that she had been basking in that atmosphere?

Most of all she was missing Ricky and she was kicking herself. Why hadn't she said yes when he had asked her to marry him? He'd probably find someone else as soon as he got to Zambia and who could blame him? She realised, with a horrible ache in her heart, that it was not at all what she wanted. What was done couldn't be undone because he hadn't been able to give her a PO Box number for his new school in Zambia. She realised she couldn't write to him – and panicked.

Blinking hard to stop the tears, Ella turned her thoughts towards home and family and picking up the threads of her old life in Caithness which seemed to have taken place very long ago in a previous existence.

At the time, in Nairobi, she had known why she hadn't been able to commit herself to marriage. It was clear that she had to go home to think very hard about the implications of abandoning her roots and making a new life half way across the world. Her original intention had been to enjoy a two year adventure before settling down to adult life in the society of her upbringing. Yes, that was what she would do. She would try very hard to readjust to life in Caithness. That lingering angst would disappear in time.

With two hours to spare before her ongoing flight to Inverness and feeling fiercely independent all of a sudden, Ella decided to book a train ticket home from Inverness to Altnabervie. She cashed her last traveller's cheque and now had ten crisp new five pound notes. They looked strange but the transaction was easy. The queue was long but getting the train ticket was no problem. Then she joined one of the long queues for the phone boxes. She'd need British coins so she dug in the sticky zippy pocket inside her duffle coat down near the hem where her Mum (again) had hidden her wee Tam o Shanter purse with the red toorie with some 'real' money 'just in case'. She found one blue fiver, three green pound notes, four pink ten bob notes (all Scottish) two half crowns, a florin, a shilling, a sixpence, a threepenny bit and five old pennies. 'That's four for the phone and one for the ladies room,' Mary had told her daughter. Ella smiled at the memory of her fussy wee mum making sure she'd be all right. She reckoned the two half crowns would be enough to tell her Dad to pick her up at five past eight. When she finally got to the top of the queue she realised she'd left in 1968 and come back close to 1971. There were no slots for half crowns or florins. What were these 1p 2p 5p 10p and 50p slots for? They'd been 1d, 3d, 6d, 1/- 2/- and 2/6d before. Annoyed and embarrassed, she humped her suitcase in the direction of the newsagent. She chose The Times and a mars bar (the first for two and a half years) and presented a ten shilling note.

'Sorry love, this was demonetised in November.'

'De... what? Oh don't worry I get it. Here.' Ella parted with one of her crisp new fivers. 'Can I have some change for a long distance phone-call, please? Thanks. It's like being a foreigner in your own country,' Ella added as she examined the new coins.

'I don't reckon this new money will catch on,' said an old lady behind Ella in the queue.

'It'd better after all this bleedin' effort,' the London newsagent replied.

When she finally got to the top of the phone queue again what she saw was 1d, 3d, 6d, 1/-, 2/- and 2/6d. That was why everyone in the queue had been ancient. Ella dug out her two half crowns and dialled the operator for the Altnabervie code.

'How much should that be these days?'

'Try a 50p. That should do.' Before Ella could ask about her half crowns, the woman rang off.

'Mackay, Hillside here,' announced the familiar voice. The half crown had worked.

'Hi Dad, it's me. Can you pick me up at Altnabervie station at five past eight tonight? You don't want to be driving all the way down to Inverness.'

'Have ye got yer ticket already? I dinna mind comin' doon.'

'Don't worry, I'm fine. I'll enjoy the journey.'

'No change there then,' Charlie Mackay said of his daughter.

'What d'you mean?

'You're needin' some thinking time, aye?'

'Probably ...' pip, pip, pip, pip... That was the end of the half crown and Ella hadn't been able to tell her Dad that he knew her so well.

There was still an hour before her connecting flight so it was time for Ella's favourite occupation - people watching. She'd keep The Times for the train. This was her next favourite occupation since she'd met Ricardo – finding out what was happening in the international world.

Looking at all the pasty white faces with hardly a brown one in sight was still strange to Ella and rather boring so she looked out for the latest fashion. She decided hot pants and woolly tights weren't for her (or that wearer over there with the big bum) and wondered if the new maxi with platform sole shoes might be nice. Was that a bloke with an earring? She'd never seen that before. You couldn't be sure what the trend was she thought; there seemed to be all lengths and odd things like cheesecloth and Chinese padded jackets. There was a girl in a kitenge top and jeans and a tan. Had she been in Africa? She did know the fashion wasn't her red duffle over the green jersey with the fairisle yoke her granny had knitted and her mum had packed 'just in case'. And it wasn't the size too big black shoes she'd bought in Kisumu to make her decent enough to go to church with Ricky's family who hadn't been impressed with her flip flops or chapals as they called them. The blue jeans would do, she supposed. She'd have to make the hundred mile trip to Inverness to spend some of the salary and gratuity from the MOD which she hadn't been able to spend in Kenya. Forget Altnabervie Drapers. She was a woman of means now with a new job to go to.

The girl in the kitenge top sat down beside her. 'Where have you been? We seem to be the only two with tans around here.'

'Oh, I know. Doesn't everybody look unhealthy?' The two girls swapped notes on their trips to Kenya as a teacher and Tanzania as a nurse and decided they were not at all ready for the British winter. Before they could exchange names or addresses, her flight had been called and she'd gone. Ella was overcome by the transience of the friendships she'd made in Africa and had to gulp back a sob as she realised she might *really* never see Ricky again.

The bumpy ninety minute flight to Inverness was half empty so Ella managed to spread out The Times to her heart's content when she wasn't being plied with tea, sandwiches or shortbread by a plump trolley dolly in a tartan suit. She quickly flicked through the National news:

'Bernadette Devlin 21 year old political activist and MP, who was convicted of incitement to riot last year, has announced her pregnancy out of wedlock thus facing the criticism of the Catholics, the very community she purports to be fighting for the rights of…' No bias there then, Ella thought feeling irritated.

'Voting age reduced from 21 to 18 on January 1$^{st}$…' 'Harold Wilson alleges MI5 have bugged his home… Mountbatten denies the existence of a plot known as Clockwork Orange or that he had ever referred to the Prime Minister as a 'menace'…Wilson says the idea that he is a Soviet spy is preposterous…' Who cares? Ella mused still much more concerned with events in Africa. The International headlines included:

UN DEMANDS NO RECOGNITION OF SEGREGATED RHODESIA

RUSSIANS LAND ROBOT ON MOON

ASSASSINATION ATTEMPT ON POPE PAUL VI

CYCLONE KILLS 500,000 IN EAST PAKISTAN

NIXON WITHDRAWS 40,000 TROOPS FROM VIETNAM

There didn't seem to be anything about Kenya. The reference to Nixon had brought Ella back to 1969 when she had met Tom Mboya, the likely successor to Jomo Kenyatta as President. It had been a few days before he was shot and he'd thanked her for her part in saving him from a previous attempt on his life. She couldn't get rid of the implication that the 'big man' referred to by the assassin might not have been Kenyatta but could have been Nixon. She hardly dared even think those thoughts. How daft, she thought. Nobody knows I know. But the fear came back for a few seconds.

It was already almost dark when the plane bumped down in Inverness. It was only three o'clock. Ella had forgotten about the short winter days. On the equator the sun is up at six and down at six all year round. Maybe it would be fun to find a long lost, favourite, thick, woolly jumper with a big polo neck and some warm boots after the endless tropical heat.

It was comforting to hear the Scottish lilt and enjoy the friendly chat with strangers as they waited for their baggage.

'Anyone want to share a taxi to the station?' a woman with a baby asked. 'There's such a chronic shortage around here.'

'I'll come,' Ella yelled quickly feeling glad of the company. She'd have to hurry to catch the train or she'd be needing a bed at her auntie and uncle's. The bogie arrived with the suitcases and Ella's was on top. She grabbed it and ran for a taxi. The driver said he'd wait for another passenger and eventually the woman and baby arrived. Twenty minutes later she was at the station with five minutes to spare.

'Fancy meeting you here, Ella.' This was Davy Brown the primary school bully, looking fat and red-faced. Ella's heart sank.

'You're looking brown.'

'Hello Davy. Where are you off to?' Ella was hoping they weren't going to be travelling companions for the four long hours to Altnabervie.

'I'm going to Aberdeen for a job interview'

'That's nice.' Relief.

'Ally Fraser's married now,' Davy said revealing that he *did* remember how Ella had got him into hot water for bullying wee Ally.

'I ken that fine. She wrote me,' Ella answered wanting to get one up on Davy and slipping straight back into the Doric.

'I bet ye didna ken she's got a bun in the oven.'

'That's lovely. I'm really pleased for her.'

'Aye,' Davy replied. Ella thought she detected a touch of embarrassed remorse but it might have been her imagination.

'Oh, there's my train. Good luck for the interview.'

'Cheerio, Ella. Thanks'

'Cheerio,' Ella called cheerfully. It didn't cost anything to be nice but she was pleased he'd gone in the opposite direction. She'd have plenty of time in her 'in between' place if there was nobody to speak to on the train. There was nobody. The journey through the darkness turned out to be four hours of agonising. What if Rick didn't write? What if he did write and her Mum and Dad had a hairy fit? Would she ever be able to bring him home? Balnahuig wasn't ready for a flamboyant Fonseca, of that she was sure, no matter how charming or handsome. Ella twisted the Zanzibar filigree silver ring he'd bought and insisted she wear on her engagement finger; she slipped it off and switched it from hand to hand again and again. In the end the ring landed up on her right hand – for the moment. She forced her thoughts to dwell on the new job at Altnabervie School. Could she survive it? She stared into the black night flashing by with the odd flickering light out to sea.

Thirty hours without sleep took their toll and she sank into a troubled slumber.

'Thu...u...rso, Thurso,' the guard called. 'All change.' Ella tumbled sleepily off one train and clambered on another juggling guitar, back pack and suitcase. Twenty minutes to Altnabervie. Only half an hour late.

Charlie Mackay waited anxiously for his youngest in his new, cream Morris Oxford. He wondered if she'd be staying long or running off again soon to marry that Kilpatrick lad, the farmer. Kenya was so far away.

'Ye're here!' he said as he met her at the door of the train.

'Aye, I'm here,' Ella teased. He was still a man of few words. There was time for a hug before the paraphernalia was bundled into the new car. Ella had forgotten how big and strong her father's hands were, the gnarled hands of a farmer, and she felt tiny beside this tall, straight-backed man with the rugged, angular features she hadn't seen for so long.

Mary had some supper ready of sandwiches, rock cakes, biscuits and cocoa, so Ella felt duty bound to eat something though she'd much rather have gone straight to sleep. Finally she just had to say, 'I haven't seen a bed for thirty six hours and five thousand miles.'

'Yer bed's as warm as pie,' her little, now grey-haired, Mum said. 'The electric blanket's been on all day to air it. Now off you go and we won't wake you in the morning.'

# Chapter 5: Too Cosy for Comfort

Next morning, Ella woke up with a raging fever and a pounding head. Mary could barely rouse her daughter and was convinced some strange tropical disease had struck her down.

'I'm sure it's just exhaustion, Mum. I'll just sleep it off.'

But Mary was having none of it so, within the hour, family GP Dr Iain Falconer was shoving a thermometer under Ella's tongue and gripping her wrist pulse point mercilessly. Fuss number one.

'If this is malaria, Isabella, you'll have a nasty few days. Have you been taking your quinine?'

'Never needed to,' Ella groaned. 'I was living at six thousand feet and there were no mozies.'

'Of course, you'd have been court-martialled if you'd been in the army,' the good doctor scolded. 'It's a good thing I've brought some chloroquine just in case, isn't it? Have two straightaway and then two a day for the next three days. Don't worry, Mary, she'll be fine.'

'I haven't got malaria,' Ella protested omitting to mention that she'd spent the last couple of weeks in hot and steamy Mombasa. 'But if it makes you happy, if I'm not better by tomorrow, I'll start taking your pills.'

'Och, ye're still as stubborn as ever ye were, Ella Mackay,' Iain Falconer added but with a twinkle. 'Mary, make sure she does.'

'I'll try Doctor but there's no guarantee that anybody can persuade our Ella to do anything she doesn't want to do.'

Ella slept for the next twenty four hours before waking up fever free, headache free and malaria free.

'Ye can just return that medicine to the surgery when you go into Balnahuig then,' Charlie Mackay said.

'I hope there's no silage in the pick up then,' Ella teased remembering the time she had presented her tarted-up self at an Altnabervie dance without noticing the smelly load behind her. She'd been in a massive hurry and blamed too much Elizabeth Arden Blue Grass perfume for masking the stench.

'I can do better than the pick up,' Charlie Mackay said to his daughter. 'Come and see.' Outside the front door, parked on the pebbles, was a maroon Morris 1100. 'Altnabervie Motors let me have it for £200. It's yours to get you to work.' Charlie was beaming with pride and Ella couldn't believe her luck.

'I'll pay you back as soon as my money comes through, Dad.'

'That you most certainly will not,' Charlie protested. Fuss number two. Fuss number three was when family, friends and neighbours were finally told that Ella had recovered from being 'awfa tired' and 'nae very weel' and would be happy to see them at Hillside. This of course was not strictly true but Ella grinned and bore it through the endless cups of tea and zillions of questions. In the end it was Jamie's wife Katy who saved the day by bringing along a projector and screen for the umpteen 35mm film slides that Charlie had had developed of their Kenyan holiday. So it was, 'No, there were no lions or giraffes in the garden. Yes, we had electricity. No we didn't have to walk to the river for water. Yes, that's tea growing. Yes you could get cars on the roads.' The questions weren't all daft but Ella was still too tired to bring her trip to life. Also her stock of wooden, sisal, elephant hair and Kisii stone gifts (including two six foot tall wooden giraffes) were still making their way to Caithness by sea. Finally Ella announced, 'I'll tell you what. Give me time and I'll get a proper presentation ready for you all – but for now, can we talk about you for a change – please.' The spotlight was proving uncomfortably warm.

Christmas was a welcome relief. Katy, Jamie's wife, did the honours with all the trimmings with Morag and Ella's help. This gave Granny Mary's nose a welcome break from being burnt on the Rayburn while examining the turkey. Morag and Howard had travelled from London with wee Thomas to stay at Hillside so the meal was to be at Jamie and Katy's house in Balnahuig village. It was a wonderful, traditional Scottish Christmas starting with the Kirk at eleven o'clock, home for Christmas lunch, presents from under the tree, the Queen's speech and a long walk in the snow. Ella's tears were mistaken for happy ones; she, hidden in her place 'in between', was wondering if she'd ever see a Caithness Christmas again with its mistletoe and red holly berries or the brisk walk with the pale sunny views over the bay. For the present, however, Ella was living in the happy dream.

Three days after Christmas, the arrival of a long wooden box from tropical Kenya threatened to cause her world to cave in. It was addressed to Mrs Mary Mackay.

'What's this? 6 Clivia miniata: 6 Schizostylis? Oh, it's the kaffir lilies from Shona Kilpatrick. How lovely! And there's a long letter.'

Ella's heart was in her mouth. Had Mike told his mother Shona about Ricardo? Was he still bitter? Would she be forced to explain? No way was she ready for this! Shona's letter was certainly long:

*Kisimot*
*December 1970*

*Dear Mary*

*As promised, here are the lilies with the scent you loved so much. I'm sure they'll bloom nicely in the warmth of your house even in Caithness. ... ...*

*I can't believe it's a whole year since you came to Kisimot. It was so special to have someone from the old country to visit... ...*

*Mike seems to be missing your Elsa desperately.... Her little dog Tana and her pups have settled in well and we all adore them. Nan has produced at least ten drawings of them already.*

*... I'm not sure if I should be writing the next part but Mike has been so insistent. He seems sure that he and Elsa still have a future together when she finally realises she can't possibly marry that Ricardo fellow. He won't say who Ricardo is so I'm guessing he's one of the teachers and perhaps an unsavoury character.*

*Anyway, I'm sure you agree that it's not for us to meddle. I think Mike just wants Elsa to know that she's loved and you know we'd be over the moon if they got together. Perhaps she will write to him. That's enough of this children's business that isn't ours.*

*I wish you could see (and smell) the frangipani right now and ...*

*... ...*

*Angus sends his best wishes along with mine.*

Shona

Ella pretended to be very busy chopping carrots for the broth while secretly contemplating the puzzled look on her mother's face as she read.

'Here, you'd better read this.'

It was a relief to hear that her little dog she'd been heartbroken to leave behind was fine but Ella was incensed that Mike Kilpatrick had the brass neck to assume that she'd ever even like him again after his outburst - far less marry him. The gall of the man! How could he get his mother to write to her mother about Ricardo and imply that he was an unsavoury character?

'What an insufferable prat that Mike is,' Ella hissed as she threw the letter on the big pine table in the middle of the kitchen and turned away to carry on chopping furiously.

'Oh dear,' whimpered a bemused Mary, 'I thought he seemed very nice and I really like his parents.'

'That's exactly what his plan is. He thinks I'll agree to marry him because our parents think it's a good idea. And no, he isn't very nice. He knows what I would say if *he* wrote to *me*. No, Mum, don't tempt me to tell you.'

There was a long pause punctuated by frenzied chopping before, very quietly, Mary ventured,

'And who's this Ricardo?'

'A teacher at the boys' school. He gave me a lift to the airport.'

'And why can't you "possibly" marry him?'

'I haven't said I *will* marry him and Mike had no right to mention him. How mean is that? He's just bitter because I dropped him.' Ella had finished chopping the vegetables and adding them to the big pot and was now subconsciously twisting the filigree silver ring which for the moment was on her right hand.

'That's a very pretty ring Ella.' Nothing much slipped by Mary Mackay but she knew she was going to have to be devious before she found out about what was obviously troubling her youngest. Some instinct told her not to show her husband Shona Kilpatrick's letter.

'Yes it is. It was made in Zanzibar.'

Four year old Thomas came tumbling in to drag his Auntie Ella off to check his melting snowman giving Ella some thinking time; Mary would have to wait. Ella suspected her Mum might be sharing her fears with her Dad and was hoping that Mike Kilpatrick's parting shot about Charlie Mackay's racist views was a fabrication brought on by Ella's rejection. If only the plan to get Ricardo and her parents together in Mombasa hadn't fallen through, she'd know what she was up against by now.

Shona's letter had backfired on Mike with the unexpected effect of galvanising Ella's thoughts. If Ricardo wrote from Zambia and he still wanted her, she'd marry him. She was sure of that now.

For the moment, all the family needed to know was that Ella had no definite plans for the future beyond settling back into life in Caithness. Both Mike and Ricardo would seem to be a thing of the past. Ella decided to try very hard to fit back in – in case Ricardo didn't get in touch.

After, Morag, Howard and little Thomas had gone it was quiet at Hillside. The house and farm ran like clockwork and Mary was delighted to spoil her daughter who soon began to feel smothered by warm electric blankets and expanded by fresh home-baking. It couldn't go on. Ella escaped at Hogmanay to attend the village dance where she caught up with pregnant wee Ally and her new husband Sandy and her old flame Rory and his wife Heather, mother of his son and an expert at the milking and driving the tractor. Ella felt strangely glad she'd missed that particular bus.

Slipping into teaching at Sinclair's Institution in Altnabervie was a bit more of a challenge than Ella had expected as she was to be covering History and something called Moral Instruction which had replaced Religious Instruction. Ella's thoughts returned to Toffee Mac her own bigoted teacher of earlier times whose demise she had contributed to. John Gunn, who still seemed to be idolising Ella, said she would get English and Geography in August after the summer holidays. He hadn't wanted to risk losing her. Adapting to new subjects wasn't a big problem after teaching so many subjects at Kipsigis Girls' School but getting used to the lack of dedication she'd become accustomed to at Kericho from the cream of Kenya's girls was a different story. It took the young teacher a little while to realise that she couldn't just wind the Caithness kids up and let them go. They had to be pushed and pulled and cajoled for the most part and it was a special day when they could be inspired. However, occasionally, with her slides and stories of Africa, she managed to do just that and at least some youngsters in a corner of Scotland could see how lucky they were to get free schooling, food and shelter and nearly everything they wanted. Ella did her job as well as she could, driving her maroon Morris 1100 from Hillside to Sinclair's via Balnahuig to pick up or travel with the Art teacher who lived in Ewan Cameron's old house. Ewan's talents had been discovered and when Balnahuig Primary School was closed, demolished and converted into two bungalows he got a huge promotion to head of a secondary school down south.

'My whole seat of learning and life's inspiration has been reduced to two fancy bungalows with well-manicured gardens. What's the world coming to?' Ella had joked with Bob and Caitlin the two Edinburgh artists who had settled in the schoolhouse. Caitlin was designing her own pottery while Bob taught Art at Sinclair's. Most important for Ella, they were an open-minded couple whom she felt she could confide in.

As the weeks went by, Ella's cheerful exterior masked her inner turmoil. She went through the motions, being polite to the new BSc Agri student who seemed to turn up from nowhere for a three month stint of practical experience at Hillside. Did everyone think he was an eligible bachelor? Perhaps he was, but Ella wasn't interested and neither was he. Then there was the double date with Jamie, Katy and Andy, a mate of Jamie's who was looking for a girlfriend. That relationship lasted through two weddings, three dances, two trips to the pictures and dinner at the Bettyhill Hotel overlooking a storm on the bay. It was never going to work so the friendship fizzled out feebly without a shred of acrimony.

'Ye're nae on my wavelength are ye Ella,' Andy had finally observed.

'Sorry Andy, ye need to find somebody better for you,' had been Ella's genuinely sad reply. 'I've got things on my mind.'

Ella took to writing down her thoughts more and more. Relieved of any domestic duties by her indulgent parents so 'she could get on with her lessons' gave her plenty of time in that 'in between' place.

*February 1971*

*I feel the clamps – invisible, intangible but intolerably real. Life, they say, is good – affluent, comfortable and easy – but stagnant.*

*Minds incline inwards, evolving into a cascade of enormous, world-shattering … trifles.*

*Youthful ideology is controlled, stereotyped and tragically limited. Boredom and apathy are ideals in themselves. The world I am in now seems small but full of fashion and innumerable impressions created and accepted. Reality is lost in a plastic echo chamber called Britain. Young maturity, post-education, pre-middle age is a world full of witticisms, alcohol and bluster - for what? The pattern is so familiar. One stage follows another with an inevitability that crushes individualism. We are all slaves to society – the society we created – or so it appears.*

*Life is a maze of give and take in personal relationships and the bigger the maze the more complicated the route becomes. Perhaps that's why we need our own little corner to settle in where our adaptability is least stretched – to make life the most pleasant – or at least the easiest possible. That must be the first sign of age creeping in.*

*When one's maze stretches beyond one's corner dissatisfaction is bred. It is the greatest stress on adaptability to accept a society so long your own but now so remote. I'm glad life's experience has lifted me out of my comfort zone but, in the same breath I damn it for robbing me of a score of years.*

Perhaps Ella was right to feel she was losing her mind. What had happened to Ricardo? Had he decided not to write? Ella was paralysed by her feelings. She still hadn't talked to anyone, except Bob and Caitlin, about him so nobody understood her anguish. This cheerful act was becoming more and more of a strain. The night after her father's birthday, she had a nightmare which caused her to wake up screaming. When she had recovered, she dug out her secret journal.

*April 10th 1971*

*In my nightmare I saw a human settlement surrounded by a greyish-green smelly glow. There were rows upon rows of box-like shacks where tiny people ran in and out at times and sometimes they went slowly into bigger, shinier boxes which smelt of sweat. Down the streets bundles of twisted metal with jagged razor-sharp cogged wheels clanked with a deafening cacophony. From time to time strange piercing squeals could be heard and the sewage in the gutter turned to red and other tiny people vomited. On a closer look I saw that some of the tiny people were pinkish-grey, some greenish-grey, some deep purplish-grey and some grey-grey. They seemed to be grouped together according to their colours and sometimes, when two groups collided there was a violent chemical reaction.*

*Then, in the distance, high above the greenish glow I saw a patch of pure golden sunlight. I felt exhilarated, dizzy and my whole being (which seemed to be pure mind) was drawn by an invisible force towards that bright glow. I felt warm and safe and the light fragrance of honeysuckle alternated with the sound of waves on a distant coral reef. There was music and laughter and the people were a deep, warm bronze, large, beautiful and healthy.*

*The bright spark faded but it's not dead.*

Next morning, Ella had to drag herself back to reality, not daring to analyse this dream. She wished Ricardo would write even if it was to say sorry there was no future for them. She had to move on before she went crazy and she had no contact address for him in Zambia. She almost wrote to his family in Kisumu but decided the repercussions of that might be catastrophic. She simply had to suffer the angst.

Towards the end of the Easter holidays Ella was gazing out of the bay window of her bedroom down the valley at the postie's red van winding its way up to Hillside when she came to the decision to put all thoughts of Ricardo Fonseca out of her mind, accept the job at Altnabervie in

August and go and have a look at a renovated cottage which was up for rent near Balnahuig. She needed to get out from under her parents' feet and with her salary she could well afford the cottage especially as her dad wouldn't hear of her repaying him for the car.

'Could I trouble ye for a cup o' tea before I set off again, Mrs Mackay – seeing as ye keep offerin'? Your Ella's got a big pile o' letters the day – and a' fae Zambia. That used to be Northern Rhodesia. Did ye ken that?'

'Aye ah did as a matter o' fact, Stanley,' was Mary's equally pompous reply. 'I wonder who could be writing to her – and I suppose you'd be wondering the same yersel.'

'Nah, nah. I ken,' the ingenuous young postman blurted out. 'The name and address are on the back.'

Mary couldn't stop laughing out loud as she put the kettle on and shouted upstairs, 'Ella! There seems to be a big pile of letters for you today – from Zambia.' Turning to Stanley the postie she added, 'I dinna think we'll find oot ony mair than that. Oor Ella keeps hersel' to hersel'.'

Mary was quite certain that, by the end of the day, half the district would have heard about how Ella Mackay of Hillside had been getting letters from somebody called Ricardo JF Fonseca in Zambia.

Ella took time to compose herself before coming downstairs. First she stuck her fist in her mouth in case a scream escaped. Then she took a deep breath, combed her hair and set her expression into one of cool indifference.

'Any tea in the pot, Mum?' As two pairs of curious eyes stared at her she threw out, 'How are you Stanley?'

'Fine, Ella – and yersel?'

'Nae bad.' … … The letters lay untouched on the kitchen table. The same two pairs of eyes moved from Ella to the letters and back again.

'It's a fine day,' Ella said her stomach fluttering and eyes twinkling with controlled excitement. Nosiness would get them no-where.

'Aye, it is that,' Stanley responded expectantly.

Five minutes later, Stanley set off down the road again less than satisfied. Mary was tempted to ask Ella when she was going to open her letters but she'd disappeared upstairs like a flash.

Almost too scared to open her six letters, Ella started by piling them in date stamp chronological order from January 25th 1971 to March 8th. The last one had taken over a month to travel. He must have written every week. Her heart leapt as she read: Sender: Ricardo JF Fonseca, Mpika Boys' Secondary School, PO Box 4, Mpika, Northern Province, Zambia, Central Africa. She wondered why all six aerogrammes had arrived together. She stared at them for a little longer and finally, with a deep breath, opened the first one.

*Mpika, Jan 24th 1971*

*My Darling Ella,*

*Hi there green eyes. How's Scotland? Hope you're missing me as much as I am you. So much has happened and these blue aero things can only handle outlines and cut sentences. I hope you got my letter from Kisumu about Christmas and Agnelo and Maria's wedding. I got a picture of Maria and me looking married – which I'm gonna display to keep the girls off. Jos went to UK and I came here – leaving only Carlos and Rosie with Mum and Dad. Will fill you in with the details when I see you. Well, I'm here at last four days late after the journey from hell. Nairobi-Lusaka flight delayed, missed the weekly flight north to Kasama, had to sleep in grotty Lusaka rest house, arrived Kasama a week later – no lift a hundred miles on dirt road to Mpika. The headmaster (definitely a prat) decided I wouldn't be coming. Finally, after another night, got lift in a kapenta (that's dry fish) lorry delivering food to my school (how lucky is that?). Anyway said headmaster (Englishman white shirt and yellow cravat job) can't believe I'm his Science and PE teacher – not surprising me being in serious need of cleaning and sweetening. He gets all pompous about me getting my travel arrangements organised – then the deputy head, an Indian guy from Durban, takes me home for a bath and his new wife feeds me the best meal ever. I'll be staying with them until they find me a house. (They haven't finished the building work and we're the first lot of staff.) Can you believe I have to start clearing the trees to make a sports ground? The schoolboys (only 200 first years) seem keen but stroppier than the Cheptonge gents and the teachers come from UK (including a mouthy Glasgow girl), India, Mauritius, South Africa, Australia, New Zealand, Trinidad, Norway, Sweden, Germany, Iran, Russia, USA, Canada, Zimbabwe, Zambia itself and Kenya (me). The mission school along the road is full of Irish. Some*

*Yugoslavs and Italians are building roads, the Swedes are opening an Agricultural College and some Chinese in green uniforms have built a camp where they're keeping pigs for food and doing some survey. No space left so love you forever and <u>write soon.</u> Your Ricky.*

'He still loves me!' The situation now had to move on. She started by moving her ring to her engagement finger. Then she put it back on her right hand.

She could just tell them she had a job opportunity in Zambia – and leave Ricky out of the picture for the moment. She decided to read another letter.

*Mpika, Jan 31ˢᵗ.*

*Darling Ella,*

*I know you probably haven't got the first letter but I'm going to write every week. God I miss you. I hope the soil of Scotland hasn't got into your soul – or were you joking? The Garribs couldn't be nicer and they're treating me like family but I can't wait to get my own place. They're newlyweds, I found out. Anyway they're painting the house I'm going into now so it should be ready in a week or two. The whole campus is still like a building site but the boys have dorms and classrooms and soon there'll be a proper staffroom and housing for all the teachers and other workers. It's really quite exciting being pioneers. I'm using this punishment called 'stumping' for obstreperous kids. They have to dig out a tree stump from the sports field for an hour. It seems to work and maybe quite soon the field will be usable. They love football here.*

*The girls' school along the road need an English teacher from September as someone's going home to Ireland. Shall I put a word in for you? You'd love it out here. There are so many young…*

*… …*

*Please write soon, All My Love, Ricky.*

'This is it. He really means it. And there's a job, Ooh.' She'd have to break the news soon. She'd have to hand in her notice and (she couldn't bear it) she'd have to tell her Mum and Dad she was off to Africa again. But not today. She wasn't ready. One more letter:

*New House, Mpika, Feb 14ᵗʰ*

*My Valentine,*

*My house smells of paint and has four chairs, a coffee table and a big (empty) double bed. Little V, married to Big V, my host, has run up some curtains for the bedroom and there's an electric cooker in the kitchen and a fully operational bathroom when there's enough water. The only thing missing is you – well – important thing. Miss you green eyes. Have you got any recipes for corned beef or spam? That's all you can buy in Mpika stores apart from beer and candles. The nearest supermarket is Lusaka 400 miles away. Somebody goes down every weekend but I missed giving them a shopping list. I haven't seen any rain in Zambia at all and none is expected until October. ...*

*...*

*Please write soon. You must have got my first letter by now.*

*Ricky.*

'He must think I've lost interest,' Ella thought and vowed to write back as soon as she'd read all six letters. She'd drive the twenty miles to Altnabervie to the main Post Office as collections at Balnahuig weren't regular – and she wanted to avoid the watching nosey parkers.

*Mpika Feb 21ˢᵗ*

*Dear Ella*

*I'm hoping I've got your right address – or that post is very slow from here to there and back. Is everything ok in Scotland? How's the job? Maybe you've decided to settle back there again.*

*I managed to get some decent food at last and guess what my next door neighbour the Tech teacher has agreed to help me to make a folding ping pong table – full size – for the schoolboys of course but for now it's filling my lounge-dining room because I still have to paint it green with a white edge and we're waiting for the paint. I have my breakfast at one end, lunch in the middle and dinner at the other end – then I clear it up and we all have a game of ping pong. Of course I'm the current champ. For some reason, someone brought a net and bats and balls from UK. My house seems to have become the social centre which I don't mind as long as they bring their own beer. …*

*…*

*There's lots of crazy company around but it's not like having you here. Sorry, I don't mean to push you – but let me know how you're viewing things. I probably need sorting out soon.*

*Ricky.*

Ella decided she'd better write soon before this love of her life started to stray. What was wrong with the damned postal system? She quickly flicked through the last two letters which both began with Dear Ella and ended without a love or I miss you. She gleaned that he'd recommended her to the girls' school and that he'd finally found an old car which he could just about afford if he spent the school holiday at home in Mpika.

She sat down straightaway and filled up an aerogramme to catch the post by 1:15. She'd have to hurry.

*Hillside, April 12ᵗʰ 71*

*Dear Ricky, (I still want to call you John Francis)*
*I've just received SIX letters from you this morning. Can you believe it? I thought you'd decided to move on which I would have*

HATED because I've missed you MORE than I ever thought I would. Mpika sounds great fun and I'm glad you put my name forward for that job.

It's been extra comfy at home with my family spoiling me. In fact it's a bit too cosy and everybody wants to know everything about everybody else's business. You should've seen the postman drooling over your pile of letters today hoping I'd tell him what was in them. The job's ok except I've got History and Moral Instruction. Imagine. The kids here are a bit tougher than my nice Kenyan girls but they're fine. People have been trying to find me a man around here seeing as I'm supposed to be 'that age' but you'll be pleased to hear I haven't taken the bait – yet – only joking.

I'm really sorry you thought I wasn't interested any more and I hope this letter reaches you very soon. Missing you loads brown eyes – and I can't wait to get out there. There'll be lots to do here though – like resigning and selling the car my dad bought for me – and horror of horrors telling my Mum and Dad. I'm really worried about how they'll take it. Out of space – all my love, Ella xxxxxxx

'Mum I just have to pop into school for something for the start of term,' announced Ella briskly. 'D'you need anything from Altnabervie?'

'Some stamps maybe?' Nothing was getting past the wily Mary even though the letters from Zambia and the one ready to post were carefully secreted away in Ella's roomy handbag.

'Fourpenny or fivepenny?' grinned Ella pretending she didn't know she'd been rumbled.

'You're out o' date lass. I'll have six 2½p and six 3p stamps, please,' said Mary with a twinkle. 'But I'm not sure about the overseas rates yet.'

Ella finished off munching a banana and headed for the door before her mother could remind her she'd missed lunch. How could she eat at a time like this? She didn't relax until the letter was sent off at the fastest possible rate which probably wasn't very fast. She decided she'd make a complaint about getting six letters at once; there had been a strike down in London so overseas mail had been stuck for weeks. She got in her car, Ricky on her mind, and remembered her Mum's stamps – which she probably didn't even need.

Then it struck her. How on earth was she going to handle this? What would she say to the family? Had Mike Kilpatrick been telling the truth when he said that Ella's Dad had confided in Angus Kilpatrick that it would break his heart if his daughter married a black? An ugly thought. This should have been the happiest moment in her life. To love and be loved and make promises for the future; isn't that what life is all about? The cloud of her Dad's disapproval and the perceived risk of her family becoming social outcasts were hanging over her but she'd have to speak out – and almost certainly change her life forever. But this was the 1970s. Mixed marriage had been going on for centuries all over the world – everywhere except Caithness. Ella recalled snippets of conversations here and there in Balnahuig and beyond.

'Did ye hear Alistair Strachan's got a Catholic wife? Naething guid'll come oot o' that.'

'Nah. It never works. Ye can tell the Catholics ye ken. Their e'en are ower close thegither.'

'Aye and the bairns winna ken whaur they are.'

Ella's stomach churned and her blood boiled. Her gentle, god-fearing family meant no harm and worried too much about what other people thought of them, and might be subjected to such ignorant prejudice. But when her sister Morag had brought home a beautiful Ghanaian student from St Andrews for the weekend, Grace by name and grace by demeanour, the family had loved her. When the comment, 'My Mam says she wouldna hae onybody like that in her hoose,' had been thrown at her at school, Ella's reply had been sharp and fast. 'Well, that's just stupid. Your Mam shouldna say stuff like that.'

Ella drove slowly back along the coast anguishing over what she should do. It was a bright spring afternoon so she parked in Balnahuig and took a stroll to watch the boats chugging to and fro across the bay. She remembered Wee Ally and the bullies who shouted 'Stinky Tinky,' at the school (which was now demolished) and how Ewan Cameron had taught the wee ones to be brave and fair.

'When all's said and done, we're all Jock Tamson's bairns,' Ewan, the dominie, had said.

Ally's whispered reply to Ella had been, 'I'm glad ah ken who ma dad is now.'

The memory made Ella chuckle. She remembered how her Mum had given wee Ally a dress and encouraged her to stick up for herself, how proud her Mum had been when her daughter had stood up to Toffee Mac her bigoted Scripture teacher, who had marginalised the Catholics and belted Ella, and how brave her Mum had been to criticise the colonial bigots in Nairobi.

From deciding to write to Ricky telling him she couldn't go through with it, she had swung in the direction of confiding in her mother.

# Chapter 6: A Surprising Confession

'Good news from Zambia?'
          'That depends on how you want to look at it,
Mum.'

Then the whole story poured out, the possible job
opportunity in Zambia, how the plans for her Mum and
Dad to meet Ricky in Mombasa had fallen through and
how Mike Kilpatrick assumed Ella wanted to marry him
and how bitterly he had told Ricky and herself about her
Dad saying it would break his heart if she married a black.
Mary Mackay could hardly keep up.

'I've never heard your Dad express that opinion Ella. I
must say I'd be surprised if he felt that way.'

'But you're not sure are you? He hardly ever says
anything about his feelings, does he?'

Mary had to agree but in the next breath she surprised
Ella with a confession.

'Perhaps you won't believe this, but back in 1930 when
I was still training to be a teacher, we got sent to London on
a two week course. I must have been about your age. There

was this young teacher like me; his name was Raj. I don't remember his surname I'm ashamed to say - I tore up every bit of evidence that he existed. I do remember he came from Kashmir and he was going home to teach. Anyway he and I spent every minute together for the whole two weeks. Yes, don't look so surprised. We were sweet on each other – and it was really hard to say good bye. Anyway, I had to come home but the following spring I made up a story about another course and spent another two weeks with him in London just before he went back to Kashmir. He wanted me to go with him and I nearly went.'

Mary stared into the distance and hardly heard Ella

'Why didn't you go, Mum?'

'Mm? … Oh, I couldn't. In those days your grandparents had given up a lot to send me to university and teachers' college and I had promised I'd teach for five years to make it worthwhile – so that's what I did. I taught at Sinclair's for the five years and I might have carried on if I hadn't married your father. He'd been sweet on me since we were at Balnahuig Primary School together.'

'Did you keep in touch with Raj after he went home?'

'For years. We exchanged photographs and letters and he kept hoping that I might go there. But then there was the letter; his family had arranged a wedding for him and that was that.'

'That must have been heartbreaking.'

'Och, I'd been half expecting it and I think we both knew I'd never go to India. So I took the box with all his photos and letters and threw it on a bonfire and poked it with a big stick until it was nothing but ash. It was an old chocolate box, I remember. Then I cried for a week. How daft is that?' Mary smiled ruefully at her incredulous daughter.

'Did you ever tell Dad this?'

'Never, but your auntie Peggy made sure he knew that I'd burnt everything to do with my old beau. She said she was trying to stop me becoming an old maid.'

'How did she work that out?'

'I suppose she was right. A week later your Dad came calling, He said if my five years teaching was nearly up, would I think about marrying him. He said he'd heard there was nobody else now.'

'D'you think he knew about Raj – you know – being Indian?'

'Who knows, Ella? I know *I'll* never know.'

Ella had been looking at her Mum with new eyes, the high cheek bones and clear blue eyes, now framed by soft grey curls – no longer blonde. She moved to hug her before the tears overwhelmed them both.

'I didn't have your bonny red hair and green eyes or your courage Ella but I was quite pretty in my day.'

'Mum, you're still pretty – and Dad's very lucky to have you.'

'And I'm lucky to have him. He's always been good to me – even though you have to dig deep to get to his thoughts – if ye ever do.'

'Oh, Mum. What do you think I should do?'

'Go with your heart, Ella. If he's a good man and you love him you have to forget about the small minds in the world and make it work. But I didn't tell you that if anybody asks.'

'I think I've already decided. But I don't know how to approach Dad. Please don't tell him yet. I need to pick my moment.'

'Fine,' Mary Mackay said firmly. 'Wait. There are a couple of things I didn't throw away.' A few minutes later

Mary came back with a bundle wrapped up in yellowing muslin. Inside was an exotic aquamarine sari with gold embroidery and a tiny carved wooden box.

'Mum that's gorgeous. Why haven't we seen it before? Oh, silly question. And what's this?' Mary was showing her youngest an exquisite gold necklace in the shape of a heart with a star in the centre.

'It's yours, Ella. I want you to enjoy wearing it. I never could.'

'That's a Hindu symbol of love isn't it? You know Ricardo's Catholic don't you?'

'I'd guessed that. And with all the Wee Frees around here, that's another battle! Oh Ella, you're a problem - but never forget I'm proud of you. Trouble maker!' Ella had never seen her wee mother looking bonnier with her blue eyes flashing and her head held high.

'You can have the sari too but there's one thing I'm keeping.' Unwrapping some tissue paper Mary Mackay revealed the word MARY worked into a delicate gold brooch with a row of diamonds underlining it.'

Ella gasped. 'Who was this guy? Mum, you were crazy not to go to him.'

'Maybe but then you would never have been born, would you?'

'And I'd never have been over the moon about being in love with Ricky Fonseca. Mum, I think I'm ready to face the world and stuff the consequences!'

'The deil tak the hin'ermost!' Mary Mackay added, half anxious but secretly enjoying the situation.

When Charlie Mackay came in from the farm for his tea, he found his wife and youngest bubbling over with an inexplicable happiness.

Life for Ella went on as normal, except for an extra spring in her step. The anticipation of another letter from Zambia and a whole new life by September was delicious. Two blots on the landscape were dragging her down; breaking the news to her father and handing in her notice to John Gunn who kept enthusing about plans for the English Department when Ella joined it in September. She decided to wait for Ricky's reply to her letter before facing the music.

*Mpika, April 28*[th]

*Hi Green Eyes,*

*I was about to give up on you but now that you've written, I'm over the moon. Love you, love you, and love you! I hope you don't mind but I've sung your praises so much that the job at Lwitikila Girls' School is yours if you can get here in August to get ready for September. The nuns are sticklers for efficiency. The headmistress is from Inverness – that's your neck of the woods isn't it? Start planning, kiddy!*
*... ...*
*All my love forever,*
*Your Ricky XXX*

That was enough to give Ella the courage to tackle her taciturn father. She assembled a few visual aids and prepared her presentation. 'Dad,' she practised in front of the mirror, 'I've met someone who wants to marry me. He's a couple of years older than me and he teaches Science and PE. He's a champion tennis and badminton player – and hockey player. (So far so good.) And he's tall, dark and handsome – emphasis on the dark – oops. I'd really like to marry him – with your blessing.' There were a few carefully chosen photographs of Ricky the sportsman, Ricky the big brother and animal lover with Rosie, Tana and her puppies and one of Ricky and Ella looking like the perfect couple.

She was poised for action.

'Is *this* the man in your life?' Charlie Mackay said as he looked over his daughter's shoulder at the photographs and depriving her of her tactical presentation. (He was in early for his tea and she wasn't ready.) His tone confirmed Ella's worst fears and she was about to deflate when her old fighting spirit returned.

'Yes, Dad. I'm pretty sure he's the one for me and I could do a lot worse – a lot!'

'What was wrong with Angus Kilpatrick's lad? He seemed to have a few prospects.'

'There was quite a lot wrong with him actually. I had a near miss there!' Ella spat out rather too bitterly.

'Oh, Isabella. This isna a good day,' Charlie Mackay said and muttered something about ringing the vet for number 42 who wasn't calving well. With that he rushed off leaving Ella demoralised and shaking with disappointment.

'Leave him to me for a while, darling,' Mary told her daughter. 'That's the worst over. He'll be thinking about it.'

'But I could have broken it to him in a much better way.' Ella was almost weeping. 'Why does my own Dad have to be such a bigot?'

Charlie retreated into his shell and threw himself into tidying up the farm until he fell off a ladder and couldn't catch his breath. Dr Macdonald responded to Ella's phone call in a flash. Within an hour the ambulance had deposited Charlie at Altnabervie Hospital. He'd suffered a collapsed lung brought on by too much smoking and over-strenuous manual work for a man of sixty two. As the family GP, Iain

Falconer felt it his duty to find out what tribulation was bedevilling his patient and friend. In the end it was Ella who was left taking the blame for the whole unhappy situation.

'Isabella,' Iain had begun, 'you do realise you're being very selfish wanting to marry that bloke. I have to say, if I had a daughter, I'd never let her marry a black man. Please don't do it. You'll ruin your family.'

Faced with such blatant emotional blackmail and racism from a so-called pillar of the community, Ella was struck dumb. She fixed the doctor with a steely gaze before marching off defiantly, without a word, but with a huge ache in her heart. She determined she would never speak to the man again. If anyone needed a mother, it was Ella and she couldn't wait to tell her what Dr Falconer had said. Mary Mackay wasn't surprised but supported her daughter with every fibre of her being.

'Don't listen to them, Ella. They're not the ones who matter. If Ricky is the man you say he is, they're wrong and you're right. But be careful. Go to Zambia. Take the job but be absolutely sure he's a good man before you marry him. Promise me that.'

'I promise Mum because that's what I've promised myself.'

Ella tried to alleviate her Dad's worries by telling him about Ricky's good points and promising to think very carefully before marrying him. She persuaded him that she might come home unmarried after a spell in Zambia but there was also the possibility of her marrying Ricky with or without his blessing.

'I'm trusting that you'll see things differently over the years – after you've met him and got to know him. Meantime, Dad, try and be happy for me. Caithness is such an isolated place. People here just haven't seen all the changes in the world,'

She wasn't getting much response and with her emotions in turmoil, Ella was in need of a great deal of 'in between' time. It was during one of those times, walking along the windy beach that Ella bumped into Rory her old boyfriend from school days. He was checking on his lobster pots.

'Since when have you been a fisherman?' Ella called out.

'Oh, it's just a hobby – but we do love a nice lobster thermidor once in a while. We dinna listen to the rumours about radiation from Dounreay.'

Rory continued, 'I was speaking to your father the other day. He tells me he's nae awfa happy about you getting married.'

'Oh, aye.'

'I was thinking, that wi a' these Wee Frees around here, maybe it's nae sae bad that he's a different colour as long as he's nae a Catholic.' One look at Ella's face told Rory what she was going to say next.

'Well, he is!' Ella yelled and broke the tension by allowing herself a good belly laugh at the situation. Rory shared the laughter and put his arm round her shoulder. 'I should've married you ma'sel.'

'We both know it would never have worked,' Ella added and the two went about their business, Rory feeling apprehensive for what he imagined was his weak and vulnerable old sweetheart but Ella feeling a bit more heartened as she could see the small-minded bigotry for what it was; trivial, petty, insignificant, paltry, inconsequential or any other word for unimportant.

This was the scene in the Headmaster's office at Altnabervie Institution after Ella had handed in her notice.

John Gunn shook her hand firmly and, for a few seconds, put his other hand on her shoulder, which was as demonstrative as it got in Caithness.

'Ella, I wish you all the luck in the world and I hope you and your young man set the world on fire. It's about time there was a bomb put under some of those ignorant bigots.'

'True. But my main worry is how badly my family are going to be burnt. Even the doctor's told me I'm being selfish to break my father's heart.'

'Well, I'm surprised at that doctor. Who is he? No, Ella, don't tell me. If I find him … he might be treating his own injuries.' Tears of relief, pain, anxiety, joy, fear and finally determined excitement streamed down his young teacher's cheeks. John Gunn felt numb and unable to help until he remembered an event from ten years before.

'Ella Mackay, you listen to me. Ten years ago you stood up to a religious bigot and won. Don't say you've forgotten Toffee Mac, the 'BIGOT THAT BULLIED THE BAIRNS'?

'Oh yes, it got in the Altnabervie paper. Thanks to your support as I recall.' Ella managed a feeble giggle.

'Now you can dot the racist bigots in the eye. You know you must. Your family will be stronger for it.' Without telling Ella, he had decided to pay a visit to Hillside farm and Charlie Mackay in particular.

Ella smiled through the tears, 'You're right. I have to go through with this. Thank you so much, Mr Gunn; you know I'd have taken the job if I hadn't met Ricky. I wish you could meet him. You'd like him.'

The young woman pulled herself up to as dignified a five foot three as she could muster and marched out of the office, head held bravely high. John Gunn felt slightly apprehensive and a little sad, but extremely proud.

'There goes another wind of change,' he thought, feeling a tiny bit responsible for it.

# Chapter 7: Cosmopolitan Capers

'I'm sure she's missed the plane, Steve. That must be everybody off now.' This was an impatient and now highly agitated Ricky Fonseca, combing his hair yet again.

'I knew she was a figment of your imagination. Which bonny Scots lass would fly halfway across the world for you?' This was Steve Thomson, water engineer employed to divine water from nowhere out of the rocks around drought-stricken Mpika in Northern Zambia. He rubbed his sore, red hairy knees and put up his hand to order another beer.

'Och, she's dumped ye for a Caithness farmer with a big hoose and a combine harvester.' This was mouthy Mhairi Moffat from Motherwell and she and her boyfriend Steve were not taking this situation nearly seriously enough for their good mate Ricky who was beside himself with anticipation and disappointment. The plane carrying his beloved Ella to him was already six hours late and she didn't appear to be on it.

They were seated at a copper table on a high balcony overlooking the runway at Lusaka Airport which just happened to be part of the bar. All three were understandably a little mellow as they had been filling in the six hour wait with the odd tipple to pass the time.

'Oh oh, who's that then?' Mhairi called out as the last passenger, a tiny figure in green with a mop of red hair and a big guitar across her back emerged from the plane and shaded her eyes from the bright sunlight.

'That's her!' shouted Ricky and started to rush off downstairs to passenger arrivals.

'Whoa there cowboy,' Steve said. 'She's going to be ages getting her baggage so I think we should have a nice cup of coffee and sober up a bit before we present ourselves.'

Ricky had been hoping they'd leave him to it now to enjoy a private emotional reunion with his beloved. No chance. He was lumbered – and he hoped Ella wouldn't mind.

As it turned out, Ricky and Ella were too wrapped up in a big welcome hug to notice what was going on in the rest of the world. Mhairi broke the silence.

'Ah don't know what you've done to him but Ricky here's got his knickers in a right twist. I think you'd better marry him and put him oot o' his misery.'

After getting over the shock of this tall, blue-eyed, raven-haired Celt with the broad Glasgow accent, Ella caught the twinkle in her eye and retorted, 'I might have to think about that. I'm Ella. Who are you?'

'Sorry everyone,' a now ecstatic Ricky remembered his manners. Ella, this is Mhairi and he's Steve. They've been keeping me company for the past seven hours.'

'We didn't believe you existed,' said Steve.

'Well I do and I'm here,' she said and when she added with feeling, 'Where's the nearest bed?' everyone laughed and when Mhairi teased her mercilessly and crudely, Ella had to explain. 'I haven't had my feet up for thirty hours and they feel like balloons.'

'We're booked into the Lusaka Hotel with half the teachers in Zambia I think,' Mhairi went on. 'Term ended two days ago.' As they walked across the car park with the luggage, Ella whispered, 'Is that the mouthy Glaswegian?'

'The very one. Sorry about that, I tried to dump them.'

'No worries. They seem fun, but maybe in small doses.'

'I've booked us the best room in the hotel for three nights with a king size bed and an adjoining shower so we can hide away from the world if that's what you want.'

'See you in the lounge at 7 o'clock,' Steve shouted as he and Mhairi went off in their own car leaving Ella and Ricky blissfully alone to drive the five miles to the Lusaka Hotel and a touch of long anticipated, much needed intimacy. In due course the two lovebirds finally showered, changed and collapsed once again on the giant double bed. After some lingering sweet nothings, Ella finally fell asleep with her feet leaning high up against the wall to drain the puff out of her ankles. Ricky just stared at her incredulously and adoringly until he too dozed off. Ella's 7am flight hadn't arrived until 1pm. They had a few hours to sleep before having to hit the cosmopolitan social scene in the evening.

Hunger was the only thing that stopped the weary lovers from sleeping through to morning (and perhaps the thought of the ribbing they might get from Mouthy Mhairi about a love in). They stumbled sleepily into the crowded lounge bar where there was a noisy 'stand around and mingle' session. There was a hush and the pair found themselves confronted by umpteen curious pairs of eyes. Ella had considered Nairobi a multinational society but this was something else; they all knew Ricky and they'd all been eagerly awaiting his girlfriend's arrival.

Ricky started the introductions, 'Everybody, this is Ella. Ella this is Reidar from Norway and Sylvie from Sweden and their little girl Birgitta's gorgeous. She speaks four languages at three. ... ... ... ... ...' After he'd got through friends and colleagues from Trinidad, Sri Lanka, Zimbabwe, Canada and New Zealand, Ella announced she'd never remember all the names but it was good to meet them all and swept the room with a welcoming glance.

'Shall we all mingle again?' A comfortable hubbub replaced the hush and Ella worked the room finding teachers from Iran, India, Wales, England, Australia, America, Germany, Mauritius, Russia, South Africa and Ireland. There was the same buzz here in Lusaka as there had been around the Thorn Tree in Nairobi. Youth and enthusiasm were bubbling over and these young people from many nations were equally convinced that they were going to undo the wrongs of the colonial past and help the local people to find their feet again and move forward under their own steam. Ella could feel the old excitement of the challenge welling up again.

Aine (pronounced Onya), whose job at Lwitikila Girls' School Ella was taking over, introduced herself; she was a thin, anxious-looking Irish girl who seemed to be carrying the cares of the world on her back.

'Can we have a talk, Ella? I'm going back to Ireland next week and I want to make sure everything will be all right.'

'Join us for dinner,' Ricky offered. 'We should be getting a table soon.' The room was slowly moving to the dining room as the hotel was endeavouring to cater for the various groups, in turn.

'Thanks. Can Breda join us too? She's nursing at Chilonga hospital.' Just as the four were settling down to a table, they were joined by Mhairi and Steve, which was likely to change the shape of the conversation. The table was already laid for six so, despite Aine's even more anxious expression, there was nothing polite that could be done.

'Shall we meet for breakfast if we can't chat now?' Ella suggested quietly. 'I can understand you feeling anxious. I hope the school got my letter and references.'

'Yes, they were fine – but it's just – you know – no interview – and are you a Catholic?'

Ella's heart sank. In the midst of all this unity in diversity and multinational cooperation, her religion might determine whether she would get her job. 'We'll talk,' she said to Aine as they joined the others. Phew.

Breda and Aine talked about their return to Ireland and how they were both former nuns looking for a new life in Cork. Before the conversation could develop, Mouthy Mhairi interrupted.

'Ah've gotta change mah joab.'

'Oh, why's that? Weren't you at Mpika?' Ella asked - politely.

'Well, there wuz a wee bit o' a communication problem. You have to be careful how ye speak. Do you know how we call naughty kids wee monkeys in Scotland and it's no a bad thing. Well the first year boys at Mpika were ae nicking ma chalk – and it's like gold dust oot here – and when ah said, "Which one o' you wee monkeys nicked my chalk?" I had a flaming riot on my hands and I had to really talk mah way oot o' it. Like explain that wee monkeys in Scotland are cute children who've only been a bit naughty like. Well. I got past that one and the boys kina understood but when it came to the next one, I was in real trouble. I'd been talkin' aboot the climax and the *denewmun* in a literary novel and when they didnae understand ah said, "I've niver seen such a row o' blank faces in a' my life." Well they thought I was saying black faces. Now blank and black are no the same are they?'

Ella was thinking they sounded exactly the same in Mhairi's accent but instead of labouring the point she simply said, 'Absolutely not; one has an n and one has a c.'

'Exactly,' the loquacious lass went on. 'I even wrote the two words on the board with the chalk the little monkeys didnae pinch but this time they were have nothing to do with my explanation. Since then I've been teaching them very quietly and they've been writin' a lot and it's been ok. but I was advised to transfer to a new school where I could start again wi' a clean sheet. I'll be takin' my wurds oot an lookin' at them before I speak now; that's for sure.'

'Did Mhairi tell you about her new camera?' Steve asked. He loved listening to repetitions of his girlfriend's endless stories.

'Oh aye. Hey, listen to this everybody.' Mhairi was enjoying playing (loudly) to the gallery which included the surrounding tables. 'I shot off my first film on my new camera and sent it off and I got a letter back from Kodak saying, *'Dear Miss Moffat,'* (The Glasgow accent had mysteriously disappeared.) *'We don't think there's anything wrong with your camera but we appear to have developed thirty six pictures of your left eye.'*

The penny dropped at different stages and sometimes with a bit of explanation but within minutes the whole company was rocking with laughter.

Next morning Ella was tempted to sleep through her breakfast date with Aine but decided it might not be the best idea so she left Ricky snoring and slipped out. Aine was carrying a large green cardboard file with a note paper-clipped to it reading, 'For Ella Mackay.'

'Good thing I didn't skip breakfast then,' Ella observed inwardly. Out loud she said, 'That looks very efficient, Aine.'

'Oh it's just the schemes of work and copies of the set lit books. The Form Fives will need all their time to get ready for their Cambridge so I thought if you had time you could get stuck in right away.'

'OK, Aine,' Ella said hesitantly thinking this was all a little over eager but when she saw 'Things Fall Apart', 'The Black Hermit' and 'Song of Lawino' she was able to put the poor girl's mind at rest. She'd read them all and set about impressing her with her knowledge of them and by asking why Dominic Malaisho the Zambian writer wasn't on the list.

'Oh, thank the Lord, Ella. I thought you might be another airhead like that Mhairi girl. She's funny but I wouldn't want her teaching my girls. Will you look after them for me?'

'I promise, Aine. I'm sure they're just as lovely as my Kenyan girls.'

'And I'm sorry I asked if you were a Catholic. How could ye be marrying a Goan like Ricky if ye weren't?' she added slipping into an Irish lilt. 'The Nuns have invited you to stay in the Convent, by the way, until your new housemate comes out from Scotland. They don't want you to be alone.'

'That's nice of them.' As Ella crunched her toast she decided it would serve no useful purpose to disillusion this earnest and conscientious girl. Ricky would be amused but Ella was quite prepared to go along with arrangements to avoid rocking the boat. She would respect the sensitivities of her employers.

Later that day, however, when, under instructions, Ricky presented Ella at the Catholic Headquarters to sign a contract, she was confronted by a worldly Irish bishop with a twinkle in his eye.

'Look, lassie. If ye don't want them to make a Roman out of you, don't you let them. As long as you're not a Wee Free. … Ye aren't are ye?' When Ella replied that she'd better not answer that question, his laughter could be heard ringing along the shiny red polished corridor.

'God love ye!'

He was wondering, with some amusement, how one or two of the more staid nuns at Lwitikila were going to handle that one.

After a spot of shopping and a siesta, Ricky phoned to arrange lunch, the following day, at the Copper Kettle.

'The food's great and you'll enjoy the company,' Ricky said leaving Ella tantalised. This meant one more evening in the company of Steve and Mhairi with the funniest episode involving Mhairi still to come. Lusaka Hotel staff prided themselves, not only in their extensive drinks and snacks menu but also in the fact that the entire expatriate teaching population seemed to have adopted them as their city pit stop. While most people were ordering lime and lemonade, wine or beer, Mhairi decided she'd like a daiquiri and some crisps. Two rounds of drinks later there was still no daiquiri and Mhairi had shared Steve's beer, Ella's lime and lemonade and someone else's white wine.

'Is my daiquiri coming soon?' Mhairi asked, remembering to be very articulate and extra polite in case she got into trouble again.

'Don't worry, madam. We're preparing it freshly and you'll love it.'

In due course, the 'daiquiri' arrived on a platter, beautifully roasted and surrounded by the crisps she had ordered. It was a small but perfectly formed duckling. The waiter looked so proud that Mhairi put forward her very best side and said loudly, 'Thank you, it looks absolutely delicious.' When he was safely out of earshot, she added, 'Is thus no anither wee communication problem, then?' and once more everyone was in convulsions. 'Excuse me,' she called after another waiter, 'Can I have a glass of white wine please?' More hilarity.

Next morning, after a subdued breakfast, the group of expatriate teachers started going their different ways, some to tourist spots and others back to their schools for the month's break after stocking up with provisions.

Ricky, as predicted, was not enamoured of the nun's offer of accommodation for Ella so was in no hurry to get back to Mpika just to have her whisked away out of reach again. The nuns had ways of finding out things and he couldn't hide Ella.

'What about visiting the Victoria Falls? What's its real name again?'

'Mosi oa Tunya, The Smoke that Fires,' Ricky informed Ella. 'We could do, if you don't mind seeing only the Zambian half. The Rhodesian border's closed and you can only go half way across the bridge.'

'Anyway we have one more day to think about it.'

# Chapter 8: The Copper Kettle

A thirty minute drive took Ricky and a curious Ella through the rural outskirts of Lusaka where, tucked away behind some trees, they found the copper kettle sign outside and copper wall hangings inside. Copper table mats and exotic flowers in mini copper kettles on each rustic wooden table completed the picture.

The rest of the lunch party were already enjoying a chilled Sunday lunchtime aperitif. Ricky joined the men in a cold Mosi (Zambia's best beer) and Ella stuck to lime and lemonade with ice. The company was as international as the menu. Firstly, 'Doc' and Samira and their son Zak introduced themselves. Doctor Ben Goldberg (Doc) was a rather battered looking forty something, Jewish by origin and South African by nationality. His very pretty wife Samira looked much younger and ten year old Zak, whom Doc was careful to introduce as 'our son', was definitely Afro-Asian but resembled his Moslem mother. Ella wondered what the mystery was there. Next were Kiran Gupta, a well built, unusually dark South African Hindu in his twenties and Amanda, a blonde, Yorkshire lass who was nursing in Lusaka. They were rather obviously in love – or she was. Then there were Joshua Sibanda and Paul Magadza, two Rhodesian students on their way to Auckland University and in Lusaka for 'politically clandestine' reasons. Also present were a handsome Zambian couple, Doctor Justin Mutambo, with a medical degree from Edinburgh, and his wife Bethsheba, secretary to Dominic Malaisho, writer and politician. Finally, Bhavin and Sunita Pindoria from Durban were there with their three little ones, Arun, Salma and Resma. They were close friends of Big V and Little V, Ricky's hosts in Mpika and had been given the task of keeping an eye on Ricky and checking Ella out. Ricky was quick to point out she'd be teaching at Lwitikila Girls' School.

'That's my old school,' Bethsheba cried excitedly. 'You'll love it but watch out for the nuns. They'll make you work your shoes off.'

'Sounds familiar,' replied Ella thinking of her previous tough times in a Kenyan girls' school.

The menu offered Zambian nshima and a variety of meat and vegetable relishes, Indian curries from many regions but mainly South Africa, Chinese dishes, pizza and pasta, burgers and drumsticks, fish and chips and roast beef and Yorkshire pudding. The background music was Miriam Makeba's click song.

'Gosh I feel like I'm in a UN think tank,' Ella said feeling out of her depth after all the introductions. Half of her was pleased that Ricky had told everyone about the part she played in trying to save Tom Mboya's life as they seemed to be showing her a healthy respect. The other half of her wasn't sure if she fitted under the heading of freedom fighter.

'It's probably as close as you could get to a think tank in Southern Africa,' Doc put in. 'It's more like a den of freedom fighters – non violent protestors of course. Why do you think this place is hidden away? Only very special trusted people are invited here.'

'Don't listen to him, Ella,' Amanda the nurse said. 'He tells the same story to all the newcomers.' Aside she told Ella, 'He's a pussy cat really and the best doctor I've ever worked with. He doesn't charge the African patients a penny if he thinks they can't afford it. But then, to fund that, he has to fleece the rich Whites and Indians, and sometimes Zambians, who love to flaunt their money - but I don't suppose I should have told you that.'

'A Jewish Robin Hood with a Moslem wife and someone else's kid. This man's a legend.' Ella said to Amanda under cover of loud conversation.

'It was Sharpeville. His first wife was shot dead and someone brought Samira to his clinic. She'd been badly beaten up and raped and before anyone could locate her family, she found she was pregnant.'

'So Doc married her,' Ella guessed. 'I suppose she felt her family would disown her.'

'Who knows? So forgive him if he starts performing. By the way the Indian food's best here. The owner's a mate of these guys.'

'What news of Big V and little V, Ricky?' Bhavin asked Ricky.

'They should be well on their way to Durban by now,' Ricky answered. 'Little V's going to stay there until the baby's born so Ella won't meet her – them I mean - until January,' he added, proudly including his new fiancée. There was great excitement over the new baby and worry about how parents and baby were going to survive the journey North to Zambia.

'It's whites only or blacks only,' Samira explained to Ella. 'If you're Asian you're the middle of the sandwich. There's nowhere to stop off along the way. You learn to carry all your meals or starve.'

'Sometimes you can get hot water for your thermos from a back entrance,' Sunita added, 'if you're lucky.'

'That's appalling,' said Ella instinctively.

'Would you like to hear about what's really appalling?' Doc added with a hint of condescension and rising anger.

'Sorry,' Ella quickly added. 'I know that's a relatively small hardship in the scheme of things. I'm afraid that aspect of apartheid hadn't occurred to me.' She felt foolish and naïve and as Doc went on to prove that he was a raconteur par excellence with his tales of colonial brutality and injustice which everyone, including Ella, had heard before; she began to feel uncomfortable with the children listening. Ricky was tightening his grip around Ella's shoulder easing her tension. Doc noticed Ella's glances at the children.

'Don't worry they've heard it all before – and seen it. Like us they're learning how to forgive.' Then suddenly his mood changed. 'Sorry everyone, I sometimes just have to get it out of my system.'

'That's OK Doc. You and yours have had it harder than most,' Bhavin said calmly. But still the charismatic Doctor dominated.

'Paul and Joshua, our friends from the Shona and Ndebele tribes of the new Zimbabwe, are garden boys soon to be PhD students. Paul's a wonderful poet too; Rhodesia and Zambia are brimming over with literary talent. Isn't that living proof of how erroneous a belief in white supremacy is?'

'Yes dear,' Samira said quietly pandering to her husband but then adding, 'but aren't you preaching to the converted?'

'I'm practising for preaching to the big wide ignorant world and I need to emphasise the richness of the culture that was almost destroyed,'

At last someone else got a word in. Paul Magadza, Shona writer, poet and about to be PhD Science scholar pitched in, 'Don't forget some of us around here haven't got independence in our countries and the young, old and innocent are dying in the fight for it.'

'And those of us who have independence are struggling to revive our traditional cultures,' said Justin Mutambo, consultant gynaecologist at Lusaka University Teaching Hospital.

'You'll have to read Dominic's book, "The Tongue of the Dumb". It's just been released,' Dominic Malaisho's loyal secretary Bethsheba announced. 'I just happen to have a couple of copies here. It's quite an eye opener.' Ella jumped at the chance of doing a deal on the spot. 'I love the African Writers' Series and I'm hoping to teach this,' she explained.

'I think the nuns at Lwitikila might approve. Dominic doesn't vilify the missionaries quite as much as some modern African writers do,' Bethsheba said.

Lunch was delicious and the conversation spiralled. By the time dessert had arrived, Kenneth Kaunda's philosophy of humanism had been dismissed as ineffectual but his statement that a country without a culture was like a body without a head was pronounced inspirational.

This led to Justin extending an invitation to the entire company, (after a few cold and sparkling Mosis) to attend the first annual revival of what he promised to be the most uplifting and exciting experience of their lives.

That was how everyone present ended up making plans to attend the Mutomboko Festival at Mwata Kazembe's Palace. This was known to be a wonderfully colourful and exciting spectacle with enormous cultural significance to the Lunda tribe in the far north west of Zambia. The Pindoria family backed out and offered to look after Zak while his parents were away.

This was not your normal tourist attraction and was considered a huge privilege. Ricky and Ella were especially thrilled as it meant putting off the return to Mpika and the clutches of the nuns.

Sunita and Bhavin invited Ricky and Ella to stay at their Lusaka home the night before the trip and the night they returned and would look after Ella's luggage and young Zak until everyone got back from the five day trip.

What a welcome to Zambia for Ella and what an unbelievably diverse group of fascinating people.

# Chapter 9: Journey to Kazembe

As the Mutomboko festival was to take place over the last weekend of July and the 400 mile journey to Luapula Province was along good, bad and non-existent roads, the plan was to leave on the Wednesday. A rather elderly minibus, thankfully four by four, although one of the wheels was strangely smaller than the other three, was commissioned, along with an equally elderly but extremely competent and wise driver. Luggage had to be kept to a minimum as most of the luggage space was taken up by spare wheels in two different sizes and two big, rusty petrol cans; this didn't exactly instil confidence but Ricky and Ella were encouraged by the enthusiasm which surrounded them.

Doc and Samira sat in front with the driver, Moses Chileshe, who had the grey hair of age but the eyes of a hawk and the tall, straight body of an athlete. Moses was a walking, driving road map, information centre, tour guide and cultural advisor on all things Zambian and he was enjoying responding to Doc's curious questioning. Behind the driver, eight of the ten remaining seats were occupied which left two seats for the pile of haversacks containing everyone's bare essentials which would have to do for the five days. Moses had a stock of refillable water bottles and plenty of packets of biscuits in a metal box under his seat. He'd seen it all before.

Outside Lusaka, Zambia appeared to be featureless grassland with stumpy trees going on for miles. There wasn't a car, cow, goat or person anywhere in sight and the still shiny black tar of the Great North Road was in perfect condition as it stretched beyond the horizon without a pothole in sight. Ella wondered how the old minibus had got into such a state.

'I can't believe how good the Zambian roads are compared to Kenya,' Ella said.

'The government's been spending a bit of the money from the copper mines,' Justin the doctor pointed out. 'You should have seen what it was like before.'

'It will not be so good soon,' Moses began. 'Until Kapiri Mposhi it is good road and then until Serenje a bit good. After Serenje we may get broken road, stony road, sandy road, muddy road or no road. Then you hang on tight,' he added with a mischievous laugh. 'Don't worry. I will find you food and a place to sleep whenever we must stop. But it will not be like the Ridgeway Hotel in Lusaka.'

The old minibus bounced along on its heavy duty shock absorbers, squeaks and rattles keeping time with the cheerful Congolese *kwassa kwassa* which was rumbling out of the tape recorder raising everyone's spirits and causing the conversation to buzz. All the characters and ingredients were there for stimulating debate. Joshua, the Ndebele Zimbabwean and Paul his Shona friend and fellow Zimbabwean were having a friendly argument with Justin and Bethsheba, the Zambian Bembas, about the best African music around and where it came from. Was it the

Zamrock'n'roll from Musi o tunya or Chimurenga from Thomas Mapfumo and the Blacks Unlimited or Tony Maonde and Los Comrados or was it Congolese soukous from Dr Nico? Paul reckoned the music had to mean something so Zimbabwean Marimba from Bulawayo was his choice. Joshua reckoned Mapfumo's Chimurenga, the music of the Rhodesian liberation struggle, was a better choice. Justin felt it was important not to let the traditional music of the tribal kingdoms disappear. Bethsheba half agreed but said KK was making a mistake to rule that more than 95% of the music on the radio had to be Zambian. She felt that would just kill people's creativity. Doc of course had to chip in and wondered what they thought of Miriam Makeba's freedom songs. And of course everyone thought she was amazing. Kiran, Amanda, Ricky and Ella had been listening attentively to this good-natured banter with amusement, asking the odd question here and there from which they discovered that Chimurenga meant struggle for freedom, Tony Maonde was a great Zambian pianist and that Zamrock was a mixture of traditional Zambian and western music often played on the kalindula – a traditional instrument like a bass guitar. Moses pointed out that none of this new stuff was a patch on what they were going to hear at the Mutomboko festival at Kazembe. The king, he said, had his own royal musicians with instruments.

'When you hear the vimbuzza drums, the ainadimba xylophone, the isanzu thumb piano and all the whistles and guns and you see all the dancing and singing and ululations,' said Moses, 'you'll think all this new music is rubbish.'

'I must agree it's pretty impressive,' Joshua pitched in being the only one apart from Moses who had witnessed this ceremony.

'What do you guys think of our African music?' Justin finally asked Ricky, Ella, Kiran and Amanda.

'It's great to dance to,' Ella said. 'Ricky and I won a crate of beer in a nightclub in Kenya for dancing to 'Sukuma'. That's Congolese rumba, isn't it?'

'Yaba. That's wonderful,' was the incredulous response.

'But I can't wait to hear the traditional stuff too,' Ella added.

'I'm sure it'll be better than bagpipes or Morris dancing,' added Amanda causing a barrage of questions about traditional English and Scottish music.

'What about western pop? What do you like?' Ricky asked.

'Brown Sugar's good,' Bethsheba suggested. 'I like all The Stones.'

'And what about John Lennon's Imagine?' added Kiran.

'My favourite's 'Bridge over Troubled Water', Samira pitched in.

'She means me,' Doc bragged.

'He's not kidding.'

'My favourite's Bread's 'Baby I'm a Want You,' Ella said.

Ricky just had to say, 'That's me, of course.'

'I'll choose Santana's 'Black Magic Woman' Joshua piped up looking fondly at Bethsheba.

After the frivolity, Kiran the serious one began pontificating on the importance of music in the shaping of worldwide human society and of course everyone had to agree. The conversation swung from Vietnam to the six day war in the Middle East to Sharpeville then American civil rights and finally rested on the second Chimurenga, the fight for the liberation of Rhodesia which was at the forefront of 1971 political thought throughout Africa and the informed rest of the world. In their minds they crowned Stella Chiweshe with her freedom songs Queen of Zimbabwean music and Thomas the Lion Mapfumo her king. Joshua Sibanda the Ndebele and Paul Magadza the Shona talked of how their music was being played at all night *pungwes* where all the peoples of Rhodesia celebrated renewed pride in their culture after decades of degradation and repression by white colonials. Paul's eyes shone with pride as he talked of the power of metaphor in the Shona poetry which disguised the message of celebration of a new era which was just around the corner. There was such optimism and good will. After the storm the rainbow would come bringing peace to the land and all its people whatever their colour. The rainbow was symbolic of the unification of all colours after the rain had cleansed the blood and the hatred. All this was rather too much for Ricky judging by the cynical expression on his face but Ella lapped it up as all this hopeful idealism appealed to her philosophical outlook on life.

'One day,' announced Doc from the front seat in a stentorian tone with pauses for effect, '... One day there *will* be a free Rhodesia with the name of Zimbabwe and one day soon there *will* be an end to apartheid there and in South Africa. It has to be. I know it will happen.'

Everyone in the bus cheered, apart from Moses who was keeping his eyes studiously on the road with an inscrutable expression on his face, Ella and Ricky remembered the talks they used to have in Kenya as they agonised about whether their interracial relationship would survive the prejudices of their respective families and communities and in one voice shouted, 'And we'll all be Cosmopolites.'

By the time various definitions of a cosmopolite had been bandied around and a consensus had been reached that a cosmopolite was 'a person whose first allegiance was to the international community but who could also be proud to be born in one country with the aim of helping that country to take its place as an equal player on the international stage', Moses had slowed the minibus down almost to a stop. The straight and perfect tarmac road was perched on a foundation so high that the sides of the road were like a mini cliff between the tar and the stony, sandy original land of Zambia. To get off it in the direction Moses wanted to go would probably result in the vehicle landing on its side or even capsizing if he didn't take a great deal of care.

'The road is good but the government need to pay for intersections now,' Moses added shaking his head and sucking his teeth. 'Very bad. Nothing is done in Zambia without KK's decision.' Very gingerly Moses manoeuvred the sturdy bus on to the dirt surface which passed as a road adding, 'Even in the bush there is nothing as dangerous as this. All is in too much of a hurry to be modern.'

Once over the 'cliff', the travellers found the surface of the dirt road was unexpectedly smooth and comfortable to travel on.

The newly named Cosmopolites had arrived in a crowded area of higgledy piggledy ramshackle wooden huts, piles of metal spare parts and tyres in various states of repair, empty crates, a lone stall selling bananas, cassava and cabbages, one hand-operated petrol pump complete with small boy to do the necessary, two small boys with buckets and cloths to clear dead insects from the windscreen and a single, large, brick building with a newly painted sign: YUSUF AND SUNS KAPIRI STORE. This was where one had to pay for the petrol. They had reached Kapiri Mposhi.

Inside YUSUF AND SUNS was a wide counter, acting as a bar, fronted by stools of different heights, materials, styles and colours. Behind the counter, presumably safe from petty pilferers, a long, shelved wall was piled high with the oddest array of consumables imaginable. A metal grill and padlocks could be seen suspended from the ceiling poised for lock up along the whole length of the bar. Yusuf seemed to be taking no chances. In one section of the shelves were tinned goods of every kind ranging from baked beans, corned beef and sardines to peaches, prunes, coffee and condensed milk. Another area displayed boxes of sweets, chocolates, chewing gum, crisps and cigarettes and finally some bottles of Coca Cola, Castle beer, red wine and white wine were displayed at the bar end of the counter. What was odd about this was that beside each product produced in Zambia, Europe or USA was another almost identical version of the brand but made in China and with a slightly different name. Wrigley's chewing gum was alongside Wiggles gum, Smith's crisps were next to Sim's crisps – and so on. Nearly every commodity had its Chinese equivalent brand. Marlboro cigarettes lay beside Marble cigarettes in the same colour and style of packet and the products that amused everyone most were the red and white wine in odd shaped bottles sporting labels with "Che Foo" written on them which Ella reckoned was an adaptation of the French "Chez Vous". Only the Coca Cola and the Castle beer seemed to have survived uncopied.

In a corner, two Chinese men in blue overalls were drinking straight from bottles of Castle beer which had come from a big, old chest freezer under the shelves. Chocolate ice lollies were also appearing from there at the request of small Zambian children with fifty ngwee to spend. Most of the other customers were local Zambians so

Moses and his multinational passengers were the centre of curious attention.

Ricky and Doc, both gregarious types, decided to tackle the two Chinese men. After a few hesitant greetings which established that the level of English conversation was going to pose a few problems Ricky asked, 'What is your job ... work ... here?'

'We build railway from Dal es Salaam to Kapili Mposhi. Tzambia rand-rocked. She need imports,' the older Chinese man said. It was Doc who worked out exactly what was going on. He didn't mean Zambia was awash with rands. He meant it had no coastline.

'Oh yes,' Doc said genuinely fascinated, 'The Tanzam railway. How far down is the line now?'

'We are through half of Tanzania. We should finish after five years. We are making leady this end now.'

'Will this be good for China?' Ricky asked. 'I see many Chinese products in the shop.'

'At first no good. Tladers say customas no want Chinese stuff so we do malket lesealch. We go home – make what they want. The ploblem with copylight they say ok if we change the name. We want to make what people wanna buy. Good? Yes?'

'Good, I suppose. We'll have to try,' said Doc. 'Can we have a bottle of red and a bottle of white Che Foo, eleven Sims crisps and twenty Marbles please?'

Moses wouldn't touch the wine and ordered a cold coke. That was how ten travellers shared two bottles of Chinese wine and each had a packet of Chinese crisps - with salt in a little twist of blue paper. Even Moses admitted he couldn't tell the difference between the Smiths and Sims crisps. It was lucky that two bottles of wine didn't stretch too far across ten because it turned out to be pretty strong.

'White before led and you're leady for bed but led before white and you'r be awr right,' Amanda piped up after a glass and a half.

What kinda rocket fuel's in that stuff?'

Everyone enjoyed some kekabs and rice, which Yusuf's never-to-be-seen wife had beavered away to produce from behind scenes; this was washed down by cold coca cola to dilute the effects of the wine.

Moses had some welcome peace along the tarred road between Kapiri Mposhi and Serenje. His petrol tank and spare cans were full again, his tyres checked and this noisy bunch of rebels asleep. He relaxed with his inner thoughts as the minibus sped across the featureless scrub on this new and perfect Great North Road. It wouldn't be long before the journey was more challenging.

Around five pm the bus rolled smoothly into the petrol station at Serenje; someone had got around to building an intersection. After filling up, Moses told everyone that he had a standing arrangement with the White Fathers at the Mission, if he was transporting anyone who needed accommodation. They weren't going to get to the rest house Mansa after all because they'd spent too much time drinking Chinese wine in Kapiri Mposhi. Would anyone object?

'I know someone there,' Ricky announced. 'I met him at Lwitikila where Ella's going to teach. Is it Father Sam?

'That's the man.'

'Won't they mind so many of us?'

'Not if we give them a donation. They always need money for the orphans. They're mostly disabled - mainly blind and deaf,' Ricky added.

'I think we should eat at that restaurant first before we land on them,' Samira suggested. Dinner at Mapontela bakery and restaurant was nshima and a tasty fish relish followed by bananas after which the gang left laden with bananas, buns and cakes for the Mission.

Father Sam Lavertu was relaxing over an after dinner brandy, with Rags his red setter, (Lags to the locals), dozing at his feet and 'The French Lieutenant's Woman' which, for the moment, seemed unable to transport him beyond his troubled existence. The day, as usual, had been filled with people with so many problems mainly due to poverty and this recalcitrant, unproductive Zambian scrubland. The rains had stopped in April and wouldn't come again until November. The overuse of *chitimene*, the local slash and burn shifting cultivation, had stamped out the nutrients from the soil and attempts to raise cattle had been ruined by tsetse fly whenever the rains appeared. Many of the men had gone to the Copperbelt to work in the mines and barely considered the villages as home any more. His heart was heavy as he thought of the blind, deaf, crippled or malnourished children at the orphanage whose families hadn't being able to cope with them either physically or emotionally. More money needed to come from somewhere. The production zones, strips of land sprouting unwilling plants, were surviving with the help of fertilisers and manual irrigation so there were enough vegetables for the children and some of the nearby villages. Maize was in short supply, however, and they had to spend far too much on bringing it in from elsewhere. Dried fish and chicken supplies were sporadic and sometimes non-existent and now that the border with Southern Rhodesia was closed, things were even worse. He was also rather alarmed at the infiltration of the Chinese. He was considering several options. Could he help start up a chicken farm or build up a goat herd so that each village could have its own milking goats? There didn't seem to be any mileage in setting up a little factory for copper or malachite goods when the main priority was producing enough food for survival. At any rate, most of the copper was exported to get much needed foreign exchange or else hijacked by a few, privileged manufacturers. He couldn't clearly see any immediate solutions to Zambia's problems. Strictly speaking, he told himself, it wasn't his problem although his conscience wouldn't allow him to shirk his responsibilities in his own corner. Kenneth Kaunda was very much in charge now, orchestrating Zambia's development from a position of complete control much as a Paramount Chief of an ancient traditional African Kingdom would. His heart was in the right place and he pulled the heartstrings of the many tribes of Zambia from behind a waving white handkerchief with which he wiped away tears, crocodile or otherwise.

Father Sam was delighted to be drawn out of his anxious doldrums by the noisy 'phut phut' of a familiar engine which meant the prospect of some company. He recognised the sound of Moses' old minibus so was confident that it was friend rather than foe arriving late at night. He wondered which eccentric bunch of visitors he'd brought this time.

Lags was barking excitedly and Joseph the houseboy was running sleepily to cope with the unexpected invasion when the ten 'cosmopolites' and their driver disgorged themselves from the minibus.

'Sorry, Father. I tried to come earlier,' Moses explained shaking his old friend's hand warmly. Ten polite handshakes followed by bagfuls of bananas and bakeries were enough to reassure the young priest and his houseboy that they wouldn't be eaten out of house and home. How strange it felt to Ella to hear that Father Sam had already met Ricky and knew about her expected arrival at Lwitikila. This vast country was full of coincidence.

'Don't worry, we've been fed and watered and these are for the mission,' Doc announced, once more the leader. The ANC rebel understood just how important the work here was for Zambia.

'I hope you won't deprive me of some congenial company over a nightcap -though I'm afraid the stock of booze is a bit low.' On cue Joseph conjured up an enormous tray with a teapot, coffee thermos, sugar and dried milk in bowls, teaspoons and ten large mugs.

'Sometimes I have five breads and two fishes but not today.'

'Just make sure you have them tomorrow, hey,' was the priest's good natured comeback.

'I'm going back to bed so don't talk all night,' was Joseph's quick retort. Turning to the guests he added, 'This one can talk for Canada *and* Zambia if you let him.'

'You can see who's boss around here,' countered Father Sam.

'Not boss - just cook, laundry man and gardener,' Joseph added and escaped while he still had the last word.

'Now,' went on Father Sam. 'Tell me about the outside world. Which cog in the big wheel of progress is everyone oiling? You look like an interesting bunch.' Moses caught his old friend's eye and nodded in agreement before downing his empty mug and heading for bed. He'd heard it all before and, as the driver, he needed to be refreshed.

From then on, for the next hour, young Father Sam orchestrated this little band of idealists, so keen to call themselves 'cosmopolites' with the skill of a conductor, teasing out their dreams of creating a better world. There were dreams of bringing wealth, equality and enlightenment to Africa, dreams of climbing the walls of convention by marrying across the racial divides, dreams of unity and harmony for Rhodesia with Zimbabwe as its new name and finally the crunch.

'Have you heard of the Spear of the Nation?'

'Why do you ask, Father?' Doc replied quietly, fear flickering over his face for a second.

'No need to worry. I wholeheartedly endorse the Lusaka Manifesto and I've read about the External Mission in the Sechaba magazine.'

'Sorry to be ignorant but what does the Lusaka Manifesto say?' Ella dared to ask. 'I've only been in the country for a week.'

Bethsheba, who had typed it out often enough, obliged with a quote. 'This would cover it: *"All men are equal and have equal rights to human dignity and respect, regardless of colour, race, religion or sex."* '

Ella couldn't remember a time that she had *not* believed that and said so.

Samira was trembling with some emotion. 'I need to tell you what happened to me.' She slipped her hand into Doc's and related the story of her attack and rape after the Sharpeville massacre. 'I was in the wrong place at the wrong time when they needed to hit out. The police opened fire and sixty died, women and children too and hundreds were injured and for what? Protesting about having to carry pass books. I'm twenty four now; my son is ten.' A hush fell. 'We are teaching him how to forgive.'

Amanda broke the silence. 'He's a lovely lad is Zak and he couldn't have a better Mum and Dad.' The Yorkshire accent added to the poignancy. Everyone was drawn to the picture of the exquisite little brown china doll of a woman who was encircled in the arm of the craggily handsome

Doctor with his prominent Jewish nose and a scar which could just be seen between his eyebrow and hairline.

'Doc saved my life,' Samira continued. 'I was unconscious when they took me to his clinic. I think he needed someone to look after. You see his wife had been shot.' Doc stayed very quiet, understanding her need to talk.

'There, that's out. Now we can move on … please?'

Amanda had told Ella about what had gone on but as Bethsheba had been spared the story; her expression had been slowly crumpling as Samira's story unfolded. Eventually she collapsed into tears and called out, 'Why you? You weren't the one who deserved that. How can you forgive them? I could never… '

'No Beth. Shh. It's easier to forgive than to hang on to all that hate. I'm OK now. Really I am. I just need people to know about it so they don't pity me any more.'

Justin, Bethsheba's doctor husband, was the one to step in. 'Listen, we're all tired. Father, where can we sleep?'

'Forgive me. Ladies, I'm neglecting my duties; you're in the luxury dorm – it's got lights and showers. Gents, you're across the quad. You'll need the torches over there by the door. Hang on. I'll show the ladies to their room and come back.' Father Sam mimed downing a night cap and pointed to an innocent looking cupboard.

Bethsheba, Samira, Amanda and Ella had followed Sam Lavertu's instructions to make up their own beds from the neat pile of items which had been carefully laid out. First they had to spread out the 'sheet bags' which consisted of one sheet stitched across the bottom and up one side by Sister Immaculata's Domestic Science class two hundred miles away at Lwitikila Mission School where Ella was going to work. Putting on the pillow slip and tucking in the woollen blanket tightly under the thin mattress completed the task. In the morning they would have to put everything in a huge Ali Baba basket for laundering. In this way the Mission could cater for the steady stream of wanderers with the least effort possible.

'And we can charge less for bed and breakfast,' he added, 'for those who can't afford donations.'

The girls were now cuddled up in their bunks but wide awake:

'These guys are going to talk all night. I think they've found a sympathiser for the cause,' Samira murmured.

'They'll never stop until they've done it,' Bethsheba added.

'They're obsessed,' Amanda sighed. 'But I hope they succeed.'

'I think you'd better fill me in,' Ella pointed out realising that she had landed in the midst of something big. This was for real. A mixture of fear and excitement was building up inside her.

'I thought you knew by the way you were talking about saving Tom Mboya's life,' Bethsheba said and when Ella shook her head across from top bunk to top bunk she went on. 'The Copper Kettle is the HQ of the Underground External Mission of the ANC calling itself the Revolutionary Council fighting for an end to apartheid in South Africa and Rhodesia. All the big cheese come there like Oliver Tambo who's been to the UN and set up ANC missions all over the world. His new secretary's a guy called Thabo Mbeki who's fresh back from Moscow. The scary bit is since the Sharpeville massacre (sorry Samira) and people like Mandela and Lithuli and Doc's brother Dennis Goldberg have been jailed it has become an armed struggle. They call it MK, short for Umkhonto we Sizwe which means Spear of the Nation. Even Nelson Mandela who was so inspired by Gandhi and so wanted non-violent protest agreed that would never work with the South African fascists. So, you see, loads more people are going to have to die.'

'But perhaps more would die if they didn't fight,' Samira added. 'God I hate this whole thing but it's still the biggest and most important fight the world has ever seen. If we can establish the Lusaka manifesto, the world will be sorted out.'

'What about revenge – and revenge for the revenge taken? Maybe it'll never end,' Bethsheba surmised bleakly. 'I don't think we'll see freedom in Rhodesia and South Africa in our lifetime.'

'Don't ever say that,' Ella almost shouted, now back to feisty Isabella Mackay. 'Apartheid is just legalised racism and most people outside South Africa and Rhodesia want to change that law too. Did you hear about the Loving versus Virginia case? This couple, he was white and she was black, won the legal right to marry and guess what - there was a 450% increase in interracial marriages between 1967 and 1970. Even the Scottish Presbyterian Church have stopped condemning interracial marriage – and that's saying something.'

'That's fine but apartheid's not just about interracial marriage. It's about a tiny minority of horribly powerful and greedy whites exploiting a huge majority of blacks, browns or any other non-white. They keep them poor to weaken them and don't want any mixing in case they get strong enough to overpower them. It's horrible.'

'True. But if the whole world unites against them, I think one day soon, apartheid will go,' Amanda put in. Everyone agreed that they hoped this would happen and the four girls, one Zambian, one South African Indian and two white British girls, settled down to try to sleep.

Ella was back in Nairobi with the sound of gunfire in the distance. She knew Ricky could be embroiled in the activism in two seconds. Despite his abandonment of all things political, he might not be able to stop himself. He cared too much. He had too much unforgotten pain. As she listened to the muffled voices of the men going on into the night she was frightened. Samira had said it was the most important fight the world had ever seen.

The cupboard turned out to be a drinks cabinet with plenty of glasses but dwindling stocks so Ricky rectified the situation by digging out a bottle from his backpack. 'Thought you might need some replenishments, Father,' he said handing him a glass of red wine.

'Ah, the ruby red globe,' Father Sam sighed before taking a sip which caused him to splutter. 'What the …,'

'Courtesy of our Chinese railway builders, I believe. Pas Chez Vous mais Che Foo,' Doc explained. 'A glass of this and a few tongues might be loosened.'

The young priest looked sideways at Doc. 'Then dare I ask if you have a family member in Pretoria? The name Goldberg … '

'You surprise me, Father. Yes, Dennis is my brother... They slapped Mandela, Lithuli, Ahmed Kathrada and the others on Robben Island but the fascist bastards (sorry Father) couldn't put my brother with the kaffirs so they slung him in the prison for whites in Pretoria.'

'I hear Oliver Tambo's got a new secretary,' Father Sam went on eager to confirm the rumours.

'That's right. Thabo Mbeki. He's very young but Oliver has great hopes that he'll carry on the fight.'

Ricky Fonseca the ex political science student was tuning in too. Everyone else seemed to be in the know and he was curious. 'Is anyone going to tell me what the Spear of the Nation is?'

At this point Paul and Joshua chipped in with descriptions of how the non violent protests had been forced to become armed struggle. This was named Umkhonto we Sizwe or Spear of the Nation in South Africa, Chimurenga in Zimbabwe or Cha Cha Cha (as Kaunda referred to it) in Zambia. Their eyes flashed as they got carried away with talk of how a way would soon be found to oust those who had created an institution which generated prosperity for one race and degraded another. Racial abuse would no longer follow the black man into exile like flies to excrement. The day was around the corner when the African gods would return to the land and all persons would live together in harmony and with equal opportunities. The two handsome young Rhodesians were fired up by their dreams of a free Zimbabwe which they hoped to see as soon as they'd returned from their post graduate studies in New Zealand.

Ella was right. Within minutes Ricky was inspired.

# Chapter 10: *Ilala Livingstone Memorial*

The ten travellers and their long suffering driver got a later start than planned in the morning but had been happy to donate a few kwachas in return for bed and frozen bread toast, marmalade and instant coffee with dried milk for breakfast all of which were hard to come by in Zambia. Nobody had expected butter.

The highly charged political bubble had burst amid the headaches but the little band of revolutionaries had added a Canadian priest, a Goan and a Scot to their list of sympathisers. Now they were all off to appreciate the traditional culture of Zambia in the shape of the Umutomboko Festival at Kazembe far away beyond roadless terrain and crocodile-infested swamps. Moses took trouble to point out that the road would have to cross into Zaire for a few miles and some trigger-happy characters might be tempted to use them for target practice.

'It might be a good idea to get your heads down if I shout. Right?'

'Right.'

'Too bloody right.'

The tar road had run out but at least there was no rain due for months so the dilapidated but tough old bus bounded across the laterite track through the grasslands for a couple of hours without any mishaps apart from heads hitting the roof and bodies slipping off seats. The dry grasslands gradually became more densely dotted with umbrella trees and soon the bus was weaving and bumping through thick miombo woodland churning stomachs and causing arms that were hanging on for dear life to ache with the strain. Travel sickness wasn't an option – so miraculously nobody succumbed. Moses tackled holes, tree roots and steep slopes alike with a confident rev of the engine, foot full down on the accelerator and a grim expression on his face. Nothing exploded.

Finally everything evened out and they were purring along a smooth, flat road hurtling towards the widest imaginable horizon. This was remotest Africa hidden from the rest of the world.

Moses, sweating profusely but now smiling, drew to a halt on a high promontory overlooking a watery wilderness, a vast spider web of streams and lagoons around the glassy expanse of silvery-blue lake; Ella felt as if they were the only people on earth who had discovered a giant inland ocean. 'I feel like we're trespassing in an ancient world,' she gasped. 'Where does the sky end and the lake begin?'

'I've never seen anything so beautiful,' Amanda added.

While the normally noisy group stood silently as if paying their respects to the earth, time stood still.

Then Moses interrupted. 'This is my homeland, Bangweulu. Do you see the dried up wetlands around the edges of the water? That's *dambo* which gives every living thing all it needs.'

'How does it do that?' Ella asked.

'The dried up soil for walls, grasses and reeds for thatch and there is enough fertile land to grow vegetables and more than enough fish and bush meat to feed the people. And the water! That water is the purest in the world after it comes through the rock into the springs – even in the driest season. They can even grow tea and rice these days.'

'You can see why the Belgians wanted to stretch a toe into the Bangweulu swamps,' Joseph said referring to the Katanga Pedicle which gives Zambia its butterfly shape. 'Look at that view. And listen.'

In the far distance, the sounds of thousands of birds, ibis, heron, pelicans, crested cranes, the strange deep honk of hippos and the splashing of antelopes racing through the shallow water could clearly be heard breaking into the stillness. Moses was the proud host showing visitors his home area.

'This place is packed full of game. When we get down there, you'll see duikers, dick dicks, red lechwe, black lechwe and the tiniest antelope the oribi – and the beautiful sitatunga. They can all survive the swamps. You can hear the hippos but you can't see them yet or the crocodiles. They're very dangerous around here as they can hide in the rushes or the floating hippo grass.'

'I heard an Irish nurse got taken last year,' Amanda told them.

'Yes. People die from time to time – especially the local children.'

'When are we due to go into Congo?' asked Ricky.

'We've been in and out again,' Moses laughed. 'It was that bit where I kept the foot down. These border police can shoot you for a couple of kwacha. Last year my friend got arrested for wearing a hat.'

Doc began to expound on how Patrice Lumumba, the first democratically elected Congolese Prime Minister, had been assassinated around the same time as the Sharpeville massacre in 1961 and how the Belgians and the Brits had caused havoc for Congo and Zambia by creating the Katanga Pedicle which cut off the Copperbelt from Northern Province. 'One day,' Doc announced, 'the world will see how wrong the colonials were and just how much damage they did.'

'Ah but,' Moses began, 'outsiders have been coming here for centuries for trading beads and cloth for copper, ivory and slaves. Arabs, Swahilis, Portuguese and Africans from other lands all came here. Some incomers were bad, others good. The Portuguese married the locals they say and Ella, your famous countryman died here.'

'Do you mean David Livingstone?' Ella asked.

'I'll take you to his memorial at Ilala. The locals – and the ancestor of the Mwata Kazembe we're going to see, had much respect for him.'

'Some miner from the Copperbelt travelled all the way across the Pedicle and the Chembe ferry in flood to try to destroy the memorial,' Joseph informed everyone. 'He blamed Livingstone for every white South African bullying *yappy* in the 1950s copper mines.'

'That man was crazy,' Moses said calmly. 'That never happened again. People knew how Livingstone fought for our people against slavery and ignorance. People still remember the three Cs that he talked about, Christianity, commerce and civilisation. Those who knew him loved him.

'Moses, you remind me of Dominic, my boss. He can see the good in people even if it isn't there,' Bethsheba said. 'Black, white or brown.'

'Which Dominic?'

'Mulaisho.'

'Is that your boss? I think I know him,' said Moses.

'He's just published this amazing book, "The Tongue of the Dumb"'.

'Everyone except Moses, Ella and Ricky seemed to have witnessed the birth of this book. Bethsheba was at pains to describe the sheer enormity of the task of finding some way to publish. In the end, as always, funding had to be found from overseas and this time, Heinemann's had obliged. 'So much writing talent in Zambia withers and dies before it reaches publication,' Bethsheba explained. 'At one point Dominic almost gave up – like so many others have done.'

What's it about? I might read it,' Moses asked, revealing that he was no illiterate taxi driver.

'It's about this little boy, Mwape, who was born dumb and soon after that all kinds of disasters from locusts to leprosy hit the land. The Nsenga people in the village couldn't decide if it was caused by the anger of the ancestral spirits at the abandonment of tribal traditions or the evil influence of witchcraft. Some people blamed the Jesuit missionaries and their African followers. In the end Mwape and his mother were chased away,' Bethsheba rattled off quickly. 'You'll have to buy the book to find out what happens in the end.'

Justin her husband laughed at his wife's loyalty to her boss, 'You're a good saleswoman, Beth, but it's much more complicated than that.'

'Don't tell them what happens, Justin. It'll spoil the story.' Beth went on. 'I will tell you there are lots of goodies and baddies and not all the goodies are black and the baddies white.'

'I'll try to get my school to order forty. Would it suit the girls at Lwitikila?' Ella asked.

'What could be better than a Zambian story by a Zambian writer questioning all the things that affect their lives?' Joshua the Rhodesian student heading for Auckland added. 'That book will make the priests and nuns think too, which can't be bad.'

Ricky and Ella exchanged rueful glances that nobody could miss.

'You agree then,' Joshua said.

'Yea, you're probably right,' said Ricky, 'but we're both thinking of how the nuns are going to whisk Ella away into protective custody until we're married. Am I right Ella?' The only reply was a coy little grin.

'Here we are, in the middle of reflecting on old history and making new history, on the brink of freedom from apartheid, about to foist an explosion of African literary genius on the world and all you can think of is getting your pecker up!' This was Doc – carving through the dreams and bringing everyone down to earth with a bump and a laugh.

'Good for you. The world's not going anywhere without peckers up, is it?' Justin added amid more smiles.

'Come on, let's go and find Livingstone's memorial,' Ella cried, raising the tone again.

An hour later, they were winding and bumping their way through woodland with the sun glinting through the trees on their way to Ilala and the famous tree under which David Livingstone's heart had been buried.

First, they all had to sign the visitors' book at Chitambo Health Centre. Ella said she might bring her grandchildren back when there was an international airport nearby some time in the distant future.

'Sorry to disappoint you,' Moses said, 'but the tree had to be cut down; they sent the bit with Livingstone's name carved on it to London. But look at the new memorial. See how they respected the man.'

An eighteen foot tall pillar had been erected in place of the tree with a bronze plaque on each of its four sides. One of these was blank. The top seemed a little uneven but it was crowned by a bronze cross.

'Why the blank space?' Amanda asked.

'KK wants to put a message there for the centenary of his death,' said Beth. 'That should be in 1973.'

'The story goes that Livingstone's companions preserved his body with salt and brandy and dried it in the sun. Then they wrapped it in calico which they coated with tar,' Moses told the visitors to his area. 'After that they tied his remains to a pole and filled a metal box with all his maps and writings and set off for the sea. It took them nine months to get to Bagamoyo on the Indian Ocean. So many people died along the way, they say, but they carried on until they could hand him over to someone who would ship him home.'

'I wonder if these companions ever knew how important their journey was,' Ella added. 'Livingstone's remains are now in Westminster Abbey and all his maps and diaries have been preserved.'

'An amazing feat,' Doc was inspired to chip in. 'A testimony to the goodwill in the heart of Africa.'

'I'll take you to Bagamoyo one day,' Rick told Ella.

'The bus only takes four days now,' Moses told them. 'That is if you're lucky.'

'That's a date then, Ricky.'

# Chapter 11: Umutomboko Festival

Moses broke the silence. Memories of Livingstone's final journey aided by the bravest and most loyal of his African companions had evoked thoughts of a complex pre colonial history of ancient empires stretching beyond the borders of countries created by European boundary commissions. What had history been unable to tell the world?

'We have to get to Mansa before dark. Come on,'

Eleven very different people, ten passengers and their driver, united by visions of the past and hopes for the future headed up to the featureless plateau where Mansa stood safely above the hot wet Luapula River valley with its lakes, rivers, rapids, wetlands, crocodiles, hippos, malaria and sleeping sickness.

In colonial times Mansa, or Fort Roseberry as it was known, had grown up around what the colonials had called the 'British Overseas Management Administration' which they had wrongly claimed the acronym BOMA stood for. The Zambians in the group were laughing at the fact that boma was an old African word for a kraal or circle of thorn bushes for keeping people and animals safe from their enemies long before the British had ever bumbled on to the scene. Doc, of course, insisted that the word came for a Persian term for 'a place of refuge'.

Good natured bantering was interrupted by the group's weary but noisy arrival at the Mansa Hotel, a two hour journey from Kazembe where the long anticipated festival was to be held.

There's no better sleep than of exhausted travellers, even in a dorm of beds with thin, narrow mattresses on metal springs with prickly, thick, woolly blankets each with a picture of one of the 'big five' game animals of Africa. Ricky was pleased with his lion.

Moses had his passengers up and on the road before dawn with a mug of thick, sweet, milky tea and a banana inside them before they were fully awake. They soon discovered why. Two hours later and a few miles from Kazembe, the mini bus was being swept along in a throng of vans, pick up trucks, battered old cars and a moving ocean of brightly clad men, women and children, babies tied on backs, toddlers perched on dads' shoulders, metal pots, baskets and bundles gracefully perched on the heads of women who walked with the confidence and posture of models on a catwalk. From time to time, groups of musicians and dancers, clad in brightly coloured uniform were practising as they marched; their performances filled the air with whistles and horn blasts, drumming and xylophones, clapping and harmonised chants, cheering and ululation as the snake like procession made its way towards the palace of the paramount chief Mwata Kazembe.

Cocooned in the minibus, the visitors were finally silent, awe struck and strangely moved. Even the Africans in the group were impressed as they too had not witnessed such a scale of excitement during their urban existence.

Moses, although he had seen the festival before, was also obviously amazed. 'Paul Lutabo said he was going to revive the Umotomboko like never before. I think he has done it. I'm sure Kaunda must have been invited. It looks like these people have been travelling for many miles to get here.'

'Nobody will ever know,' Justin, the Edinburgh qualified doctor of the Bemba tribe added, 'if this was what life was like before the colonists came.'

'In all my years in Kenya,' said Ricky Fonseca, 'I've never seen anything like this! It's like a different world.'

'Wow. It looks like Woodstock, Zambia-style!' was Ella's contribution.

'But it looks like they won't run out of food. Look, they're carrying it all,' said Amanda eyeing the giant boughs of banana bunches and the chickens and goats suspended on poles.

'Yeah, there's gonna be some serious partying,' Joshua cried gleefully. 'I bet that's beer in those big pots. The crowd seems much bigger than the time I was here before – and more organised.'

Moses brought the minibus to a halt behind a tree, on the brow of a hill, a little way back from the road and with a panoramic view of a wide river valley with sides sloping inwards in a bowl shape. Spread out before the ten excited visitors and their driver was a bubbling ocean of brightly clad Lunda people crawling over the brows of the horizon from all directions, heading for the Kazembe's Palace on the banks of the River Luapula which, they learnt, though great, was merely a tributary of the mighty Congo, which would eventually belch forth its waters into the Atlantic

Ocean, some 2000 miles along its way through the about to be re-named Zaire, once the Belgian Congo.

'You can see why the name Zaire was chosen,' Moses informed his wonderstruck passengers. 'It comes from a word that means "the river that swallows all rivers". Sorry everyone. We must foot it from here. Only take what you can carry on your back.'

Blonde Amanda, red-haired Ella and pale skinned Ben attracted curious stares as did the Asian brown Samira, Kiran and Ricky. Joshua, Paul, Justin and Bethsheba, though able to pass for locals, gave themselves away by their apprehensive expressions. Only Moses called out cheery greetings in the Lunda dialect and, after a few words of introduction, the little group of strangers were surrounded by smiling revellers queuing to shake their hands in welcome.

'Moses,' whispered Ella, as usual anxious not to offend, 'What do the three claps mean? What should I do?'

'They're a sign of respect. You must clap too to show your respect.'

A barrage of claps, nods and handshakes ensued which seemed to go on for hours before the festival-goers deemed there had been enough of a welcome extended to their visitors.

Ricky had to ask, 'What did you tell them about us?'

'I told them you were very important doctors and teachers from Lusaka who would be special guests of the Great Chief Kazembe. That is true, is it not?' Moses replied with a chortle.

From then on, onlookers and participants alike were swept along on a noisy, rhythmic current of exuberance until the massive throng had congregated around a huge 'theatre in the round' formed by the natural shape of the landscape. The more weary travellers sat themselves down on the thick grass and were soon followed by others, participants taking up their positions on the front row, having rehearsed all they needed to on their long journey from home.

The time for the ceremony seemed to be drawing near as there was an expectant hush in the air. There was what seemed like a lengthy wait before an army of motherly women came from behind the Palace with a variety of different pots on their heads, some clay, some metal, some gourds. A scrabbling around by the local visiting Lunda people produced a similar variety of small drinking vessels, including beaded baskets with handles which were held out to be filled by water from the rushing Luapula of which there was clearly no shortage. Moses had warned his foreign visitors never to forget their 'drinking cups' so they too could sport plastic or china mugs which duly got filled when it came to their turn. Joshua was clearly disappointed that there was as yet no beer in sight.

Their guests' thirst quenched, the ladies disappeared as quickly as they had arrived. After another pregnant pause, the Great Chief, Mwata Kazembe, finally graced the company with his presence. He shambled with great dignity and difficulty, due to his voluminous royal blue robes with red trimmings, into the back of the arena and on to a wooden podium where he could be viewed by all. Whistles, drumbeats and wild ululations accompanied his slow progress and stopped when he was ensconced firmly on his wide wooden throne.

Greetings in Bemba and Lunda followed in a deep, booming voice which echoed around the valley: The acoustics were amazing. Moses and his visitors were thrilled when those were repeated in English:

'Welcome to our visitors from overseas. May you witness what some of your forebears wanted to destroy. They said our customs were savage and primitive. Tell your countrymen that we too have our Morris dancers and Philharmonic orchestra. Our instruments, however, are different. But please, I am happy you are here.'

'Smile and nod,' Ricky whispered in Ella's ear as he saw the beginnings of a crestfallen look. 'He's not expecting you to purge the third world guilt of your ancestors, right here and now.' Ricky knew his anxious-to-please fiancée well and often teased her.

'How do you know? He might be.' Ella replied but there was a twinkle in her eyes.

A male dancer rushed up with the gift of an enormous feathered head dress which the already bead-encumbered chief willingly allowed to be placed on his head. A horn filled with some liquid was presented to him by a kneeling young woman. Mwata Kazembe swiftly downed the contents.

'Bet that's a slug of booze,' whispered Joshua. 'Lucky blighter.'

'What a waste,' added Kiran as the Chief emptied the last few drops on to the ground.

'That's a drink for the ancestors, you Wally,' hissed Ricky. Everyone looked suitably embarrassed. Elementary. Why didn't he know that?

'Look,' said Paul, 'Here come the crates. Dozens of them!

Sure enough, red crates each with twenty four bottles of Lion beer and Castle beer miraculously appeared from the same area behind the palace. Cheers and ululations followed as young boys moved through the crowds. Some seasoned drinkers, Zambia-style, didn't wait for bottle openers using one bottle lid to open another or even sturdy teeth. Paul had an opener in his pocket. Bethsheba was the first lady to start drinking from her bottle and she made sure Samira, Amanda and Ella followed suit – whether they were beer drinkers or not.

'I suppose it might be rude to say no,' Samira grinned, breaking lots of rules as she downed her Lion.

From then on, the music and dance were non stop. First were the xylophones and drums as spectators moved forward one by one, in hierarchical order, to show their respects by kneeling or lying on the ground and clapping three times in the air. Moses explained that higher ranking subjects need only kneel but to show greatest humility, one had to lie on the ground. When Moses went to greet his own tribal chief, he knelt. It did not surprise his companions that he was considered an important person.

As these greetings were going on, a large group of little girls performed the *cinkwasa* an energetic, gyrating and stamping dance accompanied by claps and whistles and a lone drum, which didn't drown out the harmonised song of the childlike voices. Some of these children were tiny but they looked as if they were born to dance with complicated rhythms and boundless energy. They delighted everyone but especially the outsiders.

Next came the more suggestive, yet still innocent, *cilumwalumwa* danced by the teenage girls with their new little breasts which were bare to the world although, from waist to ankle, their bodies were concealed under cotton and grass skirts topped with beaded hip belts which emphasised every nuance of their Elvis Presley type movements. Drums, whistles and xylophones or thumb pianos built the dance up to a crescendo of excitement as the singing and ululations of the girls grew louder and louder as they spun faster and faster until they sank daintily to the ground and bowed their heads for a few moments before scampering off back into the crowd.

More beer and baskets of cooked meat on sticks and chicken legs were distributed among the spectators.

Then there was a moment of silence. Mwata Kazembe himself lay down on his podium and clapped his hands ostentatiously. Silence continued until a crocodile of around ten men, women and children emerged, each with a shiny copper pot on his or her head. In one sweeping and intensely vast movement, the entire crowd lay on their sides and clapped three times. The visitors had no choice but to copy the others. The little procession marched gracefully to the edge of the bank of the River Luapula waded a few feet towards the centre and emptied the contents of their shiny pots into the rushing water before ceremoniously raising their pots above their heads at arm's length. This was followed by a volley of shots from some ancient rifles and the, by now repetitive, ululation.

'The ancestors have been appeased now,' Moses informed his visitors, 'so the festivities can continue.'

The festivities continued with the women in their twenties and thirties who had abandoned all modesty and adopted every kind of suggestive move, though still demurely covered below the waist. Their dance was *wakubasha,* a frenzy of swivelling hips, shimmy-shaking breasts, jutting chins and pure, tremulous, sexual innuendo without an inhibition in sight. Needless to say, the audience response from some quarters was equally frenetic and frisson frilled; Young men couldn't resist joining in near the fringes of the arena amid lots of laughter.

Ella and Amanda had to tip Ricky and Kiran's chins back up to close their mouths after the jaw drop.

The crescendo reached, the ululations expired, the women melted away back into the crowd; the arena was bare.

In the true spirit of African Perpetual Kingship as decreed by the ancestral spirits (a variation of the Divine Rights of Kings), Mwata Kazembe burst into the scene and took his place centre stage. More feathers were added to his headdress and he was handed his broad sword which he placed in its sheath by his side, and his decorated axe which he tucked into his many waist bands. Lion skin arm bands, bead necklaces, bracelets and anklets were fitted and finally brass bells were hung around his neck. Added to the enormously wide unwieldy *mukonzo* skirt, the restriction seemed so complete that it was necessary to usher him on to the Royal Carriage or *umesolo*, a wooden and ivory zebra skin covered chariot which would ultimately act as his coffin when his time came, according to Moses. But for now, the carriage was a means to parade him through the crowd wearing all his paraphernalia and a horribly fierce expression which was intended to symbolise the Dance of Conquest or Mutomboko – the name of the festival. Moses retold the legend:

*'Once a mighty chief, Mwata Yamva wanted his people to bring him the sun and the moon so he ordered them to build a tall tower which would reach the sky. When it collapsed the chief was furious and wanted to kill his tribesmen. The terrified tribe, led by Kazembe, were said to have fled across the great river conquering nearly all of the tribes along the way. Today, all these conquests are remembered and celebrated through the Umutomboko or festival of the Dance of Conquest.'*

The Royal Carriage, carried by eight strong men, made its way to the river where, with the sound of musket fire ricocheting across the valley, the Great Chief shambled to the water's edge and threw meat, chicken, cassava, maize and beer into the water.

'For the ancestors,' Ella said.

'Correct,' answered Ricky. 'It's not that different from the body of Christ and all that stuff, is it?'

'I suppose not,' Ella observed. 'We all need something to have faith in so why not the protection of our ancestors?'

'What's faith?' said Ben. 'Faith just allows us to believe in something we know can't be true.'

There was no chance to reply to that thought-provoker as the Chief was returning to the arena amid the cacophony of loud drums, horns, whistles and the wildest ululations of the day so far. The 'Dance of Conquest' proper was just about to begin so thoughts about faith had to be kept bubbling on the back burner.

With great difficulty, Mwata Kazembe drew his sword from its sheath and raised his axe high above his head, before beginning his dance by raising his knee and stamping his foot. Next moment he was rushing at the crowd in mock aggression, causing screams of mock fear. Clearly excited, like cinema goers at a horror movie, the crowd egged their chief on to show more and more hostility to thrill them with the fear of a fierce warrior.

With all the travelling and festivities, this spectacular extravaganza of a day had slipped away. As sunset was arriving suddenly as tropical sunsets do, the Paramount Chief raised his sword to the sky and dropped it to the ground to signal the end of the dance. He clambered back on to his carriage and was quickly whisked away behind scenes.

The crowds began to melt away slowly towards the many villages scattered around nearby but others, who had long journeys they couldn't make in the dark, were preparing to bunk down for the night around three large bonfires. A ceremonial goat had been sacrificed for the occasion and there were various other meat and chicken barbecues sizzling away. It promised to be one long party.

'I have to say the loo arrangements are a vast improvement on Woodstock from what I've heard,' Amanda announced after a longish trip up the hill to the 'long drop' which an army of people had been digging out for days. 'It's simple but effective,' Amanda went on. 'Dig a long, narrow deep hole but keep the soil pile nearby to cover up the excrement. Put a few planks across to act as a bridge and it's functional. Just build a grass fence and there's privacy – one for the ladies and one for the gents. Marvellous!'

'Until you fall in,' Bethsheba laughed. 'I've seen that happen.'

'Yuck,' grimaced Ella.

The ever practical Moses was urging everyone to get back to the bus before the fires died down and left no light to travel by, when a messenger ran after them with an invitation.

'Mwata Kazembe,' he announced in English, 'would like his Lusaka visitors to join him at his private banquet tonight but you must bring your van close by for safety. There will be much beer drunk tonight.'

Moses replied in Bemba and turned to the group, 'I've thanked him for his hospitality and he will escort you to the Mwata now while I get the vehicle.'

'Wow,' was all Samira could say. Ella wondered if there was fear in her voice.

A smartly turned out young man in a cream safari suit was draped over a brown leather sofa, crystal glass of whisky in his hand and enormous Swiss cheese plant, peculiarly not native to Zambia, framing him from behind. His glistening skin and hair and muscular physique exuded good health and squeaky cleanliness. His huge startling eyes, though now sparkling with good humour, instead of glinting with dangerous menace as they had been an hour before, were the only thing that revealed his identity. This was Paul Kanyembo Lutabo LLB (Leeds, England), successful Lusaka solicitor, and resident of the wealthy Ridgeway area along with his beautiful, journalist wife and two model children who attended the International Kindergarten around the corner. This was also Mwata Kazembe XVII, Paramount chief of the Bemba and Lunda speaking Lunda tribe whose kingdom would have covered much of Luapula Province in North West Zambia and also part of the Congo which was soon to be named Zaire – had the colonials not drawn an arbitrary line through the land and its history. This man was Monarch of all he surveyed, which nearby included the largest village in Africa, known as Mwansabombwe. In pre-colonial times the Mwata would have been revered as a Perpetual King because the ancestors had decreed it so. As such, he was never to be disobeyed. As such, the people were kept under control in a way that no other alien form of government or legislation could hope to. As a great chief, he was expected to have many wives and countless children. It would have been considered mean-spirited not to spread his wealth and royal seed for the benefit of as many as possible.

This man was also suffering from an identity crisis; with one foot in the past and one foot in the future, this attractive and affable man had to juggle his perspectives to suit the company he was in.

Eventually good manners prevailed (or perhaps he had found some energy after his energetic Dance of Conquest) and he pulled himself to his feet to greet his guests.

'Welcome, my rainbow of guests,' he boomed picking up on Nelson Mandela's use of rainbow to refer to his dreams of a multiracial South Africa, 'or can I say friends as you have travelled so far to visit us? I'm impressed. I trust you have come to observe and admire rather than disparage and destroy as some of your forbears tried to do.'

'Who, in their right mind,' Ben began, taking over the role of spokesman, 'could be anything other than inspired by such a spectacle? It is, as Kaunda says, essential to preserve and develop Zambia's traditional festivals.' After a pause, there being no response from the chief, he added, 'Mwata Kazembe.'

'Oh call me Paul, please. I was asking myself whether your reply was patronising.'

'I've never seen anything so amazing!' little Ella blurted out so obviously sincerely that everyone had to smile. 'It doesn't need Kenneth Kaunda to point that out.'

Paul Lutabo, now the Westerner, laughed. 'I'm glad you said that. Some people are slightly irritated by KK's proclamations – especially since he's strictly speaking a Malawian in the highest office in Zambia.'

There was a short but uncomfortable silence before Paul went on, 'Please, before we dine, let me show my small museum of traditional artefacts and musical instruments. I am very proud of it. You may recognise some items from the dance earlier on.'

The host, now Mwata Kazembe, led the way into a long room where every inch of wall space was fitted with glass cabinets containing numerous headdresses, costumes, armbands, bells, beads, feathers of all colours, shells, belts, weapons (including some ancient muskets), pots, baskets, horn-shaped containers and an unusual variety of drums, xylophones and other instruments made of gourds, basketry, copper, clay, malachite, wood, skin, bark or ivory. Each item was carefully labelled in large, block capitals. 'Some of these items are very old and they must be preserved. Look, this is the *mpok,* my sword in its otter skin sheath and here is my *Icisoka,*' he added, pointing to the magnificently decorated axe which he had carefully returned to its special spot in its cabinet after having wielded it with such vigour a few hours before.

'I'm sorry the *mukonzo* I was wearing today is being cleaned but please, feel free to browse. There are descriptions underneath some items – and I intend to complete the job of describing all of them as soon as I have time. Excuse me, I shall go and arrange for some aperitifs to be served.

The visitors were fascinated, discussing whether items were lion skin, deer skin, cheetah or leopard, antelope horn or elephant tusk. The names of the musical instruments were proving hard to pronounce; Bethsheba proved to have a wide knowledge of when each instrument would be used, what its name was and what it was made of.

'Do you see this old ivory tusk and that wooden bowl full of white powder? Bethsheba explained. 'If I'm not mistaken that is *ulupemba.* Tomorrow the Mwata will cover himself in this white clay of submission and sprinkle some from the tusk on to the ground.'

'Why?' asked Amanda, echoing everyone's question.

'He must humble himself before the ancestors and crawl on his hands and knees. The *Nakabutula* will then tell him if the spirits have been appeased.'

'Who's the Nakabutula?' Ella asked.

'He is the spiritual caretaker of the tribe, the link between the ancestors through the chief to the people. He knows whether or not the ancestors have been pacified. If they have not, all kinds of disaster can befall the land. It might be drought or locusts or the sleeping sickness. If people do not behave as they should, punishment is manifested through the ancestors. That is how the chief controls his tribe.'

Ricky and Ella exchanged a quick glance. What had happened to Bethsheba? Their carefree companion had taken on a glassy-eyed expression which had transported her away to a different world in which she used a strangely old-fashioned and biblical language. No one in the group dared tread along the path of asking her if she believed that.

Ella whispered to Amanda, 'She's frightened isn't she?'

'Really spooked,' Amanda had to agree.

At that point, Paul, rather than Mwata Kazembe, broke the spell by bursting into the room.

'Come this way, I have one more thing to show you.' He threw open the door at the end of the room to reveal his royal carriage in all its splendour of red cloth and zebra skins. It stood resplendent on a pedestal in the middle of its own room.

'That is my own *umesolo*. One day I will take my last journey on it. Isn't it wonderful?'

'Does that mean..?' Ella began.

'Yes, young madam, it will be my coffin too. But not for some time I hope.' He chuckled and continued, 'Come on, everyone, I've got some campari or pimms and some decent French wine. Tonight you will dine in European style with Paul Lutabo, Lusaka lawyer. Tomorrow, you will say farewell to a humble Mwata Kazembe.

Paul and his first wife, Nomsa, entertained their guests royally; Nomsa, however, said very little. When she was out of the room Paul's comment was, 'Precious, my Lusaka wife, is more comfortable in these situations but as wife of the Mwata, Nomsa is perfect.'

The two young Rhodesian men exchanged amused glances as they watched Amanda and Ella's jaws drop. This concept of polygamy wasn't beyond their sheltered experience but the reality was still disturbing.

The conversation livened up after the firmly dominant paramount chief had prised the personal details of the background and present situation of each of his guests in turn. He was puzzled by Jewish Ben married to Moslem Samira but at least Afro-Asian son Zak wasn't there to confuse matters even more.

'Right,' he announced. 'Now that we have established that we are all fighters for humanity, we can relax. Young lady with the red hair, what do you think of the country now that you've been in Zambia for nearly two whole weeks?'

'The landscape is very different from Kenya,' a diffident Ella began, 'and so far the local hospitality seems to be excellent.' This was accompanied by the most disarming smile she could muster. When there was no response except a fixed stare, she added, 'Thank you.' She wasn't sure that she was brave enough to be any 'fighter for humanity'.

'It is our pleasure. I hope you enjoy your stay in Zambia as much as you obviously enjoyed Kenya.'

'Now, you two young Rhodesians, tell us more about why you are going to study in New Zealand. Shouldn't you be helping to create this new Zimbabwe everyone is talking about?'

The ice broken, the rainbow group happily returned to the buzz of the familiar conversation they'd been indulging in for the past few days. Excellent French wine loosened the tongues and freed the inhibitions. By the end of the evening, in the minds of the young radicals, South Africa was free from apartheid and Zimbabwe had been created without one drop of blood being spilt. The 1970 bridge-building activists had climbed all the barriers crushing them along the way.

Mwata Kazembe and his wise cousin Moses didn't have the heart to dismantle their optimism. They observed silently. They saw pain and suffering on the horizon. The young zealots had chosen to see beyond the inevitable conflict – or turn a blind eye to it.

As the evening was coming to an end, a young woman with a tiny, sleeping baby tied to her back, came in and knelt by the Mwata. She spoke briefly in Lunda and left immediately.

'My youngest wife,' Mwata Kazembe explained. 'She came to say that arrangements have been made for you to stay at The Rest House in Mwansabombwe. It isn't luxurious but it is clean and comfortable. Moses, you know it very well, I am sure.'

As everyone expressed their gratitude for an excellent evening, Ricardo mentioned his pleasure at the lack of Chinese Che Foo wine.

'I wouldn't touch the stuff!' Paul Lunda confided, revealing the western tastes and sophistication he had acquired through his overseas education. 'It has been a pleasure to meet you all and I am somehow sad to see you go. I wish you well with your dreams and I hope your courage remains.'

'On behalf of us all,' Dr Justin Mambo announced formally, 'I would like to thank you Mr Lutabo. It has been a special honour to be so warmly welcomed. We know how busy you must be right now.'

Paul Lutabo bowed his head imperiously and, after the ritual handshake with everyone, he showed his visitors to the door with a sweep of his right arm. Justin was right. Paul Lutabo needed to rest before Mwata Kazembe could perform his solemn duty the following day, which was to placate the spirits of the tribal ancestors.

# Chapter 12: The Walls of Convention

The Great North Road stretched long and straight as far as the eye could see. On either side was the flat, featureless Zambian scrub with not a person or animal in sight. The new tarmac was barely worn and Ricky and Ella hadn't seen another vehicle for fifty miles.

'Wasn't that the most amazing experience?' Ella was gushing. 'But you could almost hear the sigh of relief from everybody when we left that dinner. Nice guy, the chief, but a bit scary, eh?'

'Oh, I don't know. He was probably as unsure of us as we were of him. Mzungus and Muhindis don't usually travel that far into the bundu for a traditional African festival, these days,' Ricky replied.

'Yeah, not many people can say they've been to the Mutomboko Festival,' Ella went on sticking out her chin and waving it triumphantly. 'Mind you, I got the feeling we were some sort of social experiment for the Mwata. I reckon he thought we were pretty odd. '

'I can't say I blame him. What a motley bunch of weirdos jumping on the ANC bandwagon we must've seemed.'

'I suppose so. What I couldn't get over was the transformation the next day. It was as if we didn't exist. Do you think chiefs really do have supernatural powers like Bethsheba said?'

'I think they believe they do,' was Rick's abrupt reply. 'Let's have some music – here put on some Chuck Berry.'

Rick Fonseca needed some respite from little Ella's constant starry-eyed babble. As far as he was concerned, he'd left all his political ardour behind in Kenya around the death of Tom Mboya. He'd listened to these freedom fighters at The Copper Kettle, and observed the resurgence of the Umutomboko as an outsider, but there was no point in wasting any emotion. Let them get on with it. As a Muhindi he reckoned he was going to be squashed in between the whites and the blacks in Rhodesia and South Africa. In Zambia, he'd do his job as best he could. He knew he was a damn good teacher and so did his students but the stuffed shirt of an English headmaster, Cecil Smythe of all names, saw brown, incapable skin.

For the moment, sweet Ella was happy with Chuck Berry's 'No Particular Place to Go' blaring out from the state of the art audio cassette player of his newly acquired Toyota Celica. Rick allowed himself the luxury of a little self satisfaction. He had the girl, the car, the music – and the challenge of the job as part of a pioneering team of teachers setting up a brand new boys' school for Zambia. He listened to Ella singing along to 'Sweet Little Sixteen' and thought, 'That'll show them. Nobody believes I have this Scottish girlfriend.' He was thinking of all his colleagues back at Mpika Boys' School and the staff at

Lwitikila where for six of the past eight months he'd been living his life thinking Ella had abandoned him. He hadn't exactly been unfaithful but he'd been working on it and there were one or two girls who might be surprised when this redhead pitched up.

'Oh, look, the first sign of life for hours,' Ella cried as a little goatherd waved from the side of the road. In the distance a village with half a dozen round huts and a tree could be seen and then it was gone. It was back to miles more of nothingness.

'Boring bloody countryside,' Rick grumped. 'Only three more hours to go!

'Only! We've been going for four hours already!'

'That's Lusaka to Mpika for you. We'll be there by half past two. You can see why we're so loaded up with shopping.' Every space in the car around their luggage in the boot and the back seat was piled with 10 huge loaves, 10 kilos of apples, 5 bags of carrots, 6 jars of coffee, 8 packets of rice, 25 tins of baked beans, 3 bags of chapatti flour, 6 boxes of candles, cardamoms, olives, spaghetti, peanut butter, oregano, ketchup, marmalade, shortbread, gherkins, sardines, matches, U2 batteries, weeks old copies of the Manchester Guardian and Time Magazine, a bottle of Bells whisky and 2 of Chinese Che Foo, one red and one white.

'The booze is for us, ok,' Rick told Ella. 'I don't mind what else the scavengers take as long as they pay me the right money.'

'Fine,' Ella said while making a mental note of rescuing bread, apples, carrots and coffee at least. She thought of the scrappy, almost illegible shopping lists from the expatriates stranded in Mpika. Rick had stuck them in a pocket where they would have stayed if they hadn't dropped out for Ella to find.

'Oh, I forgot about those,' the hapless Rick had said.

'What? All this stuff? You wouldn't have been very popular!'

Two o'clock found the weary couple pulling up outside a dry and dusty Mpika Stores. The petrol pump at Serenje, a hundred miles back, had only managed to spew out a few gallons before it spluttered to a halt so there wasn't enough to get back to school.

'Come and meet Kasim and have a cold coke,' Rick said, secretly anxious to show his new girl off. It was the thought of the cold coke on the parched throat that did it for Ella. She rushed out of the car.

'Do you know, I haven't seen a single drop of rain since I came to Zambia?'

'And you won't until November! Hello Monday, how are you?' Rick addressed a young Zambian who seemed to know him. 'I play darts with Monday in the club. It's an old abandoned Mzungu squash court that they put a tin roof on. Good fun and it keeps the locals eating out of my hands.'

As they entered the shop, Ella felt uncomfortable as she could feel all eyes on her. Rick said something in Gujerati and she could feel an immediate deference. The two male shopkeepers nodded and shook hands but kept their eyes averted. One rushed off and came back with a middle aged Indian lady who smiled broadly and shook her hand warmly. Acceptance. Ella was glad of her ankle length skirt and modest, short sleeved T shirt. First impressions were going to matter around here.

Rick was relieved. These guys had been teasing him about his floozy and wondered how Ella would have handled it if they'd leered at her. He needn't have worried. At the first sign of ogling she put on her imperious expression and flashed her green eyes. He remembered it well – when he wasn't exactly her flavour of the month. Definitely scary.

After filling up at the petrol pump, helped by Friday (Monday's brother), the new young couple set off on the five mile trip to Mpika Boys' School. There was no tar on the road but it was hard and smooth. For once Ella was very quiet.

'Don't worry, they'll love you,' Ricky assured her, anticipating her apprehension.

'I hope so. I can't believe I'm so nervous.'

Soon they were rolling into the school campus past the shiny new still deserted dormitories and classrooms, towards the teachers' houses. These brand spanking new bungalows each had a veranda overlooking a patch of bare ground surrounded by a wooden post and chicken wire fence. One or two little green plants were trying to emerge here and there. Unlike the girls' school in Kenya which had been securely surrounded by a thicket of high trees and locked gates, Mpika Boys' School was open to the wide expanses of Zambia.

'Home sweet home,' yelled Rick as they drew up outside one of the bungalows. This one had a plant which was all of two feet high. 'Chillies. All the water I can spare goes on this tree.'

'You call that a tree?'

'You wait and see.'

Privacy wasn't built into the teachers' bungalows and every surrounding window seemed to be an eye focussed on the redheaded newcomer.

'We're in a goldfish bowl here,' Ella whimpered.

'Who cares?' Rick replied grabbing her round the shoulders and kissing her soundly on the lips. 'That'll bring them all running to collect their shopping.' Rick opened the boot, unloaded only the booze and headed for the house leaving the car open. Ella quickly commandeered some bread, apples, carrots and coffee (for a start) and followed Rick to the house.

The front door led from a green polished concrete veranda straight into a living room which was almost filled with a full size table tennis table, complete with net, bats and balls placed ready for use. One place mat, knife fork spoon and side plate were perfectly laid near an open hatch which led to the kitchen.

'The table's nearly finished. I just have to paint a white border. Isn't it terrific? I made it for the boys.'

'Amazing,' a laughing Ella answered, 'but it'll looks a bit worn already.'

'Oh, it's been well used but I'll have to take it down to the dorms soon. Oh oh, here come the hoards. Give me that shopping list so I can keep tabs.'

Within minutes the gannets had swooped on the open boot to claim their provisions which had been much delayed because of the errand boy's trip to the Umutomboko Festival.

'Sorry,' Ella announced. 'We couldn't find couscous or black pepper.'

Rick was trying to make certain all bills were being paid accurately.

'Aren't you going to introduce us to your lady friend?' This was a gamine little, obviously French, lady with one baby on her hip and another little girl clinging to her mini skirt and staring hard at Ella.

'Meet Ella,' Rick said with a grin and left everyone to introduce themselves.

'I'm Yvette,' said the French lady and this is Amelie and the baby's Sophie. Both girls had a mop of blonde curls and brown eyes.

'And I'm Tom, her husband and their dad,' a tall north country Englishman added. He was as blond as Yvette was brunette.

'Lancashire?' guessed Ella.

'Yorkshire.'

'I can never get it right.'

A tall, pretty, demure woman in a pale peach and silver sari, hiding heavy pregnancy, put her hands together in a silent 'Namaste'. Her husband in a collarless white shirt with flowing long sleeves, white trousers and leather flip flops bowed, almost imperceptibly. Their beautiful little doll of a daughter was wearing an identical cotton shift dress to her best friend of the same age, Amelie.

'Hello. My name's Nisha. I like your red hair,' the little girl said in English with a French accent.

'Thank you, Nisha. Nice to meet you,' said Ella in her most child-friendly voice.

Two young men introduced themselves as Frank and Blacks.

'We're the only Zambian teachers on the staff. He teaches English and I teach Maths,' Frank explained.

'Good to meet you. I'm going to teach English at Lwitikila.

'They're all Irish out there,' Blacks pointed out with an infectious laugh.

'I hope we can swop teaching ideas,' Ella continued. She reflected on the rapid Africanisation of staff in Kipsigis Girls' School. It would certainly happen in Zambia.

After that, the names and faces came thick and fast. Ella remembered one or two from Lusaka, who were hoping for some spare bread, like Reidar and Sylvie and their little girl Birgitta, and Herman, the jovial Trinidadian, who had just come along for the crack and any unclaimed food. There was 'Steve' Singh.

'No turban, no wife, no money but a posh car,' he informed Ella with a mischievous chortle. Then there was Sally with her poodle in a basket.

'I've just come back on the bus from Dar es Salaam with Snowdrop in this basket and now she doesn't want to get out. She has to get carried everywhere!' After the hilarity resulting from that story, came a tall, handsome South Indian girl called Malathi and her elderly mother whom she introduced as Ama (mother); they oozed polite gratitude for the rice and cardamoms. After that came a Jewish American called Max and his pregnant Dutch wife Angelica. They desperately needed coffee and apples but were pleased to have some bread too. Next, Ella met another Indian couple, two young Englishmen and a mousey little American woman with a sly smile and a very thin husband who didn't introduce themselves. Finally, Mr and Mrs Titus from Kerala (south of Goa they explained) shook Ella's hand warmly and immediately invited her home for some chapattis made from the flour she and Ricky had brought from Lusaka.

'Sorry Mrs Titus,' Yvette called out loudly, 'I've booked them for dinner tonight. Okay for you, Rick 'n Ella?'

'Wonderful. Yvette's a great cook Ella,' Rick said in a mock whisper. 'But we'll visit you soon, Mrs T,' he added to make sure he didn't miss out on any opportunities.

'Thank you, Yvette, I can't wait,' said Ella. She was beginning to enjoy the warm welcome.

'Seven o'clock then,' Tom called and the crowd dispersed, leaving Rick 'n Ella, now an item, to bring in the unclaimed groceries.

'No, not on the table,' yelled Rick. 'Put them in the kitchen. If they're not claimed soon, we'll eat them or freeze them.'

'I hope the nuns don't find out I'm here just yet. I don't think I'm ready to be cloistered in the convent,' Ella muttered.

'Don't worry. I'm not taking you out there until next week. The term doesn't start until a week on Monday.'

Around seven, 'Rick 'n Ella' presented themselves, showered in the tiniest amount of water but in clean clothes, at Tom 'n Yvette's identical bungalow which, instead of a ping pong table, had a wooden sofa and two armchairs with soft red cushions, a coffee table, six dining chairs and a dining table. Otherwise, according to Yvette, the floor tiles, magnolia walls and beige curtains were identical to all the other bungalows on the campus. Individual taste had to be expressed through one's own possessions. Yvette had made two brightly coloured bean bags for the children, who were now fast asleep in bed, and in one corner a Zambian made copper table held a little record player. Tom had used bricks and planks to set up makeshift shelves at floor level for their collection of LPs and books. Every surface held wooden, stone, basketry or copper curios from the local markets. The children's toys were peeping over the top of a huge basket in another corner. The table was covered with a bright table cloth in an African print and sisal mats which Ella recognised as having come from Tanzania or Kenya. Candles in wine bottles and a floral table centre added the final touch to the scenario.

A young woman wearing a short mini skirt and an even shorter hair style was sitting in the corner, knitting. She didn't look up.

'Hello, Marelda,' Rick ventured timidly.

'Oh, hello. Who's this then?'

'Meet Ella. Ella, this is Marelda.'

'Hi,' Marelda managed in a clipped voice and with no eye contact.

'Hello,' Ella answered feeling rather deflated and confused.

'We invited Sally too, but she was busy tonight,' Tom said raising his eyebrows and pulling a wry face. He caught Rick's eye and glanced briefly towards Marelda. Rick let out a silent sigh and closed his eyes for a second.

'Let's have candle light,' Tom suggested rather too cheerily.

'That way,' laughed Yvette as she handed round a tray of chilled white wine, 'you won't see vot you eat.' She was sounding a little more French than before. 'Marelda brought some lovely French wine from Lusaka. Wasn't that kind of her?'

"Very,' Ella chirped, accepting a chilled glass and realising that some damage limitation was required in the situation, but not quite understanding why. 'But there's one thing missing.'

'What?'

'Where are the violins?'

Luckily everyone laughed. Tom leapt towards his LP collection and selected a touch of Mozart, 'Eine kleine Nachtmusik' to be exact, which he set at a suitably low volume.

'Perfect,' sighed Ella melodramatically.

As everyone was eyeing the extra place setting at the table, a loud 'Open the door!' was heard. Next moment, the sizzle and smell of a huge pork roast with delicious-looking crackling, came wafting in on a large tray carried by a sweaty but smiling Herman. His ample physique and Jamaican accent betrayed his love of food and his island of birth. There was a label on a stick stuck in the beast. It read 'R.I.P. Napoleon'.

'Is that who I think it is?' Rick asked.

'Yep, the rest of him is in the school freezer. We didn't want his demise to be witnessed by the boys so he went to meet his maker in the holidays,' Herman went on. 'Let us be thankful the students don't like pork.' He plonked the dead animal on a board near the open hatch. 'He needs to rest for a while before we carve him.'

'And Josephine's just had a litter of ten – all doing well,' explained Tom. 'They should keep us going for a while.'

'Please don't tell me any more,' Ella groaned, 'at least until dinner is over.' She might recount the story of her becoming a vegetarian at the age of eight when her brother Jamie announced that the Sunday roast was her pet lamb Squirquams – later.

The rest of the meal, cleverly conjured up from hard to find ingredients in remote Northern Zambia, was superb. Yvette's oven, freed from the pork that Herman had cooked, had produced fresh bread buns, □ la Tom with Yvette's French recipe, roast potatoes with garlic and rosemary and pineapple upside down cake.

Marelda, as she wanted to inform everyone, turned out to be a poor little rich Irish girl who was teaching Domestic Science at Lwitikila Girls' School. Her father, she told the assembled company, was sending substantial donations to the mission. She also had a new sports car. After passing on these exciting ditties, she had little else to say so Rick 'n Ella entertained everyone with stories of Mouthy Mhairi Moffat's daiquiri which turned out to be a duckling and her first film of 36 pictures of her left eye from her new camera. This went down well as they all knew Mhairi.

Tales of experiences and characters at Mpika Boys' School were endless, the sum total drumming up an impression of a buzz of excitement and motivation. The school had been open for eight months with only a hundred first year students. In January there would be new first and second year groups with a total of two hundred students. Building of classrooms and dormitories was still going on as was the preparation of teaching materials, texts and equipment. Tom was Head of English and Yvette was a full time mum and chef, which benefited many of the staff. Herman taught History and had already made a start on rearing pigs and chickens and cultivating some of the bare land for maize, bananas, water melon, vegetables and his favourite hot chillies. Chitemene, the local form of slash and burn cultivation, had ruined the soil, he said, so they needed all the dung and water they could find. He wasn't fussy about the source. Progress had been slow. Rick's Science teaching was coming along, now that the laboratories and some apparatus had been set up, but there was still no proper sports field as the scrubby trees around the chosen area had only just been cut down and their roots were long and very hard to dig out.

'We need some more stumpers,' Rick had announced in the staffroom, 'so, if any of the schoolboys put a foot wrong, send them to me, please.' So far, Mr Fonseca's famous punishment, half an hour's stumping for minor misdemeanours or an hour for a worse offence, had unearthed a straight running track but no football pitch. Ella was learning a lot from this dinner party conversation.

There was still little response from Marelda so Ella thought she would talk about how she had met Aine before she went home to Ireland. She hadn't got around to the bit about her bringing her teaching notes to Lusaka in case Ella needed to prepare her lessons in advance.

'You'll have to try extra hard to follow that act,' Marelda barked. 'Aine was all work and no play. She was the nuns' favourite and irreplaceable.'

'I liked her,' Ella replied with a wry smile, swallowing any resentment at the implication. There was no more response.

After Tom's excellent coffee (he always took over that duty from an exhausted Yvette), Marelda announced it was time to hit the road. After she'd gone the mood lifted.

'Is she always like that?' Ella let slip before she could stop herself.

'Only with single women. She gives poor Sally the same frosty treatment,' Yvette said.

'My guess is,' Herman added, 'it's only with other single women near Rick, here.'

'What rubbish,' Rick retorted looking sheepish and irritated. 'I wouldn't touch her with a barge pole.'

Ella decided the best thing to do was pretend she hadn't heard and began to say thank you and good night.

'Watch the traffic now,' Tom shouted as their guests set off on their 25 yard journey home across the campus. Herman's house was next to Rick's.

'That Marelda's a bundle of fun,' Ella commented once she and Rick were behind closed doors.

'Miserable cow.'

'There's nothing you want to tell me then?' Ella asked, wondering if she was taking an unnecessary risk.

'Absolutely not! Whatever anyone says.'

'OK, fine.' But it was that Caithness fine.

Next morning, a few visitors dropped in at Rick's house. Max wanted another apple because when he weighed his apples they weighed a bit less than two kilos. Rick plonked an apple in his fist and when he left, he and Ella collapsed into sniggers. Wanda, the mousey little American wondered if there was any bread left as her husband Jake had demolished the lot. 'I think he has hollow legs or worms,' she said. 'He never puts any weight on.' Steve Singh came to see if there was anything left he could buy. Finally Sally (and Snowdrop) came for the gossip having seen Rick heading off in the direction of the staffroom. Ella put Rick's kettle on, extremely thankful that there was someone straightforward to chat to – or as straightforward as anyone with a poodle in a basket can be.

'Well, how was dinner?' Sally asked unashamedly curiously which didn't seem to annoy Ella in the least. She detected an ally.

'Lovely couple, great meal and Herman was good fun,' Ella began.

'And how was Madame Défarge?'

'Knitting and scowling,' replied Ella, relieved they were on the same wave length. 'I don't think she likes me very much.'

'Nor me,' Sally went on. 'That one's been trying to get her claws in Rick for a while but she hasn't got a cat in Hell's chance. She thought I was after him too but I'm a good ten years too old for your Rick – lovely as he is. She's just got a bad dose of JFS.'

'Huh?'

'Jealous Female Syndrome.'

'Oh.'

'So, sweet Ella, there's no contest, Marelda's a fruitcake and I'm too old and off men forever, for the moment. He's all yours. Mind you, I wouldn't light the fuse on Marelda's tampon, if I were you; she's got a foul temper.'

'Thanks for the warning,' Ella giggled.

Spurred on by the laughter, Sally went on. 'Now, our own Mata Hari's a different story. D'you know that little Wanda? She'd run after anything male that breathes. It's not surprising really when you look at her skinny husband.'

'Oh come on, Sally,' Ella gulped. 'You're not telling me …'

'Only teasing. Wanda's pure poison and Rick's got too strong a survival instinct to go there. Herman tells me she tried though. He's my mate and as nothing much gets past him, I get all the goss.'

'Sally, you're evil. I think I'd better keep in your good books.'

'So far, you're there girl. Anybody that can put that cow's nose out of joint is my friend for life. Marelda, I mean. Wanda's harmless to women. Stuff the men – oops, pardon the pun. No, that doesn't work.'

'Do I really want to know what she did to you?'

'Not really, but I'm going to tell you anyway. Then you'll know what you're up against.' Sally continued. 'It was last April. We'd all arrived a few months earlier, Rick a bit later because they sent him to the wrong airport. We'd had a tough first term with everything and everyone new to the place and only half the stuff we needed. The girls' school has been established for years so the headmistress, a nun from Inverness, by the way, invited the boys' school staff to visit when the students had gone home. The idea was for the rookies to get ideas and perhaps share some materials, equipment etc. It was going swimmingly and it was a two-way affair. They were going to borrow our new magnets and compasses and we were going to borrow some of their sets of texts and so on. Then this little Irish nun comes up to Rick and says, "I hear you're a Catholic," which was ten Brownie points for him at least so he felt chuffed. Then she said, "You must be Marelda's new beau." You should have seen the poor guy's face. Then he comes up with, "I'm most certainly not her beau. It must be somebody else." So the poor lady goes all a fluster with, "To be sure now, I'm very sorry to be mistaking ye," and she scuttles off leaving Tom, Herman, Rick and me standing together. Rick was so embarrassed but we were desperately trying not to laugh. Rick put his arm round my shoulder saying it was time to go. You know how demonstrative he is with everyone.'

'I do,' Ella managed to get in edgeways, remembering the bear hugs when she was welcomed into the bosom of the Fonseca family. '

'Then, along comes Marelda, with a glass of coke in her hand, and throws it full into my face.'

'Why?'

' "That's for spreading rumours about me and Rick," she pipes up, so I say, as loudly as I can, but calmly, that I didn't know where she had got her information but I wouldn't lower myself to spread rumours about my colleague and neighbour that I knew couldn't possible be true.'

'Good for y...'

'I can be quite impressive when I like. But I was trying not to laugh. You see – I don't give a damn, and I knew everyone could tell she was lying and was just in a jealous fit.'

'How embarrassing though.'

'More for her than me. She ran off in tears and I managed to keep my dignity and say thank you for the interesting day – apart from the sticky moment. A few people laughed but I noticed nobody rushed off to comfort Marelda.'

'So, have you seen her since?'

'Only at a frosty distance, but she came to visit Rick, all tearful, insisting I had been the one telling everyone about her and Rick.'

'Did he believe her?'

'Never. She brought a bottle of whisky too.'

'I bet he couldn't resist that,' Ella pointed out.

'Right. He told Herman he wasn't going to pass up a chance of free whisky and when Herman asked him about a free woman he said Marelda had told him she was a good Catholic girl who was going to wait until she was married. That was before he'd even thought of making a pass at her – which he said he wouldn't have done anyway- because he didn't fancy her.'

'Oh crumbs,' Ella whined. 'I'm going to have to work with her. One thing puzzles me. Why did Tom and Yvette invite her to dinner when they knew I was coming?'

'They didn't. She just turned up with French wine, which is like gold dust, and her knitting, so what could they say? That's why I ducked out, but Herman couldn't because he was roasting the pork.

'Now I understand why Tom and Rick were giving each other disgruntled looks. My imagination's been working overtime.'

Rick burst in on this juicy gossip with a pile of letters and an untidily stuffed, green file.

'Rosie sends her love Ella, but I haven't opened any more letters.'

'Oh so the family know I'm in Zambia.'

'Only Rosie so far. Slowly by slowly does it. Well, Sally, have you filled her in on all that goes on around here?'

'I think I've heard enough for the moment,' Ella sighed.

'The post's just arrived, Sal. I'd have brought yours if I'd known you were here. It looks like a big pile.'

'Oh, what fun! Thanks for the coffee, Ella. Bye, Rick,' and she was off at the double.

'That got rid of her. She'd go on forever, that one, which is fine if you're not busy.

'Did she have any post?'

'Dunno. Didn't look. Oh, I'm so glad you're here. This place is full of nutcases. Just keep me away from them for a while.'

'It sounds like I didn't get here a moment too soon.'

'Oh? What's she been saying?' But he didn't look too worried.

'She told me not to light the fuse on Marelda's tampax.' Ricky Fonseca laughed long and loud before he replied, 'Good advice.'

The banter was cheerful and the mood was light but something in Ella's stomach was churning. Had she been right to come to the back of beyond for this man? What if Sally had spun her a plausible yarn? She was certainly clever enough. She was one of those pretty thirty five year olds who looked twenty one. Maybe Rick had been flirting. After all he'd thought Ella might not be coming to Zambia after all.

After lunch, she told Rick she was going to take a box of biscuits across to Tom and Yvette, to thank them for dinner. She needed confirmation of Sally's story.

Amelie was playing quietly with her dolls and Sophie was squirming in her dad's arms so Tom and Yvette were happy to hand over their baby to Ella for a while. Talking across the now fascinated baby, who was pulling her long hair, Ella said, 'It was a lovely meal. Thanks. Sally's just filled me in on Marelda's story – which is a bit unnerving. I'm not sure what to do.'

'I'd just ignore her,' Tom advised.

'I think she's just a very unhappy girl,' was Yvette's contribution.

'Do you think any of it was Rick's fault?'

'If it was, I don't think he meant it,' Tom went on. 'He seems to hug everyone doesn't he?'

'I know. All the Goans do.'

'It might have been something to do with the tennis. She's a tough old player is Marelda, like a man. For a while she partnered Ricky against me and Big V that you'll meet. When they won Rick used to hug her.'

'I can imagine that,' Ella said, feeling more relaxed.

'We still play but she's always my partner now.'

'And if you hug her, Tom, I scratch your eyes out,' Yvette said, sounding very French and ending with a giggle. 'But I'm going to hug thees leettle girl who'as come all the way to Africa for her man only to find Madame Défarge ready to pounce.' And she did.

'Sally calls her Madame Défarge,' Ella guffawed, laughing and crying with relief.

'I know,' Yvette said. 'When Sally didn't come last night, I went to find her. She said she'd seen Marelda's car so she'd give dinner a miss if Madame Défarge was there.'

'How did she know she was knitting?'

'Oof. She's always knitting since she stopped smoking. Perhaps that's why she explodes so quickly.'

'It looks like Sophie's fallen asleep on my shoulder,' said Ella who had been jiggling her up and down as she spoke.

'Looks like you're a natural mum,' Tom observed.

'Not yet. I'll leave you to it,' Ella replied, carefully handing back the sleeping infant. 'Thanks. I feel a whole lot better.'

Back with Rick, who was busy sorting out one of those dropped files. The air was purple with expletives.

'Lesson notes,' Rick explained. 'They *were* in order. The trouble is I didn't date them all.'

'That's nasty,' Ella said. 'Looks like a few hours work. Come on I'll help you. There must be some logical order. Who's going to look at them?'

'That's the problem. Cecil bloody Smythe can't wait to put me in the wrong. He thinks because I'm Indian, I'm an idiot.'

Within an hour, the file was perfect and it was obvious that Rick was good at his job – bar dropping the odd file. Ella was sorry she had doubted Rick for a moment and thought he might be feeling as vulnerable as she was but, to make certain, she wanted to know everything about everyone at Mpika and Lwitikila. 'I don't want any more nasty surprises,' she told her 'beau'.

Rick told a good tale so she soon discovered that there were two distinct camps, so to speak, at Mpika Boys' School. One small group was led by Cecil Smythe, the headmaster, whose floppy wrists, mincing steps, yellow cravat and slacks with a knife-edge crease left little doubt that he batted for the other side. Wanda knew instinctively not to try her luck there, though she and her husband were in the clique. Then there were two Englishmen, Brian and Kevin, one tall, one short, who looked macho enough but you never know. Finally, Maisie and Fred, a plump couple in their fifties who looked as if they wished they hadn't come to Zambia and couldn't wait to go home, completed the group. The rest of the staff had united to form the other group.

'I can't wait for Big V to come back. He should be back any day but Little V won't come back with the baby until January. They're good friends. You'll like them.'

'Who's the tech teacher that helped you with the ping pong table?'

'That was Steve Singh. He's a bit of a wild character. He's here on his own, for a year, from India to make some money to send home.'

'They're such a different bunch from the one in Kenya,' Ella said.

'Lots of them are only here for a year so it'll be all change in January,' Rick explained. 'Goodness knows who we'll get then.'

'What do you know about Lwitikila – apart from Marelda? I've heard enough about her.'

'Now, there's a completely different kettle of fish. For a start, there are only about five men on the staff. That includes Father O'Malley, the deputy head. The rest are nuns, ex nuns, prospective nuns and a couple of Indian Catholic married couples, two Irish couples with babies and you. Why do you think I found you a job there?' Rick joked. I did try to get you a job at Mpika but Cecil Pansy Smythe wouldn't hear of it. He said he had to be careful with Scots women after Mhairi. I think everyone thought you were a figment of my imagination.

'Fair enough, I suppose. Never mind, I'll show them.'

'I'm sure you will. Anyway it's a strange and wonderful lot that have staffed the fifty thousand new Zambian Schools since 1964.

'Is it really that many?' Ella stated rather than asked. 'Give it another few years and these kids we're teaching will be the staff – just like in Kenya.'

'Correct. Just as it should be,' said Rick.

# Chapter 13: The Nuns' Nonsense and a Wedding

The day finally came when Ella had to leave Rick's house to go and live at Lwitikila. She didn't, however, have to go into the convent, as her housemate, Kirsty, from Edinburgh, had arrived. The two girls became instant friends exchanging secrets and uniting against their strange new surroundings. Only Kirsty knew that Ella hadn't been brought up in the Catholic Church and had, through no fault of her own, made an enemy out of the Irish Domestic Science teacher. Only Ella knew that Kirsty had no intention of taking the veil as her aunt, Sister Immaculata, expected, which was why she had been persuaded to come to teach at the Mission School. Only Kirsty knew how Ella was agonising about the future and how any marriage would affect both her family and Rick's and only Ella knew that Kirsty was nursing a broken heart over a handsome Scots lad.

Both girls were dedicated to their jobs so there was harmony in the large bungalow with its elderly, colonial style chintz furniture and heavy curtains. Amos, a solid, reliable Zambian servant came with the house and job. He knew what was expected of the young teachers and was there to give them invaluable support. Kirsty was tall, with the fairest skin, bluest eyes and blackest hair Ella had ever come across. Ella told Kirsty the story of Ewan Cameron, her primary school dominie's, giant world map and his explanations for all the differences in eye and hair colour caused by migration throughout the centuries.

'You must be a pure Celt,' Ella told Kirsty. 'I bet your family are from the West Coast.'

'You're right. The Hebrides. Sister Immaculata is my mother's sister and they were born on Eriskay. My granny still lives there.'

Five hundred girls at Lwitikila and two hundred boys at Mpika meant life was purposeful and hectic so Rick only came to visit Ella at weekends. Marelda took to leaving for Lusaka on Thursday evening and arriving back at work on Tuesday morning, which meant her disgruntled colleagues had to cover for her. Sister Immaculata, the Head, said little except that Marelda was having a few problems. The nuns organised a rota for covering Monday and Friday Domestic Science lessons and everything was swept under the carpet. Marelda made one last attempt to upset the Rick 'n Ella partnership but it fell flat. Marelda said, 'Did you know Rick was married? I saw a photograph…' to which Ella quickly replied, 'Did you know that photograph is of Rick and his brother Agnelo's wife, Maria, at their wedding on 29th December last year? Rick was his Best Man.' It was time to rise above the petty nonsense.

All the ingredients for an idyllic, peaceful existence were in the natural surroundings of Lwitikila. A short walk along a pretty road was the delightful waterfall on the babbling Lwitikila River known as The Falls where one could go for a swim or some meditation. A little further away was the much protected, hot and dusty Nachikufu Cave, carved out of a quartzite outcrop, with its rock paintings depicting elephants, an exquisite antelope and human figures carrying bows, arrows and spears. This rock art is believed to date to Neolithic times, perhaps 18,000 years ago. On a quiet stroll there one day, Kirsty and Ella reflected on the ban on too many visitors which meant they couldn't take the schoolgirls on a trip. Perhaps one day someone might open up the cave as a museum with protective glass to preserve the painted wall. Meantime the two young Scots women climbed onto the outcrop above the cave and enjoyed uninterrupted views northwards across a huge, tree covered plateau. Inspired by the wide open spaces, they shared their dreams and became true soul mates.

'I feel as if we've known each other all our lives. I was wondering... Will you be my bridesmaid?'

'There's nothing I'd like better. I thought you'd never ask.'

That was how a lifelong friendship was forged. It felt so right.

The school gardens, irrigated by water from the Lwitikila River, were lush and productive despite the lack of rainfall. Enormous cabbages and cauliflowers fed the school kitchen, along with most other vegetables, especially beans, depending on which seeds or plants were available. Potatoes, the Irish nuns suggested, should be used on any newly cleared land to clean it up and make it ready for other crops. Tomato beds flourished particularly well. Maize, millet and bananas grew on large enough plantations to provide enough to feed five hundred hungry girls from time to time. There was rarely a shortage of labour unless the students were particularly well behaved. Digging was the worst punishment, akin to stumping to clear the sports field at Mpika Boys' School, followed by the lesser punishments of weeding with a hoe, pronounced as hoey, then watering. Chickens provided eggs and, when their productive days were over, special chicken and rice dinners. There were unsuccessful attempts at breeding rabbits and pigs. Nobody wanted to eat the rabbits and the saga of the pig was memorable. Unlike Napoleon and Josephine, who had enjoyed a happy married life with a successful litter of piglets at Mpika Boys' School, before Napoleon met his end, the single female pig had no name and led a lonely life. She had been acquired, at extortionate cost, from the Chinese rail workers at the Mpika Depot who needed to breed huge numbers for their spare ribs. Every day, as the school waited for specially imported pig fodder, she survived on kitchen scraps and nshima (maize meal porridge). The little Irish nun in charge of 'The Pig', Sister Josephine coincidentally and perhaps unfortunately, was extremely conscientious, almost to the point of being obsessed with the creature's well-being. She announced that 'The Pig' needed to be built up with nutritious food before she could be put to the boar and have a litter. Every morning the same question was asked.

'Is there any sign of the pig fodder yet, Sister?' Eventually, the day arrived when a lorry could be seen, in the distance, speeding towards the school in a cloud of dust.

'Do you think,' Sister Josephine asked, 'that might be yer man with the pig food?' Indeed it was 'yer man with the pig food' and he was rushed up to the pig sty at great speed. A crowd of pupils, cooks and teachers had gathered to watch her enjoy her much delayed special treat but, in front of their very eyes, poor 'The Pig' got into a flap and promptly expired. The vet was later to pronounce her dead of a heart attack.

'I blame all dese noise-makers faffin' all around the poor animal,' Sister Josephine was heard to have said after she'd recovered from the shock. It has to be reported that Kirsty, Ella, Father O'Malley and even Sister Immaculata had thoroughly disgraced themselves when the news got back to the staffroom. They'd collapsed into uncontrollable laughter. It must have been the shock.

Herman from the boys' school heard the story, laughed loudly and quickly contacted his Chinese connection at the Tazara depot. He struck a deal which involved 200 American smells (cigarettes) and a much lower price than any non-communist nun could have managed. Next day a young boar and sow were delivered to Lwitikila where they made contact with 'The Pig's' uneaten food. Sister Josephine professed undying love for Herman whose reply was, 'I think you'd better christen them quickly.'

'What d'ye tink I should call them then, Mr Herman?'

'How about Mary and Joseph?'

'Done,' a happy Sister Josephine agreed, 'but which one of the litter are we gonna name Jesus?'

The Zambian schoolgirls were as diligent and intelligent as their Kenyan counterparts but with a healthy rebellious streak against the strict regime imposed by the nuns. Their Christian names reflected the gentler aspirations of their family and included Precious, Mercy, Faith, Hope, Charity, Gracious, Unity, Freedom, Happy, Beauty, Truth, Honesty, Joy, Loveness and, the favourite, Serendipity. Sadly, she became Dippy to her friends. The choice of Scholastica and Immaculata may have been helped along for two girls who had meaningful Bemba names but not, as yet, Christian names. The boys' names at Mpika, apart from

Monday to Sunday according to the day they were born, had a more masculine significance such as the items they might need to achieve their ambitions, or the names of world famous powerful men or historical figures, so the register might include Pencil, Progress, Driver, Brains (yes), Success, Nelson (Mandela?), Winston (Churchill?), Abraham, Martin Luther, Livingstone, Wellington, Duke, King or Chief. There were a few reflective names like Honesty, Ambition, Pride or Wonder and several colours like Green, Brown or Black. The point was that these adopted names were always followed by a perfectly good and meaningful Bemba name so it mattered little.

The staff at Lwitikila weren't 'all Irish' as had been suggested, but most of them were. The headmistress, Sister Immaculata (or Catherine in real life) was a Scot and adored by pupils and staff because, though tough, she had a wicked sense of humour. Father O'Malley, an Irish Liverpudlian, was equally funny and shared a love of the 'water of life' with Ella's Ricardo as he called him. On one occasion the two flattened a bottle of Bells over philosophical conversation, or perhaps wedding plans, and Father O'Malley's comment had been. 'Oh dear, there goes another dead man. I'm glad he didn't go before he saw the priest.'

The nuns were all characters, some with more sense of humour than others. The schoolgirls had worked out exactly what God, or the school administration, had put them in charge of. Sister Josephine, of course, was in charge of pigs, chickens, rabbits and any other livestock, which included the bats in the Nachikufu caves along the road which she said, were extremely dangerous; absolutely no girls were allowed anywhere near there. The bats were in no way dangerous but the archaeological society had requested that the schoolgirls be kept away as a matter of urgency so that the cave paintings could be preserved. Sister Scholastica was obsessively in charge of hemlines and virginity (preservation of). She succeeded in keeping hemlines at just below knee level despite bad-tempered grunts from the wearers, but there was no evidence to support success or otherwise regarding the other. Sister Edmund was very English and in charge of good manners and correct etiquette. She spoke the Queen's English beautifully and provided elocution lessons for the students and suggested that some of the staff might like to attend. This didn't go down well in some corners. She was often seen hovering around the dining hall teaching the girls how to properly use cutlery and keep their elbows off the table. 'All joints on the table should be carved,' she would announce. The Bemba girls had no idea what she was talking about.

Tiny Sister Bernadette from Cork was in charge of homecraft lessons in the outlying villages where she used to take girls out with sewing, cooking, first aid and cleaning equipment. She made up for any challenged intellect by being the most spiritual of all the nuns. 'Dese Babemba people are closer to God than we are,' she proclaimed. She then went on to describe the closeness to nature and the simplicity and kindness of these good people in the villages. They could teach the rest of us greedy, lazy, selfish people a good lesson or two. Some of us, she said, have far too much and we still complain. They have nothing and they're happy. Ella, at this point, had to tell the story of how she had felt the exact same way, after a visit to the villages in Kenya and how the little Kipsigis children wanted more soor plooms from Caithness.

Sister Mary Kabwe, a local Zambian, was in charge of liaison between the non-Zambian staff and the local community. Her subjects were Religion and History with special expertise in the history and religion of the Bemba. With her help, the non-Zambians gained a little knowledge of Lesa, the Bemba Supreme Being, who symbolises the future which lies in the east; the past, symbolised by the ancestors is in the west. Any difference between Lesa and the Christian God seemed minimal to the outsiders. The concept of demi-gods of nature such as Mulenga was harder to grasp. Even harder to understand, but infinitely fascinating, were stories of the *ingulu*, the spirits of nature, who were associated with waterfalls, snakes, lions or even chickens and might come in on a cold wind from the south east. More disconcerting were the *imipashi*, the ancestral spirits, who imposed a moral code through fear. Sister Mary Kabwe was glad that her new Christian faith was able to counteract the influence of these spirits which, she said, were being manipulated by the Bemba chiefs who wanted to limit the power of women, who are traditionally very powerful in the matrilineal Bemba society. Sister Mary predicted that the Bemba people would adopt a combination of Traditional African Religion and Christianity as their form of worship. Translation of The Bible into Bemba was well underway as was the creation of new hymns with Bemba words to add to the long list of rousing hymns, which had already been translated. Lesa Mukulu and Almighty God were one and the same but there was hint of a warning that Christianity might turn out to be skin on top of the centuries old deep rooted beliefs. Time would tell.

Sister Immaculata, also known as Sister Catherine, as well as being in charge of the whole school and everyone in it, had special responsibility for catching wayward and adventurous girls. She had her own unique methods which suggested she may have been wayward and adventurous herself before she donned the veil. Her standard reply to any excuse, fib or wriggle-out from pupil or staff alike was, 'Well, now, just fancy that.' This was delivered in a gentle Highland accent but, as it was accompanied by a sly smile and a hard stare, the sinner usually caved in and confessed all.

There was one especially pretty wayward girl who had managed to outsmart Sister Immaculata time and time again by managing to sneak out to spend time with her boyfriend. News had come back from the village that the beautiful Philomena had hoodwinked her headmistress. Sister had gone to the dormitory later that evening to find that Philomena's bed was occupied by a body-shaped bundle of books wrapped in towels and clothes. Not wanting to be outdone this time, Sister climbed into the girl's bed and, confident that her plan would work, went to sleep. Before dawn and still in the dark, Philly crept silently towards her bed, relieved that her plan had succeeded again. The blisters, from digging, on Philly's hands tell the rest of the story. There was also some cruel laughter in the staff room.

Ricky at Mpika and Ella at Lwitikila worked hard but still found time for each other. The rains came in November after nine months of drought and the transient expatriate staffing saw a massive changeover in December and a whole new, equally international cast of characters at both schools began to play their part. The more colourful personalities included, at Mpika, Q.R. Blot, an eccentric Englishman with several personalities and Wayne Ploza, an Australian pothead with a single flowery shirt and one pair of floppy boots; it was usually better to be upwind of him. Big V had brought his wife Little V and new son Ravi from Durban so he was constantly chewing wine gums to help him to give up smoking around the baby. Two crazy Irish girls descended on Lwitikila with one Irish provisional licence between them which miraculously got them around Zambia, Botswana and Malawi if they remembered to use the right name when stopped while behind the wheel, which, as a result of the state of their driving, was quite frequently.

Life went on and Rick 'n Ella let it slip they were planning a small registry office wedding, before too long, with no fuss and bother. This plan had as much chance of surviving as hot pants in Heaven or at a Lwitikila school assembly; the nuns were in charge. They weren't going to be done out of a white wedding with all the trimmings. The church at the mission, with its massive state of the art cubist stained glass windows, was beautiful and available. Father O'Malley would preside over the ceremony with the help of any visiting clergymen of which there were usually many. Music would be provided by singing schoolgirls accompanied by two guitar-playing ex nuns. An exquisite bridal head dress and veil were miraculously created from net curtaining and Ella and Kirsty were sent off to Lusaka to buy suitable material for Ella's gown and dresses for bridesmaid Kirsty and flower girls, Amelie and Nisha, one French the other Indian, which would balance out the race mix in the photograph. In fact it was the perfect excuse to show off the new church and demonstrate to the world just how well Lwitikila could put on a show.

'And it would be so educational for the girls,' Sister Edmund added, predictably.

There was no ducking out. The young couple had to get organised. Invitations were printed and sent to family in Kenya and Scotland, but with little hope that anyone would be able to attend the wedding. Flights to Scotland and Kenya via Rome (for The Pope's blessing Ricky joked) were booked for straight after the wedding as this *fait accompli* had to be explained and families pacified. A high wall of convention had to be climbed over.

Most people involved gave little thought to the deeper implications as they worked hard to make the big day perfect. The whole idea had captured everyone's imagination, from schoolgirls and boys to local dignitaries and every colleague, acquaintance and friend in between. The schoolgirls suggested the traditional Bemba format of marching the couple, accompanied by a raunchy song, to the marital home, shoving them in and leaving them to it while all the guests retreat to a safe distance and enjoy some carousing. This was to be modified. All the guests would walk from the church, after the ceremony, to the house shared by Ella and Kirsty where the school girls and boys would unceremoniously push the newlyweds through the door and leave for the tea and biscuits suited to their age, served in the school canteen. Meantime the adult guests would sneak round to the back of the house where, with the help of Kirsty and her hosepipe, a lawn was being lovingly persuaded to appear in the seasonally dry scrub.

A food menu totally unsuited to remote Zambia was planned by some ambitious dreamers who didn't happen to be the prospective bride and groom. The nuns and their domestic science classes would bake and ice a three tier cake, roast a variety of meats for carving and prepare a selection of salads, pasta and rice dishes and desserts. Ricky and Ella had to work on the logistics of getting supplies the four hundred miles from Lusaka. Ricky's priorities leaned more in the direction of drinks for the day. There was also the burning question of a couple of stag parties to consider. This was all rather baffling for formerly teetotal, Wee Free, Caithness Ella Mackay who was beginning to wonder if it really was a good idea to shackle herself to this swashbuckling foreigner with a taste for Mackay's whisky. Did he think he was marrying into the industry? For some reason, Lusaka supermarkets had recently been flooded with reduced price Whyte and Mackay's whisky so Ella had teased Ricky that Charles Mackay was her father's name and, in fact, her grandfather had founded the company which of course was a total fabrication.

However, Ella had to admire her fiancé. If he wanted something done, he would pull out the stops and sit back. He was the best delegator in the world. He made useful 'connections', often over a shared beer, wherever he went. When stumping the school sports field using pupil labour was proving too slow and too hard, he somehow managed to get a local PWD (Public Works Department) digger and driver, probably with a hangover, to come and do the job in three days – at no cost. He wasn't sure if his own wedding was such a good cause as the new secondary school but he managed to persuade the owners of the only chest freezer in town. the shopkeepers, to deliver it by truck to the wedding venue and fill it with the Asti Spumante and sparkling cider that were masquerading as champagne to toast the bride and groom. Of course there was no shortage of like-minded volunteers to fetch, store, chill and 'keep safe' a variety of alcoholic beverages which in the end turned out to be enough for three weddings – although they were all to find a resting place eventually. As if this wasn't enough, a few weeks before the wedding, Zambia experienced its own 'Whisky Galore' except it was 'Tia Maria Galore' in the form of a lorry which fortuitously had gone off a bridge between Mpika and Lwitikila while on its twelve hundred mile journey from Dar es Salaam to Lusaka. The driver had disappeared so there was no proof of the allegation that he 'must have been scoffing his load'. The local Zambian constabulary, it was noted, had taken a very long time to investigate the matter. In fact by the time they turned up, the lorry was completely empty. It was also reported that the Police Station in Mpika had opened late for the next three days.

Ricky played darts with one of the local constables, an affable fellow called Mainza. The 'Social Club' as it was known, had been a roofless squash court, a relic of colonial times, until it had been taken over by a group of bored locals from most walks of local and expatriate life, and of a wide variety of nationalities. Mouthy Mhairi's Steve, the water engineer, had been a founder member and had managed to get the place on to the twenty four hour electricity grid and run in a water pipe which occasionally brought forth water. Seating and tables were provided in the shape of upturned red plastic beer crates. There was no barman so glasses were out of the question. A bottle opener on a string tied to a metal staple on the wall was all that was provided and of course all empties were returned to the crates they had come from. Payment was haphazard. Members took it in turn to buy crates and made sure they got their money back somehow, sometimes with a profit but not always. Only a few ladies were invited to attend and even fewer went back a second time. Ella went once. She stayed long enough to discover a few things like 'Kwacha' meant three twenties and a double tops on a dartboard but that wasn't as good as 'Kwacha eiiiiighty!' shouted in a loud voice. When she decided she couldn't drink the beer and there was nothing else on offer, PC Mainza came to the rescue. As he was the 'law' and therefore to be trusted, he was in sole charge of the only key to the huge padlock on the door to the 'equipment' room which had probably been the squash club changing rooms in past times. When he thought Ella wasn't looking, he slipped into the 'equipment' room and appeared with a paper cup, with coca cola written on it, which contained a mysterious liquid up to the brim.

'Try that Mrs Ricky. Our local brew.'

Ella's strategy was to say nothing and smile sweetly. She recognised the brew and was slightly irritated by the 'Mrs Ricky' as she wasn't yet married and had her own name, but this was one of those moments for diplomacy.

'Very nice. Strange how it tastes of coffee.' Indeed it slipped down nicely, helping her through the noisy testosterone-filled darts match which was being conducted through clouds of smoke from foul smelling Chinese cigarettes.

A week later, Ricky arrived at Kirsty and Ella's house with twenty four bottles of Tia Maria. There was no evidence that there was any connection with any previous recent events.

'This will be a special treat for the wedding guests,' Ricky said beaming with pride and pleasure.

As the days before the wedding sped by, excitement grew quickly but the grass grew slowly. Lwitikila was blessed with plenty of water from the river but the soil refused to deliver. Sewing machines flashed in the Domestic Science department and in Mpika where two very excited little girls were being dressed in long white dresses with tiny red flowers stitched in a sweeping curve from shoulder to hem and little puff sleeves dotted with the same flowers. One French and one Indian, Amelie and Nisha looked enchanting and were overcome with excitement over 'their' wedding. Kirsty's dress, from material she chose herself, was red and sleeveless with the same trail of flowers in white. Ella's simple white dress was high-necked, ankle length, demure, long sleeved and designed by Sister Scholastica, the one with special responsibility for hemlines and virginity. Ella didn't mind as it hid the result of some comfort eating that she and Kirsty had been indulging in so that both dresses had had to be let out two days before the big day.

As big days do, it came, but not without trauma. Mpika was blessed with twenty four hour electricity but very little water - since Mouth Mhairi had whisked Steve the water engineer off to a new job - and Lwitikila was blessed with plenty of water but electricity only between six and ten in the evening. Days were for work or prayer – especially if you were a nun.

The wedding finally began an hour late. The bride had only been the fashionable twenty minutes late, having done the Carmen heated rollers bit - between six and ten – at the Tia Maria, toe-nail painting hen party. Father O'Malley had heard the giggles and come to check that the female half of the wedding would be in a fit state for the ceremony. He'd left after a glass of Tia Maria saying he was shutting down the generator. Ricky, on the other hand, had been treated to the kind of stag party they said he would have got in Scotland. Firstly, his drinks had been spiked and then he was dressed in a Gandhi style dhoti and paraded around the teachers' campus in a wheel barrow from the school production unit. After a pathetic little dribble of a hose down outside, he was allowed to have a warm shower with the little water that was available and get into his pyjamas. But there was little chance of any sleep as the young stags continued to party in Ricky's house until he finally found the strength to throw them out. It was a sorry sight that met Ella when she finally walked up the aisle on the arm of Tom, who was playing the part of Dad for the day, complete with braces under his suit jacket. What Ella didn't know was that, once more, it was Father O'Malley who had come to the rescue. Recognising Ricky's symptoms as massive hangover combined with terror, he had sent Sister Immaculata off to fetch something which appeared in a chaste basket covered in a white cloth, clinking slightly. It did the trick. The Roman Catholic wedding, performed by Father O'Malley and in the presence of Father Sam Lavertu and the Bishop, went ahead with Ricky in one piece. Never had the hair of the dog been more welcome. The sun streamed in through the geometric shapes of the stained glass window bathing the little red and white bridal party with its red and white carnations, which had survived the long journey from Lusaka in Bhavin and Sunita's cold box, in all colours of the rainbow. The singing of the schoolgirls backed by guitars, recorded for posterity by Sister Edmund and her battery operated cassette recorder, inspired the congregation. Echoes of Bemba traditional music alternated with modern Irish hymns in perfect harmony and the vows which were exchanged were age-old and universal; the couple were pronounced man and wife as equal partners, neither subservient to the other. Ella, however, as advised by that worldly Irish bishop with the twinkle in his eye, didn't let them make a Roman out of her, because she didn't want them to. Ricky didn't mind in the least.

Meanwhile, Ricky's mates the shopkeepers, whose Moslem religion wouldn't allow them to set foot in a

Christian church, had arrived with a massive chest freezer, for the cold drinks, to find no electricity on tap. Father O'Malley, the generator expert, was tied up in the nuptial mass, so disaster was imminent. Every other spare person was either in church or busy organising the cold buffet and setting up tables and chairs around the garden with its feebly sprouting lawn, fortunately rescued by the exotic presence of high banana trees and maize plants. Temperatures were rising when the couple emerged into the sunshine to be showered with rice and whisked off on the long walk to the marital home to the sound of traditional Bemba songs, the words to which were better not translated. Father O'Malley was whisked off in the other direction to switch on the generator for the freezer and some music for the wedding waltz and the party that would go on long after the bride and groom had left for Lusaka and their flight to Rome.

The couple were finally bundled through the marital door which was firmly shut. As the singing of the schoolgirls and visiting schoolboys faded away into the distance, time seemed to be suspended.

'Can we do this Ella?'

'We've just done it Ricky. There's no going back now!'

'It's forever then.'

'Forever.'

'I suppose we have to join the others then.'

'In a minute.'

'Too late! The hoards have invaded.'

Picture the scene. Lwitikila's own entente cordiale on a global scale. Pious nuns and youthful atheists from the new world of 1970s USA and Australia chatted and joked amicably. Colonial style, pompous and very British head teacher, Cecil Smythe, conducted a polite (rather camp) conversation with his arch enemies from the BOMA who saw him as a caricature of everything negative about their former colonial masters. After a few beers they seemed to be the best of mates and were waxing lyrical over their common dream for the success of the pupils at Mpika Boys' School. The Moslems, who didn't drink alcohol themselves or eat any non-halal meat, did a sterling job of serving champagne and had even brought their own halal chicken from home to add to the buffet table. The nuns who were dressed almost exactly like Ella, and probably the entire priesthood of northern Zambia, were also present.

'I wasn't sure if it was the bride or a new Sister,' Father Sam teased. He hadn't seen the young couple since there stopover at his mission on their way to the Umutomboko Festival.

'Not surprising, Father. It's got a Sister Scholastica designer label on it.'

Other guests included the exceptionally international staffs of the two schools and a few other schools within a hundred miles, a young couple from the Swedish agricultural college, a few British nurses from Chilonga hospital, Mainza the policeman, the District Secretary, the District Governor and their ladies, the Lusaka South African Indians and the local Asian businessmen and their families. The uninvited guests had seeped in from the surrounding villages to sit at the back of the church and later came to the edges of the garden to observe how weddings were conducted in a different culture. The Italian road builders and the Chinese railway builders were not invited and didn't gatecrash. They seemed to exist in isolation and get on with their jobs.

Animated conversation over a sit down meal was followed by the traditional speeches, one from surrogate

Father of the Bride Tom in his braces, one from Best Man Big V, wishing the couple well along their difficult and brave journey and the longest one from the Bridegroom who thanked everyone south of the North Pole for all the support and good wishes. The bride smiled sweetly throughout, pleased it was expected that she should say little if anything at all. And with each speech there was another 'champagne' toast. This went swimmingly well until one of the young stags decided that Marvin Gaye's 'I heard it through the Grapevine', all eleven minutes of it, would do for the wedding waltz. Ella folded her stubborn arms. 'I am not,' she announced, 'dancing my wedding waltz to a song of betrayal.'

'Sorry, I never listen to the words. I just thought it was a good tune,' was the sheepish reply.

Eventually Bread singing 'Everything I Own' was dug out of the cardboard box of LPs and calm was restored. From then on a committee was appointed for the selection of music with suitable lyrics so such gems as Sonny and Cher's 'All I Ever Need is You, The Beatles' 'Here Comes the Sun', Bread's 'Sweet Surrender', Sammi Smith's 'Help me Make it through the Night' and Diana Ross singing 'Ain't No Mountain High Enough' soared up over the banana trees with as much volume as a portable record player could muster. Eventually, after cake and Tia Maria, it was time for the weary couple to set off on the long drive to Lusaka and a free bed at Bhavin and Sunita's house. They, in return, would be staying with their three children in Ricky's house which, with some luck and hard work, would have recovered from the stag night.

Their guests had a much better time than they did. As they left, Ploz the Oz, in a clean shirt, and the leaping priest cameraman pressed ready to process films into their hands.

Their departure was delayed by an 'Oh, oh, oh,' squeaking Sister Edmund who rushed off to get the audio cassette of the church ceremony out of the recorder for them to take home to their families. 'God love you. Such a pity your people couldn't come!' she added.

Red paint spelt out 'Follow this arrow to reach your destination' on the car bonnet. A little later a fishy smell got steadily worse until a suspicious Ricky discovered some dried kapenta in a brown bag Sellotaped to the radiator. Removing that didn't quite get rid of a lingering odour and the happy couple were too miserable to see the funny side. Half way towards their destination, exhaustion and nausea took over and the little Toyota Corolla only just managed to crawl into the car park of The Elephant Head Hotel in Kabwe. Marital rights were neither demanded nor expected which was no surprise. The brightly decorated car had been the centre of curious speculation outside the hotel. Someone had reached the right conclusion and by the time Ricky and Ella had slept the sleep of the exhausted and recovered over coffee and toast, the white car was sparklingly clean and a little boy was asking for five kwacha. After Ricky had opened the boot and got him to scrub the radiator with soap and water until there was no fishy smell left, the boy got his money and Ricky and Ella could finally laugh.

It was only then that they realised how incredibly kind everyone, including relative strangers, had been. The staff at the boys school had got together and bought them a state-of-the-art super 8 cine camera and three films to record the events of the day, the staff at the girls' school had pulled out the stops and arranged the best ceremony and reception anyone could have expected, friends had brought the red and white flowers from Lusaka and there were the most amazing wedding gifts ranging from copper tables to Poole pottery and African blankets to an Ali Baba laundry basket. They had a lot to be grateful for.

But what was waiting for them in the outside world?

# Chapter 14: Ricardo Hits Altnabervie

A short week later, the new Mr and Mrs Fonseca found themselves being picked up at 9am at Heathrow airport by an apprehensive but curious Howard, now minus a beard, brother-in-law of Ella, husband to her sister Morag and by now father of Andrew six, Maggie two and tiny May who had just been born.

By lunch time Uncle Ricardo had charmed everyone including baby May and there were sighs of relief all around. Stories of how the honeymoon couple had been conned in Rome, but not as badly as they could have been, helped to lighten the conversation and establish that Ella's Ricardo had a sense of humour but was a force to be reckoned with. While in Rome, the two had left their hotel and asked where they could find the Trevi Fountain. An obliging horse and carriage merchant had taken them all around Rome and charged them accordingly and extortionately. Ricardo had reacted badly to catching sight of Hotel Victor Immanuel through a narrow strada leading from the point where they had been dropped off. It was a two minute stroll all of twenty five yards away. Ella had laughed and cajoled her new husband saying they'd had their money's worth of a wonderful sight seeing tour and wasn't the fountain beautiful and please could they throw one coin each into the fountain? He wasn't keen to part with even more cash but he agreed eventually.

'It needs a good clean up,' Ricky had barked. 'And I bet people nick the money.'

'You're right,' a passing tourist had commented. 'Some people have magnetic poles to do the job.'

'Well I've heard they collect the money every night and it goes to charity,' ever optimistic Ella had added.

'I don't see why stupid people have to throw their money into a stupid fountain!' a dogged Ricky had continued, still annoyed at being taken advantage of.

'Didn't you see the film? Two coins mean a happy marriage and one coin over your shoulder with your back to the fountain means you'll come back to Rome.' She left out the bit about three coins meaning divorce.

'No chance of that. They rip you off here.'

The rest of the visit was spent making sure that no cash was parted with unnecessarily. Coke was drunk on the hoof as it was half the price of coke drunk while seated in a café. Taxis and horse-drawn carriages were avoided and the final hotel bill was checked carefully. This was just as well as it turned out that the hotel had tried to charge them for twelve bottles of red wine instead of two. The last straw, in Ricky's eyes was when he had to use a coin to get into the toilet at the airport and another to get some toilet paper.

'All they want to do in this place is part a man from his coins!' was Ricardo's last word as he left Rome.

However, as a good Catholic, he was glad he had seen The Pope in person at his window overlooking St Peter's

Square, even though he was a tiny dot high above everyone and speaking in Italian of which he understood not one word. A visit to The Vatican and especially the Sistine Chapel was also considered inspiring and a suitable lasting memory of the ancient city.

Safely in Belsize Park, Ella felt back in the bosom of her sister's family and her Goan husband seemed to be surviving the experience so far. Howard, however, had planned some baptism of fire at the local pub where he'd arranged to meet a few likely lads including Phil, the English husband of Morag and Ella's cousin Jean. Leaving the sisters at home putting the babies to bed, Howard and Ricky set off. First of all draft bitter was new and nasty to Ricky and secondly, the stories of Charlie Mackay, his brother Alec and the entire Mackay family giving the Sassenach husbands of Morag and Betty a terrible time weren't exactly boosting Ricky's confidence.

'Sassenach's only a slightly abusive term for us Englishmen but I don't know what they're going to call you.'

'After the treatment we got, I don't fancy your chances one little bit,' the wicked Phil went on shaking his head in pity.

'I mean black men are fine in their place but would you let your daughter marry one? That's the way they think up there, you know.'

'And wait until you meet that Granny Mackay. What a dragon!'

'She's six foot two and almost as wide, with a voice like a foghorn.'

'And she disapproves of anybody that doesn't have table manners.'

'And Ella's her favourite granddaughter. You've got no chance.'

'Thanks a bunch,' was all Ricky could manage. 'Now, don't give me any more of that cat's piss. Get me a whisky.' Had he not been watching his p's and q's, his language would have been a good deal more expressive.

By the time the lads were finished, poor old Ricky was in a proper lather. Next day found him at Howard's barber taming his bushy locks and then down to Burtons in Camden Town with Ella in tow as a fashion adviser. Not a good idea. He emerged a vision in brown, beige and yellow from head to toe. A brown corduroy jacket over a cream and brown checked shirt with a wide collar, which could be worn with or without a yellow velvety tie, topped beige bell bottom slacks, cream socks and shiny brown brogues. He looked exactly like the male model on the life size fashion hoardings only brown. Brown and black skins simply didn't exist in any catalogue, poster or hoarding. But this male model wasn't Ricky. The smart outfit was quickly hung up in its plastic suit carrier and the boy relaxed backed into his jeans, safari boots and white open neck shirt. His favourite buy however was a big chunky Aran sweater which kept out the chilly British April air.

Morag and Howard's wedding present for the new couple was the loan of their ancient, but beautifully upholstered, Wolseley car to make the long journey to Caithness and back via Leeds where Ricky's two brothers, Jos and Carlos, were braving the immigration treadmill. The wood and leather shone, the engine purred and the steering column gears slipped in like a hot knife through butter. Ricky was terrified. What if he pranged the car on the unfamiliar roads? He couldn't afford to put even one toe wrong in the face of this menacing Mackay dynasty who were so protective of their daughters. How much worse than Sassenachs would they think an Indian husband was – especially a Roman Catholic? The two Sassenach husbands had done their job well and Ricky was now bracing himself against the inevitable attack – but he wouldn't kow tow; he had too much pride. Morag and Ella were unaware of all the banter of course which meant they couldn't put the poor lad out of his misery. Ella had just put his uncharacteristic quietness down to normal apprehension in a new situation. He didn't dare confide in the equally anxious Ella in case of worrying her more so they both suffered in silence. Ella was convinced everyone, especially her father, was going to hate this new morose Ricky and Ricky could see his hopes for a happy married life crumbling beneath the steely stare of the fiendish grandmother.

Unwilling to leave the three friendly little ones and the safe comfort of Morag and Howard's home, Ricky and Ella set off to find a route out of Hampstead and far north to Scotland.

'The car will keep you away from the great unwashed British public,' had been Howard's mischievous comment as they drove off.

'Or us away from them,' had been Ricky's enigmatic reply.

'Hm,' Ella had thought, catching a wicked twinkle in Howard's eye.

After Elstree, the new stretch of the M1 with its six lanes seemed to have carved an ugly, bare swathe through the lush green beauty of the English countryside. Cars were sweeping past the Wolseley which was doing seventy in the middle lane and there seemed to be very little protection from the cars speeding in the opposite direction.

'I hate these motorways,' Ella was saying. 'They're so ugly and dangerous. I wish they'd put something in the middle to separate the cars going in different directions. And they should plant some trees to cover all these piles of rubble everywhere. All you can see is a few dandelions. Ugh. It'll be much prettier when we get to Scotland.

'Howard was saying there's no speed limit on the M1 but I'm not risking his old banger,' Ricky added.

'As long as we get to Scotland by bedtime,' Ella continued. 'I don't mind how slow we go.'

'Does that radio work?'

'Let's see if we can get Radio Caroline.'

'What's that?'

'Only the best pirate radio with the best music,' Ella told her husband who, stuck in Africa, had missed the great days of Luxembourg and Caroline. 'It should be on 259.' As the crackles subsided a familiar tune blared forth. 'Oops that must be The Archers on The Light Programme on 247.' A few more rustles and the New Seekers with 'I want to teach the World to Sing' ushered in 300 miles of Top of the Pops, 1972 style.

'I love the words, Ricky. Listen.

*I'd like to build the world a home*
*And furnish it with love*
*Grow apple trees and honey bees and snow-white turtle doves*
*I'd like to teach the world to sing*
*In perfect harmony*
*I'd like to hold it in my arms and keep it company*
*I'd like to see the world for once*
*All standing hand in hand*
*And hear them echo through the hills Oh, peace throughout the*
land
*(That's the song I hear)*

*I'd like to teach the world to sing (that the world sings today)*
*In perfect harmony*
*Yes, I'd like to teach the world to sing*
*In perfect harmony*

Isn't that the best message, Rick?' Ella gushed trying to cajole her new husband out of his obvious miserable trepidation.

'I suppose so,' was Rick's grudging reply, 'though I hope your granny feels the same way.'

'I don't know what you mean. Of course she will. My dad might cause a few problems but I can get round him. Don't worry.'

'Everything's hunky-dory in Ella's perfect world isn't it? The real world's a lot different, I'm afraid.'

'That depends what you call the real world. Why have The New Seekers been number one for the whole of 1972? More and more people want peace and racial harmony. Enoch Powell lost his job because the people that matter knew how destructive his views are.'

'But, do you really believe the people in Caithness aren't going to give us a bad time – or me at least?'

'Come on, Ricky. We've been through all this. I thought we were looking at the big picture. What's the worst they can do? Throw stones or chuck is in jail? I thought we agreed, some of us have to cross the barriers. So let's show them how happy we are.'

'I don't know. I'm imagining all sorts of things like the neighbours turning their backs on us, your father shouting and your mother in tears and your Granny asking us to leave and never come back.'

'Well you obviously don't know the first thing about any of them you big dope. They're going to love you!'

'Why do you think Howard lent us the car? It wasn't to keep us away from the great unwashed British public. It was to protect us from the nasty looks and insults.'

'That's nonsense,' Ella almost shouted but deep down she wondered if the thought had in fact occurred to her brother-in-law. 'Anyway who cares about the bigots, eh? Do we need anyone else, you and me?'

'Stuff 'em,' a more cheerful Ricky yelled as he turned up the radio to sing along to Johnny Nash and 'I Can See Clearly Now' at the top of his voice as they bombed along the ugly motorway in their shiny old car.

Mile after mile, song after song, they worked themselves into a frenzy of happiness, arming themselves against the intolerance they were certain they would face.

'I don't care how late we get there. I must sleep in Scotland,' Ella suddenly announced.

The motorway, blissfully, had given way to a quieter road with lush and very welcome trees and hedges on either side. After wrestling for control of the new experience of serving himself at a petrol station, Ricky was feeling positive.

'Which planet have you come from?' the friendly attendant had chortled.

'Planet Zambia,' Ricky had replied. 'They do it all for you there – and throw in a free screen wash.'

'At your service, sir' the lad said unexpectedly and fetched a bucket and sponge. 'Can't have you saying Planet Preston isn't as good as Planet Zambia.'

Ella was relieved to see the two young men enjoying a joke; she was sure, as she'd always known, that life with her gregarious new husband was, after all, going to be absolutely hunky-dory.

Their spirits rose as afternoon took them through the hills of the Lake District and there was the chance of crossing the border before dark. In late April, this was slightly later than in Africa with its twelve hours of daylight and twelve hours of darkness, all year round. Ella was enjoying seeing her own land through the eyes of Ricky, a stranger to it. He'd been expecting the weather to be much colder and was enjoying the warmth of the late spring sunshine.

Ella cheered as they crossed the border before dark but just before the rain started. This was Gretna Green and Ella could tell the story of youthful elopement from England where young couples couldn't marry at sixteen without their parents' permission whereas they could in Scotland. Ricky thought it was just another odd custom.

'We'll stop at the first B and B we see,' Ella said.

'You go in and I'll hide in the car.' Ricky said, half seriously.

'Don't be daft,' Ella said but did it anyway – just in case.

'Sorry, lass but I've got a bride and groom and three guests and they've brought enough folk to fill everywhere in Gretna. But I'll just give my friend Jeannie in Ecclefechan a wee phone tae see what she's got. That's a shiny new wedding ring ye've got there. What've ye done with yer man.'

'Oh, he's waiting in the car. We've been married for two weeks.'

A few minutes later, Ella and Rick were setting off for Ecclefechan to be Jeannie's first guests of the season.

'It's only ten more miles and just past the big wide main street up a hill to the left. It's got a red door.'

'What's the name of the place?'

'Ecclefechan.'

"You're joking. I can't even say that.'

'I've never been there. The only thing I know about the place is that Thomas Carlyle came from there - the existentialist from Ecclefechan. What a stupid thing to remember.'

'Who's he?'

'He was a writer and philosopher. They called him the bearded sage with the penetrating gaze. I think he was the one who fell in love with the daughter of a British soldier and an Indian princess. They say he was so besotted with her that he couldn't consummate his marriage to some other woman.'

'That's a bit pathetic. Did he at least have anything useful to say for himself?'

'Far too much about too many things as I remember. He went from the clergy to American transcendentalism and dabbled in every philosophy around at the time. A very confused man I think but he did say we should battle against out-dated customs,' Ella prattled on having hit on her hobby horse. 'Did you know that a third of the British Army officers in India in the nineteenth century married Indian women? And many of them converted to Islam.'

'I did know that, actually,' replied Ricardo the Goan, pleased that his education had enlightened him. 'I hope they treated their wives a bit better than the Portuguese sailors who abandoned theirs and went home again.'

'I bet a lot of the dusky youths and maidens at expensive boarding schools in England would have interesting family trees.'

'I'm sure. One family we knew in East Africa, the Colquhouns they called themselves, claimed to be Anglo-Indian without a drop of Indian blood in them. All these years in the tropical sun had darkened their skin they claimed.'

'And I remember a William Kirkwood who was at boarding school in Perthshire. They say his real name was Raj something or other. My school mate's cousin saw it on a letter.'

'Was your school mate dark-eyed?'

'I think he was.'

'Well it seems Mrs Ella Mackay Fonseca,' Ricardo declared,' that our little rebellion is nothing new.'

'It feels pretty scary right now. If a white woman had even gone near an Indian man back then she'd have been sent home in disgrace. '

They located Jeannie's B and B with the red door and found her to be gloriously nosey and friendly. Within five minutes she had found out everything about Ricky, his grandparents, his job and his future plans. As an afterthought, Ella was thrown, 'And where are you from?' and when the reply was 'Caithness' it was, 'Oh aye,' and that was that. It looked as if Ricardo the charmer was going to put his little Scots wife in a shadow in her own country.

The coldness of the 'not yet aired since last year' bedroom didn't match the warmth of the welcome. Damp seemed to be creeping out of the walls and bedclothes. The hot water bottle 'just in case' didn't help much beyond one foot each so the two shivering newly weds put on T-shirts, jumpers and socks over their flimsy night wear and cuddled up to try their best to fall asleep. At two in the morning Ricardo woke up rigid from head to toe with his teeth chattering so Ella had to rub some warmth back into him.

'What the bloody hell kind of country is this that you've brought me to,' he moaned through the shivers.

'I promise you,' Ella said, 'It's never been this cold.'

'Wait until that Jeannie's given us some breakfast before we complain. I'm starving,' Ricky added.

At long last morning came. Thankfully there was hot water for a shower so Ricky's spirits were almost defrosted. Porridge followed by bacon and eggs warmed them some more and by the time a nice cup of strong tea had washed it all down. they were even thanking Jeannie. The only complaints were fairly polite. Ricky said he had been a 'bit cold' and Ella said, 'I think you'd better light a fire in there for a while.' By some miracle they had left the B and B by a very early half past seven, vowing never to return.

A mile along the road, in the middle of nowhere, they stopped at a phone box.'

'Hi Mum. We're hoping to be home by tea time but can you switch on the electric blanket now please? It feels like we slept in a freezer.'

She just managed 'in Ecclefechan' before the last 10p ran out leaving poor old Mary McKay yet again incommunicado with her daughter.

'She says they slept in a fridge in Ecclefechan,' was the message Charlie MacKay got.

'For ony sake, fit next?' he grumphed on his way out to feed the cattle.

The old Wolseley bombed along negotiating the Killiekrankie corkscrew of hills and bends with ease in Ricky's expert hands. Ella was seeing her native Scotland in a new light through the eyes of her husband who seemed to be awe struck by the beauties she often took for granted. The sun came out and bathed the stunning views of loch, river and valley in a cooler, less intense light than the fierce tropical sun they had left behind a mere two weeks before.

'The light here seems to be silver rather than gold.' Ricardo observed. 'I know what they mean by Bonnie Scotland now.'

'I didn't realise you were so poetic.'

"You'd be surprised.'

So Ella told him stories of Rob Roy McGregor, the Scottish Robin Hood and tales of Bonnie Prince Charlie and Bonnie Dundee and the General Hugh Mackay from Sutherland who helped the Jacobites fight the English and might just be her close ancestor. Ricky was fascinated.

'I'll never again include the Scots in complaints about the Brits in Africa,' Rick said.

'Oh, I'm sure some of the Scots were just as guilty as some of the rest of the Brits in different parts of the world,' Ella added, realising how patriotic she must have just sounded.

'Of course,' said Rick, 'We're cosmopolites these days, aren't we?'

'Absolutely.'

They sped on past Blair Athol with its spectacular white castle in the distance and on through Glen Garry towards the bleak, blasted, deserted road near Dalwhinnie. For Ricky, on one side was the sight of his first Whisky distillery and on the other, stretched along the hill top horizon as far as the eye could see, was the biggest herd of roe deer Ella had ever seen. As the car sped by, the proud animals stood stock still and watched.

'Wow,' she said, 'wasn't that amazing.'

'Almost as exciting as the wildebeest migration,' Ricky said, adding, 'I think.'

'Perhaps more exciting,' said Ella, adding, 'I think.'

The two laughed and agreed cosmopolites shouldn't be competitive about what their native countries could offer to the world.

The deserted road snaked along a wide, treeless valley before the Cairngorms loomed up on the right.

'Look, there's snow on the White Lady!' Ella cried. This was Ricky's first sight of snow. 'We used to ski there on school trips.'

They came across a little converted ice cream van which looked totally out of place on the lonely road until they discovered that hot dogs, hamburgers, onions, mustard, ketchup, tea and coffee had replaced the Zanarelli's Ice Cream advertised in red paint on the yellow side of the van.

'Good thinking,' Ricky said to the man whose name was, in fact, Zanarelli. 'Not much call for ice cream around here, I'd say.'

'Only in June or July,' Zanarelli went on with as friendly a grin as Ricky's. 'Even then it's pretty cold,' he continued revealing the vestiges of his Italian accent. 'My brother, he decides to go back to Roma but me I like Scotland. Friendly people.'

'Same world, colder weather, eh,' added Ella getting on her cosmopolitan bandwagon.

'I s'pose,' the Italian added giving her a puzzled glance.

When the food order was ready, Mr Zanarelli piped up, 'Waneminabag?' at which Ella started to laugh.

'Your brother didn't have an ice cream shop in Altnabervie, did he?'

'Not my brother, but my uncle. Why?'

'We used to call him Waneminabag.' Ella replied with a giggle. 'He had the biggest threepenny cones in town.'

The next leg of the journey took them through Dava moor and down to Inverness.

'What on earth is that in the firth?' Ella asked as they could see an ugly tangle of grey metal girders rising out of the water.

'No idea. Let's ask at this petrol pump. Look it's 35p a gallon up here it was only 33p back south. How come?' Ricky grumbled.

They discovered that the 'thing' in the Moray Firth was a new oil rig near Ardersier. Everyone was talking about the prospect of new jobs but feared the profits would leak out to the Americans who had been brought in to teach the locals how to run the industry.

Ella picked up a newspaper to catch up on current affairs.

The journey continued out of Inverness with Rick singing along to Chuck Berry's 'My Ding a Ling' and Ella feeding him tit bits of news from the local Press and Journal which at times stretched to World News.

'They've got plans to build a bridge at Kessock –but I'm afraid we'll have to take the ferry today.'

'That'll be something different.'

'There's never good news is there? 'Three die in KKK riot in Central Park', 'Idi Amin expels Asians from Uganda', 'Heath deplores unemployment figures over a million', 'Pay and price Freeze causes Unrest', 'British Embassy Destroyed in Dublin over Bloody Sunday', 'Bombing Continues in Hanoi' – these are all the big headlines. 'Development of North Sea Oil Continues', 'Oil hits $2:50 a barrel, Organisation of Petroleum Export Countries Formed', 'Unemployment in the North East Falls Dramatically' – that's the business section. Here's a good one: 'Sirimavo Bandaranaike first woman president of Ceylon' and another one: 'Greenpeace founded to protect Earth' – that's positive.

'What was Bloody Sunday?' Rick asked picking out the most lurid headline.

'Wasn't that back in January when about fifteen people were shot in Londonderry? They blamed the British Army but they were exonerated. I suppose that's why 20,000 Irish people are throwing petrol bombs and burning Union Jacks in Dublin. What a mess." Ella rambled on adding, 'Zambia seems much more peaceful.'

'For the moment, but I suspect the Rhodesia-Zimbabwe thing's going to kick off soon,' Rick replied, once more clouding his naïve little wife's rose-tinted glasses.

'Anyway, we're here and we have a whole Caithness family and community to impress with the joys of being cosmopolites. Are you ready for the funny looks?'

'Not sure about that but we've run out of road.' The sun was bouncing off the Moray Firth as the old Wolseley joined a queue of three other cars waiting at the quayside. A rickety old boat was chugging across the water.

' What do we do here?'

'Drive on to the boat and they'll come and take our money. Oh, it's still the Eilean Dubh – it's lucky if it can hold eight cars.'

'It looks as if it's about to sink. Are you sure about this?'

'Ferry's have been crossing here for yonks – with lorry loads of sheep and all sorts. Relax.'

Fifteen smooth minutes later, they were safely on the Black Isle, heading for Ella's home.

'I can't believe it cost 50p. That's doubled!' Ella grumbled. 'Now for the best sea views in Scotland – except for that horrible monstrosity of an oil rig.'

Rick was beginning to feel more and more nervous as the expected confrontation with the Mackay clan was looming closer, and would have whipped the comb out of his hip pocket if he hadn't been driving and trying to sneak a look at all these 'bonny views' that Ella was getting excited about.

'We can head straight for Altnabervie from Helmsdale. It should be quicker in this weather,' she suggested to Rick who had no clue where anything was and would have been happier with the longest possible route home. 'We can go by Dingwall and Bonar Bridge to avoid all the ferries,' she added confusing him even more. 'My dad used to say the fairies crossed the Dornoch Firth in cockle shells - but we weren't fairies when we wanted to go on the ferries instead of the bridges.'

After Dingwall to the south east the calm Cromarty Firth twinkled in the spring sunshine while to the north west lonely, treeless hills stretched eerily into the distance. Driving away from the coast, for a while, was fast and easy on the straight narrow road as the very few other cars could be seen for miles so there was no need to fear unexpected meetings where there was no room to pass. They were soon back by the sea and had to cross the Dornoch Firth at Bonar Bridge.

'There's the monument to the Mannie o' the callous clearances,' said Ella. 'This must be Golspie.' Of course she had to explain how the Duke of Sutherland had hounded the local crofters off the land in the nineteenth century. Then, suddenly and inexplicably woodland appeared along with bends on the road.

'That looks more like a fairy castle than a Scottish Castle,' Ricky shouted out.

'That's Dunrobin, the seat of the Sutherlands. I think it's a boys' school now and it was used as a naval hospital for a while. I suppose their sheep didn't do as well as they expected.'

'I can't believe there's a place called Doll,' Rick said as the sign to it passed in a flash.

'And here's another golf course for you,' Ella replied as they swept past Brora.

Rick was charmed by the little fishing village of Helmsdale set out on a headland with its harbour lined by brightly painted fishing boats and neat streets of immaculate white cottages with similarly brightly painted woodwork. Bare hills rose sharply just behind the houses, not high but still imposing. Pretty little breakers were hitting the stony beach in the bay like moving pearl necklaces. A handsome old bridge crossed the river but before it was a large but tired looking hotel.

'Let's stop at The Bridge Hotel for a cuppa,' Ella suggested. 'It's quite posh.'

As usual, Rick engaged whoever was nearby in cheery conversation and ensured good service by 'not denying' that they might be staying a night. Ella reckoned they got today's rock cakes and not yesterday's out of it. They learned that the old Helmsdale castle had been knocked down to make way for a new by-pass bridge which would be open in a matter of weeks and the hotel manager was worried about the loss in passing trade.

Ella finally got them out of the situation by saying she hadn't seen her family for a year and it was a slow 35 miles to Balnahuig via Kinbrace and Forsinard. Promising to return, they set off across the old bridge, past the ancient ice house and headed north west through the Strath of Kildonan. Soon they had reached one of the most wild and desolate regions on the planet.

They didn't see a single car for miles. What they saw were crumbling cottages, abandoned crofts and a wide sky over a vast and silent wilderness. From time to time a loch appeared by the roadside, or a small stream crossed the tar road which was helping the travellers to pick their way safely through the wetlands.

'It wasn't always like this,' Ella explained. 'There were hundreds maybe thousands of these pre-clearance settlements. When these crofters were forced off the land, some of them went to Glasgow where the locals gave them a hard time. Others scattered all over the world but mainly Canada and New Zealand. There's a place called Kildonan in Canada. There was even a gold rush here. Some character claimed to have a ring made of gold panned from the Kildonan burn and everybody believed him but I don't think anybody else ever found any more gold.'

They soon reached the tiny village of Forsinard, close to the watershed between the south-flowing Helmsdale and the north-flowing Halladale. It felt like the top of the world.

'Please can we stop,' Ella asked. 'I want to drink in this air.'

The sounds of different birds and the slight babble of running water echoed through the silence. Standing side by side, arms around each others' waists the girl and the boy from opposite ends of the world felt alone on Earth and steeped in wordless communication. Still clinging to each other they slowly spun round to view the endless moor spreading out in all directions. Finally Rick broke the silence.

'It's the quality of light I can't get over,' Rick finally said. 'There's no dust like in Africa and the smell – mm – it's so fresh.'

'That's the peat. Let's look for that burn. They walked fifty yards from the tar where they found clear, amber water trickling from a tiny spring and disappearing into the marshy surroundings. 'That's what gives Scotch Whisky its special flavour.'

'I wish we could just stay here,' Rick whispered as his diminishing confidence reminded him he needed to comb his hair, tuck in his shirt and down one of those famous whiskies.

'Me too,' Ella whispered back, 'but we're going to have to face the music sometime. It won't be that bad.'

'What do you mean? Here we are waiting to see your six foot tall, Wee Free, teetotal Granny who told you not to bring home coffee-coloured grandchildren.'

'She was only joking.'

'That's nothing compared to your dad's likely reaction according to Howard and Phil.'

'Och, don't pay any attention to them. I'm sure they were winding you up,' Ella said firmly - though she wasn't convinced.

They weren't prepared for what was to come.

From that special place near Forsinard to Hillside Farm the fifteen miles went by at a snail's pace as Ricky's apprehension rose, keeping his right foot off the accelerator.

Meantime Mary Mackay, mother of the bride but not present at the wedding, was fussing around plumping up cushions and straightening lace-edged antimacassars on chairs. Everything had to be perfect. The pheasant casserole and the sherry trifle had been tasted and pronounced delicious. Mary would have preferred to be safe with her daughter Ella's favourite shepherds pie which she'd heard Ricardo liked too, but Granny Mackay had insisted that the newcomer from another land should be treated to something quintessentially Scottish and exotic – such were her delusions of grandeur. Charlie, as was often the case at moments of social importance, was up to his elbows in helping to deliver a new calf. This was work that could not wait. Granny was interpreting Mary's anxious sighs as unwillingness to accept her daughter's Asian husband and was laying forth in her domineering manner.

'There's no need to get yourself into such a state, Mary. If you can't bring yourself to welcome the lad into your home, I'll be happy to put him up.' This was not helpful but Mary couldn't bring herself to argue with the old lady who always ended up being right whether she was or not.

'I'm fine, Granny. It's just getting a wee bit late and now Charlie's stuck with the calving, it won't look very welcoming if he's not here when they arrive. Oh, there they are. What are they doing half way along the drive?'

Half way along the bumpy drive was as far as they had got before the old Wolseley decided to have a spectacular puncture which sent it rearing from left to right until it landed neatly and ignominiously in the middle of a whin bush with all its prickles.

'I just don't believe this,' shouted Rick, 'Right in front of everyone.'

Despite her tights being in shreds from clambering out of the car through the whins, Ella was in fits of giggles which were upsetting Rick even more.

'There must be a spare wheel and a jack in the boot,' she spluttered. 'Let's impress them with your Boy Scout skills.'

Not quite as quick as a flash, but a respectable few minutes later, the wheel was changed and the rumpled pair were back in the car and crunching across the newly replenished beach pebbles in front of the house. Granny and mother-in-law had had a grandstand view from the big bay window. Charlie had seen it all from the cowshed having delivered a wee heifer successfully and Ella's brother Jamie had driven up behind them with wife Katy and two year old Hughie in the back seat. There was no need for stuffy introductions.

'What were you doing in the whin bush?' Jamie laughed.

'That old car of your brother-in-law's blew a tyre. Goodness knows how,' Ricky explained, 'but we've changed the wheel.'

'I used to think my sister Ella could jump in a midden and come oot smellin o' roses. Looks like you're much the same, Ricardo. I'm Jamie.'

'I guessed that. Nice to meet you.' (One down, a few more to go.)

Some shy handshakes later, everyone was introduced and little Hughie broke the ice with, 'Buddy tacter boken agane,' which made everyone laugh.

'This time it's buddy Uncle Howard's car that's boken,' Katy added cheerfully. 'I wonder where he got that.' She leant towards Ricardo and whispered, 'That was his first sentence by the way.'

'It's not much of a tractor then,' Ricky replied.

When Charlie appeared later, there wasn't a trace of cow's afterbirth and he was immaculately dressed in collar, tie and jacket. Ricky had the urge to comb his hair. The two men exchanged a wary handshake and a steely gaze. Ricardo could not get Mike Kilpatrick's words out of his head. Charlie Mackay's expression was inscrutable.

'You two can never get married of course… it'll break her father's heart,' Mike had told the two of them before adding, 'He prayed she'd never marry a black… he told my father.'

Ricardo Fonseca was poker-faced.

Dinner in the dining room with the best silver and starched white serviettes was served after baby Hughie had gone to sleep in his Granny's house cot. There were no wine glasses and no aperitifs had been served. Only Ricardo had noticed. He had to broach the subject.

'Ella tells me the Mackay and Mackay and White's whisky is a family connection. Was she pulling my leg?'

'Yes,' Jamie said hiding a smile. 'You only get a drink in this house at five to midnight on Hogmanay.'

'Charlie,' Granny said coming to the rescue, 'we should treat our guest. Is there still a bottle of my elderberry wine in the cupboard? Ella, you know where your mother keeps the glasses – the ones with the bunches of grapes.'

Jamie, Katy and Ella were now all trying to stifle grins. Granny was convinced the elderberry wine was non-alcoholic; it had a kick like a mule. Ricardo the Goan, used to his daily whisky before dinner, was bemused – and thirsty. Ella had to rinse and polish the glasses to remove the dust and the only bottle of booze in the house was poured into seven glasses. Charlie made sure it was equal. It was going to be a wild night. Ricardo's heart sank as he made a mental note of getting to the nearest off licence next day.

The tipple was enough to loosen Granny's tongue and the conversation turned to her sister's days in India as a nurse.

'I'm afraid I've never been to India,' said Ricky. This was going to be a long, dry night unless he and Ella took control. They decided to entertain everyone to their tales of Rome, London and the frozen bed in Ecclefechan. Eventually, Ella bit the bullet.

'Can we get a hold of a Super 8 projector and a screen?' Ella chipped in too cheerily. 'We've managed to get the wedding films developed in London.'

Katy knew where to borrow a projector and couldn't wait to see the pictures. 'I've never seen a wedding movie before. Only albums.'

'I wish you could have been there,' Ella said wistfully.

'Me too,' said Mary, 'but it was just too far. You're father has a surprise for you though, haven't you Charlie?'

After some puzzled reticence, Charlie finally came out with, 'Oh aye. We've invited everyone for a reception at the Altnabervie Arms. Your mother has a list but if there's anybody else you'd like to invite, you'd better ring them quickly; it's a week on Friday at 7o'clock.'

'And the minister's going to give a blessing,' Mary added. There was a distinct impression of someone having had to be browbeaten into this situation.

'Thank you,' Ella said.

'We appreciate the effort,' Ricardo added.

'We really do,' Ella continued. At the time there seemed nothing more to say. Later on, in the warmth of the electric blanket which had been on all day she said, 'I think that was okay for a start, don't ye think?'

'I like your family,' Ricky said unable to hide the surprise in his voice. 'Do you think they like me? It's hard to tell.'

'They loved you. They're just not into the huggy, kissy stuff in this part of the world. Don't worry about it.'

'I'll have to train them and I don't think I can go much longer without a drink. Howard and Phil got the teetotal bit right. Wait till I see them. They had your granny down as an ogre and your father as a violent bully.'

'I told you they were taking the Mick. Howard brings his own beer and pint mug when he visits. Did you know that?'

'Now that's given me a few ideas.'

Next morning brought a nasty shock. The doorbell rang and Mary opened the door to two uniformed people, a man and a woman. They wanted to come in. Ella could hear her mother's voice, 'He's asleep' and another strange male voice saying, 'Well, could you wake him. And your daughter too.' Ella was downstairs like a shot, ruffled hair and sleepy eyed. 'What's the matter?'

'Is there a Ricardo John Francis Fonseca living at this address, madam?'

'Yes, he's my husband,' she said to the policeman and woman.

'Well, I'm afraid we have to take him in and you had better come too for safety's sake?'

'Pardon? What on earth for? And where?'

'Immigration contacted us by letter to say that Mr Fonseca may be a risk.'

'How ridiculous,' Ella retorted getting annoyed. 'He couldn't be a threat to anyone.'

'All the same, we have to make sure you both go into quarantine at Altnabervie Clinic straightaway.'

Poor Mary was as white as a sheet. What mess had her Ella got into this time? Ella rushed upstairs to tell Ricky what was happening.

'I know what this is. My X-ray at Heathrow has come up with my old pneumonia scar and they think I've got TB. It happened before in Canada when I was going to study. Don't worry.' Ella rushed off downstairs to put Mary's mind at ease. The two constables looked relieved too. Mary made tea for them while Rick and Ella got dressed.

'We'll follow you in our car, if you don't mind.' Ricardo Fonseca said in that authoritarian voice that brooked no opposition. 'Just show us where the hospital is. I'm sure we'll be out of there in five minutes when they understand the situation. It's just a shadow from a pneumonia scar when I was fifteen. I told them at Heathrow but nobody bothered to take a note of it.'

'Right you are, Sir,' the young male policeman replied meekly.

'Sorry if you got a scare, Mum,' Ricky said. 'There's really nothing to worry about. We'll be back soon.'

'Here, take a banana each. You haven't had breakfast.' Once a mum always a mum.

'They probably think we've got some horrible, contagious tropical disease,' Ella said too breezily, 'but they're too scared to say so in case they get accused of racism.'

'It's a good thing we're up here. It could have been a nasty situation down south with all these thousands of Idi Amin's rejects.'

The hospital consultant turned out to be a sensible character who was irritated by this latest bit of bureaucracy which had wasted his time. He soon sent Rick and Ella away with a reminder to keep taking their anti-malarial tablets which, to avoid further alarm, they said they would, though, like most people in highland Kenya or Northern Zambia, they had never taken them. Before they escaped from the hospital, however, they bumped into a familiar face from Balnahuig, who was visiting one of his patients.

'Aye, Isabella, he's a bonny lad but I hope he's worth a' the kerfuffle and heartache that's been goin' on aroon' here.'

'Do you know what?' Ella flashed back, the rage rising. 'We were doing just fine until you put your wooden spoon in. We've travelled half way across the world, via Rome and the length of Britain without an unkind word until we met you – and you're supposed to be educated,' and she stomped off leaving Rick with a big grin on his face, spreading his hands and shrugging his shoulders.

'That's my Ella,' he said daring to sound triumphant. 'Pleased to meet you, I'm Ricardo Fonseca, teacher and fellow human being – oh and husband to Ella Mackay, now Fonseca.'

'Iain Falconer, GP to the Hillside Mackays. I think you'll probably do.' There was a twinkle in his eye as he offered Ricardo a firm handshake. 'I think Charlie Mackay was imagining someone, shall we say, much less westernised. Now, go and sort out that lass of yours before she blows a gasket. And you make damned sure you look after her. Do you hear?'

'You can be sure I will though she's quite tough enough to look after herself.'

'Don't I know it. Ye've got yer work cut out to get round old Charlie Mackay though. Ye'd better make a steady job o' that. Good luck.'

'Thanks I'll need it by the sounds of things.'

'Mary's your ally – and surprisingly so is old Granny Mackay.'

'You seem to know more than I do.'

'Sorry, it's common knowledge around here – small village - so I'm not betraying any confidences.'

Strangely, Rick found that chat helpful. He now knew where he was and could set about charming the locals. He felt confident. Ella, however, was still fuming.

'What an ignorant bigot! What else did he say to you?'

'Enough to arm me against whatever hits the fan – and I think we're going to cope, my fiery little wife.'

Back at the farm, now hopeful that he understood the task in hand, Rick set to being as engaging, helpful and 'westernised' as possible. He mowed the lawn first, after a struggle with the mechanics of pulling the starter cord on the ancient heap of metal. Charlie was delighted as, like all farmers, he hated lawns and flowers that didn't make any profit. He decided to get his new son-in-law on to shooting rabbits and sent him off with the twelve bore.

Meantime, in search of much needed moral support, Ella rang round her old mates to invite them to the 'reception' at the Altnabervie Arms. She made a special effort to ask Wee Ally, who was now the mother of two, to sing a few songs with the band Charlie had booked for the wedding dance. They were the Alex Gordon sextet – a strange combination of violin, saxophone, accordion, mouth organ, piano and drums. There would be a few wheezes, squeaks and bangs in the wrong place but they could be relied on to belt out a good Gay Gordons and Eightsome Reel.

The rest of the guests would be relatives, neighbours and some of Jamie and Katy's mates from the Young Farmers Clubs that Ella knew too. Rick had found one guest to invite – and he was happy to introduce him to the family. At six foot four, he was known as the gentle giant. A university mate of Ella's and with the unlikely title of 1971 caber-tossing champion of Zambia, Davy Cunningham had presented himself in the middle of one of Ricardo's Mpika outdoor school assemblies on a small peeky, peeky, as such a motorbike was called in Zambia. The vision of this huge man sitting on a tiny bike, quite oblivious to the gravitas of a school assembly, caused a bit of a stir among the three hundred uniformed schoolboys but when he called out, 'I'm looking for a Ricardo Fonseca. Does anyone know where I might find him?' they all cheered.

'That's me, but you'll have to wait there quietly until I finish the assembly.'

Of course the story would improve as it was soaked in whisky and, with embellishments, it was to become almost unrecognisable by the end of the wedding shindig for Mr and Mrs Ricardo Fonseca.

As the day drew closer, curiosity was growing among the locals who had yet to meet Ella's 'man'. The rumours were flying. Johnny Brown the tailor had a story that his legs and arms were longer than the average in Caithness but he was a fine figure of a man to make a new suit for if the occasion ever arose. Ricardo's version of the story was different; he had only needed a vest but, when he dropped into the 'Men's Drapery and Tailor' and asked for a medium vest, Johnny had whipped out his measuring tape to 'make sure'. Waist, chest, hips, across back, arms and legs, outside and in had to be measured and recorded before he announced, 'Yea, medium.'

'Odd fellow,' Rick had said to Ella outside the shop. 'Do you think he's a bit pink?'

'No, just nosey – he has a wife and kids.'

Cousin Roderick Sinclair, Roddy, was the dapper, affable charmer (flash git) of the family. He appeared in full highland regalia for Ella and Rick's 'do' with his spirits in fine form. His considerable charm was going to be needed in unforeseen circumstances later in the evening. He began by warmly welcoming the maverick Davy Cunningham as the only stranger and the only other male in highland dress if you could describe a crumpled kilt with a T-shirt as such. The two were deep in mirth by the time Davy had told stories of gate-crashing Ella's Ricardo's school assembly and then playing ping pong on a table after the lunch had been cleared away. Having discovered that Rick was an acceptably good guy, he turned to him with a massive firm handshake.

'Ceud mile faille gu Caithness, Roddy Sinclair at your service,'

'If you say so… what was that?'

'A thousand welcomes to Caithness, Rick.'

'Thank you, I'm very pleased to meet you.'

From then on, the handshakes were many and the line of whisky glasses grew longer, as the guests realised that a man who liked a tipple had been sentenced to a stay of more than a few days in the teetotal Mackay house at Hillside Farm. Rick was having to exercise some self control at least until the eating, cake-cutting, and 'few words' from the minister were over. He had plans. He would bowl Ella's family and friends over with a speech of such eloquence and sincerity that any doubts about his suitability as a husband would be expelled forever. This was no problem as, whenever there are more than ten people in a room, someone with the name Fonseca has to stand up and say something even if it's just grace. This Fonseca succeeded spectacularly and his confident 'grand speech' was the talk of the district for months if not years. Only Ella knew just how many nerves he was covering up as she squeezed his hand and told him how proud she was of him. Rick allowed himself one more drink from the long line before everyone watched a hissing but otherwise soundless film of the exotic wedding in the middle of Africa, which seemed to fascinate everyone – especially after a few drinks. Ella and Rick cut short the questions with, 'Come on, let's get on with enjoying ourselves,' and as the band struck up

'The Dark Island' with a few extra twiddles on the accordion, the fairly newly married couple were enticed on to the floor for a sedate old fashioned waltz. It was almost like the real bridal waltz except the bride's posh green frock wasn't exactly a wedding dress. Next came 'Step we gaily on we go, heel for heel and toe for toe...' which brought everyone from toddlers to Grannies up for the Grand March around the room after which they could say they had been on the dance floor – even if it was only once.

Things livened up after that and Ricardo's line of glasses was growing shorter as he mastered the Gay Gordons with sister-in-law Katy and the Bluebell Polka with Auntie Meg from Inverness.

Next was the eightsome reel, a challenge for the practised native Scot. For the inebriated foreign novice, despite enthusiasm and good intentions, the world was spinning in a completely disorientated fashion though, as a sportsman, Rick's body kept upright and more or less balanced. There was a point however, when he felt his mind had toppled over in the oddest fashion. Four couples faced each other in a square formation. Ella stood with the gentle giant by her side, while Rick stood opposite, beside his attractive partner, Betsy, who had long, blonde hair. The circling, the wheel, the grand chain and the first lady in the middle went very well. As the birls with linked arms got faster and faster, little ladies were being spun off their feet - especially when it came to extra tall Davy Cunningham. Rick could see that Ella loved all this but his partner seemed to have disappeared altogether. He started looking for her all around. Beside him stood a lady with short, spiky, grey hair in place of the beauty with the blonde locks. She was smiling at him – until it dawned on her that this confused young man was gawping at her for a reason.

Cousin Roddy had seen exactly what had happened. As the temperature rose during the party, the bottom half of the sash window had been flung open and at the height of the spin, Betsy's bonny blonde hair had shot off her head and straight out of the window. Always the gentleman, Roddy stormed down the sweeping staircase, out through the revolving doors, snatched up the wig from the pavement, raced upstairs, plonked it back on Betsy's head at a jaunty angle at which point, covered in unbearable embarrassment, she fled to the safety of the ladies room. In typical Caithness fashion, the band played on until the eightsome, or in one case sevensome, reel was completed down to the last bar and bow. No one batted an eyelid. Betsy's husband Geordie, a dear man, requested a soothing slow waltz as soon as his poor wife could be persuaded to extricate herself from the loo.

A few quicksteps, jives, cha chas and waltzes later, with no more attempts at anything too complicated or fast, the evening wound up warmly with good wishes for the brave couple being served up from all directions. Some were none too sure that Rick and Ella's alliance would survive the rigours of the big, wide world but wished them all the best anyway. The older generation went home to Ovaltine and bed while the youngsters headed for a continuation of the party at Jamie and Katy's house. Good cheer and bad jokes carried on with the odd bit of singing accompanied by a moothie and a squeeze box.

'I wish Wee Ally was here. At least she can sing,' Ella whined. Wee Ally had had to go home to her babies – probably a better place to be. 'Who's going to give us a lift back to Hillside or are we walking?' Ella finally asked as she noticed Rick had given up the struggle to understand the ever-worsening jokes in a strange dialect and had succumbed to a surfeit of Scotch. He was fast asleep on the best armchair normally reserved for the master, Jamie Mackay of Benlochy Farm. Ella disturbed his slumber and they walked back. A good impression had to be maintained.

Mary Mackay, the new mother-in-law couldn't wait for the two to wake up. She was delighted that the expected ostracism from the local community hadn't transpired and couldn't wait to tell Rick how impressed everyone had been with his unexpectedly eloquent speech. Charlie had stomped off to feed the cattle as usual, without saying much. Ella had put down the lack of any speech from her dad to his normal reticence. What she didn't know was that he'd had a speech in his inside pocket which had stayed where it was.

Ella and her mum were swapping tales of funny moments from the evening when Rick finally appeared, gamely nursing a bad hangover while pretending not to have one. This was a teetotal home. He was having a light breakfast when his father-in-law came in for lunch. Rick stood up still in awe of the older man. To everyone's surprise, Charlie shook his son-in-law's hand with, 'Well done, lad. I don't know how you managed such a speech off the cuff. I was thinking the minister shouldna have asked ye to say a few words but I was wrong. I could never have done it.'

'Thank you,' Rick said without admitting that he had been secretly preparing that speech for a very long time. 'I hope I didn't let you down.' Mary thought of Charlie's speech that had stayed in his pocket.

'Not at all,' Charlie replied without adding that he hoped this man would look after his youngest but wasn't certain that society would let their marriage survive.

Ella sighed inwardly daring to feel relieved. Perhaps these two would get along eventually.

'I think Rick and I should take a drive to Smoo Cave tomorrow,' Ella bubbled excitedly. 'We'll have a meal on the way back and get here by bedtime.'

'No you won't, I've already cooked your tea,' her mum added. 'But you must show Rick what a bonny corner of the world this is.' She didn't add that they might all be the better of a short break.

Heading westwards from Balnahuig was like leaving the human world behind – although there was, just, a tarred single track road with a few passing places.

'This is spooky Scotland,' Ella told her tourist husband after they'd driven across moorland with low hills to the left and yet another bonny view of a sandy beach with cliffs and rocks to the right. There hadn't been another car for fifty miles as they headed away from the coast.

'What's Rasta doing there?' Rick said as a lone figure with dreadlocks and a little haversack could be seen marching along the road some distance ahead. As they got closer Ella could see that this man was, indeed a Rastafarian, dressed in a huge grey duffle coat but where he was going and where he had come from was a mystery.

'Shall we stop and see if he's all right?' Ella, the helpful, suggested.

'No worries, brother and sister. Too many people on my horizon in dat big smoke down there. Here my head tells me ah can live forever.'

'Good – so you don't want a lift then.'

'I got my two legs and my psychoactive and this wide, wide sky.'

'Your psychoactive?'

'Ganja, sister, my route to Zion.'

'Fine, we'll leave you to your journey then.'

'Live forever bro and sis. God go with you.'

'Taraa. Never knew Zion was so close to my birthplace.'

Look around you sister.' A touch of the forehead and a dismissive wave sent them on their way.

'Lord knows where he'll sleep in this climate,' Ricky said.

'He'll probably find one of the caves along the coast and call it Zion.' Stunned, the two drove on in silence for many miles before Ella piped up, 'Wasn't that the weirdest experience?'

Ricky and Ella would dine out on that story of the lonely Rastafarian for many years to come.

Smoo Cave took on a different tinge after the encounter. Rick hadn't known what to expect. It certainly wasn't the length of the tiny steep path winding down such a steep slope to such an enormous forty foot high cave mouth.

'It looks like the mouth of Hell,' Rick said.

'You're not the first to say that. The Clan Chief was supposed to have met the Devil here and fought him off, so the story goes, and when he sent his dog in the fires of Hell burned off all its hair.'

'Uh, huh and you want us to go in there?'

'It used to be a dwelling as well - and a smugglers cave – and a secret distillery until the excisemen found out.'

'That's fine then, I suppose.'

Ella waited until they had entered the cave and discovered the pretty waterfall and the three bore holes in the roof before she added,

'The place is haunted too. McMurdo the murderer threw his victims down these holes. You can sometimes hear their ghosts screaming.'

'Now you tell me. My God, it's freezing in here.'

'It's the spirits draining the energy from our bodies,' Ella went on gleefully. 'Never mind, the Devil doesn't come in the daylight so we're ok.'

'I think I saw a café in Durness up there. Shall we go now?'

'I'd like to go to the inner cave.'

'No way.'

'We can't anyway. You need a boat. Maybe one day?'

'Doubtful.'

A little later, over lunch, coffee and an enormous cheese and ham softie, Rick added, 'I hope Rasta doesn't decide to sleep there.'

'Come on, I *must* show you this beach before we head home.'

The two were soon running across a deserted beach of silver sands, dramatic rocks, cliffs and caves. The frothy white breakers kissed the sand and contrasted with the deep turquoise of the sea and the bright sunlight in the clear blue sky. The only clue that this was not a tropical or Mediterranean paradise was the warm clothing worn by the young couple.

'Who would believe this wasn't the Algarve or Mombasa?'

'Me,' shouted Rick through the sea breezes as he tightened his scarf and pulled up the zip of his jacket again. 'But it is bonny,' he added slipping into the local lingo.

On the way home, catching sight of an off licence, Rick decided he'd play dumb about 'teetotalitarianism' as he called it. 'It's not good for anybody to do without a drink before dinner. Let me see if I can persuade your old folks to have a 'tootie', again, getting into the lingo, for medicinal purposes.'

'You're the only one I know who might get away with it,' Ella laughed. 'And you might as well try a bottle of wine when you're at it.' That was how a bemused Charlie and Mary Mackay came to be presented with an unusual gift of a bottle of Mackay and Whyte whisky as a thank you. Mary set off to unearth the crystal tootie glasses and silver tray from the heavy oak sideboard. She was secretly delighted, not being quite as temperate and sanctimonious as her husband, given half a chance. The silver polish came out and, after a quick rinse and polish, the gleaming tray of glasses was presented.

'Ella, you'll find a bottle of lemonade in the pantry,' her mother instructed. Rick's heart sank as he imagined the thimblefuls of whisky being drowned in sweet, fizzy lemonade until Mary added, 'Rick, you can do the honours. We can't often celebrate having a honeymoon couple in our midst.'

'I'm sure Dr Falconer would recommend a tot a day to keep you healthy. Did I tell you I met him? We got along fine.' At that, ignoring the perplexed looks on his in-laws faces and the incipient fury on Ella's face, he proceeded to pour a generous whisky for everyone with not a drop of lemonade in his own.

The shepherds pie and rhubarb and custard went down particularly well, especially after Ella suggested a small glass of red wine and got the reply, 'Well, just a very wee one then.' The conversation turned to Rasta and Smoo Cave and, by the end of the evening, bonhomie had relieved the tension and the four were laughing uncontrollably at all kinds of stories ranging from Ella's and Rick's childhood to the daft things that had happened in Zambia recently, especially around the time of the wedding. Anecdotes were Rick's forte and he knew how to play to an audience.

Ella decided to give Rick a final guided tour eastwards towards John o' Groats fitting in Thurso, Dounereay and the Castle of Mey along the way. At Dounereay, Rick pronounced the nuclear power station a carbuncle on the face of the earth. At Thurso, the two newly-weds vowed to one day take a ferry to the Orkneys. At the Castle of Mey, Ella talked of her old friend Ally who had worked there for the Queen Mother. They enjoyed a ten minute stroll around the castle gardens with their abundance of enormous plants and giant orchids in a greenhouse. Before going on, they drank in the view of royal cattle on the beach, enjoying their privileged status, no doubt.

The anticipated anti-climax of reaching the much publicised John o' Groats to find only a signpost, a shabby hotel and an empty harbour prompted, 'What's all the fuss about?' from Rick.

'You'd feel pretty relieved after 874 miles on a bike from Land's End - and the hotel keeps the bar open twenty four hours for travellers,' Ella replied and dragged him off to the real most north eastern point of Scotland, Duncansby Head.

'Come on, I'll show you what most tourists never see,' she added, 'but take it easy. The old Wolseley mightn't like the road and we'll have to walk a few miles for the best treats.' Rick thought the square Duncansby Head lighthouse and the view across to the Orkneys was quite spectacular enough and worth the long hike. 'Just wait till you see this,' Ella went on dragging him across the heathery scrub towards the rising sound of seabirds.

'Careful!' she shouted, 'not too close!'

They found themselves, pleasantly petrified, staring down into an enormous, cawing, splashing gully stretching ominously downwards between sheer, black cliffs, bespatt·red with white streaks. The birdsong was deafening, the smell of fishy bird dirt overpowering and the crash of waves, on the rocks far below, alarmingly distant. What seemed like hundreds of the black and white birds were swooping, dive bombing, landing, taking off or just nestling on the many tiny ledges on the cliffs.

'These seagulls are big.'

'That's because they're guillemots. They're busy building their nests right now, hidden in the cracks. You won't see them. They often just use beach sand and you see the birds carrying bits of heather sometimes.'

'You'd think they'd build a safety barrier for those of us who can't fly though,' Rick said with an anxious glance downwards.

'They probably will one day.'

'Wow!'

'But that's not all. That was the Geo of Sclaites, by the way.'

A short walk later and Rick was saying, 'Wow, double wow.'

'That's the Thirle Door and those are the Duncansby Stacks,' Ella said pointing to an arch with a pointed head and two majestic pointed sea stacks which dominated the horizon.

'I have never seen anything like this.'

'They're amazing aren't they? I've seen these loads of times but they never fail to inspire me.'

'Can we get on to that beach?'

'Can you handle another hour's walk with a stiff climb back up?'

Down on the beach, the stacks looked even bigger but Ella was too busy picking up shells to pay much attention.

'Look. Groatie buckies. They used to use them for currency. Did you know that John o' Groats was a Dutchman and he gave his name to a silver coin called a groat?'

'Not sure if I needed to know that.' Rick and Ella were very late getting home and the only phone box on the way was out of order.

'I just thought you'd gone down to the beach near the stacks,' Ella's unconcerned mum told them after they'd apologised profusely. 'Your dinner's in the oven, by the way.'

This was followed by, 'Would ye like a tootie first?' from her dad. It was hard to say who was the most surprised.

'Only if you'll join me,' was the smug new son-in-law's reply. Mother and daughter exchanged glances behind smothered smiles.

By the time the couple were ready to head back to Zambia via London, to deliver the Wolseley in one piece, they were confident they had exploded some prejudices and forged some amicable links with family, friends and neighbours. While taking Jamie, Katy, Mum, Dad and Granny out for a meal at the Eilean Neave restaurant, Rick had even managed to introduce his in-laws to new friends he had made on his one day out with cousin Roddy, fishing and visiting the local pub, which the Mackays of Hillside were not known to frequent.

They set off on the 700 mile journey to London, content in the knowledge that the ice was broken and most of the clouds had been dispersed. There was one shadow that had crept into the back of Ella's mind and taken root. Someone had said, 'You two weren't thinking of having children, were you? That wouldn't be fair. They wouldn't be one thing or the other, would they?' Ella hadn't known how to respond and had run out of the room in a daze. Her only hope was that nobody had said the same thing to Ricky.

'Was that ok then my husband?'

'Well, I suppose they won't forget us in a hurry. I think we survived. Next stop Leeds. Jos and Carlos are waiting.'

Ella had forgotten. Rick hadn't reminded her as she had seemed so happy in the bubble of her childhood memories.

# Chapter 15: The beginning of a Tough Journey

The contrast was stark. Jos had found himself a mechanic's job and a room in a run-down house in a run-down area of Leeds, bought for a song by a Mr and Mrs Patel recently of Kampala. The house was due to be demolished to make way for a by pass but for the moment it was home. At least they were safely out of Idi Amin's way but little else could be said in favour of the peeling wallpaper, paraffin heaters and washing machine in the cold bathroom. Carlos had arrived from Nairobi with a good set of school results and presented himself at the local school to do A-levels to get himself on the next rung of his optimistic ladder to success. Cash was short so he shared that room with his brother. Life was at its best for Carlos in the public library and for Jos it was after a 30p visit to the Public Baths with its mini bar of soap and fluffy white towel – after a hard day's work which might have been better paid. He introduced a grateful Rick and Ella to that pleasure. They survived a Friday night sleeping in 'the' bed but felt guilty about depriving the boys, who had curled up on the floor. They set off in the morning for Blackpool and booked all four into a cheap but spotless bed and breakfast establishment. The boys felt they were in Heaven and the four youngsters clowned around the beach and Blackpool's amusements as far as their lack of money would allow them to. Dinner was fish and chips in a newspaper with a pickled onion each and all four slept the sleep of the dead in crisp, clean sheets and woke up more refreshed than for a very long time. Big brother Ricky and his new wife Ella dropped the two boys back at their grotty lodgings with a heavy heart. It was going to be a tough journey for them and there seemed little hope that it would be a short one and there was no indication of where it might end.

Their own journey was likely to be similar but, somehow, Rick and Ella didn't see it that way. Zambia would provide them with an interesting and successful career for a while and they couldn't wait.

The first leg of their journey took them to Nairobi airport on a lightning visit to Mum, Dad, little sister Rosie and big brother Agnelo, wife Marie and ten month old Sean in Kisumu. The short visit was to be forgiven as Rick and Ella had promised to drive north for Christmas and New Year. Agnelo picked them up, on his own, in his trusty Peugeot 404; he seemed relieved to have a break from the tensions around the Fonseca and Lobo families who, he hoped, had finally come to terms with the marriage. Baby Sean seemed to have healed all the differences.

'What on earth are they thinking of Rick and me?' Ella dared to ask.

'They haven't said much but I think they might be finding it hard. Mum did say she thought her son was going to be living out of tins.' The only possible reaction to that had to be to laugh it off. Ella's stomach, however, was churning uncomfortably.

The welcome was warm, helped along by Rosie's exuberance and the inevitable distraction of the new baby. Later, Olga included a few tips for Ella on cooking Goan food so that 'Ricardo' wouldn't starve. Unfortunately, Ella had not yet learned enough about Indian cooking to put her mother-in-law's mind at ease and she wondered if she ever would. One day she would learn that a mother-in-law's secret hope is that any woman who takes away any of her sons will never be able to cook as well as she can.

Meantime, after brief greetings and reassurances that all was well with Rick and Ella, Mum Fonseca's first words were, 'Are they all right?' and there was no need to ask who 'they' were. She was beside herself with worry about Jos and Carlos who were much too young to be in a cold, dirty, hostile country half way across the world. Rick was quick to answer, 'They're just fine. They've got a room in a lovely house and this Patel lady cooks them tasty curries every day. Jos loves his job and Carlos is doing really well at school.' This seemed to put Mum's mind at rest although Dad Fonseca was wearing a sceptical expression. Ella added descriptions of the happy times they had enjoyed on Blackpool beach and promised to send some photos as soon as they were developed.

'I always dreamt that we'd make our fortune in Kenya and the whole family would return to life in a mansion in Goa. I can't see that happening now,' Santos Fonseca announced.

'It's a different world these days, Dad,' Rick said with a touch of impatience. Olga Fonseca quietly added, 'Wait. We will see Goa again. I'm telling you.' There was a quiet determination in her voice.

'I'll come. I'd love to live in Goa,' young Rosie said but her two big brothers looked at each other and raised their eyebrows.

All too soon, the brief visit was over and the Fonsecas remembered that Rick and Ella's marriage needed blessing. A tearful Olga and stoical Santos gave their blessings and after hugs and more hugs and extra kisses for Rosie and baby Sean, Agnelo drove the new couple back to Nairobi Airport for their flight to Lusaka.

'Be happy, you two. The world is yours.'

'Thanks. And you too, bro. Look after them all back there in Kisumu.'

Ella's grateful hug was enough.

# Chapter 16: A Worthless Task?

Back in the air, en route to Lusaka, Ella reflected on the comfortable situations her London sister and Caithness brother were ensconced in while Rick reflected on the precarious and distinctly uncomfortable existence that his two brothers were clinging on to in miserable Leeds. They compared notes and discovered they were both thanking their lucky stars – but for very different reasons.

Excitement rose as they came in to land. Bhavin and Sunita would be meeting them and putting them up for the night before they set off for Mpika. They were looking forward to the three noisy kids, Arun, Selma and Resma and Ricky couldn't wait for some of Sunita's curries and soft, fluffy rotis. Their South African friends were especially fascinated by the novelty of this Indian fellow with his Scottish wife. It could never happen in RSA.

Life can be a bitch, however.

Bhavin was there; he looked uncomfortable.

'Bad news, I'm afraid. Come and sit over here for a minute.' Over there sat Sister Immaculata and Father O'Malley and when they saw Rick and Ella, they stood up apprehensively, eyes brimming with tears.

'It's Kirsty,' Father O'Malley finally managed to get out. 'We're taking her back to the family burial ground on Eriskay.'

Ella's head began to swim but Rick managed to catch her and blurt out, 'What happened?'

'There was an accident on the Great North Road. She and Vanko were both gone by the time they were found. We think there was another vehicle involved but there was no sign of it.'

'Vanko? Is that the Yugoslavian boy she's just met? No. No. It can't be true. It can't be Kirsty. Not Kirsty. She's only 22. That's impossible.'

'I know, I know,' Sister Immaculata said in a low calm voice. 'God always takes the good first.'

'I'm so, so sorry Sister,' Ella said unable to put into words what she felt but revealing her emotions through tears. 'And she's your niece. What are you going to say to her mother?'

'What I've just said to you,' the nun said philosophically. 'But this time, it doesn't help that it's my job.'

'I feel so guilty that I took her to Lusaka to buy the material for the bridesmaid's dress. That's when she met Vanko. If she hadn't chosen red... and we didn't have red flowers. If I hadn't... '

'Shh... If I hadn't persuaded her to come to Zambia. If she had only stayed in Scotland. We could go on forever with ifs and buts. I'm sure she's in Heaven. Come and say a prayer with us. You too,' she said ushering Rick and the Pindoria family to a side room at the airport where Kirsty's coffin was waiting to be loaded on to the same plane that her Aunt and Father O'Malley were travelling on. After the prayers, they looked serene.

Ella and Rick said emotional good byes and set off into the heat of Zambia, stunned and crestfallen, while the others flew off on their tragic journey, one for the last time. Bhavin's matter of fact presence helped them with the practicalities of rescuing luggage.

'I wish I had their faith,' Ella sighed wistfully. 'I can't bear to go back to the Lwitikila house for my things when Kirsty's not there.'

Busy, bustling Sunita, the chatty children and a good meal were the perfect antidote for shock and bereavement. After dinner everyone loved the Edinburgh rock and other presents with a Scottish flavour. Sadly, Ella wondered what she would do with the Swiss milk tablet that had been Kirsty's special order. She decided to give it to Sunita.

'This stuff's a bit like Indian burfi. Would you like to try it?' The children thought it was better than burfi but Sunita wasn't too sure.

'Too sugary – and no cardamom.'

'They've never even heard of cardamom in Caithness.' The little bit of laughter that followed eased the pain - for a while.

Back at Lwitikila, the horror of the shared house was unbearable for Ella. The chaos after the wedding had not been cleared as Kirsty had planned to come back from Lusaka and get it organised. She had never made it. Neither had her keys. As Ella was forcing back the tears and getting stuck into clearing up, a band of all the houseboys on the mission campus appeared and made short work of clearing the lot and buffing up the floors to a perfect shiny red, singing as they danced across the floor in their foot dusters. They had heard the news and understood why the other madam was weeping.

'You don't know how grateful I am,' Ella told them as she tipped them as generously as her purse would allow and sent them off with a crate of beer which had miraculously survived, hidden under her bed. A poignant thought occurred to Ella; Kirsty must have rescued it from the locals who considered that anything consumable which was left over at a wedding was for taking home. A last act of kindness and now she was gone.

The previous night, Rick and Ella had been unearthing bottles from odd corners of the new marital home which had finally lost its ping pong table to the schoolboys' dorms and now had a neat dining table, six chairs and a posh new wedding present of a table cloth. There was Asti Spumante in the wardrobe, cider under the pillows, beer in the socks drawer and, best of all for Rick, whisky in his underpants.

'I suppose that means they're expecting another party,' Rick said, and wished he hadn't as he remembered Kirsty. 'Not for a while, though…'

A knock at the door brought them back to life on the campus. Mercifully, there was no privacy.

'We were just about to drink to Kirsty's memory,' Rick said as their new neighbour Q.R. Blot wandered in through the always open door.

'I'll drink to that. She was a great kid. Dreadful shame.' Q.R. was wearing his conventional hat as opposed to his wild hippie hat so was demurely dressed in cream slacks, checked shirt and yellow cravat. He filled them in with the latest gossip regarding the school, especially the sudden departure of Cyril Smythe, which pleased Rick enormously. The equally quick arrival of a rather doddery, elderly Bemba gentleman who was to take Smythe's place as headmaster was interesting though disconcerting. An American couple and, significantly for Q.R., a pretty young

American girl had just arrived on the scene. Her name was Suzy May Claxton from Springfield, Illinois and she was burning with desire to change the world as of yesterday. Life at school was going to be interesting. They discovered that Q R stood for Quentin Roxburgh which he would rather people didn't know and that his parents Sir Percival and Lady Felicity of Billington Manor, Buckinghamshire were an equally embarrassing feature of his background. Q R had been expelled from boarding school and his angry parents had sent him to the local comprehensive where the local yobs had made mincemeat of his posh ways. This probably explained an apparent identity crisis. He could switch between upper-class drawl, regional Bucks, mid west American and Scots dialect at the drop of a hat and would often dress to fit the persona he adopted.

Whereas most people were amused by Q R, Suzy May was fascinated. 'I guess a shrink would say he's got a personality problem.' Suzy May analysed every situation, including the political situation in Africa, and more specifically Zambia. She was not, however, diplomatic. This did not go down well.

'Why the Hell are we educatin' these darlin', gorgeous school boys and then they're forced into conscription to fight a war that isn't theirs?' She decided to take her protest to the local Zambian District Governor and couldn't understand why she had been sent off with a flea in her ear. She had a point, the District Governor might have agreed, but a young whippersnapper of an American girl wasn't the person to advise an older man in an elevated position – especially in Zambia.

Q R, Suzy May and most of the rest of the young staff at Mpika Boys' School soon became committed cosmopolites, mainly as a result of an all through the night conversation at Rick and Ella's house when Q R had disappeared to change from his 1970s bell bottom jeans into a very 'Quentin Roxburgh' silk, paisley patterned dressing gown and checked carpet slippers. The Che Foo wine had been flowing, so Q R was in full swing. He threw out a challenge.

'We are who we are and nobody's better or worse than anyone else, I say. But what is it that we all cherish most, wherever we're from?' Answers ranged from the facetious to the deep and meaningful from peanut butter, beer, sex, doorstep milk and snow to music, friendship, love, happiness and spiritual fulfilment.

'The obvious hasn't occurred to you, has it?'

'What's that then?'

'Freedom.'

And, of course everyone had to agree. Why hadn't they thought of that? How futile everything else was etc. Then Suzy May Claxton, with a little help from a little more than Che Foo, climbed on her soap box.

'One man's freedom is another man's sacrifice. I'm sorry.' At which point the debate escalated well into the night until Ella decided to go to bed fairly certain that no conclusions were going to be reached. At 7am she found them still contemplating the world's problems with freedom and the lack of it throughout history and across the world ad infinitum.

'Anyone for breakfast?' This was not without sarcasm.

'That sounds great. Any coffee?'

Over breakfast, Suzy May announced that the most significant conclusion that everyone had come to was that it was a massive infringement of the human rights of the schoolboys to expect them to fight for the freedom of a country which wasn't even their own.

'That's the conclusion you had reached before the whole thing kicked off, Suzy May,' Rick pitched in, 'but I still say we can only assume that not all of these boys are going to fight against their will. I don't think some of us can begin to feel the pain the colonials inflicted on the people around here. That's why Zimbabwe and South Africa must be free. These young men are intelligent. They know the score and they're prepared to make the ultimate sacrifice.'

'It's wrong in Vietnam and it's wrong here; there's never an excuse for war. Ever.'

Absolutely,' Ella had to agree, 'but even I can see that man's inhumanity to man isn't going to work that out in the foreseeable future and perhaps we shouldn't say too much while we're in Zambia. Coffee? Toast? Sorry there's no butter.'

As the months passed, Ella carried on teaching at Lwitikila, where everyone was trying to smile through the broken heart of Kirsty's aunt, their head teacher Sister Immaculata. Her dedication had doubled but that little spark of humour, though present, had faded.

'A red and white wedding means blood and bandages,' was Sister Mary Kabwe's unhelpful comment. 'I've seen it before. And the car she was killed in was red. I've never trusted a red car.'

Ella wanted to scream, 'She chose the dress herself. I never meant any harm,' but the scream stayed trapped in her head burning through into her conscience. Following in the brave Immaculata's footsteps, Ella redoubled her efforts and decided to put on a full scale drama production of James Ngugi's 'The Black Hermit'. She had to pre-empt the nutty suggestion of 'The Cherry Orchard'. Why foist Chekhov and the fallen Russian aristocracy on teenage

Zambian girls when there were perfectly good examples of dramatic literature reflecting African themes?

The outdoor theatre at Lwitikila was a perfect example of rustic theatre in the round. The acoustics were unbeatable and three large dimmer spotlights just managed to bathe the stage in a romantic glow. A labyrinth of trenches and arches allowed actors to appear and disappear, and a mound in the background acted as a distant hill. Seating was on steps carved out of the earth and hardened in the sun. Cushions were needed as African drama tends to linger on long after the tale has been told. 'The Black Hermit' proved to be a challenge; the main female character, Jane, was white and had to be played by an African girl with heavy make up. The actress's name was Patience. First she had to be covered in white poster paint which had to be left to dry. After she'd muttered, 'Can I crack now?' she had to grin and stretch her mouth into all shapes as wide as she could so she could actually speak. Then she had pale pan stick slapped all over her face and neck with pink rouge, blue eye-shadow and bright pink lipstick. These added the final touches to a very convincing Jane, the white girlfriend that Remi would finally abandon when he realised that he should return to his village after university. In the play, a brush with corrupt post colonial politics had left him disillusioned and heartbroken at having been disloyal to his family.

The local Zambian dignitaries were delighted with the production and commissioned an extra performance so their colleagues in other towns as far as two hundred miles away could travel to see it. So convincing was the make up for Jane (with the help of the dim lighting) that the District Governor asked to be introduced to the young white teacher who had mastered the Bemba accent so perfectly.

It had been a superb team effort and Ella was proud to have been part of it. The message, however, was sad. Did Remi epitomise the young, educated, idealistic African who was unable to counteract the damage that unscrupulous politicians were inflicting on the newly independent African states? Ella and Rick talked long into the night again and came to the conclusion that however many honest and sincere Remis (or Ng☐gis) there were, they wouldn't have the power to topple the greedy politicians. Rick said they never would but Ella said they just might – one day. She asked the schoolgirls what they thought and their answer surprised her. In Zambia, things would only get better if the women took the helm. Some said that would never happen, others said it just might – one day.

Rick was storming ahead at Mpika Boys' School, making a difference in his own dynamic way. With the help of naughty students on stumping punishment and the driver of a bulldozer he had befriended over beer and darts, he had created a respectable 400 metre athletics running track with all the facilities for track and field events. He acquired some equipment through World Bank funding but much was improvised, like bamboo canes for high-jump cross bars. The schoolboys had built covered stands for each of the competing houses which had been named after four of Zambia's rivers, Chambeshi, Kafue, Luangwa and Zambesi. Each was a beautifully crafted, rectangular stand with strong, straight wooden poles to hold up the thatched roof. Without walls, these structures would provide excellent protection from the hot sun while still allowing a cool breeze to circulate; Rick had offered 50 extra points to the house with the best construction which had guaranteed a higher standard. Rick's inspiration had come from the Olympic success of Kenya's Ben Jipcho and Wilson

Kiprogot. He was sure he would discover some raw talent in Northern Zambia. He was going the right way about it. Sports Day came up with an unexpected batch of stars whose fitness was a result of long walks to school and a tough training regime imposed on them by Mr Fonseca, the young PE and Science teacher they loved and feared. The brightest star was Nelson Kapela who hit the track barefoot and cracked the four minute 1500 metres at his first attempt. Rick's excitement was infectious and soon the bemused boy was surrounded by sponsors and kitted out with running shoes and athletics strip and was coming up to Rick and Ella's house for extra reconstituted milk. Eventually as Nelson progressed, Rick, on a trip to Lusaka, filled a cold box with frozen steaks, just for his rising star. Ella had to cook one every day for the boy. It paid off. A new Zambian champion was born, others would follow and Rick would bask in reflected glory forever.

Positive things were happening in this corner of the world. Cut off from the rest of the world, all these busy people were unaware of the troubles brewing in Uganda, Kenya, the rising Zimbabwe and South Africa with the resultant unrest in UK. There were struggles like finding enough food to feed the rising number of boys at Mpika. There were stories of remarkable schoolboys going into O-level exams on a cup of water because the kapenta lorry had failed to arrive and the mealie meal had run out. The boys hadn't complained. They understood shortages. Even more amazing were the high marks achieved.

'Madam,' the head boy, Berrington, once said to Mrs Fonseca. 'Your brain works better on an empty stomach. The blood has to go to the stomach to digest the food if it's full.'

Finally Rick's first contract at Mpika was over and Ella's days at Lwitikila came to an end. Ella had mixed feelings. She was sorry to go but relieved to leave some sad memories behind. Kirsty had always been on her mind and she had often felt her presence, almost like a guardian angel, her spirit watching over her. She'd never forget her bridesmaid but Ella needed to move on. Rick's school needed a few teachers and had offered her a job at the beginning of the new academic year.

The two recently-weds headed for a much-needed break visiting what was left of the Fonseca family in Kenya. It was possible for their sturdy Toyota to take them the twelve hundred miles through Tanzania and Kenya all the way to Kisumu in two long days if they stuck to the tarred roads. However, stops in Iringa, to see a lion hunt at dusk, Arusha, to view Mount Kilimanjaro stretching up above an avenue of flame trees and Nairobi, to see 'The Towering Inferno' at the cinema made it a much longer but more memorable journey. There was a lot to talk about when they arrived at Agnelo and Maria's house which actually had a telephone. When Rick had phoned from Nairobi, Agnelo had taken pains to make sure that he and Ella would come straight to his house which was near the main road into Kisumu. Maria wanted to cook for everyone he said but there was something odd in his voice.

The next inkling that all was not well was the news that Mum and Dad Fonseca were heading for Goa, the homeland, taking young Rosie with them. Family disintegration seemed inevitable in Santos's mind as he watched his children scattering across the world to lands where they were becoming less and less welcome. Goa he understood – or thought he did – so that's where he would go with his wife and only daughter. His sons would see sense in the end and follow him back there. His sons didn't think so. Maria's parents had headed for Canada to be with some 'good Goans' as her mother had said. Later, when they were alone Maria confided in Ella.

'My mother's always at her happiest being a snob. Now there's nobody in my family left in Kenya, I shouldn't say so but I do feel bad about it.' The unspoken implication was that 'good' Goans meant those in the higher echelons of Goan society.

'I do understand, Maria. I dread to think what's going on in the minds of some of my folks in Scotland. I've decided to think of it as their problem, not mine. They'll be the ones looking foolish one day.'

'I wish I could believe that, Ella.'

The Fonseca family home in Kisumu had been sold which came as a momentary shock to Rick until he remembered he was now a cosmopolite. Santos, Olga and Rosie had moved into Agnelo's rambling and beautiful home in the former European area. Its extensive garden was a haven of peace, a cushion against the reality of the rapidly changing Kisumu, the once more Asian than African town in Africa. The joy of Maria and Agnelo's new daughter, Wendy, sister for Sean and god-daughter for Rick and Ella, counteracted the pain and apprehension that was filtering through into the lives of all the Asians. Tales of Idi Amin's regime across the border, once dismissed as incredible, were slowly being confirmed. Train loads of terrified and exhausted women and children were travelling through the night to Nairobi where planes were taking off for London and another anticipated nightmare. Husbands and fathers stayed behind to salvage what little they could of any assets which might have escaped seizure and Africanisation.

Rick decided to take Ella to visit some of his old mates, starting with K P Shah at Kisumu Stores. The shop sign V J and K P Shah Kisumu Stores, though faded, was still there. Underneath, scrawled in red paint was the name Kariuki's, which was doubly incongruous as it was a Kikuyu name in a Luo part of the country.

'Whoa, something's not right here. Let's have a look.' Rick marched into the old shop with Ella in his wake and asked for a box of jilebis and six samosas.

'Hapana,' was the only lethargic response - and that was without eye-contact.

'Hakuna matata. Kwaheri,' was Rick's equally curt reply. It wasn't until they were back in the car that Rick exploded. 'The bastards. The Shahs were always the first family to help anyone, black white or brown.'

'Seems like they don't want to remember that. Come on, let's get out of here.'

Rick needed to check on his old friend and set off for the Shah house; they had once been near neighbours of the Fonsecas. Passing by the home where he grew up, Rick noticed that the once famous morning glory had been pulled down. Two doors along, the Shah house looked intact but a knock at the door was not answered, although low voices could be heard inside.

Rick's news of the departure of the Shah family came as no surprise to the Fonsecas. Theirs was just another on the long list of families heading for anywhere else but Kisumu. Some, like Agnelo, who had chosen to get a Kenyan passport, were grudgingly welcomed, on condition that they pledged their loyalty to the Kenyan government and its people. Olga and Santos wondered whether Agnelo would have been better floundering in England like his brothers Jos and Carlos who only ever sent good news back to their parents; they reckoned their mum and dad had enough to worry about.

'You see, Ricardo,' his father said. 'Goa is the only safe place.'

'If you say so Dad, but with only a few words of Konkani and less Portuguese, what future is there for your sons? Rosie's young; she can learn.'

'I would hate that cold London,' Olga added. 'And without servants I'm too old to do everything.'

'You wouldn't need servants,' her Goan daughter-in-law dared to interject, adding lamely as she saw the look of disbelief on Olga's face, 'Life is much easier there.'

Olga's Scottish daughter-in-law said nothing of the struggles reported in the 1972 press of people arriving with little money and few possessions, surviving in leaky disused holiday chalets and slowly moving in to condemned slums. Olga was adamant.

'I'll never go where they don't want me. Idi Amin gave the Indians ninety days to get out of Uganda and now so many are in England, they don't want any more. Dad and I have brothers and sisters to help us in Goa.'

So, the family would split up and life would go on. The new grandchildren would be sorely missed but one day there would be reunions, somewhere.

After fond but sad farewells, Ricardo and Ella were both sorry and glad to escape to the carefree international bubble provided by the young teachers from all corners of the world who had headed for Mombasa from land-locked Zambia. Just as The Thorn Tree had been the meeting point for young expatriate teachers in Kenya, The Fontanella was the rendezvous for young expatriate teachers in Zambia. The tourist attractions of Kenya and Tanzania were the magnet for the adventurers and the Bush

Telegraph broadcast that communications could be made between 12noon and 2pm every day within the central courtyard of the Fontanella restaurant off Kilindini Road.

'Let's book into Whitesands for a few days. I could do with a bit of luxury by the sea.'

As they drove along the rocky, sandy palm-fringed road, kicking up dust, Ella recalled her previous visit to Whitesands Hotel in January 1969. Had so much really happened since then?

'You know, I wrote a song here, right over there on the rocks – before we were 'us' and when Tom Mboya was still alive and you were John Francis.

'Really, when was that?'

'After climbing Mount Kenya I spent five days recovering – from that and a few other things, like the men in my life. It wasn't long after that you had me delivering flowers and a warning to Mboya.'

'How could I forget? That was the first attempt on his life. It seems a lifetime ago.'

A shiver ran through Ella. 'It was.' As they walked through the struggling little garden of sisal plants and stunted canna lilies to the wide front door of the hotel, a vaguely familiar face appeared.

'I don't believe it. Aren't you Ella Mackay? The last time I saw you all the skin had been burnt off your nose and you were so exhausted you fell asleep before you'd even finished your breakfast.'

'Joyce. You're still here. Rick, this wonderful lady put me back together just after the 1969 New Year. Joyce you don't know how much I needed you to spoil me at that time.'

'I see you're married.'

'Oh, sorry, this is Rick, my husband. We got married in Zambia but we got to know each other just after I left you.'

'Good to meet you Joyce. It seems like you set my wife up for the *real* traumas in her life.'

'You don't know how true that is,' Ella added. The details were left to Joyce's imagination as they laughed it off. That part of Rick's dark past, they decided, was best left alone. Once again Whitesands would act as a beautiful retreat from the next group of traumas that life would present the young couple with. Together they walked by the Indian Ocean, collecting shells and putting the world's problems into perspective. Everything made sense when they looked at the big picture. What was wrong with the narrow-minded bigots who declared their mixed-race marriage a mistake? One day they would be considered ignorant and foolish. The two were convinced. After two days, Ella disappeared along the beach and came back to grab a pencil.

'Listen Rick, I've got a third verse for my song.'

'Let's pretend the world has spoken
In a universal tongue
And has made the proclamation
Eternal peace has just begun.'
**Chorus:** Let's pretend, let's pretend
That right now will never end

'Bollocks,' Rick said, 'but it's beautiful bollocks. What were the first two verses?' He smiled as she sang them but without revealing his thoughts.

Let's pretend there's no tomorrow
Let's pretend there was no past
And the moment that we're in now
Could turn out to be our last
**Chorus:** Let's pretend, let's pretend

That right now will never end

Let's pretend the bombs are banished
Let's pretend the world is free
And the boundaries have vanished
Except the mountains and the sea
'A pure philosophy, don't you think?'
'Unless you're only human.'
Ella went very quiet after that. She had gone into that
'in between' place again.

Rick loved Ella's pretty thoughts but, in his heart of
hearts, he was terrified of the deal that the world might
serve up for them. He imagined closed doors, long queues
for jobs, houses, visas or whatever, which they would be at
the bottom of, and endless snubs or snide remarks as they
tried to make a life for themselves in some, as yet unknown,
country on the planet. Ella saw none of this. She was
convinced the sea change was just around the corner. Rick
saw the assassination of Martin Luther King as the end of
all hope for racial harmony in USA whereas Ella saw it as
the beginning of a journey towards a better world. She truly
believed that he hadn't died for nothing. Rick declared he
would never, ever demean himself so far as to go and live in
what he called Enoch Powell's Britain. Ella pointed out that
the horrible man had lost his job because of his views and
they weren't representative of the general viewpoint. In fact,
she believed it was the beginning of a new era of
cosmopolitan acceptance. Rick wasn't convinced.

'Why don't we go to Australia? At least the weather's
good there. Or Canada? That's got loads of space. I have an
aunty who can sponsor us – and so have you – and you
studied there.'

'What about the 'White Australia Policy'? And too many bad memories and snobby Goans in Canada.'

'We've only got a few more years in Zambia before they'll want us to go. Most of the new graduates seem to want to teach. We'll have to go somewhere.'

'If Ploz the Oz is at the Fontanella, we'll ask him what it's like for people like us in Australia.'

'What d'you mean by "people like us"? And let's hope Ploz has bought a new shirt and boots – or had a few swims in the ocean.'

As it turned out the Fontanella was crawling with teachers who had escaped from land-locked Zambia.

'G'day. Where d'youse rock up from?' Ploz had slipped into the Aussie rhyming slang being the true blue Sydneysider discovering the ocean after six long months. 'What took ye so long?'

'Oh, this and that, mainly family. My folks have decided to head off to Goa,' Rick replied, attempting to echo the Aussie-speak – badly.

Ploz was smelling sweet or at least of salty ocean. 'I ain't been out o' the swell for long since I got here.'

'As good as Bondi?' Ella asked trying to show her lack of ignorance.

'Bondi? That's crap – full of shops and people. My home beach was Hordens near Bundeena Bay on the south side. No need for an Aussie salute there.'

'What's that?'

'Flicking flies – like this,' the Oz said waving his hand across his face. 'Hordens beach is quiet and clean. We lived five minutes away from it too. Bundeena Bay's a beaut place, right next to the oldest National Park in the world. Can you credit that? And Bundeena means the same as the old Zambia Mosi o' Tunya. They both mean noise like thunder – well almost. I reckon that's why I never got into the habit of rubbity dubs. The ocean was better fun – and bigger.'

'I see. That explains it.'

'What?'

'Nothing. Just your love for the ocean. Hey, Ploz, d'you think Ella and I could live in Australia with this White Australia Policy?'

'Aw no worries mate. That's been easin' up for yonks now. Maybe some ignorant Bogans still squirm a bit but if you keep out of their way, you'd be fine.'

'Bogans?'

'The white trash, the Westies, the guys with the mullet hairstyles that don't hold their pea brains in.'

'Westies?'

'Sydney's West End's pretty rough. You don't wanna go there. Any place else you'd be apples – sorry - that means just fine. They say old Gough Witlam's making racial discrimination illegal and he's the leader of the ALP. He might even be Prime Minister now.'

Rick and Ella exchanged glances, not quite reassured by someone who wasn't sure who his own Prime Minister was.

'Maybe we'll look into it. Thanks.'

Q R Blot was in tow with an exquisite Somali girl wearing a prominent bustle and bright lipstick. He was clearly in hippie mood. 'Zahara's showing me the tourist spots around Mombasa' he told Ella feeling the need for some explanation.

'That must be nice for both of you,' Ella replied and was treated to an almost sheepish grin. They both knew that they both knew that Suzy May Lou, his latest handbag, had made a trip home to the US of A.

Ploz the Oz's contribution was, 'Quit skitin' dingbat. Half your luck, mate. Some spots more interesting than others, I reckon.'

'Sometimes Ploz,' Ella chirped, 'I reckon Swahili's easier to understand than your Aussie slang.'

'He's just saying he's jealous,' Q R chortled, which was a pretty accurate translation.

'How about some sangers to go with the beer?'

'Bwana,' Rick shouted at the nearest waiter, 'Tafadhali, sisi njaa. Iko Chakula?'

'Chakula gani?'

'Sandwiches.'

'Cheesy, nyama na samaki.'

'D'you want a cheese meat or fish sandwich, Ploz?'

'How come you got the lingo off pat, Rick? You're no drongo, eh?'

'I was born here.'

'No way. but you're still no drongo - you guessed what a sanger was.'

'I'd definitely be a drongo if I couldn't do that.'

'Take your point.'

Ella was practising her rusty Swahili on the beautiful Zahara, having discovered the young girl's English was equally limited. Apart from finding out she was just sixteen, she was making a few other more alarming discoveries. She nudged Rick.

'Umeolewa? Nani?'

'Bwana Quentin, Memsaab. Na sema sisi taenda Englandi. Iko castle kubwa sana. Na sema mimi bibi harusi mzuri sana.'

The look of panic spread from Ella's face to Rick's.

'Kwele?' Rick began. 'Sielewi. Bwana hapana kusema Kiswahili. Hapana mzuri. Haraka haraka haina baraka.'

'Mimi hapana hawara, mimi mkewe, yeye mumewe. Angalia!' Zahara's face crumpled into a mixture of anger and dismay as she waved her finger which sported a ring of intricately wrought filigree silver – seven rings joined together with another silver twist with three silver balls attached.

'Take Zahara for a walk, Ella. She looks like she needs it. I need to have a word with Q R. Find out as much as you can.'

As Ella gently steered the very young, she now realised, Zahara out on to the street, Rick turned to Q R.

'Did you ask her to marry you and tell her you'd take her to your big castle in England?'

'I might have done. I'm not sure.'

'You bloody idiot. She thinks you're about to get married. That ring you gave her is a Zanzibari wedding ring. When I suggested it was too quickly done to be true, she said she was no concubine and you were to be man and wife.'

'Oh Lord. I thought she was just a good time girl playing hard to get. You know how it is.'

'You illiwhacker, Q R,' Ploz piped up. 'I'm no stickybeak wowser mate but what you said to get that girl in the sack ain't quite fair dinkum.'

'Would you mind translating that, Wayne?' a now almost contrite Quentin asked. 'Swahili's easier - and I've only been trying to learn that for a couple of weeks.'

'That's what's got you into this mess, you dingbat. I said I'm no killjoy but I don't think you should have conned that little Sheila. I put you down for a dingbat but not an illiwhacker.'

'What the devil's an illiwhacker?' Quentin was sounding more and more upper crust by the minute revealing his aristocratic Buckinghamshire background.

'You, mate. It's a con man.'

'I most certainly am not a con man. I mean ... I was only trying to be nice to the girl. Okay, I bought her a ring and showed her some pictures of the old pile at home. Look. That's what she thought was my castle.'

'Blimey mate, no wonder she thought she'd marry you.'

'The only thing is there's no pot of gold with it. The parents are being forced to pass it over to The National Trust.'

The point is, Q R, this girl thinks she's getting married to you. How did that happen?'

'I don't know. Well... she was teaching me Swahili and I couldn't understand half of it so I kept saying ndiyo – that means yes, doesn't it?'

'It's a pity you didn't learn hapana first. That means no. You didn't meet her family, did you?'

'Of course I did. She's only got her mother and a brother. Her father's dead. They're really poor.'

'And you couldn't understand what they were saying?'

'Right.'

'So you kept saying ndiyo.'

'Uhuh.'

'Idiot. I suppose they reckon they've got a meal ticket for life.'

'But I never meant to marry her. I mean I just can't marry her.'

'Have you slept with her?'

'Not quite. That was going to be tonight ... well, maybe.'

'Thank Allah for that. You *do* know she's probably a Moslem.'

'Of course. So what?'

'You'd have been in big trouble if any of her uncles had got wind of what you'd been up to – and the poor girl would have been ostracised.'

'So what do you reckon I should do?'

'Tell her it's over – and fast.'

'But how? I mean I don't have the language to explain properly.'

'Okay, you tell her no and Ella and I will talk to her in Swahili to make sure she understands why.'

★

By this time Ella had sussed out that Q R was in no way a suitable husband for the distraught Zahara who was no prostitute or good time girl. She truly believed Quentin was her equivalent of her knight in shining armour leading her and her family out of poverty. The whole situation was bizarre. Ella tried to explain that Quentin was too young to marry and had no money. She wanted to invent a wife for him back home but decided that story might get complicated; Zahara might not mind being wife number two. Finally Ella hoped she'd managed to ask if she and Quentin had made love; her kitchen Swahili on that subject wasn't much good.

'Memsaab. Hapana. Mimi ni mwanamke mzuri.'

'Mtoto?'

'Ndiyo.'

'Okay. That's good.' Ella sighed inwardly with relief. 'Let's go and talk to your boyfriend. Come on.'

★

By the time Zahara and Ella had got back to the restaurant, the table was crowded with a variety of teachers from Zambia.

'Hi Ella. Who's your friend?'

'This is Zahara, Q R's friend.' The complete lack of eye contact between Q R and Zahara was apparent. 'Or perhaps not? We'll be back in a minute.' She beckoned to Rick and Q R and the four walked the walk to Zahara's first broken heart and a narrow escape for Q R.

'I would do it myself but I can't speak the language. Thanks Rick. I need you to explain it gently. Then I want to take her home to her mother.'

A few minutes later, Zahara was pummelling Quentin's chest with her fists and having nothing to do with him 'escorting' her home. She just picked up her long skirt and sprinted off into a side street and was gone.

'What did you tell her, Rick?'

'The truth, you dope – that you never intended to marry her and you didn't have a shillingi to your name.'

'D'you know I *might* have married her? She was beautiful.'

'Go after her then. What are you waiting for?'

'Well… perhaps there are too many complications. What about you two? How come you got hitched?'

'I wonder sometimes,' Rick said but with a fond smile.

'Somebody has to take a chance I suppose,' said Ella, 'but it took us a bit longer than your two weeks.'

'It was only ten days, actually.'

'She'll get over it. No real harm done.'

'We didn't… you know…'

'I know, she told me,' Ella told Q R. 'It's a good thing you didn't… you know… seeing as she's a Moslem. She'd have been disowned.'

'Oh, but she *is* gorgeous.'

'Better say *was*. Let's get back to the others.'

When they joined the crowd, the questions came thick and fast but Q R stopped them with a curt, 'Just two more broken hearts. Nothing new.'

The conversation turned to lions in trees in the Ngorongoro Crater and all thoughts of the exotic Zahara dissolved into animated conversation as yet another group of starry-eyed young teachers began swapping accounts of their magical visits to the beauty spots of Africa.

Only Q R sat quietly, with a wistful expression. Nobody noticed him slip away.

'Does anyone fancy a trip on a glass bottom boat?' Rick asked. 'An old mate of mine can take you out near the coral reef – if he's still around. I haven't seen him for years.'

Within an hour, a scruffy group of eight excited young Zambian teachers, including Rick, Ella and Ploz the Oz but not Q R, were scrambling on to a small boat, having parted with some cash and been issued with a lump of bread each. Dominic de Silva, the boatman, was going through the safety routine and giving instructions.

'Don't all move to one side of the boat! Don't lean over the edge. Stay in the middle and look through the glass and, when I tell you, take turns to throw your bread over the front of the boat.'

'Why?'

'Wait and see. And quit yelling too much, hey.'

As the hot sun beamed down relentlessly, the boat chugged slowly out from the beach through calm waters which changed from blue to green to turquoise and back to navy blue. After about half a mile Dominic switched off the motor and put a finger to his lips.

'The reef is right under us,' he whispered. 'Bread, please.' As they looked down, the group saw the bread float to the surface and wedge itself against the glass like a sucker. Everyone waited. The only sound was the lap of the waves around the boat. Suddenly a shoal of tiny fish, with touches of fluorescent orange and spots of black swept under the boat, in full view, like a curtain blown in the wind. A slight increase in the ocean swell made the boat rock a little more. In a few seconds the bread was demolished and the shoal darted away into a curving dive. A closer look revealed bobbing creatures with sprawling legs and smaller groups of tropical fish of all sizes and a variety of bright colours. Tiny petrol blue fish here, jet black there, bright yellow and black stripes of angel fish sweeping past. Was that a tiny seahorse? Could that be a small octopus – or was it a squid? There was a huge star fish. Mesmerising. The whole scene was bathed in the richest aquamarine as if a coloured spotlight had been trained on the stage. Far down near the sea bed ocean plants of all colours could just be seen dancing from side to side.

'I'll take you into shallower water.' Dominic's years of experience predicted the mind of the tourist. In the clearest silver of the shallow waters, the waving coral and every tiny creature flitting in and out of the tendrils put on a colourful performance to enchant the spectators who were reduced to an awe-struck silence until one little voice whispered, 'Wow.'

Out on the reef, a few men with sisal baskets on their backs were picking their way across the coral in their hardy sandals, formed from old rubber tyres. Coral can damage feet.

'They collect shells every day and sell them to the tourists. There soon won't be many left.'

'Perhaps somebody will put a stop to it.'

'I doubt it,' said Dominic with a shrug. 'Easy money.'

All too soon, the sun was going down and it was time to head for the beach. There was a touch of anxiety over the missing Q R especially as nobody knew where he was staying. Before everyone headed off for much needed showers, they arranged to go to a lobster restaurant which Rick said served crayfish as lobster was hard to find. Perhaps Q R would pitch up at the Fontanella if they went there first for a quick drink.

There was no sign of Q R but the lure of lobster, which was really crayfish, was too strong for them to hang around waiting for him. They could try lunchtime the following day. Ella kept her uneasy feeling of doom quiet after Rick told her to stop being so daft. The crayfish was delicious as was the chilled white wine and everyone retired after a good day.

Rick and Ella were at the Fontanella long before lunchtime next day. It was eerily deserted and the coffee was mediocre.

'I've almost had enough of this place.'

'But I don't want Q R to come and we're not here,' Ella replied. By three o'clock, all their Zambian acquaintances had come and gone, including Ploz, whose comment had been, 'Aw, no need to worry. He's probably crook after a few jars.' Just as they were about to leave, a young Somali-looking boy in tattered khakis came around the tables asking in broken English if anyone knew Bwana Quentin. Rick and Ella didn't recognise Q R's other name at first until suddenly Ella shouted,

'Yes. Oh yes. Where is he?'

'Come. You come. Quick.' The boy grabbed Rick by the wrist and dragged him out of his seat. Ella shoved some money in the waiter's hand and ran after her disappearing husband who had just turned into a narrow street overhung by washing lines stretching across from high balconies on either side. Rick had understood that Q R was 'mbaya sana' but how, where or why, he wasn't sure. Had he done something bad or was he badly ill or badly hurt? The boy led Rick and Ella through a curtained doorway at the end of a long, narrow alleyway into a tiny, dark room. In the corner, what looked like a motionless pile of blankets moved and began to groan. Then it lay still once more.

'Q R?' asked Ella. 'Oh my god.' His eyes were slits in a swollen blue face and both cheeks were cut and bleeding.

'Get me to a hospital,' he slurred in a whisper. 'My ribs... all broken.'

How to get this shattered body safely to hospital from where an ambulance couldn't get to, even if there was one, presented a problem.

'Stay with him Ella, I'll find some help. You stay too. What's your name?'

'Mohammed.'

'Look after them both, Mohammed.'

'Sure, Bwana.'

Rick raced off through the alleyways in search of some hospital, clinic, doctor or nurse. Once on Kilindini Road he ducked into a nearby chemist where a tall Indian rang for an ambulance and unearthed a stretcher from behind the dispensary.

'This often happens. Come on, we need to get the guy out of that rabbit warren. Don't worry, I'm a paramedic as well as a chemist. My name's Mustapha.'

'I'm Rick. He looks as if he's been beaten up badly.'

Within twenty minutes, Q R had been carried to the back door of the chemist's shop and into a room, with one bed, which acted as an emergency clinic. Mustapha wasn't optimistic about the imminent arrival of an ambulance.

'We'll clean him up and keep him still. I think he's got a few broken ribs but he'll live.'

'Who did this to you?' Rick asked, though he had a good idea of who and why. The only reply was a mumble and another groan, before Q R slipped into unconsciousness.

'I'd better ring again,' Mustapha said. 'Maybe there's something internal going on there.'

At last the Aga Khan Hospital ambulance arrived and whisked Q R away leaving Rick and Ella feeling flat but anxious. They decided to get directions and drive over to check on the hapless friend they had grown fonder of recently. The immaculate, freshly painted, flat-roofed hospital looked exceptionally hygienic in contrast with its dusty surroundings, which was comforting. The unfortunate Q R could recover in pristine conditions if only to be given the chance to regret his recent activities.

'How naïve can you get?' Rick muttered to Ella. They found Q R hooked up to a drip and either unconscious or asleep. A nurse in a crisp white uniform and hijab told them he'd be going to theatre soon and asked if they could come back in the morning.

'Don't worry. He looks young and strong - and he couldn't be in a better place.'

'How did he get himself into such a mess?'

'Better not to ask.' With that, the crisp, clean nurse ushered them out of the room.

'He'll never be able to travel back to Mpika in that state. Shouldn't we contact his family?'

'There's no point – they'll just worry. He'll just have to take sick leave until he's better. I'll see if I can find some family friends for him to stay with until he recovers.'

Rick was feeling annoyed at his idiotic friend while Ella felt as if their holiday had been ruined. 'I don't feel much like a cosmopolite right now.'

'That's life for us citizens of the world my wife – one step forward and two steps back.'

Next day, after lunch, with Ploz in tow, they went back to the hospital to find Q R sitting up, grinning and announcing that he didn't think he'd be getting married after all.

'That was a fast recovery. We were about to contact your parents.'

'Good heavens. Good thing you didn't. I don't think Sir Percival and Lady Felicity Blot would be too pleased at the pickle I've got myself into.'

'You're joking mate,' Ploz spluttered. 'Did ya say yer surname was Blot? It's like some crazy Pom movie. Sir Percival, Lady Felicity and Quentin Blot, at your service.'

'Why d'you think I left the country? Anyway two broken ribs and a battered face wouldn't bring them here. The doctor says if I'm strapped up I can travel on tarred roads after two days as long as it's not on a camel. Could I cadge a lift, Rick? I couldn't handle the bus. Ploz, can you get my stuff from the Guest House?'

'No worries if you can tell me where it is. I reckon I'll take the bus though. You'll need the back seat to lay flat on. Besides, I'd miss all these goats and chickens and mattresses and stops every few miles?'

That was how Rick, Ella and Q R came to be not too speedy travelling mates on the return journey through Tanzania. There were no diversions but lots of pauses to view the sights along the way; that was why they were a day late for the beginning of the new term.

Q R put on his best ham performance to match his purple bruises and fading scars. Displaying his grubby bandages underneath his shirt completed the picture of the innocent victim attacked on the streets of Mombasa. All was forgiven. Suzy May had returned from USA to the sweetheart she had left for a month; she was full of sympathy for him. Rick, Ella and Ploz could be relied on to be discreet but there was no guarantee that the incriminating details would stay skipped.

As it turned out Mary Lou was to earn her passage home sooner than expected. She was guilty of caring too much and sticking her youthful, white woman's neck out, giving the local dignitaries three reasons to chop it off. What she said was fundamentally true but (under the influence of the marijuana she insisted was much less harmful than alcohol), *where* she said it, *how* she said it and *who* she said it to caused massive ripples which damaged relations between the expatriates and the Zambian officials for some time to come. Addressing the visiting Chief Education Officer in a general school staff meeting is perhaps not the place to state,

'I'm wasting my time teaching those boys who are simply fodder for the Freedom Fight. They won't even live to find out if they've passed their exams.' For good measure she had added with her usual passion, 'It's an utter disgrace. Your government should be ashamed of themselves.' The stunned silence that followed didn't seem to get through to her that she might be talking out of turn, so she added, 'We had a debate in the classroom and the schoolboys all agree that conscription should be banned.'

'If you have finished, Madam,' the CEO finally said, 'your headmaster and I will see you in his office, right now.'

As the three left, the staffroom was buzzing with, 'Silly cow,' 'Well, she's just managed to hang herself,' 'What was she thinking of?' and 'That went well'. Predictably Q R was agreeing with her but Rick's whisper of, 'Not now, for God's sake,' persuaded him to shut up. Ella was remembering a diplomat's good advice and was keeping her opinions firmly to herself.

Within the week, Suzy May was in Lusaka waiting for the next flight to New York. She hadn't left quietly, having left some confused schoolboys in the process. Of course she was right to defend them, they felt. Of course their own leaders were in the wrong. She was their English teacher who had inspired them with her youthful militancy and her passion. Some saw her as a victim; she had succeeded in portraying herself as just that. The long discussions between Rick, Ella, Ploz Q R and Suzy May were inconclusive. Ella was non-committal which infuriated Suzy May. Ella had said she wasn't there to impose her opinions on Africa; too many outsiders had done that already.

'You think we should just let them murder their own boys, then?' was Suzy May's reply.

'Don't be such an idiot,' Rick finally said. 'It's not the place of the expatriates to try to tell the Zambians what to do about freeing Zimbabwe and South Africa. Especially not a young, white, female.'

'What do you mean?'

'Think about it,' Rick added, 'especially one who smells of pot most of the time.'

Unfortunately for Ella, as an English teacher, she had to take over Suzy May's classes. New to the school, her work was cut out to get round these boys who were understandably hostile towards her. The schoolboys, though politically mature beyond their years, had been impressed by Suzy May's passion on their behalf. Ella could have solved the problem by telling them that she agreed with Suzy May. She didn't. Instead, as the concepts of apartheid, colonialism and freedom fighting came up in the context of their reading in English lessons, she opened the questions to debate while making it absolutely clear that her role, as a teacher, was to be utterly impartial. When put on the spot, she wore her diplomat's dancing shoes and came up with, 'In principle, I hate war like everyone does as it leads to death and destruction but not everyone agrees that there should never be war. Some people believe that certain problems can only be resolved through fighting. What is important is what you believe, not what I believe – so, more than that, I'm not prepared to say, in any circumstances.' After that, the mistrust seemed to melt away and the boy-men felt free to reveal their misgivings and convictions without fear that their opinions would be broadcast beyond the classroom. Ella's approach contrasted with Suzy May's indoctrination on the one hand and the antidote of dogmatic propaganda that the local Zambian dignitaries had felt duty-bound to deliver. A normal mixture of viewpoints evolved and Ella hoped that these young men were equipped to think for themselves and that they would be given the chance to do so.

Suzy May became another transient statistic, ruffling a few more feathers than most, but still soon to be forgotten. Even Q R had sighed a sigh of relief; this particular lady had been hard to keep up with.

The following three years in Mpika Boys' School recruited a rapidly changing, though dwindling, cast of young teachers from all corners of the globe, each bringing his or her unique perspective. The stronger influence was beginning to come from the even younger cast of Zambian teachers as they emerged from university and teachers' colleges.

Rick's fortunes were mixed. As predicted, dear old Mr Chikande hadn't survived too long as a caretaker headmaster. The new breed of schoolboys were educated far beyond him by the time they were in third year and soon began to run rings around him and complain about his incompetence. One memorable example of complete lack of respect was when the old man, announcing a visit by Kenneth Kaunda, President of Zambia, reminded the schools to be properly 'on uniform'. At this a particularly arrogant schoolboy, stripped off his shirt and stood on it.

'We have to be "in" uniform not "on" uniform, old man.'

This incident was promptly and firmly dealt with but it was too late. The hilarity in the school hall and this obvious show of disrespect meant that the well-meaning Mr Chikande had to beat a retreat. However, it was not hasty. It was dignified. He hosted Kaunda's visit to the school, complete with the President's tears and white handkerchief, which were as symbolic of K K as Jomo Kenyatta's zebra-tail fly whisk in Kenya. The Zambian teachers displayed the utmost respect for the elderly Mr Chikande and spent time making the arrogant young students feel thoroughly ashamed of themselves. Because of the schoolboys' behaviour, they were told, Mr Chikande had made the decision to move on. As a result, queues of schoolboys lined up to shake the hand of the old man and bid him a respectful farewell. In Zambia, youth may never disrespect their elders, however educated they may think they are. This was a lesson well learned. This was a lesson that Suzy May Claxton had not learned. There was perhaps another lesson that she, and Ian Smith in neighbouring Rhodesia, soon to be Zimbabwe, had not learned. However well meaning one's intentions, one does not presume to dictate to the leaders of newly-independent African states who have perceived that their freedom has been won through great sacrifice.

There followed three headmasters in quick succession after Mr Chikande left, each with different reasons for moving on until the post landed on Rick's doorstep.

'I need this like a hole in the head,' Rick told Ella in confidence. 'But can you handle the stress if I take it on until we leave? It's only eighteen months.'

'If you can handle it, so can I,' Ella replied but they both knew what the position implied. Resentment would be there from the young Zambian teachers who expected immediate promotion. By now, Ella was head of the English department, much to the dismay of some of her Zambian male colleagues. Luckily she had one ally who helped her to fight her corner. He was young, Zambian and he wanted to learn.

Rick, as head, would now have to walk on eggshells too; he responded by giving out various responsibilities for different aspects of the school to each of the young Zambian teachers. Within a few months Rick and Ella decided that their teaching contract with the Government of Zambia would be their last one; they let this be known. It was suggested that the young Zambian teachers should take on more responsibility as fewer expatriate teachers were being recruited. Some did. Others didn't. Pressure on relationships seemed to ease and Rick and Ella managed to jog through their last few terms in Zambia, working happily alongside their few expatriate and many new Zambian colleagues.

Rick stumbled from crisis to crisis, shooting trouble and trying to make ends meet while still making sure the, by now 600, hungry schoolboys were fed more than nshima and cabbage. Rations were short, he was told, as the border with Rhodesia was closed and the Tanzam railway hadn't been completed.

In fact the railway had been open since 1975. Petty corruption had reared its ugly head and there were all kinds of excuses for the lack of funds or the inability to honour the dreaded LPOs (Local Purchase Orders), which were so essential for the buying of everything from pencils to the local dried fish, kapenta, which was a valuable source of protein. Beans seemed to be the only other protein available. Meat and chicken were way out of reach.

On one occasion, not long after the top class had been forced to sit an O-level exam with only a cup of weak tea in their stomachs, Rick had decided he needed to be a little more proactive. Using his local Zambian contacts, he discovered that a lorry of kapenta was due to stop in Mpika en route to Kasama. He asked if it could be diverted to school where he presented the driver with an LPO for the entire load - with two signatures on it - his own and his administration officer's. This was not strictly accepted procedure but he decided to play dumb. The chances of another lorry load of any kind of food coming along before 600 boys had caused a riot at having to go hungry into yet another public exam were nil. The driver of course was delighted at the change of plan, unloaded his lorry at the school kitchen door and set off for the Rest House bar and a bed for the night.

Taking the initiative in the interest of his schoolboys was classed as misconduct so Rick was informed that he would be facing disciplinary action and possible dismissal.

By this time, neither Rick nor Ella really cared. They would soon be leaving Zambia and it was worth making sure that the boys were fed, even if it meant a hasty departure. It made all the enquiries about Australia, New Zealand and Canada more exciting. As it turned out, Rick had more friends in influential places than he realised and word had trickled down to the classrooms that Mr Fonseca was going to be sacked for hijacking a lorry load of kapenta for them. The schoolboys announced they would go on strike if he left, so there was no more talk of disciplinary action. Another unexpected result of the situation was a donation of two hundred chickens from a farmer many miles away in the Luangwa valley who had heard of the plight of the starving Mpika boys doing exams on empty bellies.

'You're lucky you know,' Ella told her husband.

'Never. It takes a crook to outwit the crooks. There was no danger.' Ella decided she wouldn't ask what it meant. 'Don't try that again.'

'I already told them I'd do it again if they didn't get their act together and send food for the boys.'

'Oh … dear.'

Meantime Ella was knee deep in what African school children love most – drama. Wole Soyinka's Kongi's Harvest was on the syllabus, a cracking tale of clashes between traditional and modern forces in African society. The politically-minded men-boys quickly drew analogies between Oba and Kongi and Chief Chitimukula and President Kaunda and threw themselves into the performance with gusto. As improvisation is a strong feature of African traditional drama, Soyinka's script and characters took on a Zambian slant which went down well with audiences. A highlight was a Malipenga dance, included to add some rhythm and colour to performances, introduced as a form of entertainment for Oba Danlola, the traditional leader in the play. The most exciting part was the lighting which flickered on and off and changed colours; nobody had seen anything quite like it. The secret was simple; never had an empty box of Quality Street chocolates come in so useful. Carefully flattened cellophane papers in front of the lens of a 16mm cine projector can create wonders as can a hand placed over the lens to create semi and complete darkness on stage. Brilliant. 'Kongi's Harvest' performed by Mpika Boys' School was the talk of the town and miles around.

Even better, however, was the hilarious Zambianised production of Nikolai Gogol's 'The Government Inspector'. Not wishing to be outdone by the previous top literature class, the boys created Bemba names for the entire cast, managing to give them meanings close to those Gogol had given his characters in Russian. Again the theme of corruption and incompetence in a small town was apt and the actors were fully aware of this. Ella could claim very little credit for the resounding success of this production; in fact, it was at times hard to fully appreciate why so many local Zambian politicians were rolling around in paroxysms of hilarity at the antics of a totally incompetent and utterly corrupt bunch of petty officials in Russia putting on airs and graces in an effort to hoodwink a Government Inspector who was in fact playing them at their own game. After the performance the delighted audience explained that the Bemba names for the characters were extremely clever and funny. Gogol would have been proud to see that satire knew no boundaries. The performance went on tour, for two performances, as far as Lwitikila Girls School, thirteen miles on tar and five miles on a dusty road away. This happened towards the dry season so the already limited water supply had practically dried up – and there was certainly no chance of a shower for a schoolboy. As a treat, the second top class were to be allowed to fill up the big bus, hired to transport the actors, so that they could be part of the audience on one of the evenings.

Lwitikila girls were proud of their school near the river with a constant water supply; one or two also had somewhat of a superiority complex. One pretty girl sitting beside a particular lad, who was feeling pretty lucky to be there, curled up her nose and asked, 'Don't you boys ever take a shower?' Washington, as his name was, swallowed his indignation, almost choking on it, until it bubbled up into a boiling wrath which exploded when the Mpika boys were on the bus home.

'Can you believe what one of those Lwitikila girls said to me?' The report of the insult led to a barrage of angry comments, not all justified. 'One of' those girls turned into 'those girls' so all five hundred Lwitikila girls were deemed guilty.

'Who do they think they are? Don't they know that we have no water? They don't know they are lucky to be near the river! They should respect us and understand.'

'We have to teach them a lesson.'

'I say we go out there… on Saturday afternoon!'

'Why not tomorrow?'

'We need to get properly organised – and we don't need to waste good studying time on such bad-mannered girls.'

This was how a throw-away rude remark escalated into a major incident which caused a huge amount of consternation and inconvenience. It began on Saturday afternoon with a stealthy exodus from the school dormitories. There was nothing unusual about that as the students were allowed out to the nearby shops. Soon small groups congregated at a pre-arranged spot and the nine mile march of two hundred boys began; this was accompanied by chants which fanned the fire of resentment into a burning fury. The first clue that all was not well was the sound of warlike grunts in the distance. Next, a cloud of dust seemed to be moving in the direction of the school from a long way off.

A man from a nearby village arrived on his bicycle panting, explaining rapidly in Bemba that the angry Mpika boys were coming across country to 'punish' the Lwitikila girls. A phone call alerted the teachers at Mpika. A few set off by car expecting to find their irate students on the road. When there was no sign of them, Sister Immaculata phoned the police who advised her to confine the girls to the dorms and the teachers to the staffroom. As the boys had to struggle up hill and down dale across dry and dusty terrain, and their chants had announced their imminent arrival, there had been time for a reception party to be prepared. Three police vans, umpteen teachers and their head teacher with a megaphone having removed the surprise element of their ambush, there was a deathly hush before pint-sized Honesty Mulenga announced in a pre-pubescent squeak, 'We want the girls! They have to apologise.'

Unfortunately, some insensitive idiot laughed before the reception committee could use their diplomatic skills and agree to a meeting between representatives of the girls' and boys' schools where a formal apology might be offered and accepted. All hell was let loose. The boys felt humiliated and around fifty of them began to storm across the fence towards the dorms before shots fired in the air by the police stopped the others in their tracks.

'Tell us what your grievance is,' the police chief shouted.

'These girls insulted us because we have no water to have a shower.'

'You mean you have come all the way here for that stupid remark. Go home now and we'll say no more.'

'No, they have to apologise.'

'We'll make these arrangements but not right now. Your foolish friends who have broken into the school are in trouble. The rest of you are not. Go back to school.' At Mr Fonseca's words, one hundred and fifty Mpika boys turned around and began to trudge back to school, feeling exhausted and a little foolish.

'I didn't think they'd agree,' Rick said, adding, 'Come on, let's sort out those other idiots before they do any damage.'

'I'm sorry sir. That's not a job for you or your staff or the Lwitikila staff. It's a police matter now. Can I ask you to keep out of the way, please?'

This sounded scary. Twenty minutes later all was resolved. Some of the lads had found their way into a dormitory and were threatening all kinds of beatings without actually resorting to any physical violence.

'It was me,' the offender called out. 'I just asked if the Mpika boys ever had a shower. I'm sorry. I didn't mean to insult them.'

'Yes, we're all sorry you have no water. You are our brothers. Why do you want to beat us?'

'Right...'

It was all a bit of an anti-climax. Everyone went home including the police who felt that a long trek home in the dark was enough punishment for the foolish boys. No more was said. The rains came a week later. The teenage boys queued up for showers as never before.

The girls were invited to attend a debate on the motion 'Does God Exist?' The boys of the debating club were dressed in newly laundered uniforms and their freshly showered bodies smelt of cheap aftershave. By a very narrow margin, it was decided that God did exist but only because he had been created by man. It was agreed that God could not have created man because such a perfect being couldn't possibly have created such imperfect creatures. Nobody lost face that way - which was important as it was the girls who were arguing for the existence of God.

Eventually the time came for Rick and Ella to wind up and leave Zambia. There had been a spate of burglaries over a period of three months with the Fonsecas being the unluckiest victims. Looking back, there were many reasons for this.

The headmaster's house was first in the line of fire and the back garden led to wide open unpopulated spaces with just enough scrubby woodland to provide the necessary cover for escaping robbers. A mile away was the now defunct camp for workers on the recently completed Tanzam railway. The news of the completion hadn't reached some remote corners of Zambia so hopeful employees were arriving in the area to find no jobs.

The break-ins were inevitable. Rick's wardrobe was cleaned out on the first occasion which put paid to the brown corduroy jacket, yellow shirt and brown brogues (designed to impress his Caithness in-laws) much to his secret relief. The second time saw the end of the record player but not the LPs. Next the bedding in the spare room and half of the contents of the bookshelf went; this made Biology and English lesson preparation a bit of a problem.

Then, one foolhardy scoundrel allowed himself to be interrupted. On their way home from a short visit, which the caller no doubt had expected to be a long trip to Lusaka, Rick and Ella could see all the lights shining at home and the curtains streaming out of a broken window. Had they had the presence of mind, they could have stopped the car, switched off the lights and crept up on the visitor. Instead, Rick raced as fast as he could up to the front door so the thief had skedaddled - leaving the back door swinging on its hinges. The intruder had forgotten to switch the cooker off. Dumped in the largest pot, was every morsel of food in the fridge. Chicken, left over rice, trifle, lettuce, prunes and even eggs still in their shells were bubbling away in some goo which smelt like a mixture of cheese and butter; the sugar bowl was empty – and the coffee jar. The concoction smelt so foul that Ella threw the pot outside to cool off. A half empty beer can, a still smouldering cigarette, an open biology text book and mud on the coffee table told a tale. Oddly, our hungry biology student had left two cans of beer in the fridge and two cigarettes in a pack which made Rick and Ella smile.

'Do you reckon he thought we might need them?'

The final straw was when Ella was left on her own one night while Rick was on a school football trip, a hundred miles away. Feeling scared, she'd locked the back and front doors, the door leading to the corridor, the bathroom door and even the bedroom door. As she was settling down to sleep, she heard someone trying to break in through the bedroom window; this would have been an easy thing to do if Ella hadn't yelled and screamed until the nearest neighbour, Mr Titus, came running and shouting at the top of his very loud voice. Again the would-be thief had scarpered.

'You all right, Mrs Fonseca?'

'Yes – but that was so scary. If he'd got in, I'd have had three doors to unlock to get out. I can't take this any more.' Mrs Titus arrived clad in a blanket, hair flying.

'Bring your blankets,' she said on hearing the story. 'You're sleeping in our spare room.' Ella didn't argue.

'I saw the little bastard. He couldn't have been more than ten,' Mr Titus said. 'Sita, we need a cuppa tea.' So Sita made tea and they all laughed at how little danger a small boy had posed but agreed that it could have been a lot worse.

'Titus, do you remember how you caught that fellow who was trying to steal your car? Tell Ella.'

'This was in Ndola, where we were visiting friends. Cars were being filched all the time so I thought I'd tie some black wool to the car door and tie the other end to my big toe, in bed.'

'You're joking. Did it work?'

'You bet, before the guy could work out how to get the engine started, I had him out of the car with his hands up his back.'

'I must tell you what happened to our Kitwe friends,' Ella went on. 'They thought their car had been stolen – from right outside their house. But next day, there it was with a note saying, "So sorry had to borrow your car to take someone to hospital. As a thank you, here are two tickets for the 'Little Theatre' matinee performance on Friday." Of course they thought, how nice, and went. When they got back their house was cleaned out. This furniture van had arrived in broad daylight, opened the door with a master key and they'd taken their own sweet time to make a tidy job of taking the lot.'

'Didn't the neighbours do anything?'

'People come and go so much, Sita; they thought it was all planned.'

'That's the copper belt these days,' Titus added. 'It doesn't surprise me. We've got another story. Our mates had packed all their worldly goods, suitcases, money passports, the lot – ready to leave for the airport to go home. They decided to pop into the neighbours to say good-bye for a minute.'

'Oh no!'

'Oh yes! It took them five weeks to get their documents together; they couldn't leave the country.'

'I suppose we should try to get some sleep.' What had slipped their minds in the middle of the night was to leave a note for Rick. His short-lived panic on finding Ella gone when he returned around eight in the morning was enough to push him out of Zambia at the first opportunity. Mr Titus came over when he saw Rick's car.

'She's fast asleep in our spare room. She's fine but a bit shaken. I wouldn't leave her alone in that house again.'

Within a day, what was left of their possessions had been packed into their ice-blue Toyota Celica and transported to a smaller house in the centre of the campus. There were no more burglaries and nobody moved into the end house for a while. After they'd left, the Fonsecas found out that a high fence and barred windows had been installed before the new headmaster would move in.

Life was easy for the next few months with few possessions in the little house that nobody else wanted to live in. Headmaster Rick and English teacher Ella worked as hard as they could for the schoolboys, one making sure they were fed among other things and the other cramming them full of good ways of passing exams which is what they wanted. When the well fed schoolboys had 'sat for' their exams, they pronounced that they had been ready and felt confident they would pass.

There was still, however, some anguish to cope with and people had reason to remember Suzy May Claxton, now back home in Springfield, Illinois. Two hours after the last Cambridge O-level, which in 1976 happened to be Chemistry, an army truck arrived to pick up the entire senior class with an 'invitation' to attend an important meeting connected with serving their nation. When Rick tried to persuade the officials to allow the boys at least a night's rest after the huge effort they had put into their exams, he was informed that the army didn't want to take the risk of any 'men' absconding overnight.

'They're only boys,' Ella wailed on hearing the story. Like so many of the other teachers who had worked so hard for the future of these students, she crumpled in a heap on the nearest chair. Nothing could have made those teachers feel worse than they did at that moment. How much worse would the parents feel when they found out?

With a heavy heart, Rick and Ella, set off for Lusaka to complete the last minute arrangements for their final departure from Zambia. Everything possible, that hadn't been tied up in red tape, had been done. The beloved ice-blue Celica had been sold (on paper), air tickets to India via Mauritius were booked, with three free days in Mauritius and an apology from Air India who couldn't arrange a direct flight to Bombay, and visas for India and UK had been bought at great expense. It was the getting out that was the problem; police checks, bank checks, exit visas, employment reports all had to be dealt with, which was a slow business. The Celica, destined to be picked up at the airport by the buyer on departure day, was staying at Lwitikila while Rick drove the red car of one of the teachers to Lusaka to be serviced. Ella still associated red cars with tragedy. Rick was not impressed. After a long journey at curtailed speed with a white-knuckled, shoulder-hunching wife cramping his style, he was very relieved to deliver the 'dangerous' serviced red car and pick up his own 'safe' blue car. His foot went down on the accelerator for the final ten miles towards home. That was until an enormous double pantechnicon decided to jack-knife into a perfect V across the path that Rick was accelerating into in an effort to overtake it in the dark. A quick swerve to the right catapulted the 'safe' blue car off the road into a ditch which sent it into a triple somersault and landed it on its roof. The engine cut out and, apart from spinning wheels, Chuck Berry yelling out, 'Sweet little sixteen…' was all that could be heard. A full minute passed.

'I've killed you.'

'I'm fine. The car's blue. Are you ok?'

'We're supposed to be having dinner at Christy's tonight.'

'Well, it's a good thing he's the doctor.'

Two hours later, having managed to crawl out through a window as the doors were jammed, the two were munching spicy Sri Lankan curry and dosas. They had freaked at the position of the car between a huge tree and a ten foot deep concrete drainage culvert, hitched a lift and had the car towed home. Christy, the Sri Lankan no nonsense hospital chief cum GP known affectionately as Doc was short on the sympathy and long on breezy get up and get on with it, so they were declared bruised but unbroken.

An often told tale was of a night of poker with Doc, his heavily pregnant wife, Mohini, and a number of teachers including Rick and Ella. Doc was having a run of luck and chose to ignore Mohini's fast increasing labour pains.

'It's baby number three. You'll be fine.'

'But Christy, we have to go now!'

'Walk about a bit. It's more comfortable here.' Eventually around 3am a wincing, groaning Mohini was bundled into the car for the ten minute journey to the hospital. All must have gone smoothly as by 10 a.m. mother was making breakfast at home while baby boy was wrapped up in a blanket in his brother's Moses basket.

'If these ladies round here can give birth in the maize fields and walk on, so can you, Mo. You're a strong woman,' was her husband's comment, delivered at breakneck speed.

Rick and Ella were given equally short shrift. 'There's no blood, not a broken bone and the car can still move. You've got nothing to moan about. I suppose blue cars are unlucky now are they Ella.'

'I'm going to hate big lorries for a while.'

Apart from a few pains and some stiffness the next day, the couple were in good spirits, counting their blessings as Doc had advised.

Father O'Malley and Sister Immaculata had heard the rumours and had hot-footed it in from Lwitikila - memories of a recent tragedy burning into their hearts. Unspoken thoughts abounded. Why did she have to die at twenty two? Why were Rick and Ella so lucky? Was everyone else thinking the same things? Eventually Ella blurted out,

'I think she's our guardian angel. I see her all the time – in her red dress.'

Nothing more needed to be said. The smothered tears said it all.

'Can you do one thing for me, please?' Sister Immaculata asked. 'Find your way to Eriskay and ask for Mrs Macdonald, the nurse. She lives in the only house on the island with a black roof. She's my mother and Kirsty's granny. Give her our love. Father knows her too and she loves him. And while you're there, take a walk to the graveyard. It's on the other side of the island overlooking the bay.'

'I promise. It's something we need to do ourselves,'

'That's a promise we won't find hard to keep, Sister,' Rick added.

'Now, can you come to our farewell 'Pass the Basket' party tomorrow evening? You can help us empty the booze cupboard.'

Then it was a rush and flurry as Rick and Ella attempted to leave Zambia with the clothes they stood in, one small suitcase each and a single haversack between them. Ella kept singing 'Got no bags and baggage to slow me down, I'm travelling so fast my feet ain't touching the ground. Travellin' ligheeeet, travellin ligheet …' One door was closing another opening and they wanted to leave things in good order behind the closed one. Joseph, who, like Arapbet in Kenya, was baker for the school staff and kept Rick and Ella in hot water, got first choice. He wanted all the perishable consumables plus the blankets, sheets, pillows, towels and cushions and the bread tins he had used so often. He later decided he'd have the spade as he'd also managed to tease some water melons and weak vegetables out of the reluctant garden. After that the giant Ali Baba laundry basket, a wedding present that couldn't travel, was filled with every conceivable household item such as salt and pepper pots, scrubbing brushes, tins, jars, rubber gloves, crockery, cutlery, electric kettle, chapatti pan, pots, bread knife, trays, washing-up liquid, can-openers (three), corkscrew, hammer, ladles, garlic-crusher, cheese board and sink plunger to mention just a few.

The little stereo player (a replacement for the stolen one) was used to play and stop the music for the 'musical lucky dip' for all the visitors which included the entire staff at the boys' school, a few from Lwitikila and some hangers on. Great excitement and a good deal of laughter accompanied the unearthing of a fish slice or a single rubber glove or a salt cellar but no pepper pot.

'I'll swop you a rubber glove for that pepper pot.'

'Done.'

In the background, Rick was blatantly cheating, making sure the neediest guests were holding the basket when the music stopped. How much more satisfying to see the excitement on the face of someone who had acquired a garlic crusher for the first time than to hear a groan like,

'Not another kettle.'

Finally every last item, apart from a few survival items for the next occupants, had been claimed, including the stereo and the laundry basket itself. Rick's dad's old radio had been sent ahead to the Fonseca brothers in UK along with some precious wedding presents with sentimental value. Even Ella's beloved old guitar had been sent home. Another one she had inherited from an American teacher had been given away to a budding schoolboy musician who used to come and play it during his free time. 'Just make sure you become a star, ok,' Ella had said. She never heard. They wondered if he had even survived the conscription.

One obscure little stick with a carved thistle head was left behind on their bed. Ella shoved her spurtle in her suitcase; it was destined to stir a few more porridge pots yet. Had she seen Sister Immaculata dig it out of the basket?

The booze cupboard emptied and the house stripped of every last thing including bedding, the couple took their suitcases and passports next door to QR Blot's house for bed and breakfast before trundling on to the Great North Road, to limp southwards in the battered blue Celica which had been deemed redeemable – at a cost. The buyer took it off their hands at a much reduced price so the two flew off to pastures exciting - even poorer than they had anticipated.

They didn't leave, however, before a last get together at the Copper Kettle where Rick and Ella passed on their good wishes to the clandestine activists who were still living in hope that they would one day see their efforts rewarded as first Zimbabwe and then Nelson Mandela and South Africa gained their freedom. They met a new member of the group whose name was Thabo Mbeki.

As they said their last farewells, Doc Ben Goldberg pressed a thick envelope into Rick's hand, which he said contained a long letter and some photographs, to be delivered in person to his Jewish uncle one of the few Jews then resident in Mauritius. It was vital, he took trouble to add, that the envelope was delivered in person.

'He'll educate you about the history of the Jews on that beautiful island.'

# Chapter 17: Air India's Apology

'Thank you Air India. We don't mind waiting for a connection to Bombay at your expense at the Mandarin Hotel, Curepipe on the Island of Mauritius.'

Rick was surveying what was left of his room service breakfast of mango hedgehog, croissant and Cona coffee. Ella wasn't listening. She was transfixed by the scene from the window.

'It would have cost us a bomb, Ella. Have you seen the tariff?'

'Mm? Have you seen the view out here?'

From a window overlooking a central square, Ella could see a potpourri of people popping in and out of temples and churches, meeting and greeting and laughing. She was looking at Mauritian unity in diversity, the blend of Indian, African, European, Chinese and Creole which had given rise to a Hindu/Buddhist temple, a Mosque, three Christian churches, Catholic, Presbyterian and Anglican, and a small Sikh Gurudwara - all within a stone's throw of each other.

'Come on let's explore.'

Minutes later they were outside in the centre of the square.

'If I could get married all over again, to you of course Rick, it would be here. We'd pop into every one of these temples for five minutes and have it done properly.'

'You're crazy.'

'Maybe, but they've all got the same message. Come on let's go into all of them. There don't seem to be any restrictions – except for taking your shoes off.'

For the next two hours the captivated couple feasted on sights, sounds, textures and smells of bright and exotic religious paraphernalia such as they had never seen before in one place; they weaved in and out of St Thérèse Catholic Church, Phoenix Mosque, a Hindu Mandir, a Buddhist temple, an Anglican church, a small Sikh Gurudwara and, hidden away, a large room which served as an area of worship for those of the Bah☐'i faith. Everywhere they went, people of different faiths were ready with explanations.

'You wanting to choose one belief?' a monk of Chinese origin asked them. 'I watch you go everywhere. That ok. God is everywhere – same guy. I don't know why so many of my relatives took Catholic religion. Why don't you buy prayer-wheel here? But it must always to spin clockwise. Sure?

So Ella bought a colourful prayer wheel and forever more remembered to spin it clockwise and to always walk round a Buddhist temple clockwise. Why? She never found out. Rick said he would stick to a rosary, if he ever felt the need. Ella pointed out that a Buddhist mala was the same thing.

Nobody in the mosque seemed to bother about a man and a woman wandering around together, much to Rick's surprise. In the Hindu temple, they held their hands in prayer, said many namastés, were offered vegetarian food and emerged, each festooned in a silk garland.

'I didn't know "namasté" meant "the light in me honours the light in you." Isn't that beautiful?'

They managed some more food in the Sikh temple and learned about Guru Nanak's philosophy of equality between all god's creatures. Bursting with good will, they were about to go back to the hotel when they came across an unpretentious brass plate, like those that might advertise dentists or lawyers. It read, '"The earth is but one country, and mankind is its citizens." (Bahá'u'lláh) Welcome to the house of the Bahá'i Faith which transcends all differences: First established in Mauritius in 1954.' Rick was suffering from religious indigestion by this time but Ella was utterly intrigued. This place couldn't have been better located. A young man with twinkling eyes and a soft voice introduced himself as Abdul Salim Krishnamurthy. Noting Rick's raised eyebrows, he laughed.

'My mother's Moslem and my dad's Hindu but I also follow the Bahá'i Faith. They don't ask anyone to renounce any other beliefs they might have.'

'That sounds about the most sensible thing I've heard in a long time. Why haven't we heard about you?'

'Perhaps you should have, judging by your accent. One of your countrymen was appointed as the first hand of the cause by the last Guardian of the Faith, Shoghi Effendi. Where are you from?'

'Caithness and I studied in Aberdeen.'

'Amazing. Dr John E Esslemont came from Aberdeen. That's where I studied by the way. He wrote a book "Bahá'u'lláh and the New Era" which is a major eye-opener for new Bahá'is in the western world – even though he died in 1925 in Haifa.'

'Isn't that in Israel?'

'That's right. This man Esslemont was phenomenal. He spoke French, German and Spanish, was an Esperantist and was learning Persian and Arabic for translation purposes when he died.'

Ella was more interested in Abdul's studies in Aberdeen. 'When were you in Aberdeen – and what faculty?'

'I finished a Science degree at Marshall's in 1975 and now I'm back teaching part time at my old college, St Joseph's which is run by Irish missionaries.'

'Good grief, you *are* a mixture of backgrounds.'

'Why part time teaching?' Rick asked.

'The pay's bad so I spend two days taxiing tourists around. Besides I want to study Bahá'i - and perhaps write a book.'

'What attracted you?'

'Would you believe I went to a memorial lecture on John Ebenezer Esslemont at Aberdeen University?'

'It sounds incredible but I'll believe you.'

'Enough about me. Looking at you two, I can see that you've come to the right place. What brought you to Curepipe?'

'Air India,' Rick said dryly. 'The couldn't find us a direct flight to Bombay so they're paying for three nights here.'

'Three nights? That's not nearly enough. Unless… What about I offer you a two day whistle-stop tour of all the best places - in my taxi?'

'How much?'

'Three hundred rupees and you buy me lunches and my wife cooks you a curry. It won't be too hot – she's Chinese.'

'Done.' Rick wasn't sure if it was a good deal but it was a nice round figure and he liked the idea of a Chinese curry. Ella couldn't stop laughing at the final piece in the international jigsaw.

'The only thing missing around here seems to be a synagogue. Our friend Doc said the only one was near a place called Beau Bassin.'

'Isn't that where we have to deliver that letter to?'

Their new friend Abdul Salim Krishnamurthy with his Chinese wife and Irish Roman Catholic and Scottish education looked at the address.

'I'll take you there but not today. Today I will take you to Trou-aux-Cerfs and you will see why Mark Twain said God made Mauritius first and then made Heaven. But lunch first. I know just the place - a bit of a drive but you'll like it.'

'Just a snack, I hope. We've done the round of the temples. And nothing too expensive,' Rick joked mindful that meals were part of the taxi fare.

'What colour's your car?' a little voice asked.

'It's a white Mazda Capella RX2.'

'Oh good.'

A sharp glance from Rick stopped the conversation. When was Ella going to get over her phobia for red cars?

May 1977 was a particularly green month in Mauritius, as the rains had been plentiful since November. The visitors couldn't have come at a better time as the drier season had begun. Abdul Salim drove them past opulent colonial mansions within lush tree-filled gardens, out of town through the greenest of tea-estates which reminded them of Kericho in Kenya and finally up a winding road towards Trou-aux-Cerfs which appeared to be a volcano. They stopped at an unlikely looking shack which had a spectacular view eastwards towards the ocean in the far distance. This was the Café des Délices. Abdul found a gingham covered table in the 'bay window with view'.

'Santé Sophie, ça va?... Is there anything you two can't eat?...' This was followed by a not quite intelligible conversation of which Rick and Ella could pick out only a few words.

'Creole. French, African, English Tamil, Urdu, Marathi, Hindi, Arabic and Cantonese – what have you – but mainly French and African from the slaves on the sugar plantations,' explained Abdul.

'You forget the bad times looking around at such sheer beauty.'

'I hope you like what I've ordered. Sophie makes the best pipi bouillon on the island – and her petit pain is straight from the oven. She grows her own pommes d'amour too.'

'Pipi?'

'A shellfish that's dug up from sandy beaches. Something between a clam or scallop or maybe oyster. They're big with the Maoris in New Zealand and the beaches around here are full of them.'

'Anybody would think you were trying to educate us. Is there anything you don't know?'

'Quite a lot but I'm showing off my favourite island today.'

They soon discovered that pommes d'amour were tomatoes, that Creole cuisine had its fair share of garlic and coriander, and that Abdul hadn't exaggerated Sophie's talents.

'That's the best clam soup and a bun I think I've ever had,' Ella announced, licking her lips and wiping her hands on a gingham serviette.

'And the bill's very reasonable too.'

'I can up the price next time then, can I?'

A short drive took them to within a few hundred yards of the rim of the crater. A lugubrious-looking lake was at the bottom of the eighty yard deep and two hundred yard across crater. They walked around the rim but didn't fancy venturing inwards. Lunch had lasted longer than they'd planned so there wouldn't be too much time to drink in the views. Curepipe was surprisingly nearby, stretching out beneath them; Abdul had taken them on a long route via the sights.

To the west was a green and shiny landscape dotted with settlements that Abdul named and his visitors forgot immediately. This stretched all the way to the ocean six miles away.

'Look east and you can just see Isle-aux-Cerfs off the coast. Look north west and you can see Beau Bassin Rose Hill and Port Louis. '

'Does serf mean slave?' Ella asked.

'No. Where did you get that from? It means stag.'

'Know-all.' But there was a cheeky grin attached to the comment.

'Watch this. Get your camera out.'

A Mauritian sunset looking west from the rim of Trou-aux-Cerfs across the Indian Ocean has to be seen to be believed. No camera could record its splendour.

Abdul Salim Krishnamurthy (Rick loved to call him that) drove them back to The Mandarin with instructions to have an early night as he'd be collecting them at eight in the morning.

'I'll tell Dawn you're coming for dinner.'

'Dawn? I thought she was Chinese.'

'She's Chen-chi. It means brilliant dawn.'

'Then I'm going to call her Chenchy.'

At five to eight Rick and Ella were outside the hotel and a minute later Abdul Salim Krishnamurthy drew up.

'I thought we'd head for Beau Bassin to deliver your letter first. What's the name and address?'

'Rabbi Joshua Ripinski, Jewish Community Centre, Leoville L'Homme Street, Beau-Bassin. I'm glad you're taking us there. We'd never have found it.'

'Unbelievable. I know this man! His wife Ruth seems quite young and they have a boy and a girl. He's been trying to get funding for a proper place of worship for the few dozen Jews on the island. He looked at a place in Curepipe. Then there's the cemetery; it's pretty dilapidated... Oh, look at that view!'

A drive through spectacularly lush, palm-studded vegetation brought them to a large, but faded bungalow set in an overgrown garden festooned with ferns and orchid-covered trees. It turned out to be Rabbi Joshua Ripinsky's family home which doubled up as The Jewish Community Centre. He was pottering in the office, his wife Ruth told them, but he'd be more than pleased to be interrupted by any friends of Ben's. She turned to Rick. 'How *is* Ben? He's my nephew – I'm the Goldberg and Joshua's his uncle by marriage.'

'He's fine, Mrs Ripinsky, doing a wonderful job in the hospital and his clinic in the township. Samira and Zak are well too.'

'Oh yes. He was very brave to take on that little family. We were very worried about how it would work out.'

'I think he felt there was nothing else he could do. They seem very happy now and Zak is delightful – very intelligent.' Ella felt that this woman needed reassurance.

Rabbi Joshua rushed in like a friendly teddy bear offering a huge handshake and a warm hug. 'Shalom, my dear Ricardo and Ella. Ben has told me all about you. How good of you to come.'

'Our pleasure. He sent this envelope.'

The old man felt the envelope and raised his eyebrows.

'Ah yes, Ricardo. This little treasure was too precious to post. He must have a great deal of trust in you. Have you any idea what's inside?'

'None whatsoever,' Ella said her eyes widening as she watched Rick's jaw drop.

'Shall we have a look then?' Out of the innocuous looking envelope, he drew a thin cardboard box wrapped in a letter. Gingerly he opened the box revealing yellowed tissue paper inside which appeared to be a rather ugly heavy pewter chain.

'Precious?' Ella didn't disguise her disappointment.

With a wicked twinkle in her eye, Ruth dashed the chain to the stone floor where it smashed into a hundred pieces.

'Painted soapstone, not pewter.'

Twinkling in the dust was the most exquisite gold chain encrusted with diamonds, rubies, topaz, sapphires, amethysts and emeralds. Ruth smiled gently as Ella gasped.

'A family heirloom,' she explained, 'which has travelled the world and through several generations. It started in Russia, I believe.'

Ella gasped. 'It must be priceless. What if we had lost it?'

'Ben must have known you'd guard it.'

'He did say it was important – but not this valuable.'

The letter contained family news for Ruth and Joshua and a clever little post script which the Rabbi read out, 'I've enclosed grandma Goldberg's old necklace. She passed away with your name on her lips, Ruth, so this is your inheritance. It's not worth much or even pretty but I'm sure it will have some sentimental value. She did miss you Ruth when you married so young and went away with your husband – but was very proud you were a Rabbi Josh. Treasure her gift.'

Ruth interrupted, 'A bit of subterfuge in case a wrong person found the necklace. How clever. This was planned at our wedding in Johannesburg in 1962. Ben wasn't much younger than me as he was my oldest brother's eldest. He couldn't understand why we wanted to come to Mauritius of all places. He'd heard the story.'

'What story?'

'Ah, Ella, not many people seem to have heard it. Ruth, can we rustle up some Mauritian coffee and Kosher croissants?'

'Ben said you would educate us about the history of the Jews on Mauritius.'

'We came by taxi. The driver must be waiting. Perhaps you remember him, Abdul Salim Krishnamurthy?'

'Of course, the Baha'i Science teacher. He tried to convert me to the Baha'ullah's word. Call him in too.'

Ruth scooped up her treasure, wrapped it in its faded tissue and rushed off to arrange croissants and coffee.

For the next enlightening half hour, Rick and Ella listened to a story related by a Rabbi who seemed much older than his forty two years.

'I was born in Czechoslovakia in 1935. Not a good time or place to be Jewish. The idea of a Jewish national home in Palestine had been bubbling away. In 1917 the British Foreign Secretary Arthur Balfour had endorsed the notion and by 1992 the League of Nations had agreed to it. But when shiploads of Jews came from all over Europe to escape their increasing plight, the British labelled them illegal immigrants. They said too many Jews would prejudice the rights of the non-Jewish Palestinians. Things were getting desperate – violent pogroms all over – ending up with Kristallnacht in 1938. Only the Dominican Republic out of 32 nations agreed to take large numbers of the diaspora. Even the US and Britain had excuses for not accepting refugees. I remember very little except the terror of running and hiding as a small child. In 1940 I remember walking for miles, getting on a train and finally going by ship to a 'safe place' as my mother said. We were going to Palestine and all would be well. When we got to Haifa, we got off our ship but were put straight back on to another ship called the Patria. I remember the long queues for hard bread and tea without sugar - and filthy toilets. My father was shouting a lot and my mother was trying to comfort him. We were to be sent to Mauritius and nobody was sure where it was. Mother was crying. As we left the harbour, there was an explosion and before long the ship was beginning to list. 250 people died they said, 200 Jews and 50 British soldiers. The British changed their minds and let most of the passengers on the Patria stay – but not all. Our little family and about 1500 others were packed off to Mauritius. We weren't treated badly. The crew and soldiers kept telling us how lucky we were to be going to such a beautiful island. We stopped off at a few places somewhere on the African coast to get food. I remember we had pineapple for days. But there were armed guards to stop us getting off which made me think perhaps Mauritius wasn't such a great place.

'What puzzles me is who tried to bomb the boat? I thought the Arabs and the Brits didn't want the illegals.' Rick asked.

'Precisely. To our shame it was our own military underground, the Haganah, who messed it up. They had planned a slow leak so everyone could be rescued and be allowed to stay but the blast was too big and all these people died. Where was I? Oh yes - when the ship finally arrived at Port Louis, we heard there were no other Jews on the island. We were the entire yishuv.'

'Yishuv?'

'Jewish community. How are the croissants?'

'Delicious.'

'Anyway, some of us had become ill on the ship. Old Yacob died the day we got to Mauritius so a funeral had to be arranged and he was buried in what is now the Jewish cemetery very near here. The Mauritians brought blankets and food and old clothes to a school hall where we were – and there were other Jews in temples and other buildings. I remember my mother crying and saying, "There is no synagogue." I think I said we would build one – but I was only five years old. Worse came. My mother and I were put in one of the iron huts the women were sent to. (I think they thought I was a girl as I hadn't had a haircut for so long.) My father was 'accommodated' in the former jail with all the other men and boys. Some of the women were wailing and stamping their feet but I remember my mother standing, head held high, silently, telling me it was going to be all right.'

'You could have been forgiven for thinking the whole world had turned Nazi,' Ella blurted out.

'To a certain extent, though I didn't understand it at the time, I think the whole world had. There wasn't a country in the world where we were welcomed without reservation. But, though we were detained here as refugees, we were looked after reasonably well. Malaria killed a few people and there wasn't always enough food so there was malnutrition. About 130 died – mostly in the first year. I made friends with a girl called Hella – her baby sister had died and then her mother. My mother tried to comfort her but nothing seemed to work.'

Ruth took over the story after she'd topped up the coffee cups.

'At some point, the authorities decided to stop segregating the sexes. Well 'whoop dee do', as you can imagine, 60 babies were born before 1945 and I was one of them. I was less than two when the war ended and the aliyah could begin.'

'Sorry, I don't understand aliyah.'

'That means a movement to the Jewish homeland in Palestine. There have been many – but let's not get into that. Anyway … nearly all of the detainees decided to go to Palestine but my father wanted to stay in Mauritius. He'd been inspired by all the mingling of faiths and the tolerance towards the Jews shown him by some of his new friends. My mother wasn't so sure. She couldn't believe Jews would be welcome anywhere but Palestine so she persuaded my father to take us (I was the only child)… take us to South Africa where her two brothers had gone to practise law, years before. Ben's father was one of those brothers.'

Rick asked, 'Where did you go, Joshua?'

'My parents took me back to Palestine where my two little sisters were born but as I grew up, I kept thinking of how I had promised my mother I would build a synagogue in Mauritius. What a crazy thought, eh? I had to come and see this island I remembered as being so beautiful with amazing pink sunrises and sunsets. There's still no synagogue and I've been here since 1960.'

'How did you meet Ruth? Wasn't she in South Africa?'

'Now, there was a happy coincidence. When I came here in 1960, having become one of the youngest Rabbis in Israel at the age of 25, I found a few crypto-Jews who had married local Mauritians; I only discovered they were Jewish when I found them at the gravesides of their loved ones. I hadn't realised that some of the young men and women had escaped from the detention. There had been so much confusion around that time. I also found some South African Jews who had decided to come and live here permanently. Nobody realised how helpful the South African Jewry had been during the war – sending food, medicine, religious items, books and magazines, you name it. One fellow was on a trip back to visit relatives he said and he was intrigued by my desire to build a synagogue. He suggested I fly back with him to see if we could rustle up some funds. The fund-raising didn't come to much as there weren't enough customers, I suppose, but I did meet a seventeen year old beauty named Ruth. There she is. We got married on her eighteenth birthday and she agreed to come to Mauritius with me and help me to build up a Jewish community – perhaps persuading those who had decided to abandon Judaism to return to the faith. I've ended up teaching comparative religion in John Kennedy College to make ends meet. Though the college is best known for Sciences, they seem to like the prestige of having a Rabbi in charge of religious studies.'

'But we haven't given up on a Jewish revival.' Ruth chipped in. 'One day the descendants of these 1500 detainees will be able to come and be welcomed into a thriving synagogue. Meantime, with the help of Jacques Duval, a Mauritian married to a Jewish girl, we are managing to maintain the cemetery and build up a small museum. But it looks like we'll be hard put to find ten adults for bar mitzvah for our Aaron and Rebecca. They're 12 and 10 now. We might take them to Jo'burg.'

'We certainly will not, my dear,' Joshua retorted. 'We'll invite everyone to visit. They can afford it – and it's much more beautiful here.'

Abdul Salim Krishnamurthy, who had been sitting very quietly, having heard the story many times before, broke in with, 'Good. Does that mean I'll get an invitation?'

'Of course. In the spirit of Mauritius, "The earth is but one country and mankind its citizens".'

'You're an incorrigible plagiarist Rabbi Ripinski but I'm sure the Bahá'u'lláh might forgive you for passing on his sentiment. Come on you two tourists, there's a whole lot of island left to see.'

Ruth scribbled addresses and phone numbers on a piece of paper entreating Ricardo and Ella to keep in touch and exuding gratitude for bringing the 'envelope' before they were bundled out of the door. Ella was coming to terms with the fact that this woman was only a couple of years older than she was and seemed to have had the experiences of several lifetimes behind her.

'It was amazing to meet you both.' Rick said shaking hands.

'I had no idea about that bit of history.' Ella added. 'I hope you get your Jewish renaissance on Mauritius before too long.'

'And may God go with the two of you. You're sure to have your own battles ahead of you. But, for now, enjoy Mauritius.'

Abdul Salim led a subdued Rick and Ella to the taxi and had the good sense to keep quiet as they visibly absorbed the enormity of the story they had just heard.

Finally Rick spoke. 'I think they're going to sell that heirloom for big bucks.'

'Never.'

'How else will they build a synagogue?'

'She won't let him do it. It's her only link with the family.'

'Come on Abdul. Where next?'

'I think we'll start with a lightning trip through Port Louis and on to Pamplemousse to see a few spectacular water lilies and trees and then we'll head for the hippy sweet spot at Tamarin to see if there are any surfers. After that we'll see how much time is left. Remember Dawn's cooking for you tonight.'

'Wonderful. You're the boss. Take it away.'

So they were whisked off around the exquisite island, much loved by their knowledgeable tour guide. He could drive around the 110 mile coastline in a few hours but didn't want them to tire of snowy white sands between deep azure seas and rich green vegetation. Mauritius had so much more to offer. The flag, he said, of red, blue, yellow and green stood for freedom, blood, sea, golden light of freedom and fertile land. The first visitors could be traced back to Dravidian and Austronesian (huh?) sailors in the 10th century, the Dutch came and named it after one of their leaders, Maurice, the French took over and called it Isle de France and then the Brits took over in 1810 and changed its name back to Mauritius but agreed to let everyone do their own thing, keep their land and carry on with French law etc. That explains why there are so many cultures and languages living in harmony – especially since 1968 when independence came. Mark Twain described Mauritius as heavenly in his travelogue, 'Following the Equator' and even though he bitterly criticised the colonials in other parts of the 'empire', he had nothing but praise for the atmosphere on Mauritius. Everyone knows about the extinct dodo of course but not many know about the rare pink Mauritian pigeon and the peach Mauritian duck with its black beak and tail. The monologue went on at speed and the picture somehow stuck in their minds but just before the point of mental indigestion was reached, Abdul Salim stopped the car and they all got out.

'Over there, the Champ de Mars, once a military bashing square, now one of the oldest race-courses in the world.'

'Do you like a flutter yourself?'

'You bet. It's a small track but the atmosphere's electric. There's Pamplemousse now.'

Ella's mind was in need of a break from the constant stream of information and within minutes, they had arrived at the ornate white gates of the Pamplemousse Botanical Gardens. 'That was quick.'

'Nothing's very far in Mauritius. It's only forty miles long and thirty miles wide.'

'Phew. There seems to be a lot in it though.'

'Sorry, girl. Shall I slow down?'

'Just a bit, maybe. Oh no, perhaps not. What's that huge tree?'

'A fig tree – but wait until you see the giant water lilies.'

An enchanting walk through palm avenues, past fiery flame trees, aromatic, sandalwood, cardamom and cinnamon trees and weeping banyans brought them to a mirror lake covered in water lilies the size of dustbin lids interspersed with flowering trees which at second glass, turned out to be reflections. Ella was struck by the exquisite blooms on a bed of ginger plants and was surprised to find it was the same plant the roots came from which had been left for two years to flower. Abdul Salim pointed out a chewing gum tree and the ornate tangled mass of the above-ground roots of a magnificent 300year old Buddha tree.

'You're right. This is startlingly exotic.'

'Thank you Ella. I must remember 'startlingly exotic' for my next spiel and our new brochure. Mauritius is quiet now, but give it a few years and we'll be the tourist hot spot of the Indian Ocean.'                                                      *v.*

'I don't doubt it,' Rick said thinking sadly that it might be the ruin of the place.

'Right. That was the garden of Paradise. Now we go for the beach of Paradise – I think. At least they have the best sunsets in the world.'

In twenty miles of blissful silence punctuated only by, 'That's a sugar plantation,' or, 'See that old mansion', the two drank in the sights of the green jewel as they drove inland. Later the vista was transformed into the blue, silver and gold of the sand-fringed sun-drenched coastline.

'Shall we get off the world and come here forever, Rick?'

'How's your French? Mine's bad.'

'Wouldn't matter.'

The taxi came to a halt on a rough piece of ground near palm trees which were providing shelter behind a silvery rock strewn beach.

'Come and see the guys who really have abdicated from their other world. I'm not promising you'll have much of a conversation though and it's a bit of a walk.'

Ella slipped off her orange flip flops and revelled in the warmth and texture of the white sands massaging her feet.

'It feels grittier than Scottish sand – and drier.'

'That's because it's coral sand. Do you know Mauritius is completely surrounded by a coral reef?'

'We do now.'

'One day there'll be glass-bottomed boats like in Mombasa. The tropical fish are even more exotic here.'

Ella caught Rick's eye and they smiled indulgently. What a salesman. Rick was stubbornly refusing to take his shoes off, declaring that he hated open-toed Jesus sandals and he wasn't a bloody hippy, when they rounded a small headland to be confronted by a commune of practically naked flower power people, stretched out on mats on the beach, sleeping off their night's excesses presumably. One or two topless girls were languishing in the shallow waters near the edge of the ocean. Nobody paid any attention to the two Indian men and the white woman.

'Let's ignore them,' whispered Ella. 'I feel like a peeping tom.'

'I'll take you further along to where some guys are actually in the land of the living.'

'Oh, there they are. The surfers you mean.'

'I like to think this is what Tamarin is famous for, apart from its salt pans, rather than those pot heads back there.'

'I hear the pot heads have hit Goa too, my little sister was telling me. The police turn a blind eye when these poor little rich guys cross their palms with some of daddy's money.'

'And that's our next stop,' Ella said, quickly adding, 'Family visit.'

A friendly, 'Hi guys. D'you wanna have a go?' came from a healthy-looking American carrying a surf board. He and his mates, Ella thought, were probably draft dodgers, ex by now as the Vietnam War had ended two years before. His next comment confirmed she was right.

'The freedom of the waves. Beats the hell out of containment hey?'

'Okay if you've got oodles of spare cash,' Ella couldn't resist yelling back at a similar American volume.

'Sorry you haven't got it, lady. See ya.'

'That's me put in my place, then.' They all laughed.

'He's right though. War stinks – especially one with no real reason,' said Abdul Salim Krishnamurthy, before adding, 'From those escaping too much of a good thing to those scraping a bare living from what the good earth provides. Let's see where our salt comes from.'

On the landward side of the main road, were several pits containing sea water pumped up from the ocean, each one higher than the other. Abdul Salim explained that the salinity increases the higher up the water goes until finally the sun has dried out the water enough for the workers to dig out the crystals and carry them to the store house. This was back-breaking work which didn't pay much.

'In the old days, they used to boil up the sea water in huge pots but that method's been abandoned for a long time.'

Ella couldn't take her eyes off an elderly woman, bent almost double, perhaps due to many years of constant brushing and scraping up of salt with a spade, unable to quite straighten up to put her full basket on her head. Another younger woman stood straight up and walked like a model. Both women smiled warmly at the passers-by.

'Bonzour, ki man yer?

'Ca va, et vous?' Ella tried instinctively before thinking, 'Oops, not French, Creole.'

Abdul's reply, 'Bjen merci,' was better understood.

'Quick snack, pink pigeons or coloured sands first?'

'Quick snack, pink pigeons and then sands please.'

Masala tea and a big samosa each, consumed by the roadside, and they were on their way to Casela Bird Park.

'Sorry we're going to have to rush the bird park if we're going to see Chamarel at its best; just before sunset the sunbeams and the shadows play their tricks.

'They were being bowled along by their tour-guide's enthusiasm. Casela's birds included not just the rare Mauritian pink pigeon but also over a hundred exotic birds from all over the world, from ostriches and flamingos to Brazilian parakeets and British kingfishers. Mauritian monkeys called macaques, giant tortoises and some deer added interest to the visit. It had been the most exhilarating day – but it hadn't quite finished.

'What do you mean by coloured sands?' Rick asked.

'D'you want the long answer or the short answer?'

'The interesting one.'

'The different colours, seven they say, were formed when volcanic rocks cooled at different temperatures and the patterns were formed by the sculpting effect of sun rain and wind. I'll leave them to speak for themselves now.'

The taxi struggled up the windy road and through a quaint village, full of palm and mango trees until it came to a halt alongside a few other cars in a clearing in the woodland. Abdul told them that small but constant groups of tourists found their way here to 'The Seven Coloured Sands of Chamarel.' The spectacle lived up to the expectations of its romantic title. Stretching out was an ocean of layers of rock weaved into beautiful patterns merging into a backwash of pink but with shades of red, purple, green, blue, orange and yellow clearly definable. The undulating surface seemed to change colour and shape as clouds moved across the sun.

'You've got here at the right time,' an American tourist with a gigantic camera told them. 'When the sun goes down, you'll see. These colours seem to dance in among the shadows.'

He was right. The Chamarel sands at sunset have a unique and unforgettable charm. All too soon, darkness fell suddenly.

Tantalising smells greeted the three weary travellers when they got to Abdul Salim's home.

'We're back, Chen-chi. Come and meet Ricardo and Ella. Guys, this is Dawn, the best cook in the world.'

'Can I call you Chen-chi?' Ella said.

'Sure, it means brilliant dawn in Cantonese – that's me.'

The evening rushed by accompanied by delicious food and tales of exotic places on Mauritius.

'It's funny how you never visit these places when they're on your doorstep. When are you taking me Salim?'

'When Kai-liang is big enough to enjoy them,' Chen-chi's husband proclaimed. 'He's only ten months old,' he added turning to his guests.

'He's sleeping but he might wake before you go. He kept me so busy today I had to make him sleep while I was cooking.' When Ella looked guilty she added, 'No no, that's every day.'

They looked at the baby album which had Kai-liang written in English in big red letters under some Chinese script that Ella presumed was his name in Cantonese.

'What does Kai-ling mean?'

'Hopeful or optimistic. We're sure he'll have a good future here in Mauritius.

'I wouldn't be surprised,' Ella replied. 'There's definitely something magic about this whole place. Maybe one day Rick and I can come here and live like the cosmopolites we say we are.'

'Cosmopolites?'

'Citizens of the world, belonging to nowhere and everywhere.'

'Ah, but there's a flaw,' philosopher Abdul Salim Krishnamurthy interjected. 'Everybody has to originate from somewhere.'

Ella had to concede. In fact she even declared her pride in being a Scot.

'At least you can say you belong there,' Rick added. 'We Goans have had our identity smudged and we're now scattered around the world. We're Catholics now but who knows what we were before the Portuguese indoctrinated us.'

'The Scots are just as much a mixture of Celts, Vikings, Normans and whatever and they say there are more Scots outside Scotland than there are in it.'

'Here in Mauritius we're such a hotch potch,' Chen-chi declared, 'that there's not much point in digging for roots. We just enjoy the variety. Isn't it the spice of life?'

'Thank you. That's just what I mean by us being cosmopolites. You two are real cosmopolites. If Rick and I have kids, they'll be more cosmopolitan than we are and so it'll go on through the generations.'

'Put like that, it sounds exciting and revolutionary. I'm full of hope for this outcome as the Báh'ái faith teaches it.'

'Unfortunately, Abdul, I still fear the dark side of human nature.'

'Yes, Ricardo, but we have to keep the ideal in our sights or down we'll go into the morass of discord. We must believe that things are improving in this worldwide society or we'll carry on in the same old, negative way.'

'I so agree with you Abdul Salim,' Ella jumped in sensing an ally and possible triumph over her cynical husband. Secretly, what Ella didn't realise, was that Rick actually agreed with most of his wife's views but had a niggling worry that she was so trusting that she was heading for heartache.

'Okay, you lot. We all like mango hedgehogs wherever we come from. Let's eat. Oh no. There's the real boss of the house waking up.' Chen-chi rushed off to fetch a delightful Kai-liang who spent the next half hour, smiling sleepily at a bunch of grinning, indulgent adults of all different colours.

'He's adorable,' Ella gushed. 'He looks like both of you if that's possible.'

'Everybody says that. I reckon he's got my brains and beauty; I'm not sure what his dad has given him except the funny nose.'

Chen-chi's sunny nature warmed the whole atmosphere and Rick and Ella were genuinely sorry to have to say good-bye. Addresses, fond farewells and promises to get together were exchanged. The following day, Abdul Salim would take them along a scenic route from Curepipe to the airport at Plaisance in the south east of the island.

'Did you know that international flights via Mauritius only started this year? You can say you were among the pioneers,' Abdul Salim told Rick and Ella as he finally deposited them at the airport. The morning had been full of even more beautiful scenes, each one unique. From Montagne Blanche the 360° view of green land stretching down to the white fringed deep blue Indian Ocean gave the feeling of being on top of the world. In the distance Isle Aux Cerfs looked like an emerald surrounded by diamonds and aquamarines on a blue background. The shades of blue and green around the shores painted a picture of the varying depths of the surrounding ocean and the encompassing coral reef which could be clearly seen from the mountain top.

'I never want to leave this place, Rick. Who knows what's waiting for us out there?'

But leave they had to, on the next step of their unpredictable and formidable voyage. It had been the most memorable apology Air India could possibly have offered.

# Chapter 18: A Hatch, Match and Dispatch in Goa

The sight of Dad, Santos and little sister Rosie, now 17, at Goa's Panjim airport was both surreal and welcome. The cosmopolites were still reeling in fantasy land from the whistle stop tour of scenic, diversely cultured Mauritius followed by an unscheduled delay in Bombay as they had missed their flight connection to Dabolim airport in Goa. They had had to be put up (again at Air India's expense) at the new, not quite completed Centaur Hotel until another flight could be arranged. An expensive telephone call to a wealthy connection in the village of Verna would hopefully have got a message to someone who could travel to Santos, Olga and Rosie's house at the other side of the coconut plantation.

This fragment of the Fonseca family had floated across the Indian Ocean from Kenya in search of a world that in some ways had stayed the same, but in others had changed beyond all recognition. Rick was meeting his mum, dad and little sister but it wasn't like coming home. Santos had envisaged all the chickens coming back to roost in Goa but instead two had flown to England where they were at least fluent in the language, one had opted for Kenyan citizenship and one was dropping in from some country called Zambia with a white wife and en route to God knows where. The latest shock to the parents' system had been the announcement that Rosie, at seventeen, had met a Goan boy from England on the beach and had got herself civil married in Margao within three weeks so that she could make plans to join him in England for a proper church wedding. The situation had been complicated by the fact that this boy's brother needed a wife too so Olga had put out her feelers in the community for a suitable candidate. The plan now was for a double wedding somewhere in middle England wherever that was – within six months, which meant that Santos and Olga might miss their baby daughter's wedding. None of Ricardo and Ella's wonderfully inspiring tales of travel and cultural diversity could compete with this trauma so a lid was kept on them for the meantime.

The young couple did however reflect Santos and Olga's sombre mood by describing the odd mixture of over the top opulence and utter incompetence that they'd come across at the Centaur. Cold, congealed, inedible curry served on delicate china laid on shiny new golden chargers hadn't been nearly as pleasant as a samosa and a cup of tea at the roadside in Mauritius. Crisp white bed linen had been wonderful but the smell of paint and lack of hot water had cancelled out the positives. The phone call to Verna from the room hadn't been covered by Air India and its cost, Olga said, would have fed a family for a week in Goa.

'Ah well,' Ricardo told his family, 'Abdul Salim Krishnamurthy said we'd have to put up with teething problems.'

'What kind of name is that? Hindu and Moslem. Hmmph,' Santos grumbled, quite unable to cope with any more changes on any horizon. 'Where you met *him?*'

'Mauritius. He was a great guy.'

Ella had to add, 'His wife Chen-chi is Chinese and she's Christian.'

Santos's frown froze the words on her lips. Any comments on how wonderful this cosmopolitan world was might not have been appreciated.

'So where's this Leonard Fernandes then?' Ricardo asked his little sister. He too was shocked that she could be married.

'Oh, he's got his own house and a job in Peterborough and his brother Blasco has civil married Caterina da Costa from Panaji so he's buying a house in the same street.'

'That sounds just great. Do you mean he's there now?'

'Yes and I'll be going there in July for an August double wedding.' The consternation on Olga's face was plain to see. After five years in Goa trying to set up a modern home with running water and electricity and a piece of land for vegetables, mango trees, a few coconut palms plus chickens and little black pigs, their last little bird was about to fly the nest. The others were expressing no wish to return to their father and mother's homeland so with Ricardo's encouragement Santos and Olga were 'reviewing the situation'.

The elderly VW Beetle had managed to get to the airport and back to fetch Ricardo and Ella but, along with the fridge, two days after the guests had arrived, it gave up the ghost. It wasn't until a month later, two days before Ricardo and Ella were due to fly to London, that it was fixed so at least they got a lift back to the airport.

Just before the monsoon in May, the weather in Goa is hot. Cold drinks are craved by pampered globetrotters. With no fridge or car and the nearest bar with a fridge a fifteen minute bike ride away, there was fat chance of such luxuries. Ella tried walking with Rosie to the bar for a chilled drink which was momentarily blissful but, by the time she'd walked home, she felt even more parched. Ricardo had more sense. To his shame, he sent nine year old Agnelo to 'race as fast as he could' on a bike to fetch something chilled; minus any device to keep it cold, the effort was wasted. Agnelo and Rosie provided the solution. They took their hapless visitors down to a shady spot at the bottom of the garden and showed them how to tie a rope round the lip of a brass pitcher and lower it into the well. Up came sweet fresh and refreshingly cool water. The best thirst quencher in the world.

Rather like the Centaur Hotel, the small family home in the village was a 'work in progress'. There was electricity most of the time which was quite unusual in the area. There was also a wet room with a shower head, a tap on one wall, a bucket, a jug and a sloping concrete floor leading to a drainage hole in one corner but there wasn't a regular water supply. Ella and Rick donned swimsuits and decided to fill a bucket from the well and use a jug to pour water over themselves in the garden; Olga didn't think this was an appropriate activity for her daughter-in-law so they enjoyed the treat only once.

'Pity,' Ella whispered. 'That was great fun.' After that it was a bucket and jug job in the wet room. There were two toilets, an eastern and a western. The eastern was the hole in the ground requiring new squatting muscles for the uninitiated and an ability to perform all kinds of tricks to keep skirts or trouser legs free from danger. Ella preferred the western which was easy to sit upon but could only be flushed if you remembered to take a bucket with you to fill the cistern. But the Fonseca's was the best, most modern house in the village for which Ella and Rick were most grateful.

As the heat and humidity built up towards the monsoon season, without constant electricity to power fans or air conditioning, the atmosphere was unbearable day and night. The only tolerable place Ella could find was flat out on the shiny, concrete floor, carefully avoiding the rough hessian mats which seemed to generate even more heat than the bedding.

Olga woke at four a.m. to get on with her cooking before the sun came up; it was a difficult and uncomfortable job to grind spices with two stones, chop meat and vegetables and light the charcoal jiko at the best of times. As the heat of the day rose it would have been impossible. The modern house did have an electric cooker but without electricity it was simply 'maradadi', as Santos said, using a good Swahili word for 'pretty but useless'.

Life was tougher than the Fonsecas had expected. There was also an impression to create, of a family having made their fortune before returning to the homeland, a family used to better conditions such as twenty four hour running water and electricity, a car but perhaps not a telephone. Such conditions were just beginning to make their way into the area of the village where they found themselves and Santos made certain the neighbours knew that his family had been used to a higher standard of living. This may not have endeared the Fonsecas to some of the neighbours and may have attracted a few shifty characters bent on relieving old Santos of some of the cash he didn't actually have.

Fortunately Olga was slightly more aware of those sharks and somehow managed to fend them off.

Ricardo and Ella soon discovered that their visit to Goa wasn't going to be as tourists. Sweaty bus journeys took them to the even sweatier town of Margao to either brave the odoriferous fish market or join long queues to get forms to get Rosie on her way to England to join her legal husband and to start the process of getting Santos and Olga along the same route to join their children. At long last, they had been persuaded that their future was not to be providing a tropical paradise in Goa for their unwilling offspring. Their baby daughter was leaving so they had to follow.

Buses were few and crowded, taxis even rarer, so Ella's 1970s mini-skirts were put to use. Cars screeched to a halt as a white girl in a short skirt hitched a lift by the roadside. When Goan husband and sister leapt out of the bushes, it was too late for drivers to change their minds.

Rick's glee at the success of this little con was almost as great as when there was a similar incident at Bombay Airport. As he told Rosie, on their arrival from Mauritius, there was a confrontation between customs officials and a plump lady who was dripping in gold on fingers, toes, all they way up her arms, legs and possibly hidden parts of her body. There was a good deal of shrieking and throwing of hands in the air while a lengthening queue was snaking its way around a chaotic customs area; Rick and Ella were in the middle but it was Ella who was conspicuous as the only white person there. Whether from a desire to avoid embarrassment, or cultivate a tourist with possible spending power or motivated by some vestige of colonial deference, an elderly airport worker homed in on Ella, put a huge cross on her suitcase and asked her to follow him through the check out. His chin dropped and his hands rose when Rick came too and she explained he was her husband. Safely through and rushing for their connection to Dabolim, Ella whispered, 'I should have said no, on principle, but I thought we would miss the connection.'

'Stuff principle, girl,' Rick added laughing. 'Make the most of it.' As it turned out, they still missed the flight, which Ella felt was poetic justice.

But here she was again, exploiting her visibility, hitching lifts from people who would never have stopped for the local hoi polloi. Rosie had deadlines. Strings had to be pulled. Without a car and only spasmodic public transport, very little could be done. Rosie was anxious she might not make the journey to Northampton in time for the double wedding.

The six week break in Verna produced a hatch, match and dispatch Goa style. Morbidly, the death was the first event. Within a week of Ricardo and Ella's arrival, eighty year old Antonio, the next door neighbour slipped away in his sleep leaving his wife in need of a huge amount of assistance in the absence of any establishment resembling a funeral parlour. The men were immediately summoned to wash and dress the body and a tailor was found to stitch the front half only of a shirt and jacket beneath which he would to be sent to his maker. Olga, Rosie and Ella rushed to the aid and comfort of widow Flavia. Rosie and Ella were given the job of emptying a huge wooden chest of all kinds of fading linen so that its false bottom could be removed to reveal the cash, saved over the years no doubt, for this final occasion. Olga was dispatched to borrow large cooking pots and to recruit cooks to prepare for the funeral feast the size of which could not be predicted except that it was sure to be enormous as no one waited for an invitation to a wake with plenty of food and a guarantee of enough cashew nut brew, feni, and its more distilled version, cajel, to float an ocean liner.

Flavia's two sons set off, cash in hand, to organise priest, choirmaster, bell ringer, candle maker, coffin, gravedigger and whoever else Rosie couldn't translate from Konkani for Ricardo and Ella. Cyclists were sent to the nearby villages to pass the word, a telephone was located for messages to more distant connections and telegrams had to be sent to Dubai and New York to the old man's son and brother. The only daughter was in Delhi and would take a day or two to come so Olga was Flavia's main support with the help of some other neighbours and even Rosie and Ella. Ella wondered about ordering flowers but these would be picked on the morning of the funeral two days later - from gardens or the wild. One of the old lady's fattened, black Goa pigs and several chickens were slaughtered and prepared so Olga could start cooking immediately. Soon the pots were full of sorpotel and chicken xacuti, filling the kitchen and the whole house with a delicious, pungent aroma. Doors were not kept shut as the aroma would come in useful to cover another less pleasant odour should the embalming process be less than successful. Later fish curry, Goa sausage pullao, fried prawns, meat cutlets, king rolls and all kinds of sweets like neuros, bolinaas, baath, kulkuls and dodols would be added to the menu. Fridges were few and electricity intermittent so care had to be taken with fish and rice especially.

For Ella and even Ricardo and Rosie, this funeral was a huge new experience. The open coffin was laid out on a table for all to file past to pay their respects. There seemed to be an endless stream of people of all generations which made it hard for Flavia to keep up the obligatory wail.

Occasionally she would stop and calmly bark out an order about some arrangement that may have been forgotten.

On the day of the funeral the bells of the Holy Cross Church rang with the distinctive knell, 'Ding, dong dong. Ding, dong dong.'

Ella felt alien but Rosie's confession that she felt the same way alleviated her loneliness within an utterly different society. Ricardo was too busy taking part in the relay system of pall bearers who, with slick changeovers, were carrying the coffin the long distance from the house to the church. A band playing funereal dirges drowned the wailing during the procession. The strikingly beautiful old church, built of golden yellow stone, was bursting at the seams with mourners despite its enormity and so full of candles and incense that it was difficult to breathe. The lengthy service was conducted in Konkani with a bit of Latin and English. The hymns were raucous in their enthusiasm except for Ave Maria which was sung in Portuguese by Antonio's little granddaughter in a sweet voice which left not a dry eye in the church.

Another trudge accompanied by mournful laments led to the cemetery where everyone threw soil on the coffin. Given the mass of people this was a lengthy process which had the advantage of almost completing the gravediggers' job.

Back at the house the eating and drinking went on long into the night as more and more mourners kept arriving from far away. Ricardo, relieved to be Rick for a while, escaped with Ella to the relatively quiet and cool verandah at the back of his parents' house - quite overwhelmed by the whole event. Olga and Santos felt duty bound to stay to the bitter end while seventeen year old Rosie had taken the opportunity to hang out with her friends.

'When somebody dies here, the world certainly knows about it.'

'I'm Goan but I don't want to die here. Imagine that hassle.'

'In Scotland I remember the whole thing being hidden away at the undertakers. Then it was in and out of the church in an hour and off to the nearest hotel for tea and sandwiches and a chat about whoever had kicked the bucket . If it was the middle of the harvest, that was it.'

'No booze?'

'Only for the reprobates, my father used to say.'

'You'd better not die in Scotland then.'

Suddenly a hush fell as people decided the wake was over. Rick and Ella went to the front door of the house perhaps to say farewell. A parade of candles in half coconut shells was shuffling away in all directions, some moving in straighter lines than others, but all subdued. There was, at last, after the feasting, a respectful, humbling silence. Three shadowy figures with bedrolls slipped into Santos and Olga's house to sleep off their excesses as it was too far to travel home.

Santos was wide awake, feeling morose, inebriated and in need of tea and a bright light to chase away the demons. Rosie was still wandering and Olga looked exhausted so Ella put a pan of water on the still smouldering jiko and fanned the embers like an expert. Santos lit what he called a Petromax lamp which was only used in emergencies given the price of the methylated spirits and paraffin.

'We used to call those Tilley lamps in Scotland but I haven't seen one in twenty five years. They're very bright aren't they?'

Santos was suffering from some harsh reality and demanded an answer to his question, 'Why did we come back to this old place? Nothing's better. Nothing's changed.'

'I don't know Dad,' Ricardo responded. 'Things have started developing. You can see it won't be long before the changes come.'

'But your mother and I aren't getting any younger and Rosie's decided she's off to London now. Agnelo's got his family in Kenya, Jos has found some Varca girl from Uganda in England and Carlos always said he'd never live in Goa. I don't suppose you and Ella want to settle here.'

'Wrong time to ask. That was some funeral. I think you and Mum should start making plans to join us in UK. What do you think?'

As Olga sat drinking the tea her daughter-in-law had made, on the 'balcao' at the now silent front of the house in the cool of the night, a look of serene acceptance spread over her face. 'Life carries on. We'll see what it brings tomorrow.' That was when Ella really understood what the quintessentially Goan 'susegad' on the 'balcao' meant. She also felt she had been allowed into the world of a strong community held together by shared poverty. She sensed there was a fragility about the society. Talk of the many who had broken loose to 'make their fortunes' revealed a barrier of resentment which would make it hard for the escapees to clamber back. Santos and Olga may not have made their fortune by some standards but they had endeavoured to create that impression. Savings were dwindling but with the help of funds sent by their four sons, they were able to sustain a reasonable standard of living which was a little better than those who lived nearby. Ricardo knew that his vulnerable parents had to get out before some of their impoverished relatives relieved them of most of what they had especially since, at sixty five, Santos was no longer working for a living.

Next morning the three young people were sent off to town to queue for the necessary forms to start the ball rolling for Santos and Olga to join their family in England. Santos had slept not a wink which meant that Olga's night had also been disturbed. She was close to tears and Santos had begun his caged lion stomp around the house. As the car still hadn't been fixed, Ella donned her mini skirt and lipstick. Within five minutes, a hopeful driver had pulled up and picked up three passengers, two of them unexpected.

Not having to wait for rare buses which were full anyway cut hours off the journey. They had soon left the bumpy palm and pedestrian fringed rural road to join the smooth tar on the outskirts of Panaji with its depressing fringe of shanty tents and shacks. Unbelievably these were permanent residences. Untidy piles of coconut shells, building stones, hessian bags of whatever, ramshackle stalls bearing foods and brightly-coloured saris lay slap bang outside the entrances to the tents which were no more than six feet away from the road and the traffic. This was a new slant on working from home; newspaper cones of rice, chillies, dried mangoes, cashew nuts, savouries and sweetmeats were waved through the car window which the irritated driver told his passengers to keep firmly shut. Rosie was worried about being turfed out on the spot so she said something in Konkani which she translated as, 'We'll pay you to drop us near town centre.' He threw his hand in the air shouting in very fast exasperated Konkani. 'He's cussing the bloody Gaudis,' Rosie said chuckling under her breath. As Ella looked out at the small thin people, the women dressed in grubby saris, the men in shabby shorts and shirts, children in rags and everyone barefoot, her first thought was that someone should help them, not cuss them.

The queue was unruly and long outside the municipal building next to the Post Office where the British Consular assistant had set up his team to deal with the many applications for vouchers to go to England. Ricardo sent the girls off to the market and charged into the mass of squashed, sweaty bodies. He was desperate for a cigarette. With his hands pinned to his sides and bodies pushing from behind and in front, there was no chance of that so he was consoling himself by trying to locate his soft pack of Peter Stuyvesant for when he hit the top of the queue and escaped. It wasn't there. In the crush it had been nicked. When he got to window he was in the wrong queue but managed to cash in on the chaos and get to near the top of the right queue.

The official must have reckoned Rick looked prosperous so he stared at him meaningfully while raising his eyebrows and dropping his head from side to side. Eventually the penny dropped and Rick's voice boomed out, 'I got no money. These forms are free. Hey, everybody, watch this guy.' The form was passed over at lightning speed by a scowling but embarrassed paper pusher.

'Most people are too scared to do what you did,' said Rosie on hearing the story later. 'Or, if they're as well-dressed as you, they cross a few palms to get things speeded up.'

'Stuff that. Nobody's getting a penny out of me. Oh,' he added with a slowly spreading grin as he withdrew a very flat but intact packet of Stuyvesant from his top shirt pocket. 'They weren't nicked.'

The next life-changing event was a hatch to follow the dispatch. As often happens, a baby boy was born on the day that Antonio, his grand uncle died. Goan Catholics may proclaim that they don't share the Hindu belief in reincarnation but old Flavia was heard to cry out in Konkani, which Rosie translated, 'He has come back to live again. May God be thanked.'

The baby was named Antonio after the deceased. For forty days the new mother would be constantly pampered and revered, confined within the walls of her home. The little family lived on the other side of the big coconut plantation on the banks of a tributary of the river Zuari which had almost dried up leaving sand-congested prawns stranded and waiting to be picked up for someone's tasty if somewhat sandy dinner. Rosie and Ella had been sent over with two dishes for the new mother, one of chickpeas and coconut and the other of semolina and condensed milk pudding which Olga had prepared. They were believed to be the best foods for producing healthy breast milk.

'It might be nice to have a baby here,' Ella told Rosie.

'Or it might not. It sounds great but some of the girls are driven mental because between their mothers and mothers-in-law, they hardly get to see their own babies. And then the two grannies start arguing about who knows best. I'm getting well away from here to have my kids.'

'Put like that….'

'Your not preggers are you Ella? It's been a few years now.'

'Not yet,' Ella replied hiding an inner anxiety. 'We need to stay in one place for five minutes first.'

To complete the trilogy of events Olga's niece added a match, only part of which Ricardo and Ella were able to attend before they headed off for London via Bombay almost in time to miss the misery of the monsoon turning everything underfoot into a quagmire. Both their escape and the wedding plans had been spoilt by the unusually early arrival of the hot sticky atmosphere and torrential downpours.

Rosie explained how she had escaped most of the rituals associated with a traditional Goan wedding, by finding her Leonard at a swimming party on Colva beach. What her parents didn't know was that he had nearly been lost in the strong backwash amid the huge breakers. He'd been so grateful to Rosie for saving him (which she hadn't) that he'd asked her to marry him and he was handsome so she'd said yes. She confessed to Ella that she had thanked her lucky stars that the current had turned and washed him up on the beach. The problem had been that the first four steps of the process, matchmaking, the meeting of the two families, the proposal and the dowry arrangements had been skipped; her parents wouldn't be happy. Leonard's parents hadn't survived the first winter in England after a lifetime in Kenya. His oldest brother had taken on the bringing up of two younger brothers and a little sister. Though heartbroken, through hard work and sacrifice, the brothers had managed to buy the house in Peterborough where Leonard was planning to take his new bride, Rosie. He had wondered if Rosie would come with a dowry. However, as the wives of Santos and Olga's two married sons hadn't come up with any dowry, it was made clear that this wasn't possible. Cirilo the eldest brother had insisted Leonard and his brother Blasco go to Goa in search of wives. He had stayed in England to earn a crust and make sure little sister Aveline finished school. Leonard felt Cirilo was a saint.

Santos and Olga finally blessed their daughter's engagement to Leonard. They sympathised with the orphan Fernandes family and were bowled over by the young suitor's charms. There would have to be a formal engagement in the presence of a priest with rings and a proper civil marriage ceremony, Goa style, before they would allow Rosie to travel to England.

Next a wife had to be found for Blasco. Olga became the *mali* (matchmaker) and she and Santos took a proposal of marriage on behalf of Blasco's family to the family of Caterina who lived in Panaji and were wealthy enough to perhaps pay a dowry. If there were any dowry arrangements, no-one ever found out about them. There had been a joint engagement ceremony and civil wedding and within a few months the two girls would travel to Peterborough for a joint wedding in an English Catholic Church; Rosie wouldn't be eighteen until September.

In Verna, the full blown traditional Goan wedding was more elaborate and Rosie and Ella could see how Hindu and Christian customs had fused into a fascinating medley of Portuguese and Indian music, dress and rituals forming its own unique blend. The local Goans took it all for granted while Ricardo, now Rick, felt it was so much mumbo jumbo.

Olga took on the role of the mali as the bride Carmen was a relative. She had approached three families with possible suitors for Carmen before finding the right one. Carmen's family lived in a humble clay house near Velsao beach near Mormugao as her father was a fisherman. Despite Carmen's undoubted beauty, families hesitated as any dowry given to a bridegroom was likely to be small or non existent. Eventually a boy called Manuel who was shown Carmen's picture insisted that she might be the one for him, with or without a dowry, so a proposal was made to his family on behalf of Carmen's family.

'Have these two never met, Mum?' Ella asked.

'That's right. That's the custom in some of our families.'

'The families don't know that Manuel and Carmen know each other,' Rosie whispered to Ella. 'They have to pretend they've never met.' The two girls giggled like naughty schoolchildren. It turned out that Carmen, while staying over at a girlfriend's house, had attended one of the many beach parties in the light of only a bonfire where she and Manuel had enjoyed a secret flirtation and had arranged to meet under cover of large groups of youngsters attending sports meetings. They had even avoided the dance floor together at several of the Goan dances, where live bands play Portuguese cum Konkani music and where the gents wear dinner suits and bow ties and the ladies long, flouncy dresses with mantillas in their hair. The two, however, did manage a few secret moments in the shadows. The youngsters were enjoying every moment of this clandestine romance but would never breathe a word to their parents. All they had to do was to say no to any proposals until the parents brought them together. The trick was to give the parents and matchmakers the impression that it had been their idea in the first place. Rosie, in her devious way, had steered her mother the mali in just the right direction.

Next came the *utor* or promise; early in the morning, according to tradition, Manuel's family arrived at Carmen's beach home hoping to be presented with a lighted candle as a sign that the match was approved. The candle (or fire stick) was carried indoors where a long discussion worked out the dowry arrangements and a long list of conditions. It turned out, despite outward appearances of poverty, that Carmen's parents had salted away a respectable sum of money for their only daughter's dowry and for some time her mother had been collecting seven of each of the items her daughter might need in her marriage such as towels, pillowcases, handkerchiefs, underpants, nightgowns or tablecloths. Olga was interested to hear that in Scotland this was called a girl's bottom drawer. It was agreed that the newly-weds would live in a wing of the sprawling home owned by the groom's parents and that the young bride would help out with cooking but would not take full responsibility for feeding the family.

A week later a formal engagement party was held at Carmen's house; two ornamental boxes containing rings and statuettes of the baby Jesus were laid on a low table. Rick and Ella were invited to join both sets of parents and a few other relatives to witness the ceremony. Under the groom's ring was a pile of rupee notes.

'That's the dowry,' Rosie whispered to her less knowledgeable big brother and his foreign wife. An elderly lady painstakingly counted the money twice glancing at Ricardo and Ella from time to time. They tried to look suitably guilty. There had been no question of Ella's family offering a dowry.

After this, events unfolded quickly. Civil registration according to the Portuguese Civil Code was necessary. Ella said she thought the Portuguese had been kicked out in 1961 and was told they had been but the Church required a colonial certificate of registration before the banns could be read in Church for three consecutive weeks.

'A lot of Catholics around here have decided to keep Portuguese passports. They feel they might have to get out as the good jobs are going to the Hindus,' Rosie said.

'I noticed that,' Ricardo replied, 'in the bank, the post office – everywhere. I'm glad you've found your Leonard, Rosie.'

'She's a clever girl, my daughter.' Santos was beginning to come round to the thought of spending his last years away from the beloved Goa which wasn't what it used to be.

To honour the souls of the departed, *Bhikarenchem Jevonn* or a Beggars' Banquet was held on the beach outside Carmen's house. Olga reminded everyone that they had done this in Kisumu for their son Agnelo and his wife Maria and of course it had been successful because they now had a healthy boy and a girl. Prawn and mango curry with rice was served on *patravallis* (plates made from leaves) and huge trays of sweetmeats made from jaggery (unrefined sugar) and coconut among other things was handed round. What stuck in Ella's mind was a strange ritual of cracking open a coconut on the doorstep. Rosie wasn't sure what that meant.

Next Carmen had to go to her uncle's house where another huge meal was consumed by many visitors. Ella was beginning to feel overwhelmed by the non-stop feasting in large groups. After lunch a group of loud *zoti* singers came marching along the beach. Zotis are special songs which accompany the *chuddo* (bangle) ceremony. A fat man, carrying hundreds of bangles of different colours and sizes shuffled up to the house. This was the *cankonkan* or bangle seller. All the ladies were present to watch Carmen's aunt choosing fifteen red and fifteen green bangles of the right size - red for married life and green for fertility. This struck Ella as a very Hindu style custom for a Catholic wedding.

'She's not allowed to do any work until the wedding in case any bangles break. That's unlucky,' Rosie informed Ella as they watched Carmen's aunt presenting the cankonkar with a bunch of bananas, a bowl of rice, a coconut and some coins as payment for the bangles. Everyone clapped and cheered, sang some more and showered Carmen with flowers to add the spectacle of fifteen bangles on each arm. She didn't look too happy. A young bride it appears should look sad at the prospect of leaving her parents.

As luck would have it, Ricardo and Ella's Bombay to London flight was on the morning of the church wedding. Ricardo couldn't wait to be Rick again and was delighted to miss yet another boozy feast. Ella was disappointed. They did manage to witness another strange ritual before they got a taxi to Dabolim airport. This was the *apros* ceremony where Carmen was rubbed from head to toe with purifying coconut juice to symbolise the end of spinsterhood. The same thing would have been happening to Manuel at his house though on a larger scale as the family was wealthier. Ella and Rick told the story of a Hindu wedding in Lusaka where the groom had been purified with yellow haldi; he had promptly come out in a rash which had stayed with him for three days. It was agreed that coconut juice was much better as it had never been known to spoil a honeymoon. Nobody had heard of such a rash. Meantime they would have to wait to hear all about the church service and the reception as well as various post wedding rituals which sounded fairly complicated. Olga told them these might involve the groom's mother fixing a gold chain and cross round the bride's neck, fireworks, lines drawn on the road to separate the two families and too many other little rites to remember. Ella's comment, 'What a fascinating melting pot of Hindu, Christian and Muslim customs,' provoked a shake of Olga's head.

In the midst of all the activity, Olga had been building a mysterious pile of goodies in the corner of her kitchen. Ricardo guessed it was an ominous pile.

'I think she's trying to send our food for the next month with us.'

'Oh Lord. What do we say?'

'Watch and listen. Mum, what's all this?'

'My sons are not going to eat out of tins only. There's a jar of rechad masala, some prawn balchao, a bottle of palm vinegar – that other stuff's no good - some sol and two packs of Goa sausage, one for you and one for Jos and Carlos when you see them. Oh and I'll get Bombay duck from the fish market and some fresh mangoes before you go – and the best cashew nuts – biggest ones. You can't get them anywhere else.'

'Whoa mother. How d'you think people in England live? D'you think there's no food.'

'Not special Goa food.' Olga looked crestfallen. 'Please Ricardo take some for your brothers – even if you want to eat rubbish food yourself.'

'But we can't take all that; we wouldn't get past customs.'

'Yes you would. Everybody does it. Ruby Mendes takes stuff all the time.' Ella was having nothing to do with this spat which Olga was winning. Rick caught up with her in the garden.

'I reckon it's forty love to your mum. I watched and listened.'

'No way. She can forget the Goa sausages and the mangoes stinking up our clothes. Maybe we can take a jar of masala if it's really well wrapped. Can you imagine what would happen if the vinegar bottle broke? She's crazy.'

'I think she's noticed our suitcases are half empty after we off-loaded their presents. And we didn't buy much here. Two spare shirts for you and a ring for me.'

During their weeks in Goa, Ricardo and Ella didn't visit the hippy beaches even once. It had been as if the 'playground of the rich drop outs' aspect of Goa didn't exist. The Goan community made a point of avoiding 'these people', an unbearable blight on their horizon, tolerated because they brought in much needed foreign currency.

Ricardo and Ella's last day was wet. Fortunately, or perhaps not, Dad's old car was roadworthy in time to take them to the airport. Mum had to be left behind by the time everyone else plus suitcases and a separate bag of foodstuffs got squeezed in.

'There's no way this food bag's going to London,' Rick whispered as they finally waved good-bye to an excited Rosie, who was expecting to see them in a few month's time, and a distressed Dad who didn't dare to hope that he might one day escape from the Goa that was no longer paradise.

It had been a tearful parting from Mum accompanied by a string of questions. What was going to happen to them in that cold country with its rivers of blood? What would they eat? When Rosie went to England would they ever see any of their children again? Would Agnelo and Maria and the grandchildren ever come to Goa? Where would she and Santos get money? Wouldn't it be best if all the family came to Goa where they would be safe? Why did everything have to change? And so it went on until Santos shut her up gently but firmly. Normally Olga was the rational one in control but her feelings of desolation and insecurity had taken over. East Africa had dealt the Asians a hard blow, England by all accounts was little better than a nightmare of prejudice and curtailed opportunities and her entire brood of five children had chosen to abandon the motherland. Even Goa felt alien as India had taken over the reigns from Portugal which meant that the Portuguese speaking Catholics were becoming marginalised in their country of birth. If her parents-in-law had been younger or more optimistic, Ella would have told them how wonderful it was to feel like a cosmopolite, a citizen of everywhere and nowhere, happy to be loyal to one's country of birth but prepared to adopt the rest of the world. But it seemed all too radical and adventurous in the face of Rick's parents' real anguish. Despite their youthful optimism over the previous few years, uncertainty over what British Society was going to serve up for them was beginning to crawl over Rick and Ella. It hadn't been a good farewell.

# Chapter 19: Pilgrimage to Eriskay

Ricardo's arrival at Heathrow airport as an unwelcome immigrant was not uneventful. Ella dragged him along with her in the queue for British subjects, as opposed to Commonwealth subjects, expecting him to be welcomed as her husband.

'I feel like Margaret and Eleanor sitting on the wrong buses in South Africa.'

'Better watch out. These girls only got driven to the nearest border. I might get put on the next plane out.'

'Sorry, wrong queue.'

'He's my husband.'

'I said wrong queue.'

An hour later having crept up the right queue, Rick was whisked off to a back room where he was strip-searched and X-rayed. Ella waited some more. The cool chill of politeness prevailed. Rick spared her some of the details of his humiliation.

They walked through the green area despite the Goan liquor and what was left of the food after they had unloaded most of it in the direction of some beggars in Bombay. Their bravado paid off so they emerged into London expecting to see Jos, Carlos or both. Santos had instructed Rosie to send a letter telling them to be sure to meet them.

'Excuse me sir. Would you be Ricardo Fonseca?'

'Yes. Who are you?'

'I'm Carlos Fonseca's chauffeur. He asked me to collect you and your wife. I'm afraid he has an important business meeting.'

'Bollocks. He's hardly out of his nappies.' Ricardo recognised the same silly sense of humour that he shared with his brothers.

'No, please sir. Come this way.'

'Anybody that drives an old banger like this can't afford a chauffeur,' Ella said taking her turn to join in the fun. A familiar figure jumped out from behind a pillar. Carlos. At twenty three he was an almost pharmacist but more to the point his 'chauffeur' friend Rahul was qualified so could afford four wheels and had a flat above the shop in Hayes quite near Heathrow Airport where he had found a job. He didn't need the flat as he was living with his parents. He hadn't found a tenant or a wife to move in with him so did Rick and Ella want to stay there until they found somewhere else? Rick and Ella did – until they saw it. It was an empty shell with a bare mattress on the floor in one room. At least it had a two bar electric fire, a bathroom and a kitchen with a fridge, a two plate electric hob and one pot for boiling water. This was back to basics.

'Lovely,' Ella sighed. 'Do you think somebody could dream up a sleeping bag and pillows?' The lads hadn't thought of that, or anything else for that matter, but within half an hour, Rahul had fetched a couple of pillows a sheet and a duvet. He'd also brought a box of coffee, milk, sugar, ginger snaps, bread, butter, jam and two each of mugs, plates, knives forks and teaspoons.

'Mum was out at work. She won't even notice they're gone. Sorry, you could've stayed with us but there are seven kids younger than me and with mum and dad working all the hours it's ... well... Rick you might be all right but I don't think you would like our mad house Ella.'

'Fine,' Ella said weakly feeling somewhat discriminated against.

'I told Rahul you wanted to find jobs in London so you'd need a base for a while – so ... ahem.' Ricardo was quick to add that they needed to visit Scotland first before starting the job hunt. This saved Ella from screaming, I wanna go home. I want ma mum. She just added, 'There's stuff we need to do.'

'Like what?' young Carlos asked.

'Like visit my parents and pay our respects to a special friend who died not so long ago.' Carlos's expression made Ella regret her sharp tone. 'But thanks for all this.'

'Will we be able to stay when we get back,' Ricardo added, 'just for a few days? We can pay rent. We wouldn't expect anything else.'

'Wait and see. You don't know how long you'll take to get jobs. There are twenty two thousand teachers out of a job.'

'We haven't even decided where we want to be,' Ella said quickly, anxious that she and Rick kept control of their own movements. Next was a meal out at a nearby Indian restaurant, where they giggled stupidly over some thin young Indian guys who kept appearing and disappearing through a hatch in the floor probably from the cellar. Carlos had decided they must be illegals and every pop out or pop in caused another fit of giggles.

'They're too thin to be legal.' This caused more hilarity and later, alone on their lonely mattress in its empty room, the slightly older and supposedly more mature Rick and Ella reflected on how cruel their laughter had been if these fellows were, in fact, hiding in cramped conditions under a floor. Ella shared her thoughts on how much the London she had known had changed and how there was no way she wanted to stay in Rahul's flat a minute longer than they had to and please could they jump on a train to Scotland the very next day. As it turned out Carlos had to get back to his studies and Rahul to work so that's what they did.

After five years of Africa, Mauritius, India and Goa, Ella was in desperate need of the familiarity of people and places of her youth. It was going to be wonderful to find people who knew all about you and your family history, people you didn't need to explain things to. Life in Britain with Rick wasn't going to be boring but it would be different. No longer could she blend in. As a couple they would be a curiosity, sometimes sought after sometimes shunned, never disregarded. Rick was optimistic, happy to explore his wife's country just as she was happy to see it through her husband's starry eyes. For the moment it was all an adventure.

Early next morning, they took the tube to Kings Cross and booked a sleeper to Inverness. Rick wanted to see Nelson's Column as they had some time to kill so, leaving their suitcases in left luggage, they jumped on the tube again to Leicester Square. Ricardo was mesmerised but came to the conclusion that if you could read, you could never get lost in London. Ella watched Rick's enchanted curiosity which delighted her. She described to him her first experience of the London Underground when, before sliding doors were brought in, the constant banging of heavy wooden doors used to reverberate around the hollow tunnel like machine-gun fire. The litter and cigarette smoke were pretty unbearable they decided but for a cheap and fast way of getting around, it was worth the discomfort. Ella managed to get them completely lost coming out of one of the many exits at Leicester Square but as there were so many new sights to devour, from the neon lights of theatre land to the pavement artists and varied shops and restaurants, it didn't matter a jot.

At one point Ricardo collapsed into giggles. 'Look at this. What kind of crazy country have you brought me to?' He was pointing to a pair of boots neatly placed on the pavement with a notice on them which read, 'BACK IN FIVE MINUTES'.

'I can't believe nobody'll nick them,' Rick went on. 'Shall we wait for five minutes?'

'Don't be daft but I suppose we could check if they're still there on the way back to the station.'

'Now who's daft?' As a compromise they nipped into the nearest café to observe from a distance over a cappuccino.

Nobody had come after twenty minutes so they decided like some things, like potholes bigger than cars, could only happen in Africa but this was a case of 'only in London'.

Trafalgar Square proved equally intriguing to Rick who had expected Nelson's column to be smaller and hadn't expected birdshit everywhere in a so-called developed country. He wasn't impressed that it was a traditional pleasure for British children to come and feed the pigeons in Trafalgar Square. Rick was, however, impressed by the sheer size and beauty of the surrounding buildings, The National Gallery, St Martins in the Fields, The Canadian Embassy and of course South Africa House where a few protesters, black and white, were attempting to bring the world's attention to the horrors of apartheid. Rick wanted to talk to them. They were surprised that anyone had paid any attention to them. After a bit of 'Rick' chat, about citizens of the world, the protesters invited them to a meeting that evening.

'Sorry, we've booked a train to Scotland but keep up the good fight. Somebody will listen one day.'

'Right now, most people seem to have no idea what apartheid is – or they don't care.'

'One day they will,' was Ella's contribution. 'Come on Rick; let's see if our boots are still there.' They left the protesters with a quizzical look on their faces. The boots were there so they left them and headed for Piccadilly Circus and pizza for mid afternoon lunch cum dinner before heading for the train. Eros fascinated Rick. He didn't believe it was made of aluminium so Ella gave up trying to convince him. He felt the statue's classical beauty didn't fit with the red buses and the gaudy adverts and Ella had to agree.

Ella had been explaining the concept of the selling of the Big Issue and how this helped homeless people to help themselves when along came a fellow with his pile of magazines shouting, 'Roll up, roll up! Queen Mother pregnant. Read all about it.' Another 'only in London' moment. Rick had to buy a copy.

'You deserve your hundred and fifty percent profit sir – for the laugh.' '

'Ta very much, Mate. They're hoping it's a boy this time – after two girls.' Ella had to explain that one.

The two giggled their carefree way back to Leicester Square station and once on the train chatted loudly without inhibition which amused some and irritated others. Suddenly, a lull in their conversation made them conscious of the enveloping hush.

'D'you think they've been listening to our every word?' Rick whispered. A sheepish grin was the only reply so they resorted to people-watching.

In June 1977, at 5pm, London's quiet commuters were a mixed bunch of races who had quickly learned to conform to the sedate silent British reserve of daily tube travel. Earlier in the day, the carriage had been full of bubbly young visitors from all over the world producing an unintelligible babel of countless different languages.

'The place is full of cosmopolites,' said Ella, 'like us.'

'I wasn't expecting this. I imagined mostly white with the odd brown or black and everybody speaking BBC English.'

'Nothing so boring it would appear. Maybe there's a market for English teachers around here.' With a germ of an idea growing, Ella was happier to set off for her native Scotland with the confidence that, if all else failed, there might be a career available in London. Rick wasn't so sure. 'I'd rather take my chances where there aren't so many foreigners putting pressure on communities. Why don't we try Scotland where people know you and there aren't so many immigrants?'

'We can have a go.' However, Ella wasn't sure that the parochial attitude of some of the folks back home would allow them to settle into the new life and career that Rick's optimism was envisaging.

Kings Cross British Rail station was less cosmopolitan; not many non-Scots seemed to be going to Inverness on the non-stop sleeper train. Rick was at last feeling in the minority and it wasn't quite as comfortable as he expected. Passers by were now rude enough to stare. Ella noticed, in Rick, the symptoms of vague discomfort that she herself had been going through as a Mzungu in Africa and a foreigner in Goa.

'The only other black guy's making the tea.'

'Get used to it. You're the novelty now.' As it was the late sleeper there was no dinner so the two decided to settle down for the night. Rick commandeered the top bunk as there was less chance of a foot in his face in the morning and proceeded to cuddle in beside Ella until she chucked him out. They would need their sleep if they were going to cope with the spotlight.

The journey rattled and hissed its way through the night echoing the anxieties and waning confidence of Rick and Ella. Were they prepared for the reactions? Was remote Caithness ready to accept these two rebels whose subterfuge consisted of being outwardly brimming with confidence?

It was late afternoon before Ella finally rang home from Altnabervie Station.

'Mackay, Hillside.'

'Hi Dad. We took the train to Altnabervie to save ye a journey.'

'We were gettin' a wee bit worried here. See you in ten minutes.' Twenty minutes of unfounded anxiety later they were back in the extended family who had gathered for their 'tea' to welcome Ella and Rick home. From Granny Mackay to Jamie and Katy's new baby Graham, a wee brother to Hughie, everyone was very welcoming so the rebels forgot they were supposed to be rebels. After a few days of pampered luxury, it was time to set off for Eriskay in an old Ford that Charlie had located in Altnabervie motors. He'd been quoted £220 but Rick managed to get it for £150.

'I dinna ken how ye did that,' was Charlie's grumpy comment. 'Jimmy Green's a gie skinflint usually.'

'He'll have to get up earlier to catch me,' was his son-in-law's smug reply. To add insult to injury, Rick was the only one in the family who could get his tank filled during the 1977 petrol shortage as he'd charmed the owner of the petrol station who had spent a few years in Nairobi.

'He probably wants to make sure I leave,' Rick said before anybody else got that in first.

Everyone understood the pilgrimage that Ella and Rick had to make in memory of Kirsty. They told everyone they had promised to visit Sister Immaculata's mother, Kirsty's grandmother.

'I take my hat off to that nun and priest that came traipsin' up here after your wedding and thon funeral,' Charlie was heard to say. 'It was an awfa tragic death o' that lassie.'

Sister and Father had travelled that long distance to assure Charlie and Mary that their daughter would be absolutely fine as Ricardo's wife. They had been right to guess that the Catholic aspect had been more of a stumbling block than race in the midst of 'Wee Free' country. Born in Eriskay near where a firm line was drawn across the Outer Hebrides between the lands of the Catholics and the Protestants, Sister understood that only too well. Charlie and Mary had warmed to them. Only very special people could travel so far in the midst of their own personal tragedy to reassure two complete strangers of the welfare of their daughter. The nun and priest had hoped they had succeeded. It would ease the pain a little.

The 1970 Ford Escort had new tyres so Rick and Ella were confident that it would survive the drive to the Kyle of Lochalsh ferry to Skye and then the ferry from Uig to

Lochmaddy on North Uist from where they could drive south to Lochboisdale on the southern tip of South Uist - just across the water from Eriskay. Simple.

'Let's just drive until we're tired and stop at the pretty places,' Ella suggested. 'We're sure to find B and B somewhere.' So they ambled through the lonely beauty of Strath Halladan where they met one car in fifty miles down to quaint Helmsdale where boats chugged across a glassy North Sea in a sunlight which was paler than the fiery tropical sun. From Helmsdale south through Brora and Golspie to the Dornoch Firth the sea twinkled but didn't rage.

'I'll take you where my dad and mum used to stop for a treat. Come on.' Kincraig House Hotel provided a luxurious setting with views of the Cromarty Firth and produced a pot of tea for two with sandwiches and home baking piled on a three-tiered silver and fine china cake stand.

'We're not supposed to finish all this, are we?'

'If you like. If you're greedy.'

Rick had one more bit of fluffy sponge and stopped.

'We don't need dinner now. We can drive until it's dark.'

'That'll be ten o'clock.'

'Oh yeah, I forgot. Fine, let's do it.'

In no time at all, on the faster road, they had reached Dingwall and were speeding past Beauly towards Drumnadrochit on Loch Ness.

'We're not going to make the last ferry across to Skye. Let's find the nearest B and B and spot the monster in the morning.'

'Good idea. Who knows when we'll be footloose like this again? Just look at this scenery!'

The winding road had emerged from trees to reveal the pale evening sun over the glassy loch which reflected the dark hills on the far bank. Rick pulled up by the roadside. The only sounds were of birdsong and the tiny splashes of ripples hitting the bank of the loch. No other cars. The dying sun kept changing the pale colours of the loch and the dark hues of the distant hills, making them seem like living creatures. It was easy to see how monsters could loom in the imagination.

'Where's everybody?'

'It's tea time.'

The two lingered, thinking their silent thoughts. Who needed the rest of the world? What did it matter if one of them would be living every day as a foreigner? But which one? Surprisingly it was Rick who spoke first, revealing that their telepathic communication was in working order.

'I could stay here, you know.'

'Aye, but a bonny view doesn't pay the bills.'

A passing car disturbed their reverie so they set off in search of bed and breakfast, drinking in the views of dramatic Urquhart Castle protruding from the trees and reflected in the changing shades of Loch Ness along the way. No roadside B and B signs appeared until a few miles south of Drumnadrochit.

'That's it!' Ella shouted pointing upwards at a traditional cottage smothered in pink roses which overlooked the loch from a point high above the road. They struggled up the windy road and parked on (or in) the pebbles outside the front door. 'Monadhliath View' was burnt into a wooden sign above the door. Another plaque depicted a wild cat and a golden eagle in the same burnt into wood style. The board by the roadside had read, 'Bed and Breakfast £6:50 Vacancies Betty and Sandy Macbeth proprietors.'

Monadhliath Cottage was the cottage Ella always used to draw she told old Betty and Sandy and where had the name come from she asked. They could see the Monadhliath Mountains they were told where the River Findhorn rose from Carn Mairg and went all the way north to Findhorn where Sandy was born. On the south east side of the Monadhliaths was Strathspey and Kingussie where Betty was born.

'From here, we feel home's not really that far away - just over the top.'

'Aye,' replied Sandy. 'Wi a helicopter we'd be there in a jiffy. Otherwise it's a gie climb.'

Rick commented on the beautiful name plaque and soon found out that Sandy called himself a pyrographic artist who worked mainly in wood but sometimes in leather. While Betty was getting a 'wee bit o' supper' ready, Ella and Rick were given a tour of the shed where Sandy's amazing work ranged from pieces of furniture to plates, bowls, name plaques and pictures.

'I suppose it was natural,' Sandy began, glad of a captive audience. 'My dad was a blacksmith and when the smiddy closed down, the old tools were hanging around for years. Not that I use any of them, now. I used to heat wire on the furnace oot the back years ago but it's a deen wi electricity now. See my wood-burning pen. It's got twelve tips of all shapes and sizes. And this is my new wood burning station. I just took a lead from the house and I can make as many smells as I like. Leather smells pretty bad but the wood smells wonderful, especially cedar, though it's sometimes too soft to keep a design. It can crumble.'

The old man was in his element and he managed to sell a picture of Urquhart Castle to Rick, who never usually bought mementoes.

Betty was an equally good salesperson. Over a supper of cocoa and rock cakes she almost persuaded them to book a few nights because the Loch Ness Monster had definitely been spotted the other day.

'My dad,' said Ella, 'always used to say that ye needed at least half a bottle of whisky inside ye to see the monster. Anyway we're on our way to Eriskay. We should have been in Skye tonight.'

In the early morning, there was a veil of filmy white condensation floating over the loch but no monster. After Betty's obligatory porridge and heather honey followed by kippers and mushrooms, toast and strong coffee, the mist had cleared to reveal a mirror-like loch but still no monster.

'Make sure you come back and see us,' Betty called as they started down the hill. The two wanderers said of course they would.

A milestone read Kyle of Lochalsh 65miles. It would be a slow 65 miles past the rushing waterfalls at Invermoriston, and the dramatic scenery up Glenmoriston past the hill of the dragon, Dundreggan, and over the old Torgoyle bridge.

It was slow because the road was single track with passing places, a nightmare for those in a rush, but perfect for two people stepping aside from a world they were hesitant to join.

Every bend produced another scene bathed in whatever light the changing sky would allow with its sunshine cloud and rain. Wet fisherman persevered on a navy blue Loch Cluanie. Ten minutes later, bright sunshine lit up the site of the Battle of Glenshiel where the Spanish joined the Jacobites in a bid to beat the English and failed. They stopped to soak up the spooky atmosphere and as they imagined the battle sounds from a dim and distant past, a dark cloud loomed above the steep-sided glen and a gentle rain began to fall and the young couple shivered.

As the narrow road snaked its way out of Glenshiel and on towards Loch Duich, the craggy peaks of the five sisters of Kintail reared up by the roadside looking too insurmountable to be the renowned paradise for climbers. Clouds swirled down and obliterated the summits and the rain pelted down as the journey continued along the north shore of Loch Duich.

The heavy shower passed, the sun appeared and along with it a rainbow grew out of the fairy tale castle of Eilean Donan, arcing across sky and loch and disappearing behind a mountain range.

'That's unbelievably beautiful,' was all that Rick could say as once again he felt compelled to pull up by the roadside.

'Even the air is a mixture of pink and purple.' Ella gasped. 'I sometimes think these picture postcards have been faked but look at this. Amazing. I wish we hadn't lost the camera. Can you believe that castle is almost a complete wreck? The family have been trying to find funds to restore it for years.'

'I hope there's a petrol pump somewhere soon. The gauge is flashing.' Fortunately they managed to freewheel into Dornie village where petrol, though expensive at 70 new pence a gallon, was at least available.

'Ye're lucky there's ony left,' the attendant told them as he cranked the wooden handle back and forth. 'We haven'ae seen a tanker for three weeks. I have tae gie ye a 10 gallon limit.'

'Will that get us to Uig?' Ella asked as Rick collected three pound notes in change. 'We're trying to get to Eriskay.'

'Och aye, easy. And there's never a shortage of petrol on the islands. There aren't that many cars.'

Ella wasn't too sure about that; they decided they could leave the car on Skye and take ferries and buses through North Uist, Benbecula and South Uist to Eriskay if necessary.

Five miles on they were in a queue of six cars waiting to board the ferry from Kyle of Lochalsh to Kyleakin on Skye. One of the two small ferries was chugging noisily back from Skye to pick them up. It looked too tiny to pack on six cars but with a hand-operated swivel platform spooning the vehicles (without passengers) on deck, eight could be transported. Passengers had to sit on slatted wooden benches protected from going overboard by a high rail but left open to the wet, cold and windy elements. Thirty breezy minutes later, seven cars and a van were deposited on Skye after a series of swivels and shunts.

Heading west along the coast with the spectacular Cuillin Hills on the left and the views across the sea to the many islands, headlands and bays of the Scottish west coast, Ella and Rick felt the magic.

The picturesque little town of Broadford with its tiny harbour and snowy white and pink houses hugging the bay had several cafés and a petrol station with an unlimited supply of fuel so they filled up with soup, a sandwich and petrol and set off confident that the car would, after all, reach Eriskay. Uig was in their sights and the ferry journey was likely to be long.

'Your lucky it's Wednesday. You've missed the 2 o'clock ferry but there's an extra one at 6 o'clock on a Wednesday. You won't get to Lochmaddy 'til 8 o'clock so I'd better send you to my auntie's B and B or you'll be sleeping in your car.' This was the very helpful ferryman with a lilting island accent who was drinking tea from a thermos as he waited for the North Uist ferry to get back for the turnaround.

'They change the crew which is a good thing. It means I can sleep in my own bed.'

Ella was trying to work out the logic of this when he added,

'You'll be needing some tea. I'd be going into the Uig Arms if I were you. There's not a lot on the boat worth eating or drinking.'

Rick decided he'd be feeding the fish if he ate too much but managed an enormous mug of strong sweet tea. Ella managed scrambled egg on toast and a smaller mug of tea.

By 5:30, the car was loaded and they had located the toilet, the bar and some reasonably comfortable leather seats. Up on deck, watching the white horses of the wake as the sun was going down, seemed like the best bet.

'You'll never get sick on deck if it's calm, Rick. Oh look at these seagulls; they're going to follow us all the way.'

It stayed light for the two hour journey but an evening chill made them glad of the extra sweaters they had carried.

Lochmaddy turned out to be another village in another bay just like the villages in Skye but without a tree in sight. As the ferry sidled up to the ferry berth and was moored to one of the huge black capstans, the lights of the village began to twinkle.

'It's Jeannie Macdonald you're looking for,' the ferryman told us. 'If I didn't have to finish off here, I'd show you the way. If you turn right at the blue house on the harbour road and go inland you'll see the B and B sign on the right about 100 yards along. Just tell her Haimish sent you.'

'Thanks Haimish,' Ella yelled back.

Jeannie was used to the last minute passing trade but had no room in the house. Would the caravan do? Her children loved it when they were banished to make room for paying guests and it was always kept spotless she told them. Her two children had gone off to boarding school in Stornoway. There was no secondary education on Uist they were informed.

'They're very chatty, these islanders,' Rick said later as they settled into the clean and comfortable caravan for the night. Jeannie came out with a tray of hot chocolate and digestive biscuits.

'You can't be going to sleep on an empty stomach. And you after a long journey.' Rick's rumbling stomach was very grateful. He'd forgotten he'd skipped dinner or 'tea' or whatever it was he didn't have. In the morning, Ella was furious with Rick for having a moonlight pee in the garden. He hadn't realised doors are rarely locked in the Outer Hebrides and he could easily have slipped into the house.

'There aren't even any trees to hide behind, dummy. What if you had been spotted?'

'It was pitch black – and look at me.'

Breakfast consisted of bacon, one egg, tea (no coffee), one slice of toast, many apologies because the supply boat wasn't due until that afternoon and an equal number of assurances that it wasn't a problem. They paid just £5 and set off with instructions that there was only one main road and if they kept going through Benbecula and South Uist it would eventually take them to the nearest point to Eriskay. What happened then would depend on the tide. Jeannie's parting words were,

"Chust don't talk about religion if you meet any of the natives. There's a definite line somewhere around Benbecula, north of which are the Wee Frees and south of which are the Papists. They're equally bad at insulting each other.'

Out on the narrow open road which stretched to the horizon through flat moorland dotted with small lochs, there was no evidence of human habitation apart from the odd lone fisherman casting his line far back from the road. The air smelt fresh and cool. Time didn't seem of the essence so the two cosmopolites paused to listen to the seagulls and savour the freedom of wide open space.

As they drove off later, over the brow of a tiny hill, they came across Hector.

A tall, imposing middle-aged man with enormous black eyebrows over blue eyes was in the middle of the road, holding up his hand, so Rick had no alternative but to slam on the brakes.

'Hector Macdonald of Clanranald - déraciné. My mother was a MacAulay and my grandmother a Lamont and a great singer.'

'A pleasure to meet you, Hector. Ella Fonseca, née Mackay, and my husband Ricardo.'

'A fellow déraciné, I suppose.' Hector was staring fixedly at Rick.

Ella decided to respond with a suspicious frown, feeling relieved that the rear doors of the car were locked. Hector, with his expensive but worn tweed jacket, ruddy cheeks, nose like a Belisha beacon and bags under his eyes as big as a highland pony's nosebag, had seen better days - and certainly better mornings after the night before.

'Goot morning,' he trilled in a well-spoken island accent. 'I once met a chentleman chust like yourself, brown he was too,' he lilted, 'but he had a handkerchief tied on top of his head. Now why might that have been, would'choo think?

'How can we help you, Hector?' Ella asked, trying to sound distant and intimidating. She wasn't intrigued. Rick was.

'Jump in,' Rick called in reply to a request for a lift to Benbecula Airport.

The air in the car was no longer fresh. Hector pulled out a half bottle of White Horse whisky from his back pocket.

'I can't pay for the petrol but I could offer you a dram – as a gesture of good will.'

'No problem Hector. It's on our way as there only seems to be one road.' Rick waved his hand and shook his head.'

'Then I shall guide you through the maze of streets and avenues on these crowded isles, by way of a thank you.'

Ella decided to make an effort. 'So what is it that you've been uprooted from Hector?'

'Ah, a lady of letters.'

'Not quite – just schoolgirl French.'

'I think I might chust have been detached from my means of remuneration - again.'

'How did you manage that?

'You'd have to consult my friend John Barleycorn on that one.'

'Sorry.'

'Don't be. I was merely the pot scrubber in the Loch nam Madadh Hotel, Lochmaddy to you – that is until last night. A bit of a step down from Professor of Archaeology at Glasgow University a few years back, eh?'

'I'd say so.'

'One couldn't tell by looking at the bare devastation now, but these magical isles have ancient history oozing from every inch of the land and water. You chust have to know where to look for it. Did you know they were once covered in forest? And that there were large townships in the centre of the land? Or that every loch had a man-made island with a crannog on it which housed an extended family? I know the whereabouts of the vestiges of every broch, crannog, wheelhouse and dun (they're chust ancient dwellings) in the entire Outer Hebrides but a fat lot of good that has done me. My family would have been rich and noble at one time, from the fishing and kelp industries, but now there's nothing left. We were descended from the Kings of Argyll. So, you see, despite my appearance, I am a true son of Somerled. Today the castles are in ruins, the lochs filled up with sand and all the young people have fled – either pushed out to the Americas or the Antipodes to make way for sheep or pulled out in search of any old job to keep them alive!'

Rick and Ella listened with a mixture of fascination and alarm. Hector was clearly unstable – the disillusioned fanatic – but there was something compelling about his story, a poignancy which could have driven him to drink.

'It sounds like you know more about your heritage than most,' Ella ventured tentatively.

'Ah my little red-headed Viking Mackay, that may be, but that makes it all the harder. I came to find my roots after studying the history of this place for years - only to find that it was my own people who had pulled them up and scattered the flowers across the world. There's nothing left but empty sadness.'

'Except a beautiful refuge from the noisy, dirty cities,' Ella tried.

There was no consoling the old man. He had another swig of whisky and went on. 'Nobody cares about these days gone by. And nobody stays here long. There's nothing to breathe back life into the place.'

'But it's so beautiful,' Rick retorted. 'All kinds of visitors would come if they were encouraged to.'

'You're right. I'm just a drunken old fool with an almost empty glass. Don't listen to me. What brings you two, very different young people may I say, to Uist?

'We've come to visit our bridesmaid. Her... she's on Eriskay,' Ella said catching Rick's eye. She had no wish to add to the angst of Hector Macdonald of Clanranald.

'Would that be Nurse Macdonald's young granddaughter Kirsty MacAulay? A desperately sad affair. Now she's one who *has* come back but only to her final resting place.' An even more dejected expression spread over Hector's face.

'We were trying to spare you ....'

'Och, there are so few people around that everyone knows everyone. At any rate, it was a gigantic funeral with people coming from all over the world. I was there myself as I have connections on both sides of the family.'

'She was a lovely girl,' Ella began feeling a lump in her throat, 'and a good friend. We never saw her after our wedding but I feel her around from time to time.'

'Ah, so you too have the sight, Ella Mackay. With that flaming hair my dear, you must have Viking blood but the name's not Hebridean. Where are you from? Sutherland?'

'Caithness.'

The old man nodded his head and went on. 'Ricardo, is it? What banished you from your homeland wherever that was and what on earth got you mixed up with a fiery red head?'

Ricardo's tone was brisk with a touch of impatience. 'My parents left Goa for a better life in Kenya - at the invitation of the British - but before their time, there was a sad history of Goa that's probably better forgotten. As for Ella and me – we met while teaching in Africa. There was a bit of a sad history there too. But we decided to concentrate on hope for the future '

Hector's sorry state didn't prevent him from getting the point.

'Am I to feel chastised, young man?'

Ricardo raised his eyebrows, almost imperceptibly.

'Ah but this was a grand place and Caisteal Bhuirg was the finest castle in all the Western Isles. The churches were called teampulls and there was one for every twenty farms. And all this showed the wealth and noble status of the Clanranald Chiefs, my ancestors. What I would give to have been alive then!'

A glimpse of the proud, handsome man Hector must once have been shone out and died away. Silence returned as Hector withdrew into himself - defeated by the disappearance of History.

'Stop the car, Rick. Let's get out! What's the point of grieving over what's dead and gone?'

The car drew up at a lay-by just short of the causeway between North Uist and Benbecula. Ella had noticed there was a discreet dustbin nearby. Ella took a deep breath.

'Hector. You say these islands are oozing history if you know where to look. Why mourn that? We don't know where these ancient monuments and dwellings are and neither do the other tourists – but *you* do. Why don't you use all that knowledge you've gained? Did you say you are a professor?

'Was.'

'Do you still remember what you learned?'

'Of course. It eats my heart out every day.'

'Couldn't you develop heritage centres for visitors? I'm sure they'd employ you.' As Hector shook his head, Ella carried on, 'What's stopping you?' The older man's shoulders lifted up in a hopeless gesture.

'I'll tell you,' Rick butted in. 'You'll find that in your hip pocket.'

'I know – but I'll need help to kick it. I'm on my way to my sister's near the airport - if she'll have me. My wife's already kicked me out and my kids don't want to know. Why is it, Ella and Ricardo, that it's easier to talk to strangers than to your own folk?'

'Maybe because strangers don't know what's gone on and they've nothing to forgive?'

'Aye lassie, ye could be right.'

'Is there anything left in that bottle?' Rick asked.

'A couple of drams maybe,' Hector guessed holding it up.

'In Zambia where we've just come from, they always pour a drink on the soil to keep the ancestors happy.'

'And then you can throw the empty bottle in that bin,' Ella added.

'I like the idea of giving the ancestors a dram but not here. Come with me, I want to show you something. We'll have to drive across the causeway first though – the one the locals built by throwing boulders in until the whole thing was above sea-level. Now, wasn't that a marvellous thing to do.' Hector drew himself up and marched towards the car. 'Let's go.'

The drive across the narrow causeway in full sunshine with the waves splashing the wheels felt like driving on top of the Atlantic Ocean. Hector shared Rick and Ella's excitement and kept chattering on about the 'ideas' that were filling his head though he wouldn't say what these were.

'We have to go off the A 865 and take the B road past the airport,' Hector called excitedly and wondered why Rick and Ella were laughing.

'If this is an A road, what's the B road like?' They soon discovered it was the same but narrower. As they came to a substantial house near the sea, Hector called out, 'That's my sister's guest house. I'll ask ye to take me back there in a while if that's okay. I'm looking for the ancestors right now; we'll have to walk the rest of the way off the road.'

They came across a moss-covered ruin with a mass of thistles growing between two gable ends and half a wall on the seaward side. Crumbling gravestones lay askew at various angles to the rough ground.

'This,' announced Hector, 'is a chapel built over an ancient teampull used by the Clanranald as far back as the 14th century. It's here that I'll share my last ever dram with the Sons of Somerled, long gone never to return!' The melodrama had to be seen to be believed and the two cosmopolites had to struggle to hide a smile. Hector was in his element. They pretended to take a swig from Hector's unceremonious bottle of cheap White Horse and watched him drink deeply. A dribble survived to appease the forefathers. It was even harder to conceal a guffaw.

Rick forced his face back into a serious expression and announced, 'That dram won't be wasted. Your ancestors are sure to be watching over you now.'

'Laddie, if ye believe that, ye'll believe that Bonnie Prince Charlie wasn't a waste of space. Unfortunately he was. Now, come and have a cup of tea at my sister Flora's house where her namesake gave the wee runt shelter.'

'Hector, you know it was Hanoverian propaganda that made him into a runt. I thought you Macdonalds were Jacobites through and through.'

'Och, ye're right but too many decent Jacobites perished to save him and he never came back to champion the cause. Too busy womanising in Paris – or drinking wine. He died a drunk you know.'

Pots and kettles sprang to mind but Hector was on a roll, folding his tall body into the car.

Flora looked surprised to see her brother and intrigued when Ella announced, 'Hector has poured his very last dram on his ancestors at the chapel ruin.'

'Oh yes. Now fancy that,' Flora said gently with a wistful look.

'But he's going to need help.'

'He knows there's a place in the Edinburgh Clinic. We'll see. He has to make that decision himself.'

'Flora, love, will ye take me there on the next flight ye can get – and tie my hands together if ye have to? I want to do it this time. I've got plans. We need to teach the tourists about the history of the isles. Please will ye help me?'

'We've been here before,' Flora told Ella in the kitchen over the kettle, 'but he seems a wee bit more determined this time. I tried to keep money from him but he chust went and got a job at some hotel, washing dishes or some such thing. Did he tell you he was a professor? Well, it's true.'

'That's pretty clear. He's got an amazing mind. There's something that really touches me about him - and I think he likes us too.'

'Would ye stay the night and set off for Eriskay in the morning? Let's see if you two can help me to get his head together over supper. I'm afraid it's only smoked salmon again and a few tatties.'

'*Only* smoked salmon. That's a treat for us.'

The evening's conversation spiralled into travel tales of Africa, Mauritius, Caithness and Goa, of cultural collisions and integrations, youthful optimism, exuberance and hope for the future, but finally the incredible sadness of the taking too soon of Kirsty MacAulay.

Five minutes after supper, Hector was snoring in his chair, but not until he'd bared his soul revealing his shame over his greedy forefathers and laid out his plans for new heritage centres and reconstructed crannogs and brochs and for developing the archaeological records in a way that he only had the expertise to carry out.

'My ancestors have spread over the world but their descendants are getting on with the future. Maybe I can preserve their past for posterity.'

The beam on his face and the indulgent smile on Flora's made his dream seem possible. Time would tell. His last melodramatic words before he fell asleep were music to Ella's soul though Rick remained firmly sceptical.

'No more wallowing in moribundity for me! It's up and on… if I can banish old John Barleycorn. You two are the face of the future. When I weaken, I'll think of you blazing a trail into a better world. May your god bless you if you have one. If you haven't, may your descendants thank you.'

After Flora had gently woken her brother and persuaded him to go off to bed, she explained how he had got into such a 'terrible predicament with the drink' as she put it. He'd been happily married with a young boy and girl when his wife had fallen for an American visiting lecturer and taken herself and the children off to Boston with him.

Hector had been crushed, but for a while had buried himself in his research.

'I suspect he thought she might come back, or that at least he'd see the children again, but when it became apparent that this was never going to happen he just kind of turned his head to the wall and gave in to the bottle. But I've got a place for him in Edinburgh so if I get two seats on the next flight out, I'll make sure he gets there before he changes his mind.'

'Has he been there before?'

'Yes, I'm afraid so but this time he seems more positive. Can you do him a favour, please? He seems to have taken to you two. Make sure you write to him. He might be in there for weeks if not months. Can you leave an address, too?'

'Well, we've no idea where we'll be, except it'll probably be London, but I can leave my parents' address in Caithness.'

'And we can always phone him. He's quite an inspirational fellow, isn't he – despite being an old soak.' Ella was about to point out Rick's lack of tact, when Flora laughed out loud. She was under no illusions.

Next morning after a hearty bowl of porridge, Rick and Ella set off southwards with instructions to look for what a sleepy Hector called 'The Paradox of the Isles' and report back to him their thoughts. They'd find her just off the A road in the north of South Uist he told them.

Ella thought she knew what he was on about but decided to let Rick find out for himself.

'And don't forget to look for Flora Macdonald's birthplace. I might be doing something about that old heap of rubble soon.'

'Wow,' sighed Rick. 'That was an experience. What a character!'

'I don't think we've heard the last of him either. Let's hope the news is good when we do hear.'

Before long, distances being short and traffic non-existent, they had driven round the coastal B road and joined the main road just as it was about to cross the causeway to South Uist. Flat land dotted with lochans to the east and wide sandy beaches to the west and the road crossing water continued. All of a sudden a thirty foot, granite statue reared up by the roadside which Rick was surprised to see was of the Virgin Mary.

'The Wee Frees in Caithness didn't build this then?'

'No,' Ella laughed, 'but a priest they called Father Rocket, if I remember correctly, had it built. Look over there. That's an RAF rocket range. They test-fired a US guided nuclear missile there in 1959 which could have got as far as Russia from Germany.'

'So this must be Hector's paradox.' The Catholic Goan part of Ricardo needed some time to stand by the statue. An elderly lady on a bicycle stopped to talk, 'We call her our Queen of Peace or *Moire Mhin Mhathar* which is the Gaelic for Sweet Mother Mary. She has saved us from the worst effects of the rocket building.' After quickly making the sign of the cross, she climbed on her bike and pedalled off without a backward glance.

'Do you remember the film 'Whisky Galore'?' Ella asked Rick. 'They made a 'Rockets Galore' but I believe it wasn't so good. I never saw it.'

'I did; my dad took me to it one Saturday morning in Kisumu in Kenya. Can you believe that? I'm sure Donald Sinden was in it.'

A few dozen more lochs along the way, they came across a sign to Flora Macdonald's birthplace and a short walk took them to a cairn of stones erected in the ruin of an old farmhouse. A few other visitors were wandering around.

'Och, there no even very sure if this is the real place,' a woman with a Glasgow accent informed them. 'They're needin' thae anchorologists tae come and dig aboot and find oot.'

Rick and Ella exchanged glances and thought about Hector.

'Stop. Time to find Kirsty's Granny,' Ella said as they drove up to a wee shoppie by the roadside. There only seemed to be jars of sweeties, tins of baked beans and Baxters soup, packets of shortbread, bottles of iron brew and a selection of cigarettes. The door was wide open but there wasn't a shopkeeper in sight.

'The boat's due in tomorrow,' a voice gently emanated from the back. 'The stock's low, I'm afraid.'

'Excuse me. Do you know where we can find Mrs Mary Macdonald?'

A tiny old lady with a huge smile shuffled through the door behind the counter and leant heavily on her elbows.

'Ah, that'll be Nurse Macdonald. She's retired now, just last year. She'll be eighty soon. She lives in the only house with a black roof on Eriskay. Ye'll be able to see it from the boat, quite clearly.'

'Thank... '

'Mind you, if you're sick, you'd be better of at the hospital.'

'Oh no we're n...

'She doesn't keep any medicines now, you see.'

'That's ok we'd just like to visit her. Thank you. Bye,' Rick said in his loudest fastest voice as he hurried out of the shop.

Ella smiled at the old lady, 'We met her daughter and granddaughter so we just want to say hello.' The old lady nodded, her curiosity satisfied. The sad look in her eyes suggested that she too had heard of the untimely demise of young Kirsty MacAulay.

'There's a small boat at every ten past and back again on the hour but there's no car ferry until Wednesday,' the old lady added. 'My name's Sheena Mackinnon, by the way.'

Ella knew exactly what the old lady wanted. 'I'm Ella Fonseca and that's my husband Ricardo back in the car already. He hasn't slowed down to island pace yet.'

'Aye. Nothing's very far away is it. It's not even lunchtime yet and I bet you've come down from Lochmaddy.'

'Only Nunton. Bye and thanks.'

'Oh, you maybe stayed at Flora's guest house.' This time, Ella just waved and said nothing. Rick was impatient and the old lady's curiosity remained unsatisfied...

'There's a boat in half an hour, if we're quick.'

'What's your hurry? Anyway, I'm hungry. Can I just go back and buy a snack. I don't see any cafes or restaurants around.'

'Don't answer any more of Old Busybody's questions then.'

'She's probably lonely.'

'Nosey, more like it. Hurry up.'

'Iron brew and shortbread. Like it or lump it.'

Eventually the road whose number the locals didn't know just ended so the car had to be parked and locked.

The boatman at the nearby pile of rocks that passed for a jetty was waiting for them.

'Is it Eriskay, ye want?' Minutes later they were chugging across the water like Para Handy with only the boatman, a newspaper, some letters, a chicken and themselves on board. They found out that the graveyard was over a hill near the church and that it wouldn't take them long to walk all around the island. Nurse Macdonald's house was pointed out and yes, it was the only one with a black roof. The houses were dotted around at random where there seemed to be a flat part of land between rocky outcrops. There was no sign of a road but there was an old car parked outside one of the cottages. The boatman switched off the engine and packed his 'messages' in a haversack and set off walking.

The silence was interrupted only by the gentle splashing of tiny waves on the shore. The reflection of the pale summer sun in the light blue sky danced across the water, and though it was warm, Ella shivered, rooted to the spot. A pony clip clopped over the horizon, unbridled and free to wander; the ocean was his fence.

Ella wondered what cruel twist of fate had ended in Kirsty dying on a deserted Zambian road. She hoped her friend hadn't lingered too long in pain but she would never know. If only she hadn't asked her to come to Lusaka to choose the material for her bridesmaid's dress. She might not have met Vanko and they might not have been driving too fast along the Great North Way. A minute later there might not have been another vehicle to smash into. Father and Sister had never revealed the details of the crash, hoping to spare them some pain, no doubt. Sometimes she felt that Kirsty was speaking to her, telling her everything was going to be fine, that she and Ricardo would be happy, that she was watching over them. It seemed so real. When she told Rick she'd seen Kirsty in her sleep, he would nod and stay quiet – understanding Ella's need to grieve.

Rick was quiet now. He withdrew and took a walk along the beach.

Ella thought of Sister Mary Kabwe the nun who had said in retrospect, 'I did think it was a blood and bandages wedding.'

If only Kirsty hadn't chosen red material for her dress. If only the flowers hadn't been red and white roses and carnations – the only flowers Sunita could find at the time. If only they hadn't gone to the Ridgeway and met Vanko. If only, if only, if only and none of these if onlys any damned use.

'I can't go and see Kirsty's granny like this. I need to find the graveyard first.' So arm in arm the young husband and wife clambered over the rocky hillock, down past Bonny Prince Charlie's beach which they recognised from a painting in Flora's house and along to the graveyard where rows of simple crosses, Celtic crosses and granite slabs nestled into a grassy slope. A cloud blotted out the sun and a light breeze brought a chill to the air. Ella could feel Kirsty's presence and stumbled across her grave almost at once. Rick didn't react but later admitted to being spooked by the eerie atmosphere.

Kirsty Jean MacAulay
Born: October 6th 1950
Died: April 23rd 1972
"Taken too soon
Is her song unfinished?
Or never ending?"

At last the tears flowed freely until Ella's unfounded guilt melted away and she could look on Kirsty's memory as a blessing. The long chats into the night came flooding back when the two girls had aired their views. The optimism of youth had seen a smooth transition from the dark days of the past and the bright days of the future. Kirsty had taught history and inspired her Zambian pupils with the words of the recently assassinated Martin Luther King. She had talked of the beautiful babies that Ricardo and Ella would make and how the world needed more people to break down the barriers of colour and creed. There would be nothing odd about feeling Kirsty's spirit all around her, pointing her in the right direction, breathing hope and courage into the difficult times she and Ricardo would have to face. They would listen to her dead friend's never ending song. Best of all, Ella could see her friend's face clearly, the blue eyes, the fair skin, slightly freckled by the African sun and the frame of blue-black hair, smelling of the silvikrin shampoo from the giant bottle she had brought out from Edinburgh. The notion of her endless presence didn't seem so strange.

Rick put his arms round her shoulders and pulled her up from a kneeling position. She rubbed her knees to remove the grass and shook her legs to ease the pins and needles.

'You've been there for ages. Let's go and see Granny Macdonald.'

'Yes, I'm ready. I'll tell her that Kirsty's memory has become a treasure. I can tell her what a good soul she was and that we'll never forget her and that nothing can harm her now and she'll always stay beautiful and never grow old and... .' The words tumbled out bringing more tears with them.

It was another house a child would draw - with a door, two windows down and two up, a chimney and a roof which should have been red but was black. Purple convolvulus festooned the door. They had to ring the doorbell twice.

'The blue one of these is your mother's morning glory,' Ella said as the door finally began to open. 'And we call the white one bindweed in Caithness.'

'And here in Eriskay it's Bonnie Prince Charlie's flower. They say he brought the seeds for it from France.' Nurse Macdonald at eighty was tall and straight with a mass ·of snowy white hair and clear blue eyes. Her hearing was good too.

Ella explained that Kirsty had been their bridesmaid and they had been to pay their respects at the graveside.

'Well now, fancy that,' the old lady said sounding just like her daughter Sister Immaculata, Ella's one time headmistress. 'Sister and Father have just left. In fact we were talking about you.'

It seemed like Granny's mind had gone. Ella and Ricardo had left Sister and Father five thousand miles away in remote Zambia. Nurse Macdonald caught their exchanged glance.

'No, I haven't taken leave of my senses. Come to the window. Look.' Sure enough, the white habit and veil of a nun and the tall, chunky unmistakable figure of Father O'Malley were perched on the same boat that had brought Ella and Rick to Eriskay.

'Their flight to Edinburgh isn't until 4 o'clock. If you help me to wash up their teacups, you'll have time for some tea and scones before you go and meet them at Balivanich.'

'Balivanich?' Rick and Ella hadn't registered the name of the village where the airport on Benbecula had been built.

'Ye'll be wanting to see them while you're all here on The Isles.'

'Yes, of course. I can't believe this. What a coincidence.'

'The Lord works in strange ways. Mind you, I'll never understand why he chose to take that bonny lass so early.'

'I had a good cry at the graveside just now, Mrs Macdonald and we're never going to forget her; she was a very special person…'

Ella's words tumbled out once more and it seemed to comfort the old lady that this young couple would be cherishing the memory of her granddaughter. Her own faith had helped her to come to terms with this and many other pointless deaths throughout her four score years. Her only comment was, 'Aye, it seems like the best go earliest.'

Rick brought up how they had met Hector Macdonald of Clanranald and how he wanted to bring the history of the islands to life and preserve it for posterity. Mrs Macdonald said she knew him and hoped he could pull himself together in time to do that before he met his maker. This lady pulled no punches.

After tea, scones and washing up because there was just time until the boat, there were good bye handshakes and waves before Rick and Ella ran down the rocky path and jumped on board. The boatman, and everyone else around, would, by now, know all about this Indian man and Scottish woman and their reasons for being on Eriskay.

'How long will it take us to drive to the airport?'

'Oh, it's not far. You'll be there in very good time for the Edinburgh flight.'

'How did you „,?'

'It's the only flight today. Did Nurse Macdonald tell you her daughter who took the veil had been visiting?'

'She did. It's unbelievable. We left them five thousand miles away in Zambia a few weeks ago. We used to work together.'

'I see.' The boatman had another piece of the jigsaw to relate to the curious community. Ella decided to complete the puzzle before any rumours spread.

'I used to teach with Nurse Macdonald's granddaughter and she was bridesmaid at our wedding. I suppose you heard that she died in a road accident.'

He seemed satisfied with the explanation.

Once in the car, Rick was in rushing mode again, anxious that they might miss meeting Father and Sister,

'Boo,' said Ella behind Sister's ear and it was a joy to hear her infectious giggle.

'We've just been talking about you,' Father O'Malley's voice boomed out mingled with laughter. That was the second time they'd heard that within the space of a few hours.

'Aw, we thought we'd surprise you,' Rick said, feigning disappointment. 'Yes,' said Sister, 'but look who's here. They're on our flight.' Walking towards them carrying trays with sandwiches and drinks were Hector and Flora Macdonald.

'Och, it's an even smaller world on The Isles,' said Ella enjoying the coincidence.

Hector was looking grey and shaking visibly but his smile was bright and the bags under his eyes were perhaps a smidgen smaller.

'I got us seats today because the flight's half empty and we'll be there by tonight,' Flora announced with a sigh of relief.

'The sooner the better before delirium tremens sets in,' Hector announced revealing that his academic brain was still in control. 'I woke up with the horrible picture of that ill-tricket beesom from Lochmaddy Hotel screaming that I was drunk in charge of the pots and pans and I had to go. I think that might have been just before I bumped into you two bright young sparks.'

'I have to say, I almost sympathise with the woman,' Rick said with a grin. 'You were well into the hair of the dog when we met you.'

'Ah but I never lost control of my faculties. Can you believe this Father? They persuaded me to part with my last dram by pouring it on the soil for my ancestors. The water of life wasted on the dead and gone. God knows what inspiration persuaded me to do that.'

'If I remember rightly,' Ella added amid hilarity. 'You swallowed a huge dram from the bottle and left half a teaspoonful for the ancestors.'

'Well. I don't remember that … exactly.'

'And do you remember your promise?'

'Was that the one to dry out and then work to preserve the history of the Western Isles for posterity?'

'That's it.'

'Rather rash. I'd need a grant for that. There's a lot to do.'

'You know Glasgow said the money was there if you could prove you could handle the project,' Flora said tentatively.

'Okay. Let everyone here present witness my pledge. By the time I'm fifty, I will be a sober man with the financial means to reconstruct a medieval crannog big enough to house a museum of the history and archaeology of The Western Isles.'

He bowed expecting applause which was politely delivered by all except Rick who told him he'd better hurry up then as it couldn't be that long until he was fifty..

'However,' he continued. 'I want you, Ricardo, and you, Ella Mackay Fonseca, to do what you must to break down the barriers of creed and colour that hold this world to ransom.'

'We can try – but please call me Rick.'

Ella declared confidently, 'I promise that one day, I don't know when, I'll write a book about just that – when the world's ready. And in that book, there'll be a character based on Kirsty MacAulay who believed so strongly in the brotherhood of man.' This was followed by another bow and more applause.

'Kirsty always called me Ricardo because she liked the name. Remember?'

Time would tell if these endeavours would be realised but, at that moment, they were sincerely undertaken, albeit with a touch of melodrama.

Conversation turned to Zambia and the serendipity of the meeting of these six people at this tiny airport on this small island. Addresses and warm hugs were exchanged as if they all six were long lost friends. As the four walked away to board the small plane Rick shouted.

'So you wouldn't recommend the Lochmaddy Hotel, Hector.'

'It's fine but you'd better not mention my name.'

# Chapter 19: Welcome or Not?

The anonymity of London felt like a release from prison after the small communities of Caithness and The Western Isles. Though the people who mattered were generous and outgoing and kept any parochial attitudes firmly buttoned up, the endless questions about their well-being and future plans finally drove Ella and Rick away.

London was the big, beautiful bustling city where they could live the life of the unfettered and the uninhibited. But they needed money and a place to live. Jobs could be found but not as teachers. Rick (the name Ricardo was now abandoned) took pride in the fact that he had never claimed the dole and never would. He never did.

'Temping' through an agency would pay rent near Parliament Hill which Ella felt was a safe part of London. A friend of a friend of Ella's sister Morag had asked them to 'look after' a small flat in South Hill Park while they were on holiday which gave them time to flat hunt. They were unaware that every time they walked past the Magdala pub on the way to the bus, they were passing two bullet holes in the wall where Ruth Ellis had shot her lover dead and become the last woman to be hanged for murder in Britain.

A small ad in the 'Ham and High' had read, '1 bed s/c flat bath/kitch/phone/TV 21g pcm' 4552121 so they had quickly found a red phone box and rushed round to an enormous Hampstead house where a little man with a big nose ushered them into a gloomy room piled high with dusty newspapers.

'Ah, the front basement in Tanza Road.'

Were they going to be living in half a cellar?

'It's a lovely clean flat with everything you need. That's twenty one guineas in advance and twenty one guineas as a deposit.'

'What are guineas?' Rick asked in his most intimidating voice. Nobody was going to pull the wool over his eyes. The man kept his head down and avoided eye contact. From a wall cupboard which had to be unlocked, he drew out an old-fashioned but highly polished black cash box with brass trimmings and handle. He selected a brass key from a large bunch of keys clipped to his waist-belt and opened the box, making sure that the lid hid its contents from his new tenants. He spoke precisely.

'A guinea, young man, is proper currency – used by gentlemen. Its value is twenty one shillings. Twenty one guineas are worth twenty pounds plus twenty one more shillings. As a shilling is now worth ten new pence and there are one hundred pence in the pound, I make that twenty two pounds and ten pence you owe me in advance - and the same again as a deposit. That makes a total of forty four pounds and twenty pence.

As Rick and Ella had only fifty pounds between them, Rick tried, 'Shall we call it forty pounds then?' That was when he discovered that you don't mess with little men with big noses in Hampstead especially when you're at their mercy and in need of a roof over your head.

'Take it or leave it. You won't find better at the price!' he barked while releasing another two keys from his waistband. He weighed them in his left hand as he waited for his money.

'I need change,' Rick snapped. He got the exact amount.

'Here's the address. If it doesn't suit, bring the keys back and I'll return your money, no questions asked – or I'll see you at six o'clock next Friday for next week's rent. I'll come to you.'

'What if we're working?'

'Phone me and I can come on Sunday – but I'd rather not.'

After they'd escaped from the lugubrious old house and their eccentric new landlord, Rick and Ella laughed loudly and looked at each other in disbelief.

'I didn't think people like him still existed in 1977!'

'What kind of country have you brought me to?'

Rick and Ella loved their bijou front basement flat which backed on to Parliament Hill fields. Wall and ceiling mirrors doubled its size and helped you forget that you had to climb, or fall, on the bed to get into the bedroom, or get out of the 'galley' kitchen before anyone else could get through to the loo, shower and sink which were of dolls' house proportions. There was, however, a new gas cooker with an eye-level grill and a friendly, red, whistling kettle to put on the hob.

Ella and Rick walked a lot; buses didn't tend to go through those narrow leafy backstreets. They walked to buy The Times Ed., to check in at The Keystones Employment Agency or to buy just enough food to survive. They had a little money from their work in Zambia but devaluation of the kwacha meant this amount was even less by the time it reached their bank in London.

Then they got their first job. The pay was £1 an hour, 2p above the minimum wage, and they worked a 40 hour week for three weeks until a BP share issue, generated by the discovery of a new North Sea oil field, was processed. On day one, they opened envelopes, day two, they were allowed to take the contents out, day three, they were promoted to the job of classifying the cheques according to value and day four, they reached the pinnacle of that particular career and were selected to check the piles and secure them with paper clips.

They blew some of the first pay packet on steak and a bottle of wine. The ex Headmaster and his ex Head of English couldn't afford to be proud. Ella sold shoes in Oxford Street, Rick organised the delivery of newspapers from a Pakistani corner shop, starting at 4 am. He worked in a cocktail bar while she filed letters in an office. They both considered taking on a franchise to manage a branch of a stationery chain. And they constantly checked the situations vacant columns.

Rick might have had the chance of a Science teacher's job but he had taken one look at the young punk rockers with their green hair, safety pins in their ears and foul language and decided teaching in London wasn't for him. Ella was told that most of the 22,000 teachers out of work were in English and Geography, her subjects.

Meantime, life had to go on. Networking had to be done and contacts made. Friends and relatives of all hues and beliefs from Scotland, the Midlands, Kenya, Zambia, Goa, Ireland, USA, Canada and even Australia descended on their little flat en route somewhere else via London. Rick and Ella didn't know they had so many friends (or, perhaps in a lonely moment, had made the mistake of posting off a cheery 'keep in touch' message to everyone in their address book.) They had soon established their identity as the cosmopolites of the street – and the neighbours were curious.

Rick had enjoyed a visit from his brothers in Peterborough and Ella had enjoyed a visit from her brother Jamie and his wife Katie who had left the kids on the farm with Granny and Granddad Mackay to come to the big smoke.

Cosmopolites need to be reminded of their roots from time to time. Feeling flat after her Scottish relatives had left, Ella dialled Flora's number on Benbecula. The progress of Hector's recovery and new project and thinking about her own plans would keep her sights set on the long term future.

'How's Hector?'

'He's chust dragged two huge boxes down from the loft and he's been spreading maps all over the tables in the house. He's driving me mad but he's still dry. Thank you so much for phoning him in Edinburgh; he had a very bad time I think but he might be through it now. He's gone to a meeting in Glasgow about a grant from the Development Board.'

'That's fantastic. Tell him we're still surviving in London but we haven't found any gold on the pavements yet. Can I write to him at your address if that's ok.'

'He'd like that. When he flags, I remind him that you and your Ricardo will be wanting to visit his new museum soon.'

Rick contacted the Goans through a cousin in South London. The community had grown enormously and was busy creating a home from home in London as they had done in Africa, Canada or anywhere else the diaspora had taken them. The dances in Catholic Church halls were flamboyant with live Goan bands, extravagant food and loads of booze. Ella joined in, up to a point, but at times felt alienated. She couldn't understand why so many people seemed to be obsessed with discussing other peoples' successes and failure. Much of the conversation seemed to be shrouded in petty envy though Ella wondered if the chinwaggers realised that. Her instinct was to clam up or talk about the weather. She persevered though, as, for Rick's sake, contacts had to be made and opportunities created. Rick's knowledge of Konkani left a lot to be desired but there were many Goans in his position. Ella remembered Rick's little sister Rosie's sad plea all these years ago.

'How can I know where I'm going, if I don't know where I've come from?'

There was a resonance which linked in with Hector and his need to preserve the history of his native Western Isles.

When Rick was bemoaning the fact that he couldn't go to concerts which his sparse Konkani was unable to cope with, Ella's comment was,

'So your Konkani's lousy. I know two songs in Scottish Gaelic and I'm not sure I understand all the words. Does it really matter? If it does, why don't you do a course and learn it.'

It turned out that it didn't matter *that* much.

Rick got dragged along to a ceilidh where he decided he and the Gay Gordons didn't get along. Rick and Ella had a huge row. Although they'd had many tiffs, this one was serious.

'Your father was right, Ella, when he said we'd be on the edges of two societies and part of neither.'

'If that's how you feel I might as well pack up and go to Caithness. I can pick up a job tomorrow without you dragging me down.'

'Oh really. Then that's what I think you should do. I wouldn't want to ruin your future. I can share a place in Peterborough with Jos and Carlos. *They* won't care about what kind of job I get.'

'That's unfair. I've never said I want you to have a high-powered job. You're the one that's putting yourself under pressure.'

'Well, I won't need to now. I'll help you pack. I'll call a taxi and after you've gone, I'll sort out the flat. I'll send you a cheque with half the deposit.'

'I'll do my own packing, thank you – but you can book a taxi to Kings Cross in an hour.'

The quivering silence that followed was aching with distress. Ella felt nauseous but nothing was going to make her back down. They had tried and they had failed. There were too many stumbling blocks and she felt too depressed to expect anything other than doors closed in their faces. Rick was consumed with guilt. What had he done to Ella? Where was the tough and happy go lucky girl he had known just a short time ago?. He remembered her uncle quoting a statistic he had hated and disbelieved. He had maintained that most interracial marriages didn't survive longer than five years. Rick and Ella's marriage had passed the five year milestone. They would have to face reality. The world, even cosmopolitan London, was not ready for them.

The taxi came and left with Ella and her suitcase. She'd managed to croak that everything in the flat was Rick's and she didn't want half of the deposit. He'd need the money. Rick had been unable even to croak. He stuffed his hands in his pockets and turned his back on Ella as she went through the door. He didn't want her to see his pain. If she had, she might have stayed. As it was, all she remembered was a cold, uncaring gesture.

For Ella, desperation set in. What could she say to her parents? How would she cope with failure in everyone's eyes? Did she really want to go through life without Rick?

Rick sat on the saggy armchair staring at the ancient TV set flickering meaninglessly. Every fibre in his body wanted Ella to come home but nothing, but nothing, would persuade him to beg her to return. He didn't know where to start looking for her. Perhaps she'd be at Kings Cross – or would it be St Pancras? He didn't know and inside he was screaming.

Ella arrived at Kings Cross feeling like a rag doll. She'd forgotten her guitar in its battered case which she'd left hanging on a hook behind the bedroom door. She missed it – but, what she missed more than anything, was Rick. She joined the queue at the ticket office and decided she wouldn't ring her parents. By the time she got to Altnabervie, she felt she'd have enough strength to pretend she was on a surprise visit. She'd think of some reason why, by then. She got as far as third in the queue.

Night had fallen and Rick was still sitting on that chair in front of that TV – motionless - when the doorbell rang.

'I couldn't go.'

'Thank God for that.'

The compromise was to embrace the London culture of the seventies. Jubilee street parties were for everyone, regardless of creed or colour and the two were young enough to hit a few nightclubs and had just enough cash to enjoy the odd theatre show, museum, art gallery or random exhibition. Life was rich but not in money.

Still they ploughed on with job applications. Ella was one of two hundred applicants for an English teacher's job at a girls' school. With recent experience only in Africa and very little knowledge of current set texts, she had little chance despite being short-listed. Rick's fourteen letters a day finally paid off when he got two job offers on the same day. Ella came home from her shift at the café to find him with an envelope at each elbow.

'9 to 5 with the civil service and very safe, or commission only but sky's the limit if you're prepared to slog and stupid enough to take chances?'

'It's up to you. Have you got the bottle?'

Ella knew there was no contest. He just needed a safety net.

The decision was still pending by the next morning so the two decided to take what turned out to be a life-changing walk down Piccadilly. A scruffy young man with long hair, earrings and a sandwich board advertising English lessons for foreigners approached Rick.

'Excuse me sir; do you need any English lessons?'

'I think I have enough of the language to cope thank you.'

'You don't need any teachers, do you?'

'Are you busy right now?'

A few hours later, Ella, armed with a pile of London tube maps (purloined from Covent Garden Station along the way), was in front of twenty young students from four continents; she began to help them unravel the complexities of 'if' in the English language. Rick, having little better to do, was her competent assistant.

The enthusiastic smiles on the fresh young faces from Argentina to Hong Kong, Mozambique, Switzerland and Zanzibar, and many other nations between, opened the curtains of uncertainty to reveal multilingual London in all its optimistic glory. If they grasped their opportunities, the young teachers decided, they would be able to fly.

Next day, as Ella set off for her new school, Rick was heading towards his high potential, high risk new job.

The parachute was in place so, confident of a warm embrace from the big smoke's great melting pot, though unsure of where they might land, the young cosmopolites jumped.

# *Epilogue*

Marble floors, petals in a bowl, smiles, chatter and icy papaya juice welcome the travellers while chilled flannels wipe away the heat and dust of the long journey, soothing the mosquito bites. Retired from long working lives, Rick and Ella have arrived at Haathi Mahal (The Elephant's Palace), Cavelossim, Goa

Two days on from packing swimsuits in a snowy London, they've had the luxury Kingfisher flying experience, survived the putrid aromas of down market Mumbai and been mesmerised by India's landscape rushing by while sampling the culinary joys of the ACC (Air Conditioning plus CHAIR) carriage on the Konkan Railway to Goa. Vendors' cries of 'Chai,' 'Coffee' and 'Samosas' are still ringing in their ears as they move from real India to tourist Goa.

But they don't quite cross over. Ella is the only non-Goan in their group of eight. Gifts of Quality Street chocolates are exchanged for recheado masala, stone ground using cashew vinegar. The family reunions are as precious as these unattainable gifts. New babies are displayed, departed relatives mourned and meals of Goan delicacies, cooked with love and washed down with cashew fenny (Goa's fire water), are punctuated with laughter and tears.

Varka Sports Club 'Fat Fat' Carnival Dance is the place to be. Opposite the white church a huge, red, illuminated arch leads into a driveway crammed with motor scooters transporting young men with girls perched side saddle, if in a skirt, or 'full on' if wearing trousers. Their taxi negotiates the swarm and deposits us at an outdoor arena three times the size of Wembley festooned by fairy lights and giant masks. Four bands play a variety of dance music and there is an air of fancy dress as people quickstep in big wigs, masks or cowboy hats. Girls in saris hover shyly, not really allowed out.

Next day a family friend taxis them to the spot, unknown to tourists, where ninety two themed floats and many costumed marchers are preparing for the 2010 Margao Carnival Parade. They feel _so_ privileged. The dazzling spectacle and exuberant, pulsating music are soon bowling us along. Brightly painted messages read, 'GOA GARDEN OF LOVE AND PEACE - KEEP IT GREEN' 'MOCHIACHEN DUKAN' (shoe shop) and 'HEAL MOTHER EARTH'. Giant monkeys, tigers, butterflies, fish, cows, chickens and even Spiderman bring their own messages. Indian cultures mingle but the overarching message is VIVA CARNIVAL VIVA GOA. Water pistols filled with the red paint of Holi spray people on the road home merging the Hindu festival with the Goan Catholic Mardi Gras.

Back on the tourist trail, they visit the Sahakari Spice farm, help bath an elephant and swim in the plunge pool of the Dudhsagar (Ocean of Milk) Falls. Beach lolling, karma spa treatments and visits to dentists, who suggest cheap Hollywood veneer smiles, reveal a different Goa.

Rick and Ella take a quiet moment to collect holy water for his ninety year old mum, now alone in England, from the spring near the church where she was married.

★

The words of Hector Macdonald 'of Clanranald' spring to mind.

'To spread our wings far and wide, we need strong roots that run deep.' No longer an alcoholic or 'déraciné', Hector has two obsessions, preserving the history of his native Outer Hebrides and following the progress of Ella Mackay Fonseca, of Viking heritage, her Portuguese Indian husband and their progeny.

Ella's wee big brother Jamie is tying the knot for a second time at the age of sixty seven – two days before their mother, Mary Mackay, would have been a hundred. It is a day full of hope that sad times will be forgotten and old wounds healed. A wedding with tartan trimmings, button holes with magnets, the Gay Gordons and a new wee girl in the family speaking to her Granny – mixing up her English with her Doric and contemplating her new Polish school friends of 2009 – remind Ella of the roots which stay firmly in the ground however far the wanderer travels.

# Fit Wye?

Fit wye div we hae tae spik Doric?
Ah speirt ma Granny yestreen.
There's nae mony fowk wi the habit
And some are nae awfa keen.

Noo, foo can ye ask sic a question?
Get back tae yer roots ma quine.
We need tae haud on tae the wordies
For the sake o auld lang syne.

But fit div we need wi thon wordies?
Naebody kens them at school.
The fowk that speak English and Polish
They think ahm a daft wee fool.

Ye're born tae this land and its language
As rich as ony ye'll find.
If ye dinna keep up bletherin,
Ye'll nae be able tae mind.

I get better answers frae English.
Ma Polish is comin on.
Gin it wisna for blethers wi you,
Ma Doric wid seen be gone.

Och Ahm sair ferfauchin ma quinie.
Ye're jist a gie wee trachle.
Ah feel ah've bin cowpt on a midden
Like somebody's aal bachle.

Granny dinna be fashin yersel.
Ah like it fin ye're cheery.
Ah loo'd yer 'Chin cherry, Moo merry'
An 'Coorie doon ma dearie'.

Noo see, that's fit wye we spik Doric.
A bairnie learns he belongs.
When ye hae yer babies mah quinie
Sing them thae bonny wee songs.

The roots may be there but the 21$^{st}$ century mind can fly to any corner of the globe. Ella contemplates a cosmopolite's best friend.

## Cyber Transport

Ahm tappin awa at the keys
An weaving ma thochts intae dreams.
Tho the words tumble oot wi ease
Life's nae aye fit it seems.

Thon cyber space jines the hale earth
Aboon aa – except for the bairns.
Frae Wick tae New York doon tae Perth
It grasps their main concerns.

Life's floatin aboot in the sky.
The dot com buses leave frae here.
Nature's sweet joys are aa passed by
Nae touched by ee or ear.

The world wide web's noo in control
Nae jist o daily arrangements
But o hert an mind – and o soul
And human derangements.

Some sites are gie lugubrious
Ye'd need tae be unco canny.
Gin they're nae quite salubrious
Ye micht meet Net Nanny.

Noo 'googlemail' an 'face book friends'
Jine up fowk in iv'ry nation.
Speedy wikepedia sends
Instant information.

It eest tae be pen and paper
An 'snail mail' ca'd the postie's load
Wi a thon trock an the caper
Full binner doon the road.

Noo the postie's pyok's aboot teem
A new kina transport is here.
Alang the invisible beam
The messages ding clear.

Ahm here in ma wee but and ben
An skypin awa tae the bairns.
On Seturday mornin at ten
It grasps *my* main concerns.

★★★

Eliza Jane Goés was born on a farm in scenic Lower Speyside, Morayshire where she enjoyed a happy childhood feeding orphan lambs in spring and being part of a strong community where everyone knew everyone else. From tiny primary school and small secondary school, she took a brave step towards Kings College, Aberdeen University where she gained an MA in English, Geography and Moral Philosophy. After getting a PGCE, she was about to take a job at her old secondary school when she spotted a request for teachers in East Africa. This began a long journey which hasn't yet ended.

The Cosmopolites is her second novel, a sequel to Fusion. She also writes short stories, travel articles and poetry, some in her native Doric, to remind herself of her roots.

She and her husband live in North West London and their daughter and her fiancé live and work in Bristol.

# Acknowledgements

Many thanks to the following for the advice, encouragement and inspiration:

Swanwick Writers' School, Derbyshire,
www.swanwickwritersschool.co.uk

Watford Writers, www.watfordwriters.co.uk

Elgin Writers, SAW (The Scottish Association of Writers),
www.sawriters.org.uk/clubs

The London Writer Circle (South Bank)
www.londonwritercircle.org.uk

Kenton Monday morning group.

These writing groups do a wonderful job. I must also thank Emma Darwin for persuading me to 'murder my darlings' and 'dump or develop', Frida and Colin Davies for reading the first draft of the first Chapter – which is now very different, The Writers' Workshop for keeping us up to date with free advice and competitions and of course all those agents and publishers who actually got around to reading, acknowledging and rejecting my submissions. Where would we writers be without them?

Finally, thank you Simon Potter www.fast-print.net for showing me a whole new perspective within the publishing industry – shared, at some point, by such authors as Rudyard Kipling, Alexander McCall Smith, Beatrix Potter, John Grisham and countless others.

(I can't name all the family and friends who deserve thanks in case I miss someone out - but you know who you are.)